FULL MOON
OVER
AMERICA

Also by Thomas William Simpson

The Gypsy Storyteller

This Way Madness Lies

FULL MOON OVER AMERICA

THOMAS WILLIAM SIMPSON

A Time Warner Company

Warner Books, Inc., 1271 Avenue of the Americas, New York, NY 10020

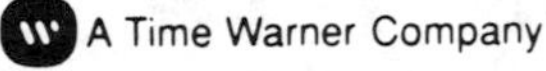

Printed in the United States of America
First Printing: August 1994
10 9 8 7 6 5 4 3 2 1

Library of Congress Cataloging-in-Publication Data

Simpson, Thomas William, 1957–
Full moon over America / Thomas William Simpson.
p. cm.
ISBN 0-446-51808-5
1. Presidents—United States—Election—Fiction. 2. Twenty-first century—Fiction. I. Title.
PS3569.I5176F84 1994
813'.54—dc20 93-50110
CIP

Book design by L. McRee

For the Fox, the Bull, Beezer, Brown Dog, and Dirty Dick.
Thanks, bros.

And again, for Lorelei.

Everything that deceives may be said to enchant.
—Plato, *The Republic*

In order to enjoy the inestimable benefits that the liberty
of the press ensures, it is necessary to
submit to the inevitable evils that it creates.
—Alexis de Tocqueville,
Democracy in America

MAP OF MACKENZIE AND TAMARACK ISLANDS

By Willy MacKenzie May 5, 1978

TAMAQUA RIVER VALLEY

By Willy MacKenzie March 23, 1997

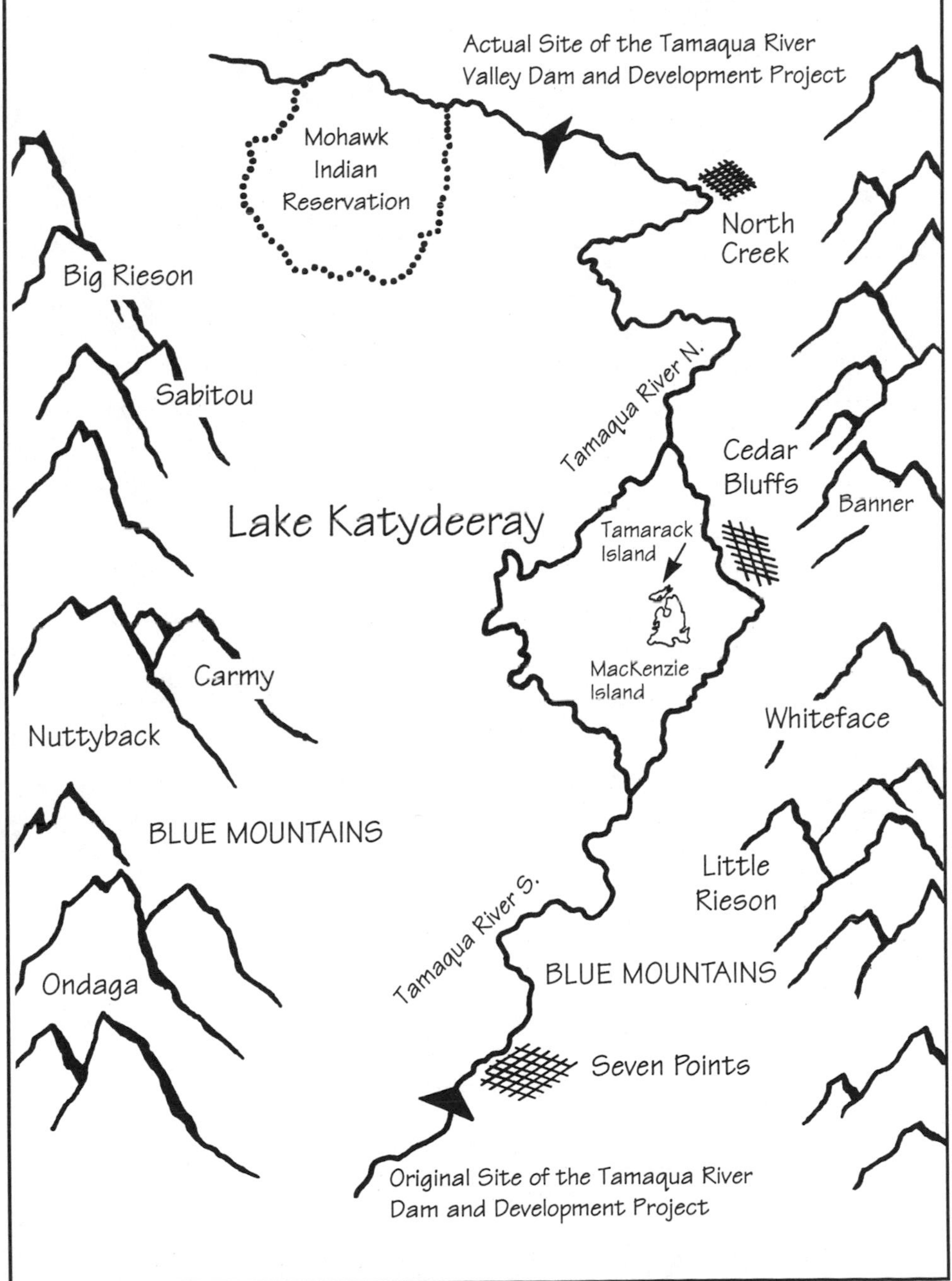

FULL MOON OVER AMERICA

6:01 A.M.
JANUARY 20, 2001
MACKENZIE ISLAND
THE INAUGURATION OF THE FORTY-FOURTH PRESIDENT OF THE UNITED STATES

Good morning. Jack Steel, national political correspondent for American Network News, reporting live from MacKenzie Island. Glad you could join us.

Today we gather as a nation, as citizens of that nation, to celebrate one of our oldest constitutional responsibilities. In six hours, at high noon, the executive branch of government will change hands as it has every four years since General George Washington took the first oath of office back in the spring of 1789.

Today's inauguration, however, will be unlike any other in our country's two-hundred-and-twenty-five-year history. First of all, the swearing-in ceremony and the celebration afterward will not take place in our nation's capital. This year our new president will take the oath of office in the living room of his family's home right here on MacKenzie Island in the heart of the beautiful Blue Mountains.

Until late last evening the president-elect had planned to take the oath on the steps of the United States Capitol. But concern for his own personal safety, and for the safety of his family, caused him to alter his inaugural plans. In the president-elect's view, the situation in the District of Columbia remains dangerous and extremely unstable.

Second, we are, for the first time in our reasonably long and distinguished history, inaugurating a president who has been elected directly by the people. The electoral college, as ordered by ratification of the Twenty-ninth Amendment to the Constitution on April 17, 1997, has been abolished, cast aside after two hundred years as not reflective of the adage "One man, one vote."

And third, as many of you already know, the president-elect is only thirty-two years old. William Conrad Brant MacKenzie is still more than two years shy of the presidential age required by Article II of the Constitution as ratified by the thirteen original states. Underage but still here, poised to lead our country into the next great century. . . .

I asked Willy about his age last night during an interview we held just before he announced his decision to hold his inauguration here on MacKenzie Island rather than down in Washington, D.C.

JACK STEEL: Mr. President-elect, what about your age? How do you respond to this assault on the Constitution?

WILLY MACKENZIE: This is a government of, by, and for the people. At least that's what they taught us in school. Of course, they taught us an enormous amount of untruths in school, so maybe government of, by, and for the people was just one more deception. I see it this way: The people, of their own free will, voted me into office. So now Congress should get on with the job of amending the Constitution so that the voice of the people can be made legal and binding.

J.S.: Let's be frank here. Do you think we will have a peaceful change of power tomorrow at noon? You know as well as I that an air of violence hangs over the country.

W.M.: When hasn't an air of violence hung over this country, Mr. Steel? This nation was conceived in violence. It has been held together with violence. It has repeatedly resorted to violence to solve its problems and subdue its enemies. I would suggest that violence between these shores is an accepted, even an encouraged, practice.

J.S.: But you do not want your own inauguration marred by violence.

W.M.: Of course not. But I think the gravity of the situation has been exaggerated. If people want to believe what they read in the newspapers and hear on the radio and see on their televisions, I can't stop them. If they accept the crap you people feed them, then I understand why they might think the United States of America teeters on the brink of chaos and dissolution. I've heard all about the military coups and the assassination plots and the civil unrest that'll take place the moment I take the oath. I think it's mostly nonsense, extra heat to bring the pot to a boil.

J.S.: But how do you respond to these rumors? And to the threats that you will be dead and buried, at least politically, before the end of your first day in office?

W.M.: I respond by saying that not every person who voted is happy about my being elected President. But when in our history has every single citizen been happy with the man who wins? I won the most votes, and in a democracy, even a democracy as hypocritical as ours, the guy with the most votes wins.

Let's take a quick look at the final numbers. Apathy, as usual, reigned supreme in the November elections. More than half of all eligible voters did not even bother to go to the polls. And so, in the end, the results of election 2000 looked like this: 28,612,483 votes for Willy MacKenzie; 28,499,212 votes for the incumbent, President Anderson Montgomery; and 26,917,111 votes for the other major party candidate, Stephen Thompson. Definitely one of the tightest races in modern times.

President Montgomery demanded a recount, and not surprisingly, he received not one, but two complete reviews of every vote cast. All three times the numbers came up the same. The president showed not a moment's grace in defeat, refusing to acknowledge the winner either publicly or privately. His snub reminds us that the MacKenzie-Montgomery feud, going back now nearly twenty years, continues to simmer with malice and bad blood.

For Willy, victory was sweet. As a third-party independent, his name on the ballot in only forty of our fifty-one states, Willy was given virtually no chance of winning by the preelection pollsters. They wrote him off as another in a long line of protest candidates. No one, including Willy himself, thought he had a chance of emerging victorious.

"I'm just out here," he told us, "to let you know what I think. I think the tides will ebb and flow. I think the sun will rise and set. I think the earth will circle the sun, the moon will circle the earth. I think the United States of America is on a collision course with itself, and that we have only ourselves to blame for the cataclysm to come. I think the race will be won by the individual who pauses to reflect and contemplate the cycles."

The crowds, cynical and sick of the old rhetoric, loved Willy's allusions and his dreamy mysticism. By the time he hit the campaign trail he was already famous for his best-selling book on the environment and for his antics on the roof of the National Art Gallery. His unusual and eccentric style took root and blossomed among the disgruntled masses. I ought to know. I was there. I watched it happen.

During the campaign, Willy insisted he did not even want to be president of the United States. "At night I pray to the Great Spirit," he told every audience he faced, "that I will not be elected. I should not be elected. I have no idea how to be president. If you give me the job, I'll probably only screw things up worse."

Concerned citizen, or savvy twenty-first-century statesman? That's a tough call. It is a question that has been debated now for months. Perhaps today we will find an answer. We have six hours to do so, six hours of coverage before the swearing-in ceremony. We have put together an in-depth biographical profile of Willy MacKenzie and his family. We will begin by looking at how the MacKenzies first made their fortune, how they came to own this valuable piece of island real estate. We will also peruse some of the president-elect's journals in an effort to better understand this man who will soon become our forty-fourth commander in chief. Willy is a writer by trade, a modern-day combination of John Muir, H. D. Thoreau, and Will Rogers. What you might not know is that most of his life Willy has kept a journal, a private record of his thoughts and feelings, his comings and goings.

But right now we're going to turn to Willy's great-grandfather, that eccentric turn-of-the-century robber baron, Mr. Ulysses S. Grant MacKenzie. From there we will move through the twentieth century, weave a sort of socioeconomic-political quilt depicting the growth of a modern nation and of one particular family in that nation, the MacKenzie clan. Along the way we will see if we can discover how and why our president-elect, the man destined to lead us into the twenty-first century, earned the moniker "the Last Innocent Man in America."

★ ★ ★ ★ ★ ★ ★

It all started up in the Blue Mountains back in the steamy hot summer of 1899. Four drunken fat cats from New York City stumbled out of their guide boats and waded ashore. You might not have known it that day, what with the four of them dressed from head to toe in brand-spanking-new fringed deerskin, but those four titans of industry and commerce were worth close to a hundred million tax-free dollars—real cash at the close of the nineteenth century.

"Are you shittin' me, Mitchell?" asked Ulysses Simpson Grant MacKenzie, the Scottish lion of shipping and stock manipulation and a great lover of obscenities large and small. "This is a goddamn island?"

"*Oui*, Monsieur MacKenzie," answered Mitchell Sabattis, the venerable French-Canadian guide who knew the lakes and rivers of the Blue Mountains better than any man alive.

"I'll be a son of a bitch," said U. S. MacKenzie. "It's as big as a goddamn continent."

Well, maybe not that big, but it had taken those four fat cats and their guides the better part of two days to paddle around it.

"And you say them damn redskins still own this fancy piece of real estate?"

"*Oui*, Monsieur MacKenzie. The Mohawk."

"Well, why the hell haven't we stolen it from 'em yet?"

Mitchell shrugged. "The island has been in the hands of the Mohawk since they warred on and won a great victory over the Oneida back before the days of the Iroquois Confederation, long before white men ever came to this part of the world."

U. S. MacKenzie elbowed one of his cronies in the ribs, then let loose with one of his famous booming belly laughs. From Wall Street all the way up Park Avenue, the sound of that laugh usually meant MacKenzie had just chiseled someone out of something, anything from a man's last dollar to his dignity. "Let's cut the crap, hey, Sabattis? We all know there wasn't anybody here before us white folks rolled into town."

Mitchell Sabattis hated Protestants. He did, however, enjoy the way the rich ones threw around their money. "No, monsieur, I suppose not."

"So what do them Injins call this place?" The earth trembled when Ulysses spoke. His voice was loud and deep and came up out of his barrel-shaped chest. U.S. stood over six feet tall and weighed in at two hundred and ten pounds.

"Wassanamee," answered Sabattis, his head bowed, "Land of a Million Souls."

U.S. spit a wet wad of tobacco juice in the dirt. "Wassa what? Ahh, hell, forget it. Don't tell me. Don't wanna know. I'm gonna buy the whole damn island anyway and change the name to something an ignorant, uneducated son of a bitch like me can pronounce. Something simple like . . . like MacKenzie, yeah, MacKenzie Island. Got a nice ring to it, hey?"

U.S. reached into his Blue Mountain guideboat and grabbed an unopened bottle of whiskey. He walked a few meters to the nearest tree, a small tamarack slightly bent against the prevailing northwest wind. "In the name of rich, loud, and obnoxious white men everywhere," he shouted while his cronies cheered, "I claim this prize for the MacKenzie clan and hereafter call this place MacKenzie Island."

That night, after the sun had set on that long, hot summer day, after the guides had made camp and served supper, U.S. and his buddies decided to do some deer hunting. Now it's best to understand that these were city boys, born during or just after the Civil War and bred in some of America's largest East Coast and midwest cities. They had taken up wilderness sports only after a fashion. Not one of them had ever slept out of doors before this trip. But among their well-heeled circle of acquaintances down in Manhattan, hunting and fishing and camping were all the rage. The acquisition of a wilderness "camp" had also recently become popular. All the fattest of the fat cats had "camps" in the Adirondacks or the Blue Mountains. So, of course, U.S. wanted one as well.

Ulysses and his well-oiled pals decided to hunt the whitetails by a rather ruthless method known as hounding. This savage means of bringing home the venison was normally practiced, as Mitchell Sabattis tried to tell his employer, "only by poor mountain peoples in desperate need of meat to feed their starving families."

"Don't hand me that whiny-ass socialist stuff, Sabattis. Just go and get them dogs a-huntin'."

So Sabattis and the three other wilderness guides, all French-Canadians, leashed their bloodhounds and set off for the interior of the island. U.S. and his cronies waited with their whiskey bottles and their shotguns in a large clearing not far from the water's edge.

Who were these other fat cats, anyway? We can only speculate. Harvey Firestone, the rubber magnate, might've been there. Maybe J. D. Rockefeller, Jr. Some say Henry Ford was on hand, although others claim Henry never took a vacation his entire working life. So we're not absolutely sure who accompanied U.S. into the wilds for that summer fortnight of boozing, hunting, and land plundering.

We are sure, however, what happened when those hounds flushed a herd of whitetails and drove them into the clearing where the fat cats loitered: wholesale slaughter. That warm, moonlit summer night turned black with smoke as an endless eruption of shotgun blasts roared across the peaceful sweep of Wassanamee Island. The Mohawk might have called their island the Land of a Million Souls, but that night not one of those souls found a moment's peace.

After three days of hounding, their appetites for slaughter finally sated, the rich white men ordered their guides to take them back to civilization. Before parting, Mitchell Sabattis made a quick count of the dead whitetails. He came up with ninety-three carcasses, all but four of them left to rot under that sweltering summer sun. Each of the fat cats had picked a buck to haul home as his prize, proof to the boys at the club that he was indeed a great white hunter.

Back in Cedar Bluffs, the small town servicing that part of the Blue Mountains and Lake Katydeeray, U. S. MacKenzie slammed his fist down on the oak bar of the town's only tavern.

"No more excuses, Mitchell. I want that island. If you ain't gonna get it for me, I'll give the job to someone who will, someone with balls bigger'n poppy seeds."

It was late. The other fat cats and their guides had retired to their rooms above the tavern. Only MacKenzie, Sabattis, and the barkeep remained. The barkeep was fat and jolly. He kept the whiskey flowing. Never in his eleven years as a tavern owner had he seen men spend money as freely as these gentlemen from the big city. They threw fifty- and hundred-dollar bills around easier than he threw kindling on a cold fire.

"But Monsieur MacKenzie, as I tell you now many times, others have tried to buy Wassanamee. All have failed. Even your own government. The Mohawk refuse to sell. Important ceremonial hunting grounds on the island. Those whitetails you killed—"

"Yeah?"

"The Mohawk do not take that many in a year."

"That's their problem."

"No, monsieur, you do not understand. The Mohawk take only what they need, kill only as many as necessary to live. Also, they believe on Wassanamee the Great Spirit dwells."

"Great Spirit my ass. The only thing that's gonna dwell on MacKenzie Island is the son of a bitch you're lookin' at. I'm gonna build me a goddamn wilderness palace on that island, already got me a site picked out."

Mitchell Sabattis knew his arguments were in vain. He knew this Monsieur MacKenzie with the big mouth and the bulging pockets would never be able to understand the ways of the Indians. Still, he had to try. "The Mohawk also have tribal burial grounds on the island. Very sacred. Many generations interred there."

U.S. swallowed a jigger of whiskey, then chased it with a long draft of ale. The man seemed able to pour alcohol into his body without pause and without evidence of drunkenness from dawn till dusk and then, if necessary, from dusk till dawn.

"Aww, shit, Mitchell," he said after the drink had settled, "I'm gettin' awful damn tired of your whinin'." U.S. slammed his beer mug down on the bar and tapped his index finger twice against the French-Canadian's chest. "Now this is what I want you to do: go see the head of these Mohawks, their goddamn chief, they probably call him, and you find out how much this chief wants for his island real estate. Just ask him, Mitchell. It ain't all that complex. Just ask the man how much.

Every man has his price, and hear me when I tell you this redskin won't be no different from other men."

Ulysses Simpson Grant MacKenzie was born in New York City the day after General Ulysses Simpson Grant made General Robert E. Lee kiss his high black riding boots down at Appomattox Courthouse on April 9, 1865. His father, Benjamin MacKenzie, a Scotsman from the Highlands north and west of Edinburgh, named his boy after the Civil War hero as a show of respect for his newly adopted country.

Before the war Benjamin had worked for Cornelius "the Commodore" Vanderbilt, first as a shipping clerk, later as a stock analyst, and finally as a general confidant. When Cornelius decided the future lay in railroads, Benjamin borrowed money to buy several of Vanderbilt's steamships. Exactly what transpired has never been fully realized, but it appears that Cornelius lent the money to his trusted employee. It has been suggested the Commodore did this because Benjamin had caught his boss doing funny things to underage boys. To keep Ben from spilling his guts to Horace Greeley or some other gutless newspaperman, Cornelius gave several of his steamships to MacKenzie in return for remaining mute about his perversions. This scenario, however, is probably just the fantasy of some yellow journalist's imagination. The more plausible explanation for Benjamin MacKenzie's sudden rise from mere employee to shipowner was his quick mind and his uncanny ability to predict subtle swings in the stock market. Ben made money for Cornelius, so the Commodore rewarded him with his very own fleet of ships to ply the waters up and down the East Coast.

Benjamin made money off his ships, but not as much money as you might think. There was intense competition in the Boston–New York–Baltimore corridor. Ben was not a natural capitalist. He may have been good with numbers, but when it came to driving his employees and breaking the backs of his competitors, Ben proved himself a pussycat. He aged rapidly once he became an owner, and he often spoke of how he wished he had never left his father's sheep farm in the foothills surrounding Ben Nevis.

Benjamin nevertheless provided a good and pleasant life for his wife, three daughters, and one son. They lived in a modest brownstone in lower Manhattan not far from Washington Square Park. Young Ulysses received an excellent education. As he grew older, however, U.S. liked to play the role of the unsophisticated, uneducated, ignorant immigrant who had crossed the mighty Atlantic alone without a nickel in his pocket and, in just a few short years, had worked his way from rags to riches. He even learned to speak with a thick Scottish brogue to authenticate his imaginary background.

Ulysses grew up hearing firsthand about the great financial feats of Gould and Cooke and Carnegie, men who had made millions building steel mills and oil refineries and railroads clear across the prairie and the mighty Rockies to California. These men were heroes. They would stop at nothing to accomplish their goals. They pushed themselves to the limit for excessive profits and also for the glory heaped upon them by their less affluent countrymen.

And so, in the brutally cold winter of 1886, when Benjamin MacKenzie, despondent and some say feverish, jumped into the East River with an anchor chained to his leg, his boy Ulysses was ready to take charge. The sharks immediately circled the offices of MacKenzie Shipping on Lower Broadway, but U.S. was there to fight them off. They said a twenty-one-year-old had no business running a shipping company of that size, but he told them, using his wonderful way with profanity, exactly what they could do with their attitudes.

The day after they dredged Benjamin's body off the bottom of the East River and stuck him in a hole out in Brooklyn, U.S. went to see William Henry Vanderbilt, the Commodore's son and now head of the family business since the old man's death a decade earlier.

"Uncle Billy," U.S. asked, "how do I make the big money? What's the trick?"

Billy Vanderbilt, maybe not his famous father's egotistical equal but a pretty slick and savvy businessman in his own right, paused a moment before answering. He took enough time to light himself a fat cigar. "Ulysses, my boy," he said as he puffed out some giant white smoke rings, "there's no trick to making money. There's just one small business adage you need to know, only one worth a damn. It goes like this: Seek out the competition, and then, with all your courage and all your strength, cut off their balls and watch them bleed to death."

That's exactly what U.S. did. The weakest sisters plying the waters between Boston and Baltimore he simply bought outright. He did this by floating bonds, watering down stocks, fixing the books, and lying boldly about the value of MacKenzie Shipping. Several small companies that refused to sell suddenly found themselves victims of calamity. Not a shred of evidence exists, but anyone who has studied the shipping wars during the last decade and a half of the nineteenth century knows that Ulysses MacKenzie resorted to industrial terrorism to gain an advantage over the competition. Taking his cue from the likes of Andrew Carnegie, Leland Stanford, and the great Pierpont Morgan, U.S. decided to take more drastic actions to insure his own financial future. He hired scoundrels to burn the competition's ships right down to the waterline. No one was killed, but property damage was estimated in the tens of millions of dollars. And before the fires had even stopped smoldering, U.S. stepped in with his checkbook and offered to buy the ruined assets for pennies on the dollar.

When the smoke cleared, only a handful of shippers remained. Ulysses decided the time had come for a truce. He called a meeting of owners and told them he wanted peace. "This has to stop," he said as he strode around his teak-paneled conference room, stopping here and there to put a firm hand on a competitor's shoulder. "We don't need all this violence and destruction. It's not productive. So I suggest we settle our differences."

"And how do we do that?" his wary competitors wanted to know.

"By fixing prices at artificially high levels and driving into the ground any son of a bitch who tries to undercut us."

The idea immediately brought smiles to the faces of the fat cats around the table.

"Cooperation," U.S. announced, "not competition, is the key to our financial success."

They all thought this made perfect sense, so U.S. rolled in the whiskey and the port and the fine Cuban cigars. They all lit up and toasted their newly founded secret society of ship owners in cahoots against everyone else.

This secret society, both unethical and illegal, held together for many years before anyone caught on, in this case muckraker Lincoln Steffens, who in 1907 published a scathing account of MacKenzie and other New York shippers. Steffens claimed MacKenzie and his cohorts had been fixing prices, dictating freight costs, and violating the Interstate

Commerce Act of 1887 for twenty years. U.S. just laughed and denied the charges. By this time he had made millions and diversified into other areas: stocks and bonds, railroads, real estate, even hotels.

It took almost a year, but Ulysses finally got his island in the north country. On July 4, 1900, he sat down at an old wooden table in the Cedar Bluffs Saloon. The table wore the carved initials of a hundred drunken patrons. The saloon smelled of stale beer and smoked tobacco.

Directly across from the capitalist sat Nathan "Tear in His Eye" Brant, chief of the local Mohawk Indians, a proud and very serious young man who never smiled in the presence of an adversary. The two men had no way of knowing, but some decades down the road they would have a common descendant—none other than our president-elect, Mr. Willy MacKenzie.

They stared at one another through the dim light of that dusty bar. All was quiet. Several minutes passed. Nathan wondered if he should spit in the eye of this rich white man and walk out. All over the country he knew Indians were selling off their ancient tribal lands. The practice seemed despicable, totally against the beliefs of his ancestors who had nurtured for thousands of years the attitude that all the great gifts of the universe lay with the land. Without the land man was nothing. But his people had voted to sell the land, to give up the island, and he was here, reluctantly, to carry out their mandate. So Nathan dropped his eyes and signed his name several times on a thick stack of legal documents.

Ulysses MacKenzie smiled and did the same. He then ordered a round of whiskey for everyone in the house. "Nate, Chief, you old dog," he said after everyone had a drink, "no doubt about it, you really took U. S. MacKenzie to the cleaners on this deal. Not many men get the better of this tough son of a bitch, but you did, Chief, you sure as shit did."

His words were just more horse trading. U.S. hadn't paid the Mohawk chief any amount close to what the island was really worth.

In the MacKenzie entourage that warm and muggy summer day was Mitchell Sabattis, who in the end had done the deal and earned himself a hefty commission. Also present were several lawyers and financial advisers, U.S.'s wife, Penelope, a pretty New York socialite who had been out to the island once and vowed never to return, and their seven-year-old son, Lawrence Van Rensselaer MacKenzie, who didn't know it then but who would spend most of his adult life serving in the United States Senate.

In Nathan Brant's entourage were several lesser Mohawk chiefs, as well as half a dozen of his own legal and financial advisers. Chief Brant was taking no chances with this shifty paleface who wanted Wassanamee. For six months the chief had refused even to negotiate a sale with the Frenchman Sabattis. But then the numbers began to climb so high, he could no longer ignore what the money might do to invigorate his people. In time, as U.S. had predicted from the beginning, the Indians simply could not afford to say no.

So in the end the island went to the rich white fat cat. Most of it, anyway. A survey estimated the size of the island at approximately seven hundred and fifty acres, depending upon the water level of Lake Katydeeray. Of this the Mohawks retained just under seventy-five acres at the extreme southern end of the island, where they had sacred burial grounds. The deal also included a much smaller island off the northwest shore known as Tamarack. (See map.)

Immediately after signing the contracts, U.S. went to work. Actually, his laborers went to work. He stepped out of the Cedar Bluffs Saloon, and there they stood: a virtual army of masons, carpenters, woodcutters, and architects, even a team of cooks and waiters to prepare and distribute the vast quantities of food needed to keep the construction crews fueled.

And never one to miss a chance for some free publicity, U.S. had also invited a couple of New York newspapermen along to record the event for posterity. During the first few weeks of construction, every tree that fell, every stone lifted into place to form the enormous foundation, every discussion between the boss and his draftsmen, were witnessed and recorded by reporters for the *New York Tribune* and the *New York World*. Their accounts were then telegraphed to the city, where the masses consumed with great interest the wilderness exploits of their hometown hero, Ulysses Simpson Grant MacKenzie.

The men worked like dogs all summer and into the fall. A great tent city emerged around the construction site. Some nights as many as a hundred men gathered around the open fires to eat their pork and beans and drink their watered-down beer. The woodcutters came from the Blue Mountains, but the skilled workers came from the cities. The Irish carpenters were brought in from Boston, and many of the masons were Italians from Staten Island and lower Manhattan. Every day there were arguments and fistfights, and one night an Italian stone worker named Giovanni knifed to death an Irish joiner named Mick after Mick called Giovanni a wop. A riot nearly ensued, and for several weeks afterward U.S. had to maintain order on the island with a small armed battalion of hired hands.

Work on what quickly become known as the "Great House" progressed nevertheless. A steady supply of food and material arrived via barge from the brand-new dock U.S. had built on the Cedar Bluffs waterfront. New businesses sprouted up in the small town as a result of the construction project. A hardware store opened. So did a restaurant, a whorehouse, and a second saloon. Every Saturday night, after receiving their paychecks, the construction workers headed for town. They spent their week's pay on tools, cheap whiskey, loose women, and bad food. By Monday morning most of them didn't have two quarters left to rub together. And the stupid slobs didn't even know that each and every one of those new businesses was run by a front man for their boss, U. S. MacKenzie. He doled out the wages, then sucked almost every penny back into his own coffers through the ancient economic rite of supply and demand.

If you take a look at the map of MacKenzie Island, you will see exactly where U.S. built his wilderness "camp." All the fat cats called their mountain retreats "camps" in those days, and so what if the MacKenzie "camp" had twenty-six rooms, twelve-foot ceilings, sixteen fireplaces, and a dining room big enough to seat twenty without anyone even bumping elbows.

"If Astor and Vanderbilt want to call their mansions in Newport 'cottages,' " U.S. roared at anyone who cried foul, "I'll damn well call my place a 'camp.' "

The Great House was completed in early August of 1902. Construction continued on the boathouse and the dock and the elaborate gardens, but that August the family spent its first night together on MacKenzie. Penelope, despite her earlier claims never to return to the island, was on hand with her mother, her sisters, several cousins, her son, and a whole slew of servants.

They ate a fine meal prepared by a famous French chef. They drank a case of expensive French burgundy. Ulysses made a speech. Most of what he said has been lost over the years, but he made one declaration that evening once considered by an editor of *Bartlett's*: "The stupid son of a bitch who said money can't buy happiness oughta come sit at my table."

After dinner the family and their guests retired to the enormous front porch, where they watched the sun spread its shimmer across Katydeeray before slowly slipping behind the peaks of the Blue Mountains to the west. And in the morning, their very first morning on the island, at the crack of dawn, while everyone else tried to sleep off the effects of too much wine, U.S. performed what would quickly become his Scottish ritual, something he did virtually every morning he awoke in the master bedroom suite overlooking the lake.

Ulysses, you see, was not a great sleeper. He rarely slept more than three or four hours a night. Always he was up and out of bed with the first light. So on the island he would don his full Scottish regalia: his kilt bearing the MacKenzie tartan, argyle jacket with epaulets, matching Balmoral, a pigskin sporran stuffed with cash, a nickel-plated *sgian dubhs* concealed in his hose, and, of course, his full complement of bagpipes. Down the wide front stairs and out onto the front porch he would march. He would fill his bags with air, do a bit of tuning, and then break into a rousing display of "Scotland the Brave."

As a younger man Ulysses rarely visited the island except during the summer months. To escape the torrid New York City heat in July and August, U.S. traveled north. Often he invited his fat cat buddies to his island retreat. Usually once a year, traditionally over the Fourth of July so they could celebrate the nation's birthday in the bosom of their families, the fat cats brought along their wives and children. These long weekends were usually marked with fireworks displays, wild pigs roasted on an open spit, and kiddie games like the three-legged race on the long sweep of lawn leading down to the water's edge.

Other times the fat cats left their families at home and brought along only their shotguns and fishing poles. These forays into the wilderness were punctuated by excessive amounts of boozing, farting, belching, and the random killing of wildlife.

However, the most famous trips north by Ulysses and his cronies took place when the fat cats arrived with their lady friends. Every fat cat had at least one mistress; more virile fat cats like U. S. MacKenzie had several. He tried to be discreet about his extracurricular sexual activities, but everyone, including his wife, knew he fooled around. Some of the old-timers in Cedar Bluffs still tell stories of the wild orgies out on MacKenzie Island, when a fisherman would row past that sweep of lawn between the Great House and the lakefront and see clearly a dozen overweight, middle-aged men and a dozen attractive young women stark naked and laughing while they engaged in a vigorous round of leapfrog.

When Ulysses first saw the town of Cedar Bluffs in 1899, the population did not exceed one hundred people; maybe fifteen or twenty families lived in the immediate vicinity. But U.S. had a vision. He knew city dwellers from Boston and New York needed to escape the urban chaos. He knew they needed some peaceful place on a clear, clean mountain lake that was both accessible and affordable. So Ulysses built a railroad to meet their needs and maybe make himself a few bucks along the way. It was just a ninety-mile spur off the main line, but it brought folks directly into the heart of the Blue Mountains, right smack into downtown Cedar Bluffs. To feed and house these urban explorers, U.S. built a grand hotel on the Cedar Bluffs waterfront. The Tamaqua River Valley had never seen anything like it. For three dollars a night guests got a room and the opportunity to sit on the wide front porch and look out across Lake Katydeeray at the Blue Mountain peaks. They could sip cool drinks and gossip about Mr. MacKenzie. His enormous island loomed half a mile offshore. Everyone who came to Cedar Bluffs soon knew who owned the island and the railroad and the hotel and most of the other business establishments in town as well.

Whenever U.S. pulled into Cedar Bluffs in his private Pullman, most town residents turned out to have a look. Often he brought along someone famous. Charlie Chaplin spent time on the island. So did Sarah Bernhardt and Enrico Caruso. A baseball fanatic, Ulysses once had Tris Speaker and Ty Cobb on the island at the same time. Supposedly, or so the story goes, the two legendary hitters got in an argument, and Cobb hit Speaker over the head with a croquet mallet.

A man who proudly stated he never wasted time reading books, U.S. nevertheless cultivated acquaintances with many of the country's foremost writers and journalists. Samuel Clemens, Carl Sandburg, Ring Lardner, and Clarence Barron all signed the leather-bound guest book kept on a special oak table in the front foyer of the Great House. But perhaps the most famous visitor to MacKenzie Island in that early era was Teddy "the Rough Rider" Roosevelt. He spent nearly a month walking the island and nursing his wounds after Woodrow Wilson whipped him in the 1912 presidential election.

"Don't worry about it, Teddy," U.S. told him as they drowned their sorrows in a bottle of the finest Scotch money could buy. "We'll kick that goddamn socialist's ass first chance we get. It might take us a few years, but mark my words: we'll damn well win back the White House before it's all over."

6:16 A.M.
JANUARY 20, 2001
MACKENZIE ISLAND
THE INAUGURATION OF THE FORTY-FOURTH PRESIDENT OF THE UNITED STATES

Last night, after the president-elect announced he would not go to Washington to take the oath of office, a collective panic raced through the ranks of the news media. Willy's sudden and unexpected change of venue left thousands of journalists stranded in the capital with nothing newsworthy to report. Many of them are frantically heading north for the Blue Mountains even as we speak.

Until they arrive, I will do my best to keep you informed and entertained. I have only a bare-bones crew here with me on MacKenzie Island, but we feel ready and able to take on the task at hand.

An agreement has been reached by the major networks and cable news services that will allow us to broadcast live from MacKenzie Island on an open feed. Access to this feed will remain open until the various news organizations have their own teams in place.

That said, I would like to turn our attention to the president-elect's journals. Soon after his election, Willy sold the rights to his journals to a prestigious university press. I am fortunate enough to have in my possession a prepublication galley of these journals. I recently obtained this galley through sources requesting anonymity. I have agreed to honor this request. But today, this morning, I plan to share some of Willy's journal entries with you. I feel they will help all of us better understand this young man who would one day be president.

In their complete state Willy's journals occupy literally thousands of pages. Starting at the age of ten, he wrote one or more pages almost every day for the next twenty years. It would serve no one's interest to read this tidal wave of words in its entirety, so I have taken it upon myself to edit the journals into something digestible. I will offer you bits and pieces from his youth, show you Willy at work and at play. Later I will serve up generous portions of Willy's journal as he wandered aimlessly across the country in the mid-nineties. But let us turn now to his very first entry, dated June 21, 1978.

* * * * * * *

Today is Wednesday, June 21, 1978. It's right around five o'clock in the morning.

My name's Willy MacKenzie. My whole and complete name is William Conrad Brant MacKenzie, but most folks around here just call me Willy. I'm 10 years old, and sometimes I wake up before it gets light. What I aim to do when this happens is write stuff down in this brand-new notebook. I'll just write down whatever comes to me. Maybe stuff that happened yesterday or stuff that might happen today or tomorrow. I'll keep a journal, not a diary like girls keep because somehow a diary seems like secret sissy stuff, love stuff, and I don't aim to have much to do with that.

See, I got Indian blood in me, Mohawk, same as Mama, and she says the reason we don't know more about our Indian kinfolk is because for thousands of years they lived without writing anything down. Strange I know but that's just the way they did things. Seems they didn't have an alphabet so they passed on whatever needed passing on just by telling someone, usually someone younger in case the older one died. Mama says this way of doing things left for some awful confusions. By writing everything down I figure I'll keep the record straight.

Normally what I do first thing every morning is pull on my dungarees and flannel shirt and walk over for a visit with my great-grandfather, Mr. Ulysses Grant MacKenzie. I'm not going this morning though because yesterday they hauled Ulysses over to the hospital in Cedar Bluffs so the doctors could get a look at him. Papa says there's nothing much the matter with him except that he's one hundred and thirteen years old and doesn't know more than about one day in seven who he is or where he is or even what season we might be celebrating.

Ulysses lives in the apartment over the boathouse. He's lived there a while now, since back before I was born. Papa brought him out to the island after he suffered a stroke. The doctors told Papa Ulysses probably wouldn't last out the year. Fifteen years later and he's still going strong.

Most folks around here have pretty much forgotten Ulysses is even up there, but not me. I like going to see him, listening to him mutter. He says all kinds of wild stuff, has these dialogues with himself where he yells and stamps his feet in one voice, then says how sorry he is in another voice. It all sounds like a nightmare to me, only he's wide awake. Mama says he suffers from guilt, and all the muttering is just Ulysses reflecting on bad things he did as a younger man. Sometimes he gets to screaming so loud I have to go over and put my arms around his neck to quiet him down.

Once in a while, once a month or so, I'll walk into his bedroom up above the boathouse and find him sitting in that old wooden rocker staring out the window at the dawn. "Mornin' to you, Willy, me boy," he'll say, just as though he'd been expecting me to drop by. "Been out dancing with that pretty little girl of yours, have you?"

I'll blush and tell him no way and he'll poke me in the ribs with those big bony fingers of his and then laugh so loud the boathouse'll shake and Nurse Tully'll come running thinking old Ulysses is finally headed for the next great mystery.

"Outta here, Tully," Ulysses will order, "me and the boy got business. We don't need your lily white ass snoopin' around."

Business is usually a game of Parcheesi or a hand of crazy eights. Or maybe we'll just sit there at the window and watch the loons fish the cove. I love to watch the loons fish the cove.

July 27, 1978

Yesterday morning, after breakfast and my visit with Ulysses, me and Dawn (that's Dawn Tyler, my best friend, even though she's a girl and all) sat on the front porch looking out across the lake at the Blue Mountains and thinking out loud about what we might spend the day doing. I thought we might go fishing, but Dawn thought we should turn ourselves into monarch butterflies—big, bold, colorful ones with bright orange wings and long black bodies. So we did.

Without another word we sprouted wings and flew off the porch. We went around the side of the house and through the small orchard of apple and cherry trees. Beyond the orchard we flew over a wide stretch of goldenrod dotted with patches of royal blue blazing star. A cool breeze blew across the meadow, shooting us off in opposite directions. I closed my eyes and let the wind take me.

Beyond the goldenrod, tall white lupines filled a corner of the meadow. I battled a crosswind trying to reach the flowers. After tacking back and forth, I finally lit upon one of the lupines with a shoot nearly ready to burst open. My eyes grew wide. And then the flower bloomed, so fast I hardly saw it happen. Almost invisible, lighter than air drops of nectar slipped by my nose. The sweet smell made my eyes smile. I made a wish the lupine would just keep blooming, forever and ever.

Sensing a change in the wind, I left the lupines behind. I flew over the prettiest but scariest wildflowers in the whole meadow—buttercups and morning glories. I swooped down for a closer look. And sure enough, a sudden downdraft caught my wings and plunged me into a thick mass of morning glories. My body got only a scratch, but in that jungle I couldn't take off, couldn't even raise my wings.

"Dawn!" I shouted. "Dawn! Dawn!" But she couldn't hear me. She'd flown off on her own, something we promised later on never to do again.

The thought of centipedes and field mice grabbing me from behind and ripping off my wings made me turn in circles and carry on like some stupid moth flying around a torch flame. But panic only drove me deeper into the green vines. I could see the sky through the buttercups, but it looked so far away. Strange noises surrounded me. I shook and shuddered from fear. Finally I commenced flapping my wings, faster and faster. And soon enough I cut through those buttercups, up and over the meadow, free again. A brisk tail wind caught me and blew me over the goldenrod to where the meadow meets the forest, to Dawn.

"Willy! What happened? You're white as a sheet."

I told her my adventure, starting when that lupine burst open. I exaggerated some, but Dawn knows when the truth's being stretched so she just listened. When I finished my tale she told me hers.

"Soon as we flew off the porch," she said, "I felt sure the miterwort had finally bloomed. I headed straight for the forest. I kept flying right through the trees, somehow knowing which way to go without even thinking about it. After the rain this morning a whole lot of flowers had opened up, so the woods were alive with colors and smells. I passed right over some tiny angel wings and some yellow trilliums, but I didn't stop for anything."

"Not even to look at that eagle's nest we found in the spring?"

"Nope, not even for that. Just past the old oak tree holding that nest, I saw something sparkling on the ground. I swooped in and spotted a whole new patch of miterwort nestled between two thick roots. Tiny raindrops clung to the petals. And then a sunbeam shot through the leaves and flooded the miterwort with all this beautiful golden light. I couldn't take my eyes off it."

"Sounds like something special," I said. "Wish I'd seen it."

"That's okay you missed it, Willy. I saw it for both of us."

I thought about that for a while, and then we just sat there quiet for a spell before shedding our wings and starting down the path for Wannehatta Falls.

Wannehatta Falls, which Mama says means Enchanted Falls, got their name from the Mohawk Indians who used to hunt and fish on the island. Now they come to the island but twice a year to pay their respects at the tribal burial grounds down on the south shore. Mohawk from all over the country come to MacKenzie to worship at the graves of their ancestors. And since we have dead relations there, Mama and I go to worship too.

Dawn can't go because she doesn't have any Indian blood in her.

6:22 A.M.
JANUARY 20, 2001
MACKENZIE ISLAND
THE INAUGURATION OF THE FORTY-FOURTH PRESIDENT OF THE UNITED STATES

So even at that tender age Willy had a fertile imagination. I certainly didn't have the creative instincts to turn myself into a monarch butterfly at the age of ten. Did you? And I definitely didn't have the skills or the patience to sit down and write about it. But Willy did.

And he has been writing ever since. In fact, there was a light on over at the Great House just a few minutes ago. I thought the president-elect might be up before dawn working on his Inauguration Day speech. Rumor has it that he will spend most of his time ruminating on what he calls the three essentials: earth, air, and water. But the light switched off a minute after it switched on.

Inauguration morning has been very quiet here on MacKenzie Island. We've been up since five o'clock without hearing a sound or seeing a soul. My small crew (cameraman, audio man, producer, and two interns) and I occupy a cluttered utility room in the boathouse directly below the apartment where Ulysses MacKenzie lived during Willy's youth. We have been on the island for three days awaiting the MacKenzies' departure for Washington, D.C. Now that Willy has decided to hold his inauguration here, well, you can imagine how we feel about our great good fortune at being the sole media representatives for this historic event. We stuck it out long after the other crews, restless and uncomfortable, headed south. I was ordered by my superiors to pull out as well, but my intuition told me to stick around a while longer.

Conditions have been rather primitive. We've been sleeping on the floor in our down bags and eating mostly out of tin cans. The MacKenzies have not been the most hospitable hosts. They probably would have preferred to see us leave their island. But we've made room for ourselves and our equipment among the gear-oil cans and the fishing tackle and the wooden rowing oars and the life preservers. It is a chilly but bearable fifty-nine degrees in here. An hour or so ago we fired up the wood stove with some dried split oak we found out back. Little by little the room begins to warm.

Outside the temperature is a blustery eighteen degrees Fahrenheit. Snow looms in the forecast. A steel gray sky hangs low over the Tamaqua River Valley. The National Weather Service informs us that a severe winter storm is fast approaching the Blue Mountains. It should hit sometime this morning. But for now, all is quiet and calm.

Not so down in Washington. We understand the nation's capital is a hotbed of activity, even at this early hour. Tens of thousands have gathered in the capital to protest for and against the new president. After Mr. MacKenzie's announcement last night that he would not travel to Washington for his inauguration, a nasty brawl broke out on the Ellipse across from the White House. One person was killed and dozens injured as Willy's supporters battled his foes.

All through the night lights burned as the power brokers met behind closed doors in the White House, the Capitol, the Pentagon, and the Supreme Court. Over and over they asked the same question: What can be done about Willy MacKenzie?

With the swearing-in ceremony just five and a half hours away, a degree of urgency rarely seen in the capital city has taken hold. It's as if our political, judicial, and military leaders believe an atomic bomb will explode at high noon if the ascendancy of Willy MacKenzie to the highest office in the land is not defused.

But while they debate the issue and decide what course to take, let us go back for a closer look at Ulysses S. Grant MacKenzie and his turn-of-the-century wheelings and dealings.

Ulysses S. Grant MacKenzie spent only a few weeks a year on his island retreat in the Blue Mountains. His wilderness "camp" was primarily a status symbol to impress his wealthy pals. U.S. preferred the swirl of activity in the ever-expanding, ever more cosmopolitan town of New York. Manhattan was where he lived and worked. He owned a lavish brownstone on Park Avenue staffed by half a dozen servants, most of them recently arrived Irish immigrants whose low wages and sparse living conditions made them little more than indentured servants.

Robber Baron Row, as Park Avenue was known at the time, housed many of the nation's wealthiest and most influential bankers and businessmen. U.S. knew them all. He might not have been as rich or as powerful or as famous as the Morgans or the Goulds or the Harrimans, but he nevertheless traveled in similar company. He belonged to and frequented such pillars of monetary might as the Union Club, the Metropolitan Club, and of course the New York Yacht Club. Ulysses was certainly no social bon vivant (he couldn't tell sherry from port or *ris de veau* from *côtelette de veau*), but in those days refined taste mattered not one whit as long as you had large piles of cash trailing you wherever you went.

Perhaps even more important to his position in New York society than his impressive bankroll was his marriage. Ulysses did not marry for love so much as for the deep blue blood running through his young bride's pale and fragile body. Penelope Van Rensselaer came from an old Dutch Knickerbocker family whose ancestors had arrived even before Peter Stuyvesant. The Van Rensselaers no longer had much money (years of decadent living and an absolute refusal to work for wages had taken care of that), but they nevertheless retained an air of aristocracy, being as they were a member of the city's original Four Hundred club created by Mrs. William B. Astor.

Penelope, two years younger than Ulysses, married him in June of 1888 on her twenty-first birthday. It was not love at first sight. For months she had tried to ignore both his money and his infectious charm, but in the end U.S. proved far too persuasive.

Her parents did not approve of "the young ruffian from the north country with the filthy mouth," but they finally relented to his proposal after he promised not to use profanity in their company. The fact that young MacKenzie was worth several million dollars no doubt aided them in their decision.

The wedding was the social event of the summer, drawing close to five hundred guests and costing Lawrence Van Rensselaer in excess of thirty thousand dollars, a sum U.S. helped cover behind closed doors. Immediately after the reception, Ulysses and his new bride steamed off on a three-month tour of Italy, Greece, and Egypt.

Once back in New York, the honeymoon swept into the past, Penelope proved a handful. Spoiled rotten from birth, she refused to get out of bed before noon, treated servants like slaves, drank whiskey and wine, smoked cigarettes at the dinner table, and worst of all, for Ulysses anyway, she had a great disdain for sexual intercourse.

"For chrissakes, Penelope, what the hell is wrong with you?"

"There's nothing *wrong* with me. I just don't feel like it tonight."

"You never feel like it."

"I wouldn't say never."

"Well, goddammit, almost never."

"Perhaps I don't feel like it, dear, because you are rough and vulgar and insensitive."

"What the hell does that mean?"

They were married almost five years before Penelope finally became pregnant. And less than one week after she gave birth to their son, Lawrence Van Rensselaer MacKenzie, she informed her husband it would be her first and last pregnancy.

"The hell it will."

"The hell it won't. I found the experience both painful and humiliating," she told him in a voice suggesting the onset of postpartum depression. "I absolutely refuse to go through it again."

"Oh, you'll go through it again," Ulysses informed her. "You'll go through it as often as I say. I want me a house full of kids, and your job is to give me what I want!"

The issue, as you might imagine, became a source of considerable conflict between Mr. and Mrs. MacKenzie. No one knows, of course, exactly what goes on behind the closed door of a married couple's bedroom, but we know for certain that Larry Van Rensselaer MacKenzie, the future United States senator, had no legitimate siblings.

On a slightly less dependable note we have this rumor to pass along: More than one of those Irish household servants claimed that Ulysses occasionally raped his young wife. No evidence of this sexual violence exists however, so perhaps the rumors are just the oral hate mail of vengeful domestic help.

As wedded bliss slipped from his grasp, U.S. moved more and more in a wide circle of women who had announced the demise of the Victorian era. A great wave of sexual freedom washed over the country as the new century dawned. Ulysses did not hesitate to get his feet wet. In fact, U.S. dived in headfirst, putting together a whole harem of young beauties to help him exercise his sexual fantasies and perversions.

Among his cronies, his financial peers, U.S. was famous for his bawdy tales, his wild imagination, his sense of humor, and his propensity for predicting the future. Many of his well-heeled contemporaries were dry, dull, and humorless. They did little else but work in their never-ending pursuit of more profit. For them, U.S. was like a gift from heaven. He made them laugh, and for this ability alone they loved to have him around.

"Let me tell you ugly rich white sons of bitches something," he began one afternoon as they sipped their fine French cognac in the mahogany-paneled sitting room of the New York Yacht Club over on the East River. "Don't get used to your velvet smoking jackets and your fancy limousines and your dainty imported fish eggs. The world, boys, is fast changing out there. The muckrakers and liberal do-gooders and social reformers, men who we well know copulate with monkeys and she-goats, are out to see our kind burned at the stake, tarred and feathered."

Just this brought tears of laughter to the eyes of the fat cats lounging about the room on leather sofas and easy chairs. They, of course, found themselves invincible. As far as they were concerned, they had built the damn country. In just a few short decades they had turned the United States of America into the world's premier economic power. Sure, they lived like royalty, enjoyed the very best society had to offer, but they had no doubts whatsoever that they deserved their wealth and their power and their fine mansions and their private Pullmans and their cheap immigrant labor. So they just laughed at their friend's prediction while they ordered the tall black manservant to stoke the fire and replenish their fine crystal snifters with more expensive French cognac.

"Go ahead and get your jollies, you fat, stupid bastards," U.S. told them, his huge face hiding a grim smile, "but I'm speaking the truth here today. Within our lifetimes, right before our eyes, our homes on Park Avenue and our retreats in Glen Cove, Newport, and the Blue Mountains will be overrun by wild hordes of coloreds and lowlife Eastern European types who think the pope's pits don't stink. I tell you the streets will be full of looters carrying off our Louis the Fourteenth furniture and our fine Italian art. The banks and the counting houses will be overrun, pillaged, burned to the ground! We will be tethered together by our testicles, dragged through the streets, peed on by the teeming masses."

More laughter from the fat cats, followed by some fine Cuban cigars. Oh, how they loved those cigars from our island colony in the Caribbean. This was fine stuff, they all thought, excellent entertainment, well worth the high price of membership.

"Anarchy, goddammit!" shouted U.S. as the laughter ebbed. "I'm talking social anarchy here. I'm talking a complete breakdown of law and order. Our women and children will be raped and beaten and sold into slavery to some wild-ass Zulu tribal chief in the heart of Africa. We'll have to hire mercenary armies to go in and get them out."

More laughter as they snipped the noses off their cigars and powered them up with long wooden matches held at arm's length by Jesse Jefferson, grandson of a Virginia cotton slave.

Ulysses enjoyed entertaining his cronies, but his remarks had not been made simply in jest. For years U.S. had been reading the signs, taking the pulse of the nation, figuring out all the angles. He knew the era of running roughshod over the little people was fast coming to a close. The politicians had their small and grubby fingers in the pie now and things would never be the same again. There would be no more lying and cheating and stealing as there had been in the good old days.

Ulysses knew that successful business enterprise in the future would favor those who controlled the people who framed the legislation and passed the laws. For years he and his robber baron buddies had been paying off judges and politicians. But payoffs, he knew, were no longer a guarantee; favors simply went to the highest bidder.

"To insure loyalty," U.S. told his closest financial advisers, "we will need to handpick our representatives. Of course, whenever and wherever possible we should take and hold office ourselves. By cutting out the middle man we can make and enforce the laws as we see fit."

As far as Ulysses was concerned, the country was being run by a bunch of lily-livered, weak-kneed socialists who didn't understand that what was good for business was also good for America. Since McKinley's assassination the White House had been inhabited by two-faced sons of bitches who promised one thing and did something entirely different. First Roosevelt had proven himself a closet liberal. Then Taft and his group of pseudo-Republicans had stomped all over poor J. D. Rockefeller, forcing the old codger to break up and sell off large chunks of his Standard Oil trust.

"Goddammit," U.S. howled from one boardroom to the next, "if Rocky ain't safe to make a buck, you can be goddamn sure the rest of us ain't, either. We'd better watch our backs. This government's getting too damn big for its own britches."

And then times went from bad to worse when Woodrow Wilson moved into 1600 Pennsylvania Avenue. Ulysses could not believe it, felt the end must soon be drawing near. In 1913 Wilson forced the Federal Reserve Act down the country's throat. Immediately the social zealots who ran the Federal Reserve Board put the lid on the banks and the money supply.

Barely pausing to catch his breath, Wilson and his pal Congressman Henry Clayton of Alabama instituted the Clayton Antitrust Act. This strengthened the government's power to control trusts and monopolies.

"Pretty damn soon," U.S. ranted at members of the Senate Committee on Labor and Public Welfare, "it'll be a goddamn crime in this country to make a profit!"

The senators, one of them, anyway, had other crimes in mind. "Mr. MacKenzie," asked Senator Robert La Follette, preeminent social reformer of his time, "is it true, sir, that you employ young children to stoke the fires and clean the crappers in your steamships?"

Ulysses sat ramrod straight in his slightly too tight Prince Albert frock coat. He looked his accuser dead in the eye. "Sir, I hire any man willing to work."

La Follette did not hesitate. "Is it true, Mr. MacKenzie, that you pay these children less than a dollar a day, sometimes as little as three dollars a week?"

"I pay the going wage, sir. No more, no less."

"I see, Mr. MacKenzie." La Follette glanced at his papers, then leaned forward. "Now can you tell us if it's also true that recently one of your employees, a Mr. Rankin, a deckhand, fell and broke his leg on one of your ships while swabbing the deck?"

"I have over a thousand employees, Senator. I can't be expected to keep track of every damn one of them."

"Perhaps not, Mr. MacKenzie. But as I understand it, Mr. Rankin received absolutely no compensation for his injury and was, in fact, fired because he failed to report to work the day after his leg was broken."

Ulysses had heard enough. He grew indignant. "I've done nothing illegal, Senator. If you pansy asses want me to take care of every son of a bitch who gives me a day's work, then I might as well put my ships in dry dock and close up shop. I pay a man a day's wage for a day's work. What more does he want? What more do you want? You want me to hold his hand and wipe his ass from the cradle to the grave?"

La Follette was not intimidated. "The power and strength of your shipping trust insures high profits and low wages, Mr. MacKenzie. We want you to consider the possibility that perhaps you are playing the game with a rigged deck and benefits like workmen's compensation might not be too much to ask."

Ulysses guffawed at the senator's suggestion and was soon excused.

But the crowning blow came when, in an act U.S. saw as tantamount to treason, the three branches of government banded together and inflicted upon the people an annual income tax

"How do you idiots expect the economy to grow," Ulysses asked the Senate Banking Committee, "when you sit here on your high horses and demand we pay you a percentage of our hard-earned money?"

The senators were attempting to solicit from Mr. MacKenzie information on exactly how much income he derived every year from his various business interests. But U.S. was having none of it. He slammed his fist down hard against the polished oak table. "It's an outrage, I say, an outrage! Not twenty years ago the Supreme Court of this country declared taxes on personal income unconstitutional. Unconstitutional! Now you arrogant windbags chuck the Constitution and cram your goddamn desires to live off the public dole down our throats. You ought to be ashamed. Ashamed, I say, ashamed!"

Ulysses would not relent. The senators needed their henchmen to remove him physically from the committee room.

His tone of voice and choice of words may not have been appreciated, but what U.S. had said at the hearing was true. In 1895 the Supreme Court had indeed declared the collection of personal income taxes a violation of the Constitution. But on February 3, 1913, the Senate overturned that ruling when they ratified the Sixteenth Amendment. Summed up, it read: Congress shall have the power to levy and collect taxes on incomes without regard to any census or enumeration.

"Chicanery," U.S. called the amendment and the tariff act that soon followed, "pure chicanery! Out-and-out goddamn thievery!"

U.S. declared war. And not the violent, idiotic kind of war breaking out in Europe. That kind of war was for fools and glory seekers. If they wanted to kill themselves off with guns and grenades and mustard gas, that was their business. Ulysses didn't mind lending his capital and leasing his large fleet of ships at highly inflated prices, but the nature of the conflict itself did not mean a thing to him. Government intervention and too much taxation, however, did. These were issues worth fighting over.

U.S. went to his newspaper pals to get his message across. It was no easy chore. Most of the editorial boards had taken up positions against the mighty industrialists, preferring to state the case of the common man. Ulysses felt betrayed. In a speech at the Waldorf-Astoria before a packed house of the city's business leaders, U.S. warned, "This, my friends, is only the beginning. If we let them get away with this income tax crap, they'll only demand more of our profits later. Free-market capitalism will cease to exist. So I say we nip their greedy claims on our cash in the bud now, before it's too late. I say we rise up and demand an accounting!"

More and more Ulysses sounded like a man running for public office. And indeed, he was. He sought a seat in the United States Senate, where he felt certain he could rally his cause and set the country straight.

Unfortunately, another important event had taken place in 1913, this one in early April, when the Seventeenth Amendment was ratified into law. Prior to this, senators had been appointed by their state legislatures. This system, as you can easily imagine, stank of political corruption and dirty money. Many a senate seat was acquired through blackmail, payoffs, and various other forms of political treachery. The Seventeenth Amendment called for senators to be elected by popular vote within their own states. The Senate, as a governing body, fought tooth and nail to suppress this amendment, but in the end, after a long and bloody battle, the upper house was forced to accept the inevitable. The masses had spoken.

"Son of a bitch," announced Ulysses when he heard the news.

The amendment put the brakes on the MacKenzie political juggernaut. He had the goods on many members of his state legislature, enough so that his desire to serve in Washington would have been a sure thing. But when he hit the campaign trail in 1914, he found an untamed electorate. Spend though he did (upward of three million dollars), he was his own worst enemy. Every time Ulysses gave a campaign speech, he wound up stuffing his foot in his mouth. He tried to let on as though he cared about other people besides rich white Anglo-Saxon Protestant males, but the powerful industrialist, closing in on fifty, had no control over his tongue.

At a rally in midtown Manhattan he proclaimed in a gruff and self-righteous voice: "Old Abe Lincoln said we need government of the people, by the people, and for the people! Well, let me tell you, that old bearded son of a backwater bitch was exactly right. We got too many lazy politicians down in Washington telling us when, where, and how to take a crap. I say enough's enough. I say the business of the United States is business, not government. And the sooner we all realize it, the sooner we can all get back to doing what we do best: making money!"

Nope, Ulysses didn't have the touch. He received only a small percentage of the popular vote. He had no choice but to retire from the political arena. For several years he did exactly that. He went back to copulating with loose women and profiteering off a war in which literally millions of young men died defending little more than his right to earn excessive profits.

A month after the war ended, in December of 1918, Penelope MacKenzie died at the age of fifty-one in the terrible influenza epidemic that claimed the lives of more than half a million Americans. Her husband cried at her funeral, but those in attendance doubted the sincerity of his tears. Ulysses had no great love for his wife and was probably glad to see her go. For years they had been emotionally, if not legally, separated.

Her son, Lawrence, on the other hand, cried without inhibition.

Larry loved his mother, thought her the most wonderful woman in the world. To put this absurdity into perspective, Larry also thought his father was the most wonderful man in the world. He was, you might say, blind to the realities of the universe. And always would be.

Larry had been educated at the best schools money could buy. He had traveled to all the great cities of Europe. He had visited Persia and the Far East. He, of course, would never have to worry about money. But all this education, world travel, and affluence could not change the one basic flaw in Larry's character: his goodness. He was as good as his father was bad. He smiled at the world, not in an arrogant or condescending fashion, but simply because he found it much more natural to smile than to frown.

Larry was tall and very handsome, and some said dashing, even debonair. His mother had taught him how to dress and how to treat the ladies. An extrovert by nature, Larry won the hearts of all who crossed his path. He was one of those people you just couldn't hate. Even though he had been born with the proverbial silver spoon in his mouth, he never displayed any of the mannerisms associated with the idle rich. Larry had not a mean-spirited bone in his body, and rarely, if ever, was he heard to utter a bad word about anyone. He always looked on the bright side of things. Some folks took one look at Larry and saw an optimist. Others, like his father, took one look and saw a natural politician.

A few days after Penelope's funeral Ulysses asked his son, "So, Lawrence, what are you going to be when you grow up?" Larry was twenty-five at the time.

"Geez, Dad, I don't know. I guess I haven't really thought about it much."

"Well, son, maybe the time has come."

Larry nodded. "I guess I figured maybe I'd just go into business with you?"

"Not a chance. You don't have the stomach for it. They'd eat you alive."

"You think so, Dad?"

"I know so, son." And then, "Have you ever thought about running for office?"

Larry looked puzzled. "Well, no, I haven't, but it sounds like it might be fun."

Ulysses rubbed his hands together. "Yes, exactly. It'll be fun. Fun and good times."

* * *

A run for the House of Representatives was considered in 1920, but two events moved Ulysses to change his mind. First was the announcement by Senator James Branford that he would not seek reelection after completing his term in 1922. And second was the ratification of the Nineteenth Amendment, which gave women the right to vote. Ulysses took a close look at these developments and decided to forgo the House. He felt certain with the incumbent out of the picture and women going to the polls for the first time, he could send his boy directly to the United States Senate.

One small problem: At the time of the election, in November of 1922, Lawrence would be only twenty-nine years old, one full year short of the age required by the Constitution for election to the Senate.

"I don't know, Dad. Seems like a problem. Maybe we should settle for the House."

"No way!" roared Ulysses. "Never settle. Never give an inch. Never. I ain't gonna let a little thing like the Constitution stand in my way."

"But Dad," argued Lawrence, "I don't see how I can be older than I am."

"Let me worry about that, son. You just keep smiling."

"Yes, sir."

So what did crafty old U. S. MacKenzie do to solve his small tactical problem? He had his son's birth certificate and all other appropriate records altered to show the year of the boy's birth as 1892 rather than 1893. The change didn't take much: a few thousand dollars and a little muscle flexing. It was a small moment of business as usual in America.

Years later, as we all know, Willy's backers in his presidential bid would also face the problem of an underage candidate. But the MacKenzie for President Committee would not resort to tampering with birth records and falsifying legal documents. No, they simply took the high road. They used a much more modern approach to political action. They announced their total disregard for the constitutional demand requiring a president be at least thirty-five years of age. And then they held high huge banners of their favorite campaign slogans: "Stop Us If You Can!" "Vote Willy and Win!" And one of the most famous presidential slogans of all time, right up there with "Tippecanoe and Tyler Too" and "Nixon's the One." We mean, of course, "Vote MacKenzie—the Last Innocent Man in America!"

November 22, 1979
Thanksgiving

Thanksgiving's a fasting day here on MacKenzie Island. We don't eat any food and we only drink water. We do this on account of Mama, who says the Pilgrims who first celebrated Thanksgiving were the beginning of the end of the Indians and she wants no part of that celebration. So while all my friends over in Cedar Bluffs are busy eating turkey with mashed potatoes and gravy and pumpkin pie I sit up here in my room and think about my troubles.

Fasting's not the real reason I hate Thanksgiving, though. I have two other reasons for that. First off because it means that today is the first whole day I spend without Dawn. She left yesterday. In the winter the Tylers live in Florida. They won't be back till spring. Maybe even summer. We write letters and once in a while talk on the phone but it's not the same. Every year Dawn begs her mother to let her stay (she hates Florida, says the kids are all stuck up down there) but so far anyway the answer is always no, you're too young, maybe next year.

The other reason I hate Thanksgiving is because it means that soon we'll leave the island for the winter. I only go as far as our house on High Street in Cedar Bluffs but that's plenty far enough.

Cold weather moves into the Blue Mountains in early December and by Christmas Katydeeray is frozen solid. Mama has always refused to live on the island in the winter. She says it's just too lonely and isolated out here with the leaves all gone and the windows all closed up tight against the wind. I guess I don't blame her but I sure hate leaving. The only one who stays is Papa. Even Sanders and Alice move over to the mainland. And Ulysses, he's hauled up to the nursing home next to the hospital, where he has a room all to himself. But Papa, he doesn't budge. He's been wintering on MacKenzie for over thirty years and says he's got no plans to stop now. Oh, he'll come over to town for a visit every couple days, once in a while to spend the night, but mostly he'll stay on the island chopping wood and keeping the fireplaces burning.

I'd rather if we had Thanksgiving in the spring, after the ice melts, after the trees bloom, after we come back to the island, after Dawn gets home. By then we'd have something to celebrate.

February 13, 1980
High Street House

It snowed last night. Enough so they called off school. I went to bed staring at the moon and woke up to over a foot of fresh powder. Almost scary the way it came without making a sound.

After breakfast me and Henry Bender carried our cross-country skis down to Water Street. I told him I wanted to ski out to MacKenzie to see Papa. Henry said he'd go along. So we strapped on our skis and shoved off. Neither of us had ever skied out to the island before. And I might as well mention that we weren't supposed to ski on the lake at all, what with the ice maybe not being safe.

Besides Dawn, I guess Henry is my best pal. He's a big kid, not too bright. I've heard it said around town his folks can't read or write. Mama says that's not a measure of how smart someone might be. She says we can't all fly jet airplanes but that doesn't mean we can't dream about soaring with the eagles. About some things Henry is pretty smart. Like he knows how to use a magnifying glass to start a fire with dry leaves. And he's only eleven but already he knows how to change the oil in his father's pickup. I don't know how to do that.

Anyway, we got only a stone's throw offshore and Henry said, "I ain't goin' no further, Willy."

"Why not?"

" 'Cause I'm cold and scared and afraid of falling through the ice."

I was cold and scared and afraid of falling through the ice too, but I didn't let on. "You're a sissy, Henry Bender."

"I am not."

"You are too."

"Am not."

"Are too."

Henry's twice my size and strong as a bear cub but he hates to fight. "I'm goin' home where it's warm," he said.

"If Dawn was here she'd go with me."

"I ain't Dawn," Henry said, then he turned and skied for shore.

"Go ahead home!" I shouted into the wind. "I'm going out to the island anyway." I stood there and watched Henry ski back to town. I stood there so long I commenced shivering. To stop shaking I pounded my hands against my arms. But the wind tore right through my jacket. So I turned and started skiing. It was like some invisible string pulling me, drawing me out to MacKenzie, and so what if I was cold and afraid of falling through the ice? It was something I had to do.

It's not really all that far but boy oh boy, it seemed to take forever. Part of the reason was that wind. Seemed like for every two feet I skied forward that wind blew me three feet back. But finally I reached the island. I skied through the channel separating MacKenzie from Tamarack and then off the lake and right up onto the front lawn.

I heard Papa before I saw him. I heard the whack whack whack of his ax chopping into a tree somewhere out behind the boathouse. For a minute or two I just leaned on my poles and rested near the front porch while I watched the smoke silently spill from the stone chimneys rising up massive out of the roof of our house.

Once I caught my breath I skied around the side of the house, down along Loon Cove, frozen and perfectly still, past the boathouse, and up the slope to where the hardwoods grow. This is normally where Papa takes his trees for burning. He only takes the ones that are dead or dying, says it's not right to kill any healthy living thing unless it comes down to your survival or its.

He sat on a stump putting an edge on his ax. Papa doesn't use power tools. He hates the sound of chain saws, says they scare the daylights out of every living creature within ten miles. "And besides," he says, "easier and faster's not necessarily better."

I thought about calling out to him, but instead I just stopped and watched. I could see him pretty good through the trees, mostly birches, black oaks, and red oaks. The temperature was way below freezing, probably right around ten degrees, fifteen at the most. But Papa, he sat there on that stump wearing nothing but a T-shirt, a pair of overalls, and his leather work boots. I couldn't figure out how he didn't up and freeze solid right on the spot. He wears a bushy beard in the winter, says that keeps him warm. He'll shave it off come spring. Mama'll make him.

I could say Papa's big, but that wouldn't describe the man proper. He's a giant, to me anyway, as tall and broad as that hundred-year-old white pine growing over by the old icehouse. He's got muscles in his arms and chest and back that swell up like boulders every time he just reaches to pick up a shovel or his knife and fork. I wonder if I'll ever grow to that size.

"You going to hide back there and gawk, boy, or you want to come out in the open where a man can get a look at you?"

I just about fell over from surprise. I don't know how he saw me. He was turned clear away, couldn't've heard me. But somehow he did, so I swallowed hard and skied down through the trees, stopping a good distance from where he sat. Papa scares me, but not that much.

"Trouble in town, boy?"

I shook my head.

"Your mama all right?"

I nodded.

"She know you're out here?"

I considered lying but knew better. "No sir."

"You skied across by yourself?"

I swallowed hard again. "Henry Bender chickened out."

"So you came across by yourself?"

I saw then that not only did he wear nothing but a T-shirt, but he was sweating pretty good to boot. Beads of perspiration ran off his forehead.

"What's the matter, boy? Cat got your tongue? Be the first time in my memory if it does."

He meant I have a tendency to talk too much. "Yes sir," I said, "I skied across by myself."

He stood up, filling the forest, and sank that razor-sharp ax into the meat of a red oak. "And do you think that was a good idea, boy? You think your mama will be happy when she finds out?" He didn't sound mad, just matter-of-fact.

I thought about my answer, but not for long. "No sir."

"Don't the two of you have some kind of a rule about skiing on the lake?"

"Yes sir."

"And don't you have that rule because of warm spots where the lake doesn't freeze and you could fall through and never be heard from again?"

I swallowed hard once more and nodded. "Yes sir."

"All right then, unstrap those skis and take off your jacket."

I thought maybe he was gonna tan my hide but I'd've been surprised if he had on account he's never done that before. Threatened to but never actually done it.

Soon as I got my jacket off he handed me the ax. "Time you learned how to use this tool, Willy. Any boy old enough to disobey his mama is old enough to chop, haul, and stack wood."

Which is exactly what I did, for most of the rest of the day. It wasn't long before I'd stripped down to my T-shirt too. Some kind of hard work all that chopping and hauling and stacking.

The funny part is, Papa thought all that hard work was punishment for skiing out to the island. I didn't tell him different. I didn't tell him that I didn't mind the work one bit, not even after I thought for sure my arms would fall clean off my body from fatigue. I didn't tell him that was the best day I'd had all winter long or that first chance I got I'd be skiing out for more of the same.

We worked side by side for hours, and even though he said only a few words, I could feel him telling me stuff all day long. Without opening his mouth he taught me how to swing the ax, how to keep it sharp, how to make a tree fall where you want it to fall. A man doesn't need to say a word to say what needs to be said. No, I didn't make that up. I heard Papa say it once to Sanders.

Late in the afternoon we put away the tools and went into the kitchen. Papa had coffee and I had hot chocolate. We ate most of a pecan pie Mama had sent out the day before.

"Can I stay over tonight?"

"No."

"But I could chop and haul more wood in the morning."

He drained the coffee off the bottom of his mug. He likes it black and thick as roofing tar. "In the morning, boy, you won't be able to raise your arms high enough to take a wizz."

He was right, I can't. They feel like a couple of lead weights hanging off my shoulders.

"Besides," he said, "I have to get you home. Your mama will be worried sick."

So we skied back across the lake, me following in his tracks. The sun went down and the moon came up while we made the crossing.

I was dog tired, thought for a time I'd have to ask Papa to carry me. But I struggled on, and finally, long after I should've died from exhaustion, we reached the house here on High Street.

Mama was worried but not too mad. She forgave me as soon as she saw how pooped I was. I had some bean soup and went straight to bed, where I slept as hard as I've ever slept in my whole life.

6:43 A.M.
JANUARY 20, 2001
MACKENZIE ISLAND
THE INAUGURATION OF THE FORTY-FOURTH PRESIDENT OF THE UNITED STATES

A few minutes ago here on MacKenzie Island we saw a most remarkable sight. In the first faint traces of dawn on this short winter's day, I watched the president-elect, his brother Sanders, and their father, Conrad, march out of the woods behind the boathouse. From the axes and bow saws the MacKenzies had slung over their shoulders, I knew they must have been out cutting trees and splitting firewood. It was quite a show.

I had assumed they were still inside sleeping, resting up for their big day ahead. But Willy, Sanders, and Conrad must have slipped out for a few early morning chores before any of us even crawled out of our sleeping bags.

As soon as we spotted them, my cameraman, Fred Lorry, and I scurried from the boathouse to intercept Willy before he could reach the back porch of the Great House. Deep snow and intense cold impeded our progress. I didn't get five feet before I sank into a drift as high as my waist.

The MacKenzies had on snowshoes. They easily passed over the fine white powder. And they seemed impervious to the wicked chill in the air. They wore nothing but boots, canvas trousers, and hooded sweatshirts. Old Conrad, seventy-six, didn't even have on a pair of gloves. I, in contrast—and believe me, I hate to admit this—had on

Gore-Tex gloves, a heavy wool sweater, a goose-down parka, and a cashmere watchman's cap. Even bundled up like an Eskimo I felt the cold seeping into my bones.

I struggled through the snow to reach the president-elect. Just before he reached the back porch I fired off a few questions.

> JACK STEEL: How are you feeling this morning, Mr. President?
>
> WILLY MACKENZIE: I'm not the president yet, Jack.
>
> J.S.: But you're ready to take the oath?
>
> W.M.: Ready and willing.
>
> J.S.: Have you finished your inauguration speech?
>
> W.M.: To hell with my inauguration speech. Is that camera on? Are we live?
>
> J.S.: I believe so, Mr. President.
>
> W.M.: Then I'd like to say this: The implication made earlier that I decided against a Washington inaugural is not accurate. As you well know, I had every intention of taking the oath of office on the steps of the U.S. Capitol. But everything has been done by the present administration and by certain powerful members of Congress, the military, and the media to prevent me from doing so. I am essentially being held prisoner here on MacKenzie Island.

I tried to get Willy to comment further on these accusations, but he refused to say anything more. He removed his snowshoes, slapped the snow off his pants, and climbed the steps to the back porch. Without even turning around and waving to the camera, he followed his brother and his father into the kitchen and slammed the door.

I was not surprised. Willy MacKenzie has often refused to answer our questions. He does not have a high opinion of the press. He has on more than one occasion referred to us as a pack of wild carnivores.

I have known Willy for more than four years now, since before the formation of the Committee to Make Willy MacKenzie President, so I know he can be a cool and cantankerous son of a gun. I wouldn't put much stock in his insinuation that he is being held prisoner here on MacKenzie Island. I think he's probably just feeling the pressure of the moment.

We'll try to get another word with him later in the morning. But right now I think we should take a look at the early political career of Willy's grandfather, Larry MacKenzie, the first MacKenzie to hold public office.

* * * * * * *

On November 7, 1922, Lawrence Van Rensselaer MacKenzie was elected to the United States Senate. He was only twenty-nine years old even though his falsified voter registration card claimed he was thirty. His father, Ulysses, had spent untold thousands, untold hundreds of thousands, perhaps untold millions, to make his boy's election a reality. It probably also helped that Larry campaigned as a reformer, as a man interested in cleaning up the system, in elevating the common folk economically, socially, and politically.

In truth, however, no matter what he said, at least in those early days, Larry MacKenzie didn't give a hoot about anything but having a good time. Ulysses hired the best penmen in the business to write Larry's speeches. Larry gave those speeches with fire in his eyes but with barely a clue in his brain as to what the speeches meant. He took naturally to the campaign trail. He loved the hustle and bustle. Larry had an easy smile, gleaming white teeth, and a handsome, happy face. The public believed what he told them. And when his opponent, a short man with a bulbous nose and an enormous chip on his shoulder, accused Larry of being nothing but a pawn of the high and mighty, Larry simply dismissed the charge with a wave of his hand and said exactly what his handlers had told him to say: "Nonsense, sir, utter nonsense. No one tells Larry MacKenzie what to say! I am my own man, sir, a man who has glimpsed the past and sees clearly the need to forge a new future!"

During those more innocent times, high-minded rhetoric such as this, when used at the appropriate moment, could be very effective. People sopped it up. They believed the fifty thousand MacKenzie campaign posters plastered on practically every billboard, telephone pole, and trolley car from one end of the state to the other: "MacKenzie Is the Future! A Vote for MacKenzie Is a Vote for You!" They sent the young man to Washington with nearly sixty percent of the popular vote.

"Atta boy, Larry," Ulysses shouted to his son at the victory bash in the ballroom of the Waldorf-Astoria, "I knew you could do it."

Larry stood at the podium, smiling and waving to his troops. "I couldn't have done it without you, Dad."

Ulysses slapped his boy on the back. "That's true, son, very true. So that's why I'll be telling you how to cast your votes."

Larry drank off a tall glass of French champagne and nodded. "Sure, Dad, whatever you say. You're in charge."

Larry, you see, did not equate political office with the casting of votes. How he would vote or what he might vote on had never occurred to him during the campaign. Larry loved the applause and the cheers and the way the masses flocked around him whenever he entered a room. He had little interest in the actual duties or responsibilities of a United States senator. If his father wanted to tell him how to vote, no problem, he could deal with that. Larry had already decided to do whatever he had to do to keep his political fortunes burning bright.

Ulysses bought his boy a brand-new brownstone in the recently rejuvenated area of Washington known as Georgetown. The house stood at the end of Whitehaven Street not far from the Naval Observatory, just across from Dumbarton Oaks Park. From the third-floor balcony, where Larry liked to entertain the ladies in the late afternoon, he could sip his Scotch sour and look out across the flatlands at the wide and muddy Potomac. Usually these ladies were invited to dine. Dinner was always a sumptuous spectacle at the MacKenzie residence, prepared by Corrina the Creole cook and served up by Canin, the handsome black butler who had been educated in the classics at Howard University but had been unable to find equal employment opportunities because of the wanton racism still deeply embedded in the national psyche.

An invitation to dine at the MacKenzie home on Whitehaven was considered practically on par with an invite to the White House. In those days D.C. still ran amok with rich fat cats holding public office. But only Lawrence Van Rensselaer MacKenzie combined money with youth, great good looks, and the finesse and breeding to throw a truly splendid dinner party. Larry quickly became the toast of the town, and, after hours anyway, no one gave a damn how he cast his votes.

Every day Congress was in session Larry rode in a limousine down Pennsylvania Avenue, past the White House, to Capitol Hill. His office in the Richard Russell Senate Office Building on Constitution Avenue was remodeled in solid cherry and staffed by a bustling contingent of professional bureaucrats financed almost entirely by his kind and generous father, Ulysses. No one else on the Hill had a staff half as large as the small army the MacKenzie camp put in place upon Larry's arrival in D.C. Even in this day of bureaucratic overload, the MacKenzie staff would seem both large and zealous. There were two ultraconservative Ph.D.'s on board to wade through the swamp of legislation pending and already on the books. Four Ivy League–educated lawyers occupied prime real estate in the senator's office space, where they gathered daily to discuss ways of watering down existing laws and entirely blocking bills that might impede the way U. S. MacKenzie preferred to conduct business. Larry also had peons on staff who took care of all the mundane, unpleasant chores of a senator. There were people to answer the mail, handle the press, and manipulate his public image.

Chief among this lower echelon was Kirby, the little guy from Brooklyn whom Ulysses had hired to keep tabs on his son and to make sure Larry did not get himself into any—how shall we say this?—delicate situations. Kirby was not particularly well educated in any formal sense, but he had plenty of street smarts: exactly the kind of fellow Ulysses liked to employ. At least once, and sometimes as often as five times a day, Kirby reported directly to his boss up in New York on the comings and goings of Senator MacKenzie. Young Larry couldn't take a leak or pass wind without Kirby telling Ulysses about it.

Lawrence MacKenzie was the forerunner of the modern United States senator: he looked good, he had a great staff, he knew how to handle himself in a crowd, he did what he was told, and he had few if any deep-seated convictions. And best of all, Larry loved the job. It made him feel important, and with all those people on staff, he didn't have to work very hard. The whole enterprise was little more than a game to the Honorable Lawrence Van Rensselaer MacKenzie, a game he played in those early years with the enthusiasm of a little boy.

Larry soon became known as the Beau Brummel of the United States Senate. He wore fashionable, well-tailored, handmade suits. His hair, long and wavy, was always perfectly coifed. His shoes, made of the finest Italian leather, held a shine so bright that his fellow legislators used to stroll past his desk and twist their mustaches in the reflection made by the senator's wingtips.

In a chamber filled with grumpy old men suffering from gout and suppressed guilt, young Lawrence seemed almost to float down those aisles so rich in history and debate. Closer in age to the page boys than to his colleagues, Larry often looked like the proverbial kid in the candy shop. During his first term in office, some say, he never once stopped smiling. He had an excellent seat in the Senate chamber, on the Republican side, of course, right on the aisle. As the junior member from his home state, he sat near the back, but Larry enjoyed that because he got an excellent view of the proceedings, and when sessions grew too long or too tedious he could slip through the nearby cloak room door for a cigar or, if late enough in the afternoon, a nip of Scotch from the silver flask he kept in the charge of Senate doorman Issac Bennett.

In that era before C-SPAN, senators actually used to spend a fair amount of time inside the Senate chamber. When Congress was in session they would gather for hours to debate and argue and eventually vote on one piece of legislation or another. During his first term, Lawrence rarely argued with anyone. He preferred to sit there and suck up the atmosphere. Eye contact with any pretty ladies up in the visitors' gallery was one of his favorite pastimes. When that got boring he would stare at those two life-size oil paintings of Thomas Jefferson and John Adams hanging on the front wall. He would daydream about one day doing some great and wonderful deed so that a group of senators in the future would hang his portrait in the Senate chamber.

"Wake up, Larry," his Democratic colleague from Massachusetts, who sat directly across the aisle, whispered to the senator one afternoon when Larry had his head back on his shoulders and his eyes half-closed.

Lawrence snapped to attention. "I wasn't sleeping," he explained.

"I was trying to read what it says up there on the ceiling on the Great Seal."

"*E Pluribus Unum*, Larry. Something you Republicans should keep in mind."

Lawrence thought it over. "*E Pluribus Unum?* Right. What does that mean again?"

The senator from the Bay State shook his head. "Out of many, Larry, one."

Larry looked at his colleague, then back up at the ceiling at that enormous painting of the Great Seal of these United States. He saw an eagle clutching an olive branch in its right talon, a cluster of thirteen arrows in its left talon, and in its beak a red scroll with the Latin *E Pluribus Unum*.

"Yes, exactly," Larry told his colleague with no great certitude, "out of many, one."

During the 1920s Washington, D.C., was still a sleepy little town, rather provincial in its size and scope. F.D.R. and his army of bureaucrats were still a decade away. The business of governing the nation had not yet become our principal preoccupation. Power rested in the hands of a few, and the many blindly trusted those few to do the job with integrity, compassion, and circumspection. A war for independence, a civil war, and a world war had all been fought, but still the United States remained essentially a nation of political innocents.

Up until the worst years of the Great Depression, Larry MacKenzie simply did not know how most of his constituents lived. He didn't know, for instance, that one of his hand-tailored cashmere frock coats cost more than one of his father's deckhands earned in an entire month of hard labor. He didn't know that one out of every five full-time workers in the United States was under the age of sixteen. And when, in 1924, he voted yes for legislation making all American Indians citizens of the United States, Larry did not know that the vast majority of those Indians had no desire whatsoever to have this honor bestowed upon them.

Larry's knowledge lay in other arenas. The social graces, for instance. His mother, Penelope, had taught him well. He was charming and witty and outrageously adept at making the ladies laugh. No dinner party was complete without Senator MacKenzie. Democrats or Republicans, it made no difference; Larry swung either way. "Protect the poor," he'd tell his Democratic hosts. "Protect the rich," he'd tell his Republican counterparts.

Prohibitionists or folks who liked a little libation now and again, both sides could count on Larry. "Satan's elixir," he'd tell the former. "Worst damn law we ever passed," he'd tell the latter, referring, of course, to the Eighteenth Amendment, which had made the manufacture and distribution of alcoholic beverages illegal.

Larry was like a willow tree: firmly rooted in his own innocence and his daddy's wealth and yet able easily to withstand the heavy political winds by swaying from side to side without stiffening and breaking against the onslaught; the perfect politician.

On December 31, 1924, New Year's Eve, Senator Lawrence MacKenzie slipped his hand inside Rebecca Whitman's green velvet gown. The couple sat on the leather sofa in Thaddeus Whitman's teak-paneled library. Thaddeus Whitman was Calvin Coolidge's undersecretary for the interior and one of the most trusted members of the president's staff. His annual New Year's Eve bash was attended by most of Washington's elite.

"Please, Senator MacKenzie, sir," giggled Rebecca, who had probably consumed too much spiked punch, "someone might walk in and see us."

It should have been Kirby, U.S.'s errand boy, who walked in and saw them, but Kirby had been physically expelled from the Whitman mansion for not having the proper invitation or the proper attire.

And too bad, because the honorable senator from New York had hold of the young Miss Whitman's right breast. It felt firm and smooth. The nipple stood up hard and erect. The senator did not want to let go. "Don't worry, Miss Rebecca, I locked the door."

The senator was thirty years old, although everyone thought he was thirty-two. Miss Whitman had recently turned twenty. She was pretty but very proper and had the reputation for being a snob. Actually she was just sheltered and very shy.

"Still," she said, her voice not quite steady, "you really shouldn't."

The senator moved his hand to the left breast. It felt slightly smaller, but just as silky smooth. "You've been well endowed, Miss Rebecca."

Rebecca subdued a giggle. The senator put his left index finger on her mouth. Her blue eyes sparkled and grew wide. The senator replaced his finger with his lips. Miss Whitman moaned, then suddenly stiffened and attempted to move away to the far side of the sofa. "Oh, Lawrence, really, we shouldn't."

The senator followed. "But Rebecca, I assure you, we should."

And while the cathedral bells rang in the new year, while the guests inside the Whitman mansion cheered and made toasts and offered resolutions they would not keep, the senator pulled down his pants and Miss Whitman pulled up her gown.

Just about exactly seven weeks later, Larry sat in his office smoking a cigar and feeling very good about himself when the undersecretary of the interior, Thaddeus Whitman, knocked on his door and entered. A few flakes of snow covered the undersecretary's overcoat.

The senator stood. "Sir, come in. What brings you up to the Hill today? Had no idea you were coming."

"Personal business, Senator MacKenzie."

Larry offered Thaddeus a cigar.

Thaddeus refused and got right to the point. "You, sir, have violated my daughter. I demand satisfaction."

The days of dueling had faded into the past. Hamilton and Burr on the banks of the Hudson was a distant memory in the history of the nation. What the undersecretary wanted was quite simple. He wanted the senator to marry his daughter before a scandal broke and screwed up the political lives of all concerned.

And so, after a brief powwow with Ulysses, who ranted and raved about his boy's sexual indiscretions, that's exactly what Lawrence agreed to do.

Soon enough Ulysses decided it was all for the best. "Dammit, son, it's high time you took a wife. You're too damn old to be wandering through the political jungle with your pants down."

Larry and Rebecca married on the fourth day of March, a cold and windy afternoon, at the First Episcopal Church in Georgetown. Though barely even acquainted, they agreed to love, honor, and cherish until death did them part.

September 3, 1980

Yesterday we celebrated the eighty-seventh birthday of my grandfather Lawrence. We celebrated it even though he died twenty-two years ago. He died back before I was born so I never knew him except through the stories Papa and Sanders have told me. Everyone says I look just like him, same eyes and mouth and smile.

Grandfather Lawrence was a United States Senator. I've seen his name in some of my history books at school. This one book had real nice things to say about him, called him a statesman, said what a great American he was. But this other book had some pretty mean stuff to say.

I asked Papa about this, about which book told the truth.

Papa looked me dead in the eye and said, "Best not to believe anything you read or hear, Willy; least not until you have the facts firsthand."

I need to try and remember that.

Anyway, we celebrated Lawrence's birthday out by the flagpole. Papa raised the flag to half-mast and we all sort of stood there for a few minutes with our heads bowed. I was there, and Dawn was there, and Mama, and Sanders and Alice too.

After a time Sanders and Papa and I went up into the boathouse to fetch Ulysses. He made a ruckus about not wanting to leave his bed, but we finally managed to carry him downstairs and wheel him out to the flagpole in his old wooden wheelchair. I could tell he didn't have the foggiest notion what was going on. At first he just sat there frowning, but then a cricket jumped up on his wrinkled old hand. That made him smile. I felt better after that. Ulysses is a hundred and fifteen years old, some say the oldest living American.

September 21, 1980

Almost midnight. Final day of summer's drawing to an end. I hate that.

This morning, early, Dawn and I were over on the other side of the island, near where Wannehatta Falls flows into Katydeeray, looking for Indian arrowheads, when we saw a sight I'll be having nightmares about for sometime to come. That's why I'm writing in my journal now, so I don't have to turn off the light and lie here in the dark.

Dawn was the first to see it, then me. It was a huge fish washed up on the rocks. At first it just looked like an old log. We climbed over the rocks to where the fish floated dead in the clear, shallow water. It was a gigantic fish, easily the biggest fish I've ever seen, and I've seen some pretty big fish pulled out of the waters of Lake Katydeeray. He must've been four feet long and fatter around below the gills than my neck; a good thirty-five or forty pounder.

"That's one ugly fish," said Dawn. "What kind is it?"

"Northern pike," I said, just to let on like I knew.

"No way, Willy. I've seen northern pike and they don't look like that."

"Oh yeah? Then what do you think it is?"

Dawn has this way of looking at me that burns holes right through my head. "I don't know," she said, "but it's no northern pike."

I looked at the fish. It just floated there, dead. It gave me the willies.

After a while Dawn asked, "I wonder why it died?"

We turned the fish over with a stick but couldn't find anything wrong like bites or wounds, and it didn't look like it had taken a plug or a fly, so I said, "Beats me."

"We should ask Sanders. He'll know."

So wishing like crazy I knew, I followed Dawn along the shore to Looking Glass Cove. On the way I wondered if I'd ever know all the stuff Sanders knows.

At the back of the cove we started up the long, steep hill that leads away from the water to the cabin where Sanders and Alice live.

Dawn broke into a run. I made chase but couldn't catch her. She runs faster than me, always has, runs like a whitetail.

Halfway up the hill we stopped to catch our breath. We could see Sanders sitting on his wide wooden porch in that old overstuffed chair with all the stuffing falling out. As long as it's not too cold or too rainy he sits there with his typewriter set between his legs on one of those metal trays with the folding legs. I've watched him a million times. He'll read over the words he just wrote, then he'll look out at the lake and the mountains, and finally, after he's got it all straight in his head, he'll go back to the words and start in again on the typewriter.

Sanders is my half brother. We have the same father but different mothers. He's got a few years on me, though, twenty-one to be exact. He's almost as old as Dawn's father. He writes and edits articles for The American Observer, the magazine he and Alice publish. The American Observer is all about living in the country and observing wildlife and keeping the earth clean. Most everybody in these parts reads it. I hope someday to write for it.

Sanders knows plenty about this neck of the woods. He spent a lot of time on the island as a kid, not as much as me because for a long time he lived with his mother down in New York City. But when he got older and could decide for himself, he came up here to MacKenzie to live with Papa, "The Great Silent One," as Sanders calls him.

Sanders knows all about the rivers and the lakes and the mountains, and about the birds and the animals and the fish that live around here. He knows the history, too, going all the way back to the Indians, clear up through the arrival of the first French fur trappers and the coming of the Jesuits and the settling of the English. He's told me plenty. He knows more about the Tamaqua River Valley and the Blue Mountains than anyone else I know. Well, that's not true, lots of folks around here know more than Sanders does, but most folks in these parts don't talk much. Need a crowbar to pry their mouths open. Papa's not the only one. Mama's the same, although she can talk a blue streak if you catch her in the right mood.

Dawn and I ran the rest of the way up to the cabin. We were both breathing hard from the long climb, but right away Dawn started telling Sanders about the fish. She told him how big it was and how dead it was and how I said it was a northern pike but she knew it wasn't.

Sanders looked over at me and smiled. Then he started to laugh, a big, rip-roaring laugh that sometimes I practice when no one's around. Some folks say old Ulysses used to laugh like that.

"So," he asked, "is this fish still down there for all to see?"

"Sure," I said, "right at the foot of the falls."

"Then we best hightail it down there and have a look." He stood, jumped off the porch, and loped down the hill. We followed hot on his heels.

After a quick inspection of the dead fish Sanders said, "This here is a muskellunge. Musky for short. You called it close, Willy. Muskies are part of the pike family but they look and behave a whole lot different from their cousins, the northern pike. Muskies stay pretty quiet most of the time, a pretty lazy bottom fish, really, but when they get to feeding, watch out, they get downright nasty. They'll bite your hand or your foot clean off."

"Really?"

"Indian lore has it that a Mohawk brave once grabbed a musky with his bare hand, and that fish bit that poor Indian's hand right off at the wrist. Mohawk didn't bother much with musky meat, though. They thought it had a dirty flavor, like it had been living in the mud. But I've heard it said by others that musky meat has a finer flavor than free-running salmon. So who knows? We all have our own way of figuring things. Maybe the Mohawk were just sore about their brave getting his hand bit off."

"Are they all so big?" I asked. "This is the biggest fish I've ever seen come out of Katydeeray."

"They grow to a good size," said Sanders. "But I've seen bigger muskies than him come out of this lake. Some years back I watched a pair of fishermen pull up to Compton's Landing with a musky that weighed in at fifty-three pounds."

"Well, how come I haven't seen one of these muskies before this?"

"It takes some time to see everything, Willy. You have to keep your eyes open and your mouth closed. Any angler looking to catch one has to put in plenty of hours behind his pole, plus have quite a string of good luck going, before he can pull in one of these monsters."

"But this one wasn't taken by a fisherman," said Dawn.

"Nope, I'm afraid not."

"So what killed him?"

Sanders stood there for quite a spell studying that big old dead fish. We waited so long for an answer I thought maybe he'd forgotten the question. But then, just as I was about to ask again, he said, "I don't know for sure, but I'd bet my finest fly rod that acid rain was the culprit."

"Acid rain? What's that?"

Sanders took another look at that dead musky. "It's sort of a change in the chemistry of the lake water."

"What do you mean?" I asked, feeling all of a sudden sort of nervous.

"Well, Willy, I don't understand it all myself yet, but basically it's polluted rainwater that falls into the lakes and rivers and messes up the chemical balance."

Before I could ask what that meant, Dawn piped up. "Why's the rain polluted?"

"That's kind of complicated," said Sanders. "See, factories that produce lots of energy, like steel mills and rubber factories, have these tall smokestacks that burn coal and then spew sulfur dioxide into the air. When the sulfur gas combines with natural chemicals up in the atmosphere, it slowly changes into sulfuric acid. And when this acid mixes with precipitation it falls back to earth and often winds up in our streams and rivers and lakes."

I was just about to say it's all too complicated when Dawn said, "I think I get it, but why don't the factories just close down their smokestacks?"

Sanders got a big kick out of this, let off a pretty good laugh. "Real good question, Dawn. Be nice if it was that simple."

Then all of a sudden we heard Mama say, "Yes, it would."

We looked away from that dead fish and there was Mama standing not a willow switch away with a big pile of wildflowers nestled in her arm. We had been concentrating so hard on this acid rain stuff that we hadn't heard her come across the meadow to the lake edge.

"But," she continued, "the paleface never knows he has his arms in the fire until they're already burned black."

I knew Mama meant white folks as opposed to Indians when she said palefaces, but I wasn't real sure about the arms in the fire part.

"I think you've had enough talk of dead fish and acid rain and smokestacks spewing poison into the air for one day," she said to Dawn and me. "Why don't we go search for some nice fresh dandelion greens for a supper salad? Be a lot more constructive than all this running off at the mouth."

So that's what we did. We collected some greens and we watched a bald eagle soar without flapping his wings practically from one end of MacKenzie to the other and we laughed at a pair of gray squirrels chasing each other through the hemlocks.

But all that good stuff hasn't made me forget the bad stuff, including that big old dead musky floating in the shallows. Mama must've seen my light on and figured I was up worrying because just a few minutes ago she came in and gave me a squeeze and said, "You don't need to fret about any of this, Willy. Just a waste of your time."

I know she just wanted me to relax and go to sleep, but I know too that as soon as I turn off the light and close my eyes, I'm gonna fall into a nightmare featuring the fishes of Katydeeray dying a painful death. To avoid that nightmare I might just stay awake all night long with my Magic Indian.

I've had this Magic Indian friend since I was a little kid, like three or four years old. He stays outside on the window ledge till I need him, and tonight it looks like I'm gonna need him bad.

The Magic Indian wears a loincloth and has one of those Mohawk cuts with a band of hair running from front to back across the middle of his scalp but no hair at all on the sides. He doesn't smile or say much, but he can fly, and whenever I get scared and can't sleep he puts me on his back and we go for a flight out over the lake and down the valley and sometimes even up and over the peaks of the Blue Mountains. Once we stayed out till after dawn and when Mama came to get me up for school my bed was empty.

"Where've you been, Willy?" she asked after I finally got home and went down for breakfast.

I hemmed and hawed and kicked at some dust on the floor before saying, "I was out flying, Mama, with my Magic Indian."

She looked at me long and steady, and for a time I thought for sure she'd give me a tongue-lashing for lying, but then she turned back to the stove and from over her shoulder I just barely heard her say, "When I was your age, I called him my Flying Indian."

6:56 A.M.
JANUARY 20, 2001
MACKENZIE ISLAND
THE INAUGURATION OF THE FORTY-FOURTH PRESIDENT OF THE UNITED STATES

The story of the Magic Indian reminds me that we need to stay in touch with Willy's Native American roots. We haven't given that side of his family much attention yet, but we'd be fools to avoid the obvious. If we want to grasp the intellect, the passion, and the vision of our next president, we would do well to better understand his American Indian heritage.

Willy MacKenzie carries around with him no small amount of Indian blood. His great-grandmother was a full-blooded Mohawk. They called her Sarah, but she preferred her Indian name, Swift Cloud, for her fast-changing moods and explosive personality. Swift Cloud was the daughter of Nathan "Tear in His Eye" Brant, the Mohawk chief who negotiated the sale of Wassanamee Island to U. S. MacKenzie at the beginning of the twentieth century. Swift Cloud married Guy Sabattis, son of Mitchell Sabattis, the French-Canadian wilderness guide. They lived together in the Iroquois tradition and raised their children as members of the Six Nations Confederation.

Their youngest child they named Maia. Maia married Matheny Carver, a doctoral student who had come to their village to do research for his thesis in native anthropology. Their first child was born on August 6, 1945, the same day the United States of America dropped an atomic bomb on the Japanese port of Hiroshima. They named the girl Emily, and later, after her character had blossomed, they gave her the Indian name "Keeper of the Fire" because they felt she possessed the spirit of the past.

Today, in just a few hours, Emily will become the mother of our country's forty-fourth president. And in another of the day's rather unique twists, Emily Brant MacKenzie will also become her son's vice president, the first female to hold that powerful post in our nation's history.

I asked her about this in an interview yesterday morning.

> JACK STEEL: How do you feel, Mrs. MacKenzie, now that you are soon to become vice president of the United States?
>
> EMILY MACKENZIE: I feel fortunate and enthusiastic. But I also feel it's an honor long overdue, both for Native Americans and for women in general. Two hundred and twenty-five years without a single female president or vice president is, quite frankly, a little difficult to believe.
>
> J.S.: There has been quite a lot of opposition to your nomination. Many people believe you wield an undue amount of influence over your son. It has even been suggested that it will be you who runs the executive branch, not Willy.
>
> E.M.: That suggestion comes primarily from paranoid and powerful white men who feel their power and their control slipping away. It is high time we took away that power and that control and gave someone else an opportunity. The answer to your question is, yes, my son listens to his mother, but in the end he heeds his own counsel.
>
> J.S.: But it is true, is it not, Mrs. MacKenzie, that you have publicly admitted that you see yourself and your son not as citizens of the United States, but as members of the Iroquois League of Nations?
>
> E.M.: I see myself as both. And I will do my best to serve both entities as vice president of the United States.

The first presidential inauguration of this new century continues to astound. Moments ago both National Public Radio and the Associated

Press announced that the chief justice of the United States, Sandra Day O'Connor, will not, repeat, will not, administer the oath of office to the new president. As speculated but not confirmed until this morning, the chief justice refuses to play any part in the swearing-in ceremony.

In her brief statement, just released from her heavily guarded offices at the Supreme Court, Ms. O'Connor, who became the country's first female chief justice two years ago after Chief Justice William Rehnquist retired following several unsuccessful attempts on his life by pro-choice advocates, said: "The election of William MacKenzie to the highest office in the land makes a mockery of the Constitution. This man is not old enough to assume the presidency under the constitutional laws of the United States. For this reason, and for this reason alone, I will not participate in his inauguration or, in keeping with tradition, administer the oath of office."

Chief Justice O'Connor may be using the Constitution to remove herself from this mess, but most Court observers believe her decision has more to do with politics and personal safety than ethics. Any connection whatsoever to Willy MacKenzie is seen as a political liability. Most senators, congressmen, and other power players inside the Washington Beltway have avoided the president-elect as though he harbored some fatal and contagious disease.

Politics, however, is only part of the reason they have kept their distance. Fear for their physical well-being has also played a part in this scenario. Chief Justice O'Connor offers a striking example. Last week I went to the Supreme Court to interview Ms. O'Connor. A year ago, even six months ago, I would have marched right up the steps and into our nation's grand marble house of justice, pausing only long enough to pass through a simple metal detector. But when I visited last week I found the building under the protection of young, very well-armed marines who frisked me and demanded I state my business. Scary stuff when you have spent your entire life under the wings of a free and open democracy.

This siege mentality sweeping our political and legal institutions obviously predates the arrival of Willy MacKenzie to the national scene. His election has only intensified an already ugly situation.

Assassination plots on Willy's life have been flying since the election results became official last November. Every radical from Maine to Maui has threatened to put an exploding bullet right between Willy's eyes. These nuts seem to fall at every extreme of the political spectrum. Both ultraliberals and -conservatives want Willy dead.

And they're not the only ones. The nation's first military grab for power poses a very real threat. Not only has Willy accused the military of virtually every atrocious crime under the Stars and Stripes, but he has also publicly stated his desire to cut their manpower and their munitions in half and in half again. And to add insult to injury, he has also said the armed forces will be used to clean up refuse along the nation's highways, lakeshores, and beaches. And not just the privates, but the lieutenants, colonels, and generals as well. In times of peace our military manpower will be put to work refurbishing our decaying infrastructure.

Let's go back now and take a look at the early years of the man Willy has chosen to run the refurbished Department of Defense: his own father, Conrad Whitman MacKenzie.

* * * * * * *

The day after their wedding, Lawrence and Rebecca MacKenzie sailed south to the Caribbean for six weeks of fun in the sun. A few months after they returned from their honeymoon, in the late summer of 1925, Rebecca quietly disappeared.

When she reappeared, on January 1, 1926, Rebecca held an infant in her arms: Conrad Whitman MacKenzie, the father of our president-elect. He was an enormous baby, weighing almost sixteen pounds on the day of his first public appearance. Senator MacKenzie's office had released a statement earlier in the week stating that Rebecca had given birth on Christmas morning.

In fact, Conrad Whitman MacKenzie had been born back on September 27, 1925. But in yet another effort by the MacKenzie clan to dictate the terms of their births, Ulysses insisted the official record show his grandson entered the world a full nine months after the marriage of Lawrence and Rebecca.

"I don't want any two-bit reporter adding up the numbers," he told his son, "when you make your run for the White House. Any suggestion whatsoever you had fathered that child out of wedlock could spell curtains for your presidential bid."

Lawrence had no desire to run for president (that was his father's dream), but he allowed Ulysses to pay off the right people to have his son's birth date changed to that of Christ's, in the year of our Lord nineteen hundred and twenty-five.

Regardless of when he was born, Conrad Whitman MacKenzie might just as well have been born a prince. The boy who would one day sire our next president had a loving mother and a doting father. His mother took him to the White House, where he spit up on Gracie Coolidge's lap; then, after his bottle, he emptied his tiny bladder onto Calvin's favorite reading chair. His father took him into the Senate chamber, where he wailed in the middle of a pro-labor speech by his grandfather's old nemesis, Robert La Follette.

Back at the brownstone in Georgetown, Senator Lawrence MacKenzie and his beautiful young bride, Rebecca, settled, believe it or not, into a wedded bliss that sustained itself for almost all of the next thirty years. Larry fell madly in love with his wife the day Conrad came into the world. His relationship with Miss Whitman had started with nothing more than a flirtation, but when he saw that smiling infant he tasted his first drop of eternity.

"You know, Becky," he said to his wife, who had battled most of a day to bring Conrad into the world, "it's all starting to make sense to me now: the sun, the moon, the stars, Ulysses, me, Conrad. If you think about it, it's incredible, absolutely amazing."

But Rebecca wasn't so sure. In fact, she didn't give it much thought; she had passed out from the sheer exhaustion of her labors.

Lawrence was not a deep thinker, but he thought long and hard enough that day to realize what he wanted more than anything else in life was to make his wife and son happy. And so that's what he set out to do. He came to know his wife, and in no time at all he discovered a fine and pleasant woman with many exceptional qualities.

And unlike his father, who once slept with a different woman every day for forty days and forty nights just to prove he could do it, Larry never fooled around once he slipped that ring onto Rebecca's finger. It could be said the senator and his wife became downright boring after the birth of Conrad, what with all their domestic felicities.

They did, however, experience several months of melancholy after the miscarriage of their second child in the spring of 1928. But a year and a half later, on the day of the Great Crash, October 29, 1929, a baby girl was born, strong and healthy. They named her Patricia after Rebecca's mother.

Patricia's grandfather, Ulysses MacKenzie, was not on hand for her birth. He had left some six months earlier on a trip around the world. "I'm sick and tired of working fifteen hours a day six days a week fifty-two weeks a year," the sixty-four-year-old multimillionaire told his son. "There's more to life than making money."

So he filled a leather duffel bag with legal tender of mostly large denominations, and off he went. He took the *Fresco Express* from New York to San Francisco, then a luxury liner from San Francisco to Honolulu. After a month in the islands he sailed on to Fiji and then New Zealand. From Auckland he sent his son this terse message: "I have come halfway around the world," he wrote. "Big fucking deal." Then he moved on to more important matters. "The economy's going to hell. I can feel it in my bones. The shit's about to slam into the fan. So listen up, Larry, and listen good: Sell all stocks, even at a loss, and cash in all bonds. Stuff the money in the mattresses. Hide it in the closets. Bury it in some deep hole. I don't give a good goddamn what you do with it just as long as you get it away from those stinking stockbrokers and those thieving bankers."

In early September of 1929 Lawrence passed his father's message on to the family's principal financial adviser. But Ian Foster thought pulling out of the market with prices falling was a very bad idea. So he waited. He felt sure things would turn around. Well, as most of us already know, things did not turn around. Prices kept falling, lower and lower, until finally the bottom fell out, causing individuals all over the country who had large sums invested in the stock market to leap out of tall buildings and put bullets between their eyes.

Ulysses MacKenzie did not lose his entire fortune, not by a long shot, but at the close of the market on October 30, 1929, his assets were worth about half of what they had been worth the day before. He received the news while in Burma playing blackjack with a colonel in the British army and several extremely wealthy Burmese pimps. Their marathon session lasted into the wee hours of the morning, during which time four quarts of Chivas Regal were consumed and a dozen young Burmese lasses violated between hands. Ulysses lost close to a thousand dollars that night, but after he learned what had happened on Wall Street, the old boy said, "The thousand pissed me off, I could've killed that smiling limey, but the paper millions, shit, I didn't even feel it beyond a slight burning in my bowels."

Ian Foster felt it. Ulysses knocked out most of Ian's teeth with one blow upon his return to New York on the day before Christmas of that disastrous year for Wall Street investors. "Get yourself some false teeth, Ian, you stupid English twit," the Scotsman shouted at the man with the bloody mouth, "then pack up your pencils and get the hell out of here!"

The MacKenzies spent Christmas at U.S.'s magnificent home on Park Avenue. The butler served Scotch imported from north of Edinburgh. The cook prepared pheasant and ham with all the trimmings. Ulysses told about his adventures in the South Pacific, India, Kenya, and Egypt. He bounced his four-year-old grandson, Conrad, and his two-month-old granddaughter, Patricia, on his knee. After dinner Ulysses and Lawrence retired to the study, where they smoked aromatic Cuban cigars and sipped fine French brandy.

"I was wrong, son," Ulysses told Lawrence.

"About what, Dad?"

"About the money."

"No, you weren't," insisted Lawrence. "You told me to tell Ian to sell. He just failed—"

Ulysses waved his son off. "No, that's not what I mean. Before I left to travel the world I said there was more to life than making money."

"Oh, yes, that. I remember now."

"Well, I was wrong. Dead wrong. As wrong as I've ever been about anything. The only goddamn thing worth doing in life is making money. The rest is a waste of time."

"But, Dad, you're almost sixty-five years old. Don't you want to retire, enjoy your twilight years? I mean, even though we took a beating in the Crash, it's not as if we're about to starve to death."

"Retire! Enjoy my twilight years! For chrissakes, Larry, I'll retire the day you stick me in the ground, not a second sooner. I plan to make up the money we lost and then double it, maybe triple it. Hell, everyone's running around with their tails between their legs, acting like this little economic downturn is the end of the world. Perfect time to kick some butt, if you ask me. Billy Vanderbilt taught me a long time ago that any stupid two bit a-hole can make money during good times, but the real honest-to-God, mean-as-sin, down-and-dirty ass kickers can make money even in bad times."

The senator nodded.

The MacKenzies sipped their brandy, puffed their cigars.

"So," Ulysses asked, "how's things in Washington?"

The capital, as the new decade dawned, smoldered. With the economy in a shambles and the politicians running for cover, the name of the game had become point your finger and blame the other guy. Hoover, who had entered the White House in 1928 with high hopes and his ever-present zeal for the benefits of hard work, was suddenly, for the first time in his long and distinguished career as a public servant, in the doghouse. No way could he have stopped the inevitable. Policies and national habits long in place when he stepped into the Oval Office nine months before the Crash were the major cause of the country's economic slide. But don't try to explain that to the fickle voting public. Herbert, who had wanted so much to be the good guy, the benevolent and kindly leader, found himself holed up in the White House as the nation and the world slipped ever deeper into the financial doldrums.

Mr. Hoover was not the only public servant to suffer. If Senator MacKenzie's first term had been an amusing and painless political debut, his second term, beginning in 1928, proved somewhat more distressing. Tough times faced the nation, and certain high-ranking members of the Senate felt the time had come for Larry to step up to the plate and carry his weight. No more naked sunbathing on the Capitol roof, no more catnaps in the chamber because little Conrad had been up all night with a fever, no more avoiding participation in the committee system. For six years Larry had been a member of just one committee, the Commerce Committee, and that only because Ulysses had slipped the committee chairman a generous campaign contribution to secure his son a seat. Behind closed doors Larry was told to shape up.

Initially, the Republican leadership in the Senate followed Hoover's lead by calling on Americans to battle economic hardship with personal initiative and individual grit. Hoover did not trust government intervention to cure economic ills. He believed in business enterprise and private charity. But by the early 1930s it was clear that people all across the country wanted, even expected, their government to help them survive these difficult and troubled times.

Rebecca MacKenzie agreed. She was an avid reader of liberal-minded periodicals. She had read about the jobless and the homeless and the helpless. She knew about the Hoovervilles springing up across the nation. She knew about the farmers facing foreclosure and the dirt-poor families roaming the countryside in search of food and work and shelter.

During dinner at their luxurious house in Georgetown, Rebecca would tell her husband about the plight of the poor. At first he barely heard her; his ability to grasp any reality but his own had always been difficult. But finally, after Becky had been bombarding him for months about the wretched conditions facing literally millions of Americans, Larry cleared the cobwebs. It happened in the middle of his second term, in the middle of his thirty-seventh year, in the middle of the night. Senator Lawrence MacKenzie popped up out of a sound sleep and saw the whole world spinning out of control. He gave his wife a shake. "Becky, sweetheart, wake up! Something has happened!"

He told her he had seen the light. Together they wept. She held him close. They kissed in the darkness of their warm, safe, secluded bedroom. And in no time at all, they were both sound asleep again, dreaming their guiltless dreams.

The senator did not become a liberal Democrat overnight, but he did help sponsor such Republican economic cure-alls as the Reconstruction Finance Corporation, the Relief and Construction Act, and the Federal Home Loan Bank Act. These programs, however, proved too little too late. The Great Depression deepened. Roosevelt creamed Hoover in the November elections, and the Democrats rolled into Washington for what proved to be the beginning of two full decades of executive and legislative dominance.

Larry, his political antennae all a-quiver, felt the tide turning, the storm approaching. So with his wife's encouragement, he declared himself a Democrat not long before the start of his third election campaign in the spring of 1934.

"This has been an agonizing and difficult decision," he told a gathering of supporters at the Plaza Hotel in New York City, "but I realize now my true calling is to assist and protect the weak and downtrodden in our society. If I can help even one man find a job, even one woman feed her family, even one child stay warm on a winter's night, I will feel as though I have done my constitutional and Christian duty."

The press proved skeptical, casting aspersions that perhaps Senator MacKenzie's lofty sentiments were politically motivated. But the skeptics died away as the election grew closer and Larry at every opportunity hammered home his theme about helping those who could not help themselves. And in the end, regardless of his true motivations, the voters accepted Larry's conversion and embraced his message. In November the two-time incumbent easily defeated his Republican opponent, winning two votes out of every three cast.

In the end there remained only one loud and boisterous dissenter: Larry's dad, the aging but ever volatile Ulysses S. Grant MacKenzie.

"You're a goddamn traitor, boy! Not so long ago you agreed with me when I suggested we take all the Democrats out behind the barn and shoot 'em. Now all of a sudden you think their shit don't stink. You think their highfalutin liberal ideas are gonna save the day. Well, I think you got shit for brains. This do-gooder Roosevelt and his choir boys are a bunch of closet Bolsheviks. Son of a bitch is gonna overregulate, overadministrate, and overtax us right into oblivion."

"Something has to be done, Dad," Larry protested. "People are suffering."

"Jesus Christ! You think this goddamn New Deal's going to solve the problems of the world? You think suffering's some new phenomenon of the twentieth century? Suffering's as old as syphilis, boy. Maybe older."

"Why is it wrong to want to help?"

U.S. shook his head and guffawed. "We're a sick and selfish species. The only way we help others is through first and foremost helping ourselves. We don't do a damn thing without expecting something in return. That's just the way it is. You say you want to help. How? By giving every son of a bitch in town a key to the candy store? Do you know what happens when you do that?"

Lawrence did not like being lectured, so he dropped his eyes and shrugged.

"I'll tell you what happens. Pretty soon the goddamn candy runs out. And you know what happens then?"

Lawrence shook his head.

"War, you little twerp. War war war."

"War?"

"That's right, boy. War! Mark my words. I've been a student of history all my long life, and I tell you, these crooks and liars who govern, they're all the same. They all resort to the same old bullshit once they get their asses in a jam. And they'll do it this time, too. Before it's all over, before this economy turns itself around, they'll have our boys fightin' again, fightin' and killin' and dyin', same as they did a few short years back, and countless other goddamn times before that."

"I really don't see armed conflict on the horizon, Dad. The League of Nations might've run out of steam, but the major powers in the world now have open lines of communication."

"League of Nations! Open lines of communication! What crap are you feeding an old dog now? You wanna be a pretty-boy Democrat, go ahead, boy, follow the crowd, be a sheep. You're just like the rest of these liberal windbags: you want to take that famous line 'All men are created equal' and act like it was more than just a fancy political slogan created by some sharp and greedy power brokers who wanted to break away from England so they could slice up the great American pie among themselves. And you call yourself a MacKenzie! Shit!"

May 2, 1981

Last night after supper I went out and sat on the front porch. I looked out across MacKenzie Island and Lake Katydeeray at the Blue Mountain peaks. Most of the lower peaks in close to the lake I've already climbed: Carmy, Sabitou, Little Rieson, Banner. But farther out, in the distance, still covered with snow, rise some of the highest peaks in the Blue Range—Nuttyback, Big Rieson, Ondaga, and Whiteface. I'm still waiting for my chance to climb those peaks, still waiting for Papa and Sanders to tell me to strap on my pack.

After I'd sat on the porch a spell Mama came out and joined me. We sat there for a while without saying much, but then I got to thinking about something that had happened at school. "We've been studying the Iroquois again, Mama."

"Oh? And what lies have they been telling you now?"

"Did the Iroquois really use torture on their enemies?"

Right off I could see Mama didn't like this talk. "Tell me what they told you, Willy."

"Well, let's see. Mr. Ambler, our history teacher, he told us the Iroquois would take a sharp piece of wood and push it through a prisoner's Achilles' tendon. Using the piece of wood like a needle, they'd draw a length of catgut through the hole. Then they'd tie a bunch of prisoners together with the catgut and march them back to the Iroquois village. The lucky ones got buried alive in big pits. The unlucky ones got sacrificed. The Iroquois'd strap them to a pole in the middle of the village and each member of the tribe would come by and whack them. The kids used sticks to gouge out flesh from the prisoner's legs. The women burned the prisoner with hot coals. And the men, the braves, to prove their manhood, would scalp the prisoner, then pour boiling water on the bloody wound."

Mama listened to my story without making a sound. I was surprised she let me tell it all without interrupting. When I finished she asked, "You're telling the truth, Willy? This is what your teacher taught you about the Iroquois?"

I nodded but looked away. "Mostly," I said. "Maybe some of it I found in a book."

"And what else did this Mr. Ambler teach you? What else have you read in that book?"

The look in her eye made me wish I'd never brought it up. "Oh, I don't know, some other stuff, but the part about the tortures is the part I remember best."

Mama stared for a time at the yellow moonlight flickering off the lake. Finally she said, "Hear me, Willy, and hear me good. The white men who write these things and teach you these things want you to hate the Iroquois. They want you to think the Iroquois were a savage and uncivilized people.

"Yes, it's true, the Iroquois did torture their prisoners. The men were fierce warriors. They had no fear of blood or death, and absolutely no compassion for their enemies. During part of their history there were many wars. And for them, war had no rules. You either fought and lived or you fought and died. So yes, Willy, the Iroquois did practice torture. Most North American Indian tribes did."

"So they really did scalp their enemies?"

"There was more to it than just the savage brutality of the act. The Iroquois believed, Willy, that the terrible cries of the prisoners helped ward off evil spirits and famine and disease. The tribal leaders also believed that torture was an excellent means of deterrence, of preventing war. As word spread of the wild and vicious treatment of prisoners at the hands of the Iroquois, the other tribes thought long and hard before going into battle against them. In this way the Iroquois frightened their enemies into submission. The use of torture was one of the principal reasons why the Iroquois Nation became the largest and most powerful Indian nation on the continent. And they held power until an even more brutal enemy arrived."

"Who was that, Mama, the Cherokee?"

"No, Willy, it was the European, the white man."

"Did the Europeans use torture too?"

"Yes, Willy, they did. Mankind has a history of torture, of inflicting pain on the weak and the defeated. Do not let these white men make you think for one second that their ancestors behaved any better than your ancestors. In many ways the white men were worse. They had no respect for any living thing. They killed without reason, without remorse. They killed out of fear. Man is a brutal beast, Willy, and only when he learns love and compassion does his enemy stand a chance."

I felt confused and kind of hollow inside, like it might be nice to lie down on the porch and close my eyes. But instead I asked, "How come men torture each other, Mama?"

"Because they're crazy, Willy. Crazy as loons."

"Are women crazy too, Mama?"

"No. You don't need to worry about women, Willy. There are a few bad apples, but not many. It's the men you need to worry about. They're the ones who do the pillaging and the torturing and the raping and the killing. Keep your eye on them."

I just sort of sat there nodding with my mouth open. The sky was clear and high. We studied the constellations. Mama pointed out Orion. I pointed out the Big Dipper.

After a time I said, "I'm almost a man, Mama. I don't want to pillage or torture or rape or kill."

"That's fine, Willy. I'll remind you of that once you get a little older."

June 6, 1981

Yesterday was my birthday. I finally hit thirteen. A very big birthday around here. It means I get to operate some of the smaller speedboats, especially the Gar Runabout, so I'll be able to go over to town whenever I feel like it. Not that I'll go all that often. Like Sanders says, there's a whole lifetime of learning right here on the islands. Still, it'll be nice to know I can go if and when I want to.

Yesterday was a great birthday even if I did get an old-fashioned scolding from Mama for messing up her garden. We had a party here on the island. About a dozen of us. Mostly guys, a few girls. Would've been more girls but Dawn's still in Florida. Too bad, she might've kept me out of trouble.

We grilled venison burgers and then everyone sang Happy Birthday, Willy, and then we ate the chocolate cake Mama'd made. After the cake we played some games: hide-and-seek, dodge ball, spud, stuff like that. But then a few of us, Henry Bender and me mostly, got a little stirred up and started racing around like a couple of headless chickens. It wasn't long before Henry went racing through Mama's garden and I went racing in after him. Without really meaning to, I guess, we trampled some bean plants and busted down some corn stalks.

Mama waited until everyone had gone home. Then she grabbed me by the ear and marched me out to the scene of the crime. Now I have to say that maybe half a dozen times at the most in my first twelve years have I seen Mama mad. Oh, she spouts off from time to time about one thing or another, but she has to be pushed mighty far to get an honest-to-goodness mad on.

But yesterday, look out, she was as mad as a yellow jacket. "Looks to me, Willy MacKenzie," she said, pointing at the damage, "like a wild animal's been let loose in here."

I stood there trying to ignore the pain in my ear and the broken corn stalks laid out before my eyes. Mama twisted my ear a little further and for a good four or five minutes we just stood there quiet as trees on a dead calm summer day as though waiting for the garden to maybe heal itself. I knew something was coming but wasn't real sure what.

"Using my garden for a playground, young man," she said finally, the tone of her voice sending a shiver down my spine, "is a disgrace. It shows disrespect for me, and more important, for the earth. Now I want you to stand here until it's too dark to see, and think about what you've done. I don't want you to move a muscle or let your eyes wander. I want you to stare so long at those damaged plants that you become one of them, that you feel their pain."

Then Mama let go of my ear, turned, and walked away. I heard her footsteps on the back porch, then the screen door opening and slamming closed. I wanted in the worst way to turn and take a look, but no way did I have the guts. So I stood there without hardly moving an inch, exactly as ordered.

The days last a mighty long time up here this time of year, doesn't even begin to grow dark until near ten o'clock. Then for another hour or so it's only sort of dark, so I guess it was close to eleven before Mama opened the back door and told me to quit my vigil and come inside.

She sent me up to bed without supper after telling me a boy who destroys crops doesn't deserve to eat. I thought she was probably right, but my stomach was growling nevertheless. "It'll do you good," she said as I made my way slowly up the back steps.

I lay in bed thinking about that chocolate birthday cake down in the fridge when Mama stepped quietly into my room. I saw right off her mad was all used up and put away and she had some Indian stuff on her mind.

"Our ancestors, Willy," she said as she sat on the edge of the bed, "taught us that nature should not be disturbed without sacrifice and without ceremony. Every morsel of food we put in our mouths is a gift from nature. But we have to earn these gifts. And we begin by respecting the earth. Do you understand?"

I nodded. "Yes, ma'am."

"Have I told you about the Three Sisters, Willy?"

"I don't think so."

"What did you see this evening when you stood before the garden?"

I gave her the answer I figured she wanted. "I saw the plants I'd wrecked."

"But what kind of plants?"

"Corn . . . beans."

"Anything else?"

I shrugged.

"Squash, Willy, you also trampled some squash. Corn, beans, and squash—those are the Three Sisters. For hundreds of years the Three Sisters have kept our people alive. I grow other crops as well, fruits and vegetables, but these three are the essentials, the ones that give us sustenance and strength. The earth enjoys providing us with the Three Sisters. It does so willingly as long as we return the favor with pure air, clean soil, and fresh water. Do you understand what I am telling you, Willy?"

I nodded. "I think so."

"Good. So in the morning you will help me repair the damage. I will teach you how to plant and nurture the Three Sisters. Agriculture, the tilling of the soil, was always women's work in the Iroquois tradition, but I think it's time men, and boys like you, began to get their hands dirty as well. Just a few weeks ago we talked about how the Iroquois used torture against their enemies. You told me that day, Willy, that you wanted to avoid pillaging and torturing and killing. But do you see now how easily things change, how quickly you can go astray?"

I thought it over and nodded again. "Yes, ma'am."

"All right then. Tomorrow I'll show you how to plant the corn first. Then, in a few weeks, after the corn stalks have sprouted and gained strength, we plant the beans and the squash. As the summer grows warm the vines holding the beans and the squash will wrap themselves around the corn stalks and head for the sun. It is a perfect system, Willy, and one that, if you learn it well and give respect to the earth and the air and the water, will keep you always from going hungry."

We both heard my stomach rumble. "I'm hungry now, Mama."

She stood and moved toward the door. "Self-imposed hunger is good for us, Willy. It makes us understand and appreciate a full belly and the sincerity of our thoughts. Now go to sleep, and dream of a bountiful harvest." She turned off the light and left.

I made no move for that chocolate cake in the kitchen. Instead I thought about the Three Sisters and how I couldn't wait to tell Dawn all about them. She's due home in just a few days.

7:23 A.M.
JANUARY 20, 2001
MACKENZIE ISLAND
THE INAUGURATION OF THE FORTY-FOURTH PRESIDENT OF THE UNITED STATES

And so we begin to understand the cultural schizophrenia facing our president-elect. On the one extreme he has this Old World white Anglo-Saxon Protestant chain draped around his neck, and on the other extreme this New World Native American culture facing him every time he looks in the mirror or into his mother's eyes. It must have been tough on him as a kid, and probably it only got tougher as he grew older. But let's face it, this dichotomy is one of the things that has made Willy MacKenzie an interesting and intriguing character.

And it just might make him an extraordinary and effective president as well, if he gets the opportunity.

But before we take a closer look at Willy's Indian heritage, we first need to report on a fast-breaking story that has just come over the wire. It seems the chartered express train carrying diplomats, foreign dignitaries, and several hundred members of the press north to Cedar Bluffs for the inauguration of William Conrad Brant MacKenzie has been delayed, perhaps even waylaid. Unconfirmed sources claim the train has been stopped and boarded by military personnel, either troops from the United States Army or the United States Marine Corps. The exact location of the train is not known at this time. We also do not know of any reason why this action may have been taken.

However, it has already been suggested that certain high-ranking members of Anderson Montgomery's administration might be involved. For weeks the Montgomery administration has been putting pressure on foreign governments to keep their ambassadors and high-ranking officials from attending the inauguration. They have cited safety and security as their reasons for applying this pressure, but my sources indicate all the arm twisting has had more to do with undermining the president-elect's power and credibility.

Does this activity indicate a possible coup by President Montgomery in this, his final hours as head of state? Has he enlisted the help of the military to maintain power? Are they prepared to oppose the inauguration of Willy MacKenzie through the use of force, through the application of violence? If so, why have they stopped a train from reaching its destination? What do they expect such an action to accomplish?

All of this, of course, is mere speculation. Perhaps that northbound train has simply experienced some mechanical difficulties. Or maybe ice and snow have blocked the tracks. We know a vicious winter storm has swept across the area and is set to pound these Blue Mountains within the hour. A coup is certainly not the only explanation.

We will provide you with additional information as it becomes available. But right now seems like an excellent time to go back and delve into a little native history.

* * * * * * *

When the first Europeans entered the Hudson River Valley in the 1600s, they found a group of Indians unlike any they had encountered before. These Indians were highly organized and very adept at both warfare and diplomacy. They were the Iroquois, a confederation of five tribes that dominated the territory stretching from the Hudson River west to Lake Ontario and from the St. Lawrence south as far as present-day Pittsburgh. On the eastern border of this confederacy lived the Mohawk. On the western frontier lived the Seneca and the Cayuga. And in the middle lived the Oneida and the Onondaga.

Before the creation of their confederation, for a period known to the

Iroquois as the Time of Darkness, the five tribes lived in an almost constant state of war. Generation after generation learned to kill or be killed. They had no concept of peace. Living by an axiom similar to one many of us know well: an eye for an eye, the Iroquois spilled blood as easily as they quenched their thirst. They practiced torture, cannibalism, and human sacrifice.

But then among them was born a red-skinned baby whose story has many similarities to that of Jesus of Nazareth. According to the legend, he was conceived of a virgin mother, and at a young and innocent age he set off into an unknown world to spread a message he did not fully understand. A dozen Iroquois sages will recount his story a dozen different ways, but the one fact that shines through in all accounts is this young man's intestinal fortitude. He had guts. With blood flying all around him, with dead and dying bodies strewn everywhere, with warfare and treachery the political reality of his time, he stood up and called for peace.

Over the centuries the sages have given this man many different names. Deganawidah is the one we hear most often. Another is Hiawatha, although many say Hiawatha was a disciple or even a mortal incarnation of Deganawidah. One thing is clear: The Hiawatha of Iroquois fame, of Iroquois immortality, had nothing whatsoever to do with the poem of the same name by that pompous ass and consummate racist white man, Henry Wadsworth Longfellow.

Whatever you call him, Hiawatha brought peace to the five nations and was ever after known as the Creator of the Great Peace. If he lived today, he would be a famous diplomat, a supreme statesman. Every president and prime minister would want him in their cabinet. He took five diametrically opposed nations that had been at war with one another for countless generations, and in the course of just a few years, he had them not only on friendly terms, but actually forming one of the world's first-known federations.

But how many of us have ever even heard of this Indian Hiawatha? He seems barely to exist at all in contemporary textbooks used to teach our children the history of North America. Is this a simple slip, a mere lapse of memory, in the long chronology? Or is something more sinister at work in the omission of this important Indian from our historical record?

* * *

Let's take a quick look at how Hiawatha achieved his Great Peace. It's important we do so for two reasons. First, because it has been suggested that our president-elect is directly related to this ancient character, perhaps even Hiawatha's reincarnation. And second, because the polls have shown that many of the people who voted for Willy did so because they believed he might bring the same miracles to our era that Hiawatha brought to his. "Go ahead and laugh," they said, "but with everything so screwed up environmentally, socially, and politically, we could do with a savior carrying a miracle or two around in his pocket."

Hiawatha used many of the same tools still used today by modern politicians: flattery, manipulation, cunning, and compromise. Hiawatha knew what he wanted, and through trial and error he learned how to get things done. He had great oratory skills and excellent powers of persuasion. Over time he brought together the chiefs of the five tribes and stroked their egos. He told them how wonderful they were, how powerful, how perfect. And then, because he knew they relied heavily on mysticism to explain the mysteries of life, he told them he had been sent by the Creator, by the Great Spirit, to bring peace and harmony to their people.

The chiefs scoffed at this pronouncement. They demanded proof from Hiawatha that he had been sent by the Great Spirit. Hiawatha did not hesitate. "I will climb that tall pine growing along the cliff above the roaring river," he told the chiefs, "and when I reach the top you will chop the tree down. If I survive the fall into the river's rapids, you will know I am the emissary of the Great Spirit sent to end the wars and stop the famine."

The chiefs snickered among themselves, then agreed this was a suitable test. No way did they think the stranger could survive the fall.

Up Hiawatha climbed, to the very highest branches. The towering pine tree was chopped down. It toppled over the cliff and into the raging river. All those present saw Hiawatha fall into the rapids and slam against the rocks. He disappeared beneath the swirling current. The chiefs stood atop the cliff, their smiles barely hidden. They knew for sure the stranger had perished, drowned in the river's fury. They labeled him a fraud and turned their backs.

But the next morning, as the chiefs prepared to part and resume their cycle of war and death and revenge, into the camp strolled Hiawatha. He looked unharmed, not a scratch on his person. At first they thought he was a ghost. But when he pricked his finger he bled. Thus began the Great Peace.

The Iroquois had no alphabet, no written language, but they nevertheless created what can only be called a constitution. This oral log represented the laws and the responsibilities of the five nations. The Mohawk, Oneida, Onondaga, Cayuga, and Seneca agreed to stop killing each other and to begin living according to the rules and regulations of the constitution. Their agreement called for cooperation among the five tribes. They would share their territories and hunting grounds. They would come to one another's aid if invaded by an outside enemy. They agreed to set up trade and guarantee free and safe passage. And at least once a year they sent representatives to a central location to discuss problems and to further their alliance.

It was this League of Five Nations that was in effect when the first Europeans entered the Hudson River Valley in the early seventeenth century. And although the white man has done his best to wipe the Iroquois off the face of the earth, to impose upon them, as upon all native peoples of this continent, a brutal and calculated genocide, this same league, though small and seemingly powerless, still survives today.

In fact, many believe the league is about to take control of the most powerful political office in the country, perhaps on earth. Certainly the powers that be all across this mighty land believe this to be true. That's why they're running scared, holding last minute meetings behind closed doors, possibly planning to blow MacKenzie Island right off the map with a couple of Tomahawk cruise missiles.

There is, of course, a very interesting irony here. In order to share this irony with you, we will have to step back a moment for a visit with Benjamin Franklin. That's right, Ben Franklin, the old-timer who sort of discovered electricity, who signed the Declaration of Independence, and who adorns every single one of our worthless one-hundred-dollar bills.

Mr. Franklin led a remarkable life, one worthy of kudos in many different arenas. But today we are interested in his work with the United States Constitution and its predecessor, the Articles of Confederation. We know Ben had a firm and heavy hand in the preparation of both these vital documents that gave rise to a new nation. We also know he had firsthand knowledge of the Iroquois and their League of Five Nations (actually six by this time, due to the entry of the Tuscarora tribe, circa 1722).

In his inimitable and often sarcastic style, Mr. Franklin once voiced these words to his fellow delegates at the Second Continental Congress: "It would be a very strange thing indeed if six nations of ignorant savages could form a capable union and execute that union in such a manner that it has subsisted for ages and appears indissoluble; and yet a like union should be found impracticable for a dozen English colonies to whom it would seem an even more practical and powerful necessity."

We know for a fact that Benjamin Franklin, Alexander Hamilton, James Madison, and the other framers of the Constitution used the League of Iroquois Nations as a model to assist them in their struggle to create something more than another Old World monarchy. There can be no disposition on this point. In many ways the League of Six Nations was the progenitor of these United States. This is undoubtedly a tough pill for many of us to swallow, especially considering our homicidal attitude toward these people, but it's a new century and a new age, so we will simply have to grin and bear the truth.

7:37 A.M.
JANUARY 20, 2001
MACKENZIE ISLAND
THE INAUGURATION OF THE FORTY-FOURTH PRESIDENT OF THE UNITED STATES

I'm sitting here wondering how Willy fits into this irony. Certainly his mother schooled him well on the brutal and calculated injustices the white man perpetrated upon the red man over the past four hundred years. But let us not forget that Willy is predominately a white man, an Anglo-Saxon. The MacKenzies are an ancient Scottish clan, and to this day the majority of the president-elect's blood comes from that chilly, damp land to the north of England where men are stoic and stubborn, and fiercely independent.

What does all of Willy's mixed blood, ethnic duality, and genetic schizophrenia mean to the future of this country? Willy, like so many Americans, is a blend of different cultures, diverse backgrounds, and geographic incongruities. Where do his loyalties lie? Whom does he trust? Is he a red man or a white man? An Anglo or an Iroquois? A Republican or a Democrat? A bleeding-heart liberal or a blue-blood conservative? Is he truly the last innocent man in America or just another political opportunist cashing in on a society in turmoil?

Above all, who is Willy MacKenzie? And can he get the job done?

We have looked at some of his early journal entries. We have witnessed small moments from his mostly idyllic childhood. We have experienced his creativity and his imagination. We have met his family and his friends. But the boy is growing older. The boy is fast becoming a young man.

I would like now to turn to an entry written in the early summer of 1982, when Willy was fourteen years old. For the first time he will refer to the Tamaqua Valley Dam and Development Project. He could not possibly have known it at the time, and yet if you study his words carefully, you will see that he somehow senses the project will have tremendous impact on his life in the years to come. I believe the moment Willy overheard his father and his brother discussing that hydroelectric dam, his innocence was forever after shattered.

* * * * * *

June 22, 1982

The first full day of summer. I wouldn't mind if it was the first day of summer every day. Mama says some of our Iroquois ancestors could hold time in the palm of their hand to keep it from slipping away. I sure would like to possess the power to do that.

I was up and at it early this morning; wasn't even light yet when I went down the hall and knocked softly on Dawn's door. She's been living with us all winter and spring, but next week her parents return from Florida so she'll be moving back across the channel to Tamarack. That's only a couple minutes by boat but I'll miss her just the same.

This morning she wasn't real glad to see me. She doesn't like getting up as early as I do so the second I stepped into her room she started yelling at me to get out and not come back till the sun showed over the Blues. I made a run for the door before she threw a book or something at me.

Halfway down the stairs I heard voices: Sanders and Papa. Sanders hasn't been around for a few days, away on business was all anyone told me. I wondered what he was doing over at the house so early, so I crept down the stairs a little further to listen in on their conversation.

"Well, Pop," I heard Sanders say, "I can tell you one thing, that was no wild goose chase."

"You learned something?"

"I learned the rumors we've been hearing might hold water."

Papa shook his head. "I had a feeling this new Administration might be trouble. Front man like that, you know they have a secret agenda."

I could see Papa, but not real well through the spindles of the carved wooden bannister. He wore nothing but a plaid robe and a pair of boxer shorts. His cheeks and chin were white where he recently cut off his winter whiskers, but the rest of his face was red and worn from the sun and the wind. Papa prefers to be outside. He says it's not natural for a man to hang around indoors. Claims it's the cause for most of the world's ills.

"So what are they cooking up for the valley this time?" he asked.

"I heard talk," said Sanders, "of a hydroelectric dam as big as anything east of the Mississippi."

"Hell," growled Papa, "the government's been talking that line since the fifties, no, the thirties. FDR wanted to build a dam on the Tamaqua to put the unemployed to work. Ulysses and Lawrence killed that project dead in the water."

"All I know is what I heard, Pop."

"And what did you hear?"

"I heard talk of a plan to harness the power of the Tamaqua River downstream from Katydeeray. Sounds like they're pretty well along in their thinking. They've studied the environmental impact on the river valley. It's possible water levels on the lake could rise as much as forty or even fifty feet."

Papa stayed quiet for a few seconds, then I heard him say, "Talk's cheap, son, especially in that town. It's the only thing they do doesn't cost us money."

"Might be more than talk, Pop. The Army Corps of Engineers has been in the valley."

Papa stroked his chin and sighed. "All right," he said, finally, "let's get some coffee."

They turned and started for the kitchen. The door closed. I quickly crept downstairs and along the hallway. I pressed my ear to the door but couldn't hear a word they said.

I stood there for a minute or two thinking things over but that got me feeling troubled so I slipped out the front door, ran down to the boathouse, jumped into the old birch bark canoe, and paddled across the channel to Tamarack. All the way I kept thinking about Katydeeray rising forty or fifty feet. Seemed to me that would put most of the island underwater. That thought didn't sit real well, made me nervous as a polecat, so the second I landed the canoe on the Tylers' beach, I hopped right out and started running.

Pretty soon I was clear over on the other side of Tamarack, where Dawn and I have been building a lean-to since we got back to the islands in April. Before we started the lean-to we walked over just about every square inch of MacKenzie and Tamarack looking for the perfect site. Finally we made our decision. The lean-to sits at the head of a small, deep cove where the tamaracks and the oaks grow practically right down to the edge of the lake. We can look out across the cove and watch the sun go down behind the Blue Mountains.

Almost eight weeks we've been working on the lean-to but we still have a long way to go. We got the floor down and the sides on, but we still have the roof to do and Dawn wants a fireplace so we'll have a place to cook and keep warm.

So I set to work, first cutting oak saplings for the roof, then hauling stones for the fireplace. But all the while I was distracted because I kept hearing Sanders in the back of my head talking about how Katydeeray could one day rise forty, fifty feet. It made me wonder if I might be wasting my time. I mean, if the islands are all of a sudden underwater, why bother building anything?

All that happened before breakfast. After breakfast Dawn and Mama and I took the launch over to town. The Tamaqua Valley Arts and Music Festival starts soon and we volunteered to help set up.

The Arts and Music Festival draws thousands of folks from all over to Cedar Bluffs. The whole town takes on a different look. All the streets, from Lake Street up to High Street, will be closed to traffic. Two bandstands will be set up: one on the corner of Main and Lake and one on the corner of Main and High. Bands from all over the state come to perform at the festival.

And along the six blocks separating the bandstands there will be dozens of booths set up by craftsmen selling their wares. There will be painters, sculptors, wood carvers, photographers, all kinds of interesting folks to meet and talk to about one thing and another.

This year Dawn and I will be competing in the fiddle contest. I'm not much of a fiddler but Dawn has a good shot of winning first prize in the sixteen and under division.

Anyway, soon after we got to town, Dawn went up to High Street to help with the bandstand while Mama and I set up the booth where she'll be displaying her paintings. She's been selling her paintings at the arts fair for years, since before I was born. Mostly she paints watercolors. She does landscapes of Katydeeray and the Blue Mountains. But what she likes best to paint are portraits. She's painted me dozens of times, usually all dressed up in the traditional clothes of the Mohawk. Mama says the Mohawk have been recording their history through paintings for over a thousand years.

You can tell Mama has Indian blood just by looking at her. She has golden-brown skin, not from being baked by the sun, but just natural, like finely sanded tamarack. She has big, brown, oval eyes and long, straight, dark hair she braids in a ponytail and lets dangle down her back.

We worked on the booth a while, hammering nails and getting the plywood walls straight, but all the while I was thinking about the stuff Sanders and Papa had to say earlier. So finally I said, "Mama, we need to talk."

"So go ahead and talk, Willy."

I looked around, made sure no one was listening, then said, in kind of a panic, "I mean we need to talk, just you and me, in private."

Right away she caught on. She has that sense, knows what I'm thinking just by the tone of my voice. So less than a minute later, we started up Main Street for Wilson's Hotel. Wilson's used to be called the MacKenzie Hotel when Ulysses owned it. He built it back in 1905 and owned it up until the Great Depression came and folks all but stopped coming to these parts. Ulysses closed it down and boarded it up. And then, I don't know exactly when, he sold it to Homer Wilson, whose son Harry still runs the place today.

Mama and I found a booth near the back and ordered lemonade. "Now what's the matter, Willy MacKenzie? You're as nervous as a whitetail caught in a light beam. Been that way all morning."

I know better than to mess with Mama. She likes straight talk. Still, I felt the need to ease my way in. "Do you know where Sanders has been the last few days?"

"Sure I know," she said. "He's been down to Washington."

"How come he had to go to Washington?"

"Something to do with an article he's writing. He went down to do some research. Why?"

Before I could say anything Mr. Wilson brought the lemonade. He and Mama talked for a few minutes about the festival and the weather. After he went away I asked, "What kind of research?"

Mama sighed. "Willy, maybe you should just tell me what's on your mind?"

I squirmed around in my seat for most of a minute before I finally said, "I heard Sanders and Papa talking this morning."

"You heard them talking about what?"

"Well," and I squirmed some more, "I'm not exactly sure about what. Stuff."

"Maybe you should be a little more specific."

"I don't know. Engineers and hydroelectric dams and Katy-deeray rising ninety or a hundred feet. Stuff like that. Scary stuff." I took a quick look into Mama's eyes. "Sanders and Papa seemed pretty upset."

"And now you're upset?"

I didn't look at her but I nodded.

A minute or two slipped away before Mama said, "It all has to do with time, Willy."

I looked at her, confused. "Huh? I don't get it. What do you mean?"

"I mean all of us during our lives live through good times and bad times, sad times and happy times, troubled times and peaceful times. It's not always easy to know what time it is, Willy. Sometimes it's very difficult. Sometimes you have to trust others to know what time it is. You can trust your father. He knows. He has his ear to the earth and is as close to nature as any white man I have ever known."

I waited for her to say more but she didn't, so I asked, "What about the lake, Mama? What if it starts rising and MacKenzie winds up underwater?"

She thought over her answer for quite a spell, then looked straight inside me. "You're not a child anymore, Willy. You're a man now, or will be very soon."

That wasn't the answer I expected, definitely not the answer I wanted, but I knew it was the only answer I was going to get.

Later, on the way home, Mama asked me if I wanted to pilot the launch back to MacKenzie. I couldn't believe my ears. I've never been allowed to drive the launch before. Called the Penelope, after my great-grandmother, she's the oldest boat we own. Ulysses had her built by the Turner and Mayfield Boatworks down in Seven Points way back in 1926. She's thirty-nine feet from stem to stern and was originally built to ferry guests back and forth between Cedar Bluffs and MacKenzie. Like the other old wooden boats in the boathouse, Papa keeps the Penelope in A-1 condition.

Every plank of teak shone and every brass nail on her sparkled as Mama slipped out of the leather seat and handed me the controls. "Take the long way home, if you want, Willy."

By the long way she meant around the south side of MacKenzie.

I thought that sounded like a good idea, it being such a pretty evening with the sun getting ready to dip below the Blue Mountains to the west and the sky just starting to turn orange and the surface of the lake quiet and shimmering.

I settled in behind the wheel and worked on getting comfortable. I didn't do much to change the position of the throttle. Mama's slow but steady speed suited me fine. No way did I want to smash up the Penelope on some shoal and rip out the bottom and never be allowed to drive her again.

Mama went back to sit with Dawn. I kept glancing over my shoulder. The two of them sat back there talking and laughing. I didn't look for long because I had to keep my eyes on the water ahead.

After a while I pushed the throttle just a hair forward, not even enough to increase our speed but enough to make me feel like I was the one piloting the boat. Off our starboard bow I saw the whole western shore of Katydeeray. There's nothing out there but stands of timber and meadows filled with wildflowers. No towns or houses or cabins or anything made by man. Just the land. And the state owns the land, meaning the people, and a few years ago a law was passed protecting the land from developers and miners and lumbermen. But what about a law protecting it from a dam?

I looked over my shoulder again to make sure Mama and Dawn saw all those wildflowers. But they didn't see a thing. They were leaning shoulder to shoulder, heads thrown back, sound asleep after our long day of labor. I thought about calling out, waking them up, but suddenly I got this powerful urge to protect them, to keep them safe, to let them sleep while I motored us home. And then I realized why Mama had handed over the controls of the Penelope to me. It was a test.

I settled in to do my best. I put us on a course for home. It was the longest crossing of my life, but I made a good, safe job of it. And when I motored into Loon Cove, Mama and Dawn still sleeping, the engine barely purring above an idle, I saw Papa standing on the dock outside the boathouse. By the look in his eye I could tell he had mixed feelings about seeing me at the helm. But he didn't budge, didn't say a word, didn't begin to tell me what I was doing right or doing wrong. I've watched him dock the launch a million times, so I had a pretty good idea what to do. I think he knew that.

I decided not to pull the Penelope into the boathouse. Partly I feared slamming her against the pilings, but mostly I just didn't feel confident enough yet to drive her through those narrow doors. So I eased her in close to the dock. Papa reached down and grabbed the gunwale. I cut the engine, threw out the rubber fenders, and stood up feeling a whole lot taller than I had this morning.

"You bring 'er all the way over, Willy?"

"Yes, sir," I said, beaming. "All the way from town."

"How did she handle?"

"Beautiful, Pop," I said, remembering what Sanders always said after he drove the launch. "Like a dream. Like a beautiful dream."

He smiled. I climbed out and together we tied off the boat to the steel cleats along the dock.

7:46 A.M.
JANUARY 20, 2001
MACKENZIE ISLAND
THE INAUGURATION OF THE FORTY-FOURTH PRESIDENT OF THE UNITED STATES

The day after the Tamaqua Valley Arts and Music Festival, Willy recorded in his journal that Dawn had indeed won first place in the fiddle contest. He also reported that he'd placed sixth out of twelve fiddlers. He wrote:

Yup, I came in sixth. Not too bad. I can be satisfied with that. I had some stage fright at first, then settled down and did some pretty fine fiddling. But Dawn, she played like a demon. Fiddled like a fiddler twice her age. Of course, she had to win, had to take the blue ribbon. She's so competitive, anything but a victory would have killed her.

I find this brief passage from the journals extremely illuminating. Willy and Dawn were only fourteen years old at the time, but this entry provides us with a high degree of early insight into their personalities and their relationship.

Just before we shared that selection from the journal, I had a brief confrontation with the president-elect. I was outside at the time, stretching my legs and passing water after half a dozen cups of black coffee, when all of a sudden Willy came up behind me. He held a pan of bacon grease in his hand. When I turned around and saw the scowl on his face, I thought for a moment he might throw that grease right in my face.

Unfortunately, my cameraman, Fred Lorry, was not out there with me to record this conversation, but I have a very clear recollection of the exchange between myself and the president-elect.

WILLY MACKENZIE: How the hell did you get my journals, Jack?

JACK STEEL: Mr. President! How are you?

W.M.: I didn't come out here to exchange pleasantries with you, Steel. I want to know how you got hold of those journals.

J.S.: Quite legally, I can assure you, Mr. President. You signed a contract to make them part of the public domain.

W.M.: You little weasel.

I had to laugh at this insult, considering the fact that I am almost six feet tall, just a hair shorter than Willy.

J.S.: I think we're presenting the journals in a fair and unbiased light.

W.M.: Fair and unbiased, my ass. My contract states very clearly that I have full and final editorial control over the finished product. You have obtained an uncut manuscript. I warn you, Steel: be very careful with my prose.

J.S.: Sir, I have only the highest regard for you and your work. I have no desire to illuminate you in any but the most positive light.

W.M.: Bullshit.

J.S.: I'm sorry you feel that way, Mr. President.

W.M.: I also do not appreciate the way you're characterizing my family. You're being very subtle and very sly, Steel, but nevertheless manipulative. You've made Ulysses sound like nothing more than a filthy rich SOB who would do anything to get what he wanted. And you're portraying Grandfather

Lawrence as weak and corrupt, a man with the moral fiber of a chimpanzee. These were fine and decent men who deserve better.

J.S.: All right, Mr. President. What would you like us to say about them?

W.M.: That they were good, hardworking men who cared about their families and about their country. But you won't. That would be too kind, too simple, too boring.

J.S.: I'll say exactly what you want me to say, Mr. President.

W.M.: You won't, though. You'll skew it and twist it. Just like this conversation we're having. You'll go back to the boathouse and tell the American people your version of what we said out here.

J.S.: Are you suggesting, sir, that I might lie?

W.M.: Does a bear crap in the woods?

I stood there with my mouth open, speechless and offended by his remarks, while Willy poured that bacon grease practically right over my boots. Then he turned and headed back to the Great House. I watched him go, then glanced up at the sky. It looked and felt as though the snow would begin falling any second.

And now that snow has started to fall. Just a few seconds ago. So let's settle back and take a closer look at the formative years of Conrad Whitman MacKenzie.

* * * * * * *

The rift between Ulysses MacKenzie and his son, Lawrence, after the senator switched his political allegiance from the Grand Old Party to those bleeding-heart Democrats did not open very wide or stay open very long. Ulysses, for all his bluster and gruffness, was at heart a softie when it came to the loyalty and tradition of family. Larry was his only son, Conrad and Patricia his only grandchildren. Blood, you might say, proved thicker than even the staunch Republican party line.

Especially where it concerned Conrad. Ulysses saw himself practically reincarnated in the young man. Physically the grandson resembled the grandfather to a T. Old and extremely grainy photographs of Ulysses taken in the 1870s, some by famed Civil War photographer Matthew Brady, could easily be interchanged with those taken of Conrad in the 1930s. By the time they reached their teenage years, both MacKenzies had broad shoulders, impressive manes of wavy brown hair, and big booming voices.

"Oh, yeah," he told Conrad many times during the boy's early years, "you're gonna do some damage out in the world. No doubt about it, you're a MacKenzie through and through, right down to the quick. Just remember, there ain't nuthin' tougher, nuthin' rougher, nuthin' meaner than a full-blooded MacKenzie. And don't you ever forget it."

Conrad assured his grandfather he never would.

U.S. tried to impose his powerful personality upon every phase of Conrad's upbringing, but his son and daughter-in-law often stood in his way. Their choice of schools, for example, proved a constant source of contention. Larry and Rebecca enrolled Conrad at a rather liberal coed boarding school out in the Virginia countryside west of D.C.

"For the love of God," pleaded Ulysses, "think about what you're doing. That place is a goddamn beehive of radicalism. I've seen the textbooks they use. Pure communist ca-ca. And the idea of a MacKenzie going to school with fillies. For chrissakes, they'll destroy the boy's concentration. He won't do a damn thing but think about bedding those young lasses."

Conrad did spend large amounts of time daydreaming about sexual intercourse. But so do most healthy young men. It's part of the passage into manhood. Still, all his carnal fantasizing did not prevent Conrad from doing well enough in school. He proved an adequate student, applying himself mostly to history, social studies, and civics.

Conrad, however, preferred to explore his potential out on the playing fields. Like his grandfather, young MacKenzie was fiercely competitive. Football was his favorite sport. He loved the contact, loved to carry the pigskin into the middle of the line, stiff-arm would-be tacklers, break into the open field, and run for glory.

In the spring Conrad wavered between tennis and baseball. His mother wanted him to follow in the tradition of the Whitmans and become a tennis player, but Ulysses, on the sly, tried to convince Conrad that tennis was a game for sissies and old ladies. "Hell," he told his grandson, "they run around in their underwear swatting at that stupid ball like they're catching butterflies or something. And they're always shouting across the net how it's thirty–love and love–forty. What the hell kind of a way is that to keep score?"

Ulysses did not stop there. He had learned long ago in business to always cover his backside. So a few weeks later, just before the start of the spring season, U.S. invited Conrad up to New York for the weekend, "to meet," he said, "a very special guest."

And who do you think showed up for dinner Saturday night at U.S.'s Park Avenue mansion? Only the greatest baseball player of all time: George Herman "Babe" Ruth. The Babe had retired from professional ball by this time, but he still knew how to tell a great tale. "So," he began in his loud, boisterous voice, "I hear you're thinkin' about playin' tennis rather than baseball. Good game, tennis, but not half as good as taking a swipe with a Louisville slugger. Why, I remember back in the second game of the twenty-seven series against the Pirates when I come up to the plate with the bases loaded in the bottom of the ninth, two out, losing four to one, and I take the first pitch, a curve, for a called strike. Boy did that make me mad. So mad I swung with all my might at the next pitch and missed it by a country mile. I practically had fire spewing from my nostrils, what with the fans at the stadium yelling and screaming. I could hardly hear myself think. I stepped out of the box, knocked the dirt off my cleats. Then I took a good long look at that pitcher, a young southpaw from somewhere down in the woods of Carolina. Kid didn't even shave yet, still had pimples. So I kept starin' at him, and pretty soon I got under his skin. Soon as I did I started scratchin'. Finally I stepped back up to the plate. He threw the next couple pitches in the dirt, frazzled he was. Then he came right down the pipe with a hummer. I unloaded on that sucker and hit it into the upper deck out in center field."

"A grand slam?" asked Conrad, who hadn't taken a breath since the Babe had stepped through the front door.

"That's right, son, a game-winning slammer, a four-bagger."

All Conrad could do was shake his head. After dinner the Babe gave Conrad a signed baseball glove. And needless to say, Conrad, much to his mother's displeasure, tried out for the baseball team that spring and quickly became the starting left fielder.

Conrad didn't know it, but a lot of folks around the country had far more important things to worry about than whether to play baseball or tennis. He didn't know because his father was a United States senator and his grandfather was filthy rich. This combination of wealth and power insulated the young man from the realities of his age.

By 1937 FDR had been elected and then reelected to the White House, but still the economy stalled and sputtered. Businesses continued to go bankrupt. The shipping business was all but dead, what with so many factories and so many industries shut down for lack of orders and unemployment at an all-time high. By cutting his operation to the bone and laying off more than half his employees, Ulysses continued to turn a profit. But those profits proved a pittance compared with what he had been making earlier in the century.

"I've said it once," U.S. told Larry one night over dinner at the almost deserted New York Yacht Club, "and I'll say it again: War's our only way out of this mess. You can't legislate people back to work. That's a Band-Aid for a bloody goddamn knife wound. Believe me, another war is the last thing I want. But you see, boy, war puts people to work. War makes people rich, especially people like me, so we push for war all the time, extoll its virtues as the great economic cure-all."

"That may be true," said Larry, "but I still think we learned our lesson last time around. All across Europe and Asia and America, countries are signing neutrality treaties and nonaggression pacts. I think we're entering a generation of peace and prosperity."

"You're so damn naive, Lawrence. Just like your mother. She thought all you had to do was get up in the morning and go make yourself a few million bucks. She didn't know you had to lie and cheat and steal, that you had to screw your enemies, wipe out your competition, sell your soul to the devil. There ain't no peace, never has been, never will be."

And as evidence, before they ordered dessert and a decanter of port, U.S. pointed to the Italian invasion of Ethiopia in 1935 and to the Rome-Berlin Axis created by Adolf Hitler and Benito Mussolini in 1936. "Maybe just a couple of insignificant historical footnotes," said Ulysses, "but I got me a gut feeling bigger things are in the wind."

Six months later, in March of 1938, Germany annexed Austria. In 1939 the Nazis marched unopposed into Czechoslovakia. Later that same year Hitler sent his boys across the border to have a visit with the Poles. Next thing we know, Great Britain and France have cut through all the appeasement nonsense and declared war on the Third Reich.

"I hate to say I told you so," said U. S. MacKenzie to his son out on the back porch of the family brownstone in Georgetown, "but I told you so. For ten years I've been warning you about this. But you morons down here in Washington refused to listen. Or maybe you just didn't want to listen. You thought your damn Social Security Acts and your Welfare Acts and your Fair Labor Acts would be enough to make everyone happy, fat, and stupid."

"I don't think you're being fair about this, Dad," replied the senator. "There's nothing we could have done to stop this maniac Hitler. Nothing."

"Bullshit. France and Great Britain and the United States could have stopped the little Bavarian years ago. But the assholes who make these decisions didn't want him stopped. They wanted the little psychotic to keep pushing. This whole thing is all mapped out ahead of time, Larry. You're just too damn dumb to see it."

They sat back and puffed leisurely on their fine Cuban cigars. The senator had come to expect talk like this from his father. The old boy loved to ramble, to spout off his latest theories on what made the world tick. Ulysses found conspiracy everywhere he looked. He'd grown old and rich conspiring against his adversaries, browbeating his competition into submission, so naturally he assumed the rest of the species operated in a similar fashion.

"I don't want to sound disrespectful, Dad," said the senator, "but I think this time you've gone overboard. You're teetering very close to paranoia with this theory of worldwide political collusion."

"Paranoia, my ass," Ulysses grumbled. "You just wait and see, boy. History will prove me right."

Before Lawrence could respond, young Conrad, a strapping fourteen-year-old, came running out onto the porch. "Is it true, Dad? Are the limeys gonna battle the Nazis? Is there gonna be a war, Dad? Is the U.S. gonna fight?"

"Not a chance, son," answered his father. "This is a European conflict. The United States will most assuredly remain neutral."

Conrad looked glum. But right away his grandfather began to laugh. For the next several minutes Ulysses just laughed and laughed and laughed.

Senator MacKenzie gave this response, of course, because immediately after France and Great Britain had declared war on Germany, Roosevelt had announced a policy of neutrality for the United States. Larry was simply espousing the national party line.

"Neutrality, my butt," announced Ulysses after he had laughed himself out. "We'll remain neutral just long enough for the old cripple to get himself elected again."

In 1940 Lawrence MacKenzie easily won his fourth term to the United States Senate. More important, FDR won his third trip to the White House. Along the way Roosevelt did his best to fulfill the predictions made by Ulysses: he signed the Selective Service Act, he cautiously but decisively began to lift the veil of U.S. neutrality, and in June he okayed the sale of surplus war materials to Great Britain. Without a doubt the country's decade long slide into armed conflict was reaching a point of crisis.

There would be many more political maneuvers before the United States reported its first combat casualty. There would be Roosevelt's sentimental speech about the four freedoms: freedom of speech and religion, freedom from want and fear. Talk of these freedoms brought tears to the eyes of patriotic Americans across the country. Others, however, U. S. MacKenzie included, saw the four freedoms as just more political flag waving.

Then came lend-lease, wherein the United States, still officially neutral, agreed in principle to finance the war for both Great Britain and the USSR. Yes, the USSR, our old adversary, had suddenly become the lesser of two evils, to the tune of some seven billion dollars in military loan guarantees: a spit in the ocean in this era of the two-trillion-dollar budget, but no small pittance in 1940 dollars. Soon after this move, Roosevelt issued the Atlantic Charter with Mr. Churchill, which said, in effect, that although the United States would remain neutral, it would take whatever actions necessary to preserve safe passage on the open seas.

"Smoke screens," insisted Ulysses, "nothing but smoke screens. Roosevelt's as slippery as an oil slick. One move at a time he draws us closer to the brink. And like sheep being led to the slaughter, we just stand by and wait for it to happen."

On the first Sunday in December 1941, the big blow struck. Historians have been debating the Japanese attack on Pearl Harbor for close to sixty years. For decades American schoolchildren were taught the attack was an unprovoked military exercise carried out by a nation bent on destroying the United States. This portrayal, however, does not tell the whole story. For several years prior to the attack the United States had been skirmishing with the Japanese on various economic battlegrounds. The two countries were hardly kissing cousins. Add to this all the evidence suggesting certain high-ranking military and government officials had detailed knowledge of the attack on Pearl Harbor minutes, hours, and in some cases even days before the incident, and you begin to understand why U. S. MacKenzie made the following remarks immediately after he learned of the attack:

"Suckered, I tell you. The American people have been royally suckered. Every damn one of us. I'll give you hundred-to-one odds that bastard Roosevelt saw this whole damn thing coming. And now the son of a bitch finally has the war he's always wanted."

Ulysses sat in the living room of his son's Georgetown brownstone. He'd been playing pinochle with his son, his grandson, and his granddaughter when suddenly Lawrence had to excuse himself to take an urgent call from his Senate office. When he returned a few minutes later he informed his family of the catastrophic events halfway around the world. Senator MacKenzie listened to his father's angry response about the people being suckered, then off he went in his limousine to a long and difficult session on Capitol Hill.

For more than twelve hours the members of Congress sat in session to study and debate this latest international crisis. Important and influential members of Roosevelt's administration came to the Senate chamber to drum up support for a strong and immediate response to the decimation of the Pacific fleet.

It easily proved the most arduous day of Lawrence MacKenzie's political career. When he finally arrived home, long after midnight, he looked haggard, worn to the bone. His father, his wife, and his two children awaited his return. He made this brief announcement before dragging himself up to bed. "Tomorrow morning, the United States will formally declare war on the nation of Japan."

And so, of course, we did.

And a couple of days later, just to get everybody lined up on the right side, just to make sure the teams were evenly divided, the Germans and the Italians, who had already signed the Axis Treaty with the Japanese, declared war on the United States. We, in turn, immediately declared war on them.

And away we went.

"But everyone's enlisting," insisted Conrad Whitman MacKenzie. "Why can't I?"

"Because you're only sixteen years old!" screamed his mother, Rebecca, who had rarely been heard to raise her voice above a whisper.

It was Christmas morning 1941 in the MacKenzie house, just two and a half weeks after Pearl Harbor. It was also Conrad's birthday, his sixteenth, or so he believed.

"So what?" Conrad argued. "I don't care how old I am. I'm old enough to fight. I'm old enough and plenty strong enough to kill Japs or krauts or I-ties or whoever else they want me to kill."

"Who exactly are *they*?" Ulysses demanded to know.

"Huh?"

"Who do you mean when you say *they*?"

Conrad thought about it. "I dunno," he told his grandfather. "The generals and the admirals and the president."

"Oh," said Ulysses, the sarcasm running down the sides of his mouth, "right. I get it now. The generals and the admirals and the president."

"Dad," implored Lawrence, "please, don't. It's Christmas."

But the old boy would not be silenced. "You stupid little twit. You don't know these generals and admirals from Adam, but you sit there and tell me you're willing to kill people you've never met, people who've never caused you or your family harm, kill them dead just because these chickenshit military men who hide back in their bunkers told you to do it."

"It's the right thing to do," insisted Conrad. "Don't try and pretend like it's not. The Japs attacked us, we didn't attack them."

U.S. shrugged off his grandson with a wave of his hand and turned to his son. "There you go, Senator. The youth of America has spoken. You bastards up and down Pennsylvania Avenue can feel proud. You've done your jobs well. You've got these hot-blooded jackasses with the smarts of pigeonshit all riled up and ready to kill the enemy. Merry Christmas!"

Conrad, in the great MacKenzie tradition of lying about one's age, tried to enlist in the U.S. Navy in January of 1942. He did this after the Japanese invaded the Philippines and sent MacArthur and his troops fleeing for their lives across Bataan and Corregidor. His attempt failed, however, when the recruiting officer, following standard operating procedure, phoned up Mrs. MacKenzie and heard the following from the young recruit's mother: "If you allow that boy to join the navy, I will personally come down there and destroy your manhood."

So for the next year all Conrad could do was follow the war in the newspapers. He read stories of great heroism from North Africa to the South Pacific. If the day's hero was a soldier fighting in the desert, he wanted to join the army. If ships were involved in the day's combat, he wanted to join the navy. During the battle of Midway, which raged all through the first week of June of 1942, Conrad wanted desperately to be a fighter pilot. Night after night he dreamed of taking off from aircraft carriers and battling Jap Zeros to the death.

But his true and final calling came when he read the powerful and vivid accounts of the United States Marine Corps fighting to capture and hold the island of Guadalcanal in the South Pacific. Day after day, week after week, month after month, the fighting raged. The marines battled the Japanese for every square inch of that island's real estate.

Conrad, because his father was a senator and because he knew all the staffers in his father's office, possessed detailed topographic maps of many of the islands in the South Pacific, including Guadalcanal, New

Guinea, Guam, Saipan, and Bougainville. Conrad pored over these maps for hours, late into the night after everyone else in the house had gone to bed. By studying the maps and reading the newspapers, he could follow the Allies as they moved into an offensive posture and began the long haul north to Tokyo. And every night before he turned out the light, he prayed he would get his chance to fight before the battles came to a close.

Christmas morning 1942, on what he believed was his seventeenth birthday, Conrad walked downstairs and into the living room, where his grandfather, his mother, his father, and his little sister had already gathered to open their holiday gifts.

"Merry Christmas, Conrad," said his mother.

She moved to hug him, but he stepped back and said, "I'm joining up. Don't try and stop me. Tomorrow I'm enlisting in the United States Marine Corps."

Ulysses, unable to control himself, cracked the boy a good one on the side of the head.

August 19, 1983

Ulysses died this morning. He was one hundred and eighteen years old.

I went out to the boathouse to see him, just like I've done a million times before, but this time, when I shook his shoulder to bring him awake, he just lay there without moving. I knew right off he was dead, but I didn't go fetch anyone, not right off. I just pulled up a chair and sat beside him.

Sitting up here in my room, thinking it over, I keep wondering what I'll do early in the morning now that I won't have Ulysses to visit. Makes me think dying is tougher on the living than the dead.

August 22, 1983

We buried Ulysses yesterday. Now he rests between his wife, Penelope, and his son, Lawrence, up in the family graveyard on the high ground out behind the boathouse. Nobody was invited to the funeral except for blood relations: Pop and Sanders and me. That's the way Ulysses wanted it, said so right in his last will and testament, written way back in 1965 on his one hundredth birthday.

Pop stood between Sanders and me, and for a long time we didn't say a word, just stared down at the hole in the earth. I started to feel older standing there, although older might not be the right word; sadder might be a better word. I started to feel sadder.

"Pop," I all of a sudden asked, "are we absolutely sure Ulysses is dead?"

Both Pop and Sanders looked at me like I'd gone around the twist, but for some reason I had it in my head that he'd magically come back to life, maybe never left it.

They didn't say anything so I asked, "You think maybe I could check?"

"Ulysses is dead and gone, Willy," said Pop. "Now let's get on with it."

"Hold on, Pop," said Sanders. "I think if Willy wants to see if Ulysses is really dead, well, we should let him have a look."

I saw Sanders wink at Pop, then Pop shrugged and said, "Okay, fine. Go ahead, Willy, knock yourself out."

I thought about declining the offer but knew I had to make sure. So I climbed down into that hole, worked the top off the coffin, and took a look inside. Old Ulysses lay in there looking whiter than the paper in this notebook. I swallowed hard and pressed my index finger against his neck. I tried but couldn't find a pulse. Then I put my ear right up against his mouth and listened. I tried but couldn't hear a sound. Then I put my mouth flush against his ear and shouted, "Ulysses! It's me, Willy, your great-grandson! Can you hear me!?"

Ulysses didn't flinch, didn't move a muscle.

"Satisfied, Willy?" I heard Pop ask.

I shrugged. "I guess so."

Pop and Sanders each let go with a small laugh, but I didn't think it was one bit funny. I put the top back on the coffin and climbed up out of that hole. "Well, come on," I said, kind of irritated, "if we're gonna do it, let's do it."

"Hold on there, Willy," said Pop. "We have some business to take care of." He pulled a piece of paper out of his pocket and read: "In the beginning God created the heavens and the earth. Later he created light and dark, land and sea. Next he created birds and fish and the other beasts. Then God created humans. And one of the humans God created was Ulysses Simpson Grant MacKenzie, who was born into a good family who worshiped in the Church of Scotland and followed the teachings of Jesus of Nazareth and John Knox of Glasgow. Ulysses lived nearly six score upon the earth, a mighty long time for any man to live, and in that time he saw amazing things; some good and glorious, some horrible and downright evil. He leaves behind a grandson and two great-grandsons, and of the many small but powerful profundities he would like to pass down to his kin, he has decided to depart with these few brief words: 'Life, in the end, is mostly confusion; a battle to overcome foolishness. Stand tall and don't take any lip.' "

I waited for the rest but Pop grew quiet.

After a time Sanders asked, "That's it? That's all the old boy wants to tell us?"

Pop nodded. "That's it." He folded and put away the piece of paper.

Sanders picked up two shovels and handed one to me. Together we shoveled the fresh black earth back into the hole. I began to cry as those clumps of damp soil exploded on the top of my great-grandfather's coffin.

Later, on the way home, after Sanders said so long and took the path back to Looking Glass Cove, Pop asked, "You okay, Willy?"

"Sure, Pop, I'm fine."

"You'll miss him, won't you?"

I nodded and asked, "You think you'll live as long as him?"

"I don't know, Willy. Unusual for anyone to live that long."

"What about the island?"

"What do you mean?"

"You know, the dam and all?"

"We're doing our best, Willy."

"I know, but what I mean is, if they build the dam and flood the valley and the island winds up underwater, what'll happen to Ulysses?"

"That dam will probably never happen, Willy."

"That's what you keep telling me, Pop. But let's just say it does."

Pop stopped walking and turned to face me. "If it does, Willy, we'll have to dig up Ulysses and Lawrence and the rest of the family and take them wherever we go."

"And where will that be?"

He started walking again. "That's not even worth talking about, Willy. What you're doing now is worrying. You're worried about losing your prized pike before you even have him on the line. . . . Now come on, boy, we've got a day's work ahead nailing those new planks to the dock."

August 24, 1983

Late yesterday afternoon I kissed Dawn for the first time.

It happened over at the lean-to on Tamarack. We'd been working for hours, hauling stones for the fireplace. We were both sweaty and tired. We sat on an old log we'd rolled down to the lake. The sun began to set behind the distant peaks of the Blue Mountains.

"Dawn?"

"Yeah, Willy?"

"I didn't tell you this yet, but . . ."

"But what?"

"Day before yesterday, when we buried Ulysses . . ."

"Yeah?"

"I kept thinking he wasn't dead. Like we were burying him alive."

Dawn looked over at me, and I had the feeling she knew just about everything in the world, and then she said, "Only his body's dead, Willy. You were just burying his body. His spirit's still alive and well. Same as always."

"What makes you say that?"

"Because it's obvious. You can't kill a spirit that wants to live, the Bible says so. Besides, we'll keep Ulysses alive forever by talking about him and thinking about him. Just like we're doing now."

That made pretty good sense, so I relaxed some, and then, all of a sudden, for some strange and unknown reason, I turned my head, leaned forward, and kissed her right smack on the mouth.

She looked surprised. "Willy, what are you doing?"

"Nothing." Then, without even thinking, I did it again, harder and for even longer this time.

When I stopped she laughed.

"What's so funny?"

"Nothing," she said. "Just you."

"Me? Why me?"

She didn't answer. She sat on that old log and drew her legs up close to her chest. I decided to do exactly the same thing with my legs.

We sat there like that, quiet and all, for a few minutes, while the last rays of sunlight scattered across the lake. Then Dawn turned and kissed me. Right out of nowhere just like I'd done to her. Her lips were soft and moist. We both had our eyes open. I had this strange feeling we were at the beginning of another great discovery. We're only fifteen but all our lives we've been discovering things together. Like the taste of wild carrots. And the sound of ripe apples hitting the ground in late autumn. And the cool smell of wild mint. And the sight of a thousand Canada geese heading south over the lake. And the call of the loons. And now the feel of our lips touching.

* * *

Later, after supper, I sat with Mama on the front porch. She likes to sit out there in the dark for a while, thinking things over and calming her thoughts before she goes up to bed.

"Mama," I asked, "could you tell me again about that old Iroquois tradition?"

"Which one, Willy?"

"The one about younger folks marrying older folks."

She turned and looked at me, and in the light coming through the windows I saw her smile. "I swear, Willy MacKenzie, I never know what you'll say next. Now why is it you want to know about that?"

"I don't know. I just wanted to hear about you and Pop."

"Well," she said, "the Iroquois did have a tradition. Not everyone followed it, and your father and I didn't necessarily marry because of it, but it's out there for all to consider nevertheless."

"How does it go again?"

"Your ancestors believed the strongest marriages were forged between an older man and a younger woman. Or vice versa. It didn't really matter as long as the older person brought wisdom and security to the relationship and the younger person brought passion and a sense of adventure."

"Like you and Papa?"

She smiled. "That's right, Willy, although sometimes I'm not sure who brought what."

I wasn't sure what she meant by that, but I let it go because I had something else I needed to ask her about. "So if Dawn and I were to get married we'd be in big trouble seeing as we're almost exactly the same age?"

"You and Dawn are too young to get married."

"I know that, Mama, but I'm just saying if we were to get married, you know, someday, it probably wouldn't work out, on account of her being only a couple months older than me."

"You never know, Willy. The Iroquois didn't get everything right, not by a long shot. You and Dawn might get hitched and be as close as a couple peas in a pod."

I turned away from her and smiled into the darkness.

7:59 A.M.
JANUARY 20, 2001
MACKENZIE ISLAND
THE INAUGURATION OF THE FORTY-FOURTH PRESIDENT OF THE UNITED STATES

I wish we had a videotape of young Willy MacKenzie climbing down into that grave, prying open that coffin, and shouting into his great-grandfather's dead ear. Pretty strange stuff. Even for a fifteen-year-old.

Now, remarkably, eighteen and a half years later, that same Willy MacKenzie is preparing to take command of the ship of state. I can see him through the boathouse window, hunched over his desk up in the study on the second floor of the Great House. He appears very vulnerable, a perfect target for a sniper's bullet.

Willy wrote a good deal of his journal right there at that desk, late at night or very early in the morning. But I doubt he's working on his journal now. I think he's putting the final touches on his inaugural address, deciding how to soothe the scared and disgruntled egos of the American masses.

Willy's become a pretty fair speech maker. He writes all his own material, except for some occasional help from brother Sanders. Unlike politicians of the past, Willy does not use slick speech writers or pollsters to determine content. He just jots down a few key phrases on a piece of paper, then steps up to the microphone and goes to work. With Willy what you hear comes from the gut; you never get the sense he's just lipsynching someone else's words.

I see it's eight o'clock now, so the president-elect still has four hours to mull over what he wants to tell us. It looks, however, like he might wind up delivering his address in the middle of a blizzard. The snow has started to fall in earnest now, and the intense cold and the absolute absence of wind suggest to this old weather vane from the rural Midwest that a long and steady storm has swept into the Blue Mountains. The National Weather Center predicts two and a half to three *feet* of fresh powder will fall before this system moves out of the Tamaqua River Valley. You might as well put another log on the fire while we delve further into the life of Conrad MacKenzie as America engages in yet another world war.

* * * * * * *

Senator MacKenzie and his wife, Rebecca, tried repeatedly on Christmas Day to talk their son out of enlisting. They begged him, pleaded with him, even made a brief attempt to buy him off with a new convertible. But Conrad, as stubborn and ornery as his grandpappy, held fast. He told them they had no right to stand in his way. He did need their signatures, however, since he was still considered a minor.

When Rebecca mentioned this fact to him, Conrad swelled out his chest and scowled with indignation. "How dare you threaten me? You raised me to think for myself, to be independent. This isn't some rash decision. I've been thinking about joining for a whole year. I want to join. I want to fight. I want to serve my country."

So just before midnight, exhausted and defeated, the senator and his wife reluctantly signed the consent form. Early the next morning Conrad presented the form to his recruiter.

"You've made a sound and honorable decision, son," said the Marine Corps sergeant. And then he barked, "Report for duty one week from today, seven hundred hours sharp. Don't be late!"

Conrad saluted and raced out of the recruiter's office. He didn't waste a second. As soon as he got home he called Sally. His parents didn't know about Sally. His buddies didn't know about Sally. No one knew about Sally.

Sally Colt sat next to Conrad in English class. The two had been making goo-goo eyes at each other since September. They had missed entire lectures on such great works of American literature as *The Grapes of Wrath*, *The Sound and the Fury*, and *Babbit* because their eyes and minds could not stop wandering.

Sally was the great-great-granddaughter of Samuel Colt, inventor of the single-barreled pistol back in 1835. Sally's father, Troy Colt, worked in the Roosevelt administration as a munitions expert. He was responsible for making sure the tens of thousands of U.S. soldiers heading overseas to battle the Japs and the Nazis and the Italians had the appropriate firepower to bring victory to the Allies.

Sally, undoubtedly because of the rousing displays of patriotism around the Colt family dinner table, believed firmly in the war effort. (Whether or not the Colt family patriotism was based on ideology or on the soaring value of a share of Colt common stock on the New York Stock Exchange is open to debate. It is a fact, however, that almost every single officer in the United States military carried a Colt .45 on his person.) But regardless of motive, in her spare time, along with her mother and sisters, Sally prepared packages full of cigarettes and candy and razor blades for GIs stationed everywhere from Auckland to the African desert.

We have no way of knowing exactly how much influence Sally Colt had on Conrad's decision to quit school and join the service, but she probably did little to dispel his desires.

"Hello?"

"Hi, Sally, it's me."

"Conrad! Hi."

"I did it."

"You didn't!"

"I did."

"When?"

"This morning."

Sally caught her breath, then asked, "Can you come over?"

The two had only ever kissed. Conrad had never even touched Sally's breast. But all that changed before New Year's Day 1943. Sally was a mere wisp of a young woman, barely tipping the scales at one hundred pounds and standing just sixty-two inches high. Conrad, with his enormous shoulders, towered over her. With her blond bangs and perfect little mouth, she seemed almost like a doll wrapped in Conrad's arms. He did his best not to crush her. Virgins both, they, like countless other young American couples facing the outbreak of armed conflict, took a crash course in copulation. The first time they did it on an old and musty mattress in the Colt family attic out in Arlington, Virginia. It took only a few minutes. Sally absorbed the pain to her pelvic area like a good soldier. And at least a dozen times over the next six days they worked to increase their carnal knowledge.

"I love you, Conrad MacKenzie," said Sally the night before he became a United States Marine.

"I love you back, Sally Colt," said Conrad, who wanted now more than anything to just stay home and diddle his sweet coquette.

Alas, Conrad's Uncle Sammy called. After all, Conrad had asked for an invitation. And so on January 2, 1943, young MacKenzie passed his physical and was immediately sworn into the corps along with several dozen other pale and anxious recruits.

That night, with Conrad shorn of every lock of hair and his family seated around the dining room table for the boy's last supper, old Ulysses rumbled, "I hope you live through this goddamn war, you stupid little son of a bitch, because the day you get home I'm going to personally break every goddamn bone in your body."

Because of the war Ulysses was making money in tremendous quantities, more than he had ever made before. The government had leased, for outrageously high sums, virtually every single ship, boat, barge, and tug owned by MacKenzie Shipping, Inc. The Great Depression had miraculously come to a halt. Ulysses, however, paid little attention to the profits jumping off the daily tally sheets. Now in his seventy-eighth year, even though he looked and moved like a man half his age, U.S. had developed a new passion.

Churchill and FDR, meeting in Casablanca, agreed to continue fighting until the Japs and the Nazis had been crushed. "That's easy for those two old farts to say," grumbled Ulysses, "they ain't getting shot at, they ain't nineteen years old and dying in some hellhole ten thousand miles from home."

Larry tried not to listen. He preferred to toe the party line. The entire Congress preferred to toe the party line. Even when Roosevelt introduced the country's first withholding tax on personal income, only a smattering of dissent could be heard from either the House or the Senate. The entire Capitol, beneath that great rotunda, stood mute. In fact, that great edifice to democracy probably could just as well have been closed and locked during the war years, so silent were its voices, so impotent its powers.

Mr. Roosevelt claimed his withholding tax was a temporary measure to help pay for the war effort, a measure he assured the American people would be repealed once the peace had been won.

"Horseshit," shouted Ulysses. "Total and complete horseshit. This goddamn country is becoming like feudal England. The peons pay their lord and master their hard-earned bread so he can go out and raise armies and ride around the countryside fighting for glory. What's next on Franklin's agenda? Knighthoods for his generals? Lord Douglas? Sir Dwight? Maybe we should just proclaim Mr. Roosevelt king of the Americas."

And later he confided to Lawrence, "I won't pay. I'll burn the damn money before I'll give it to these money grubbers and warmongers. No, on second thought, I won't burn it, I'll bury it! Up on MacKenzie Island. In stainless-steel boxes. I'll bury fives and tens and twenties and fifties and hundred-dollar bills. Thousands of 'em, millions of 'em, for chrissakes. I'll show these sons of bitches they can't spend U. S. MacKenzie's money to kill off untold numbers of boys and innocent civilians."

"But Ulysses," pleaded Lawrence, "it's for a good cause, a just cause."

"You stupid peckerhead, that's what they always say. Since the beginning of time it's always been for a good cause, a just cause. Well, I say bullshit. I say you'll feel different when they ship your boy home in a pine box or without any legs or with his brains all scrambled."

By late spring 1943, Conrad, homesick to beat the bandit one day but restless to find and kill the enemy the next, was still stateside. He had not yet laid eyes on even one Japanese soldier. At boot camp down in the swamps of Parris Island, South Carolina, Conrad had been all fire and glory. The youngest soldier in his company, he had quickly proved himself with strength, speed, and endurance. Maybe he didn't excel in the close-order drill or the about-face, but send him out onto the obstacle course or on a thirty-mile forced march and he practically begged the DIs for more abuse. And on the firing range he proved himself a veritable one-man army. He'd been shooting ducks and pheasant and rabbits up on MacKenzie Island for nearly a decade, so he knew how to handle a firearm. The corps loved a raw recruit who could shoot straight.

The corps also loved young men whose characters had not yet taken root, whose minds they could bend and manipulate. At seventeen, his innocence and his ignorance stamped right across his forehead, Conrad walked willingly into the lion's den. The drill instructors, foaming at the mouth, quickly sank their teeth into young MacKenzie. Using the ancient Marine Corps rite of breaking the backs and spirits of its new recruits and then rebuilding and reinventing those backs and spirits in the name of God and Country and Corps, they methodically turned Conrad into an able-bodied and well-disciplined killing machine.

Standing a fraction of an inch from Conrad's face and yelling at the top of his lungs, the drill instructor would inquire, "Tell me, Marine, are you a totally worthless pile of human excrement?!"

"Yes, sir!"

"Marine, are you the lowest form of scum on the planet?!"

"Yes, sir!"

"Marine, do you drink your own piss and eat your own shit?!"

"Yes, sir! If so ordered, sir!"

"Marine, if I kick you in the balls and shove a grenade up your ass, will you squeal like a pig?!"

"No, sir!"

"Why not, Marine?"

"Because I am a United States Marine, sir!"

"Bullshit! You're human excrement!"

"Yes, sir! Whatever you say, sir!"

"When your commanding officer orders you to kill a whole squad of Jap soldiers with your bare hands, you'll do it, right, Marine?!"

"Yes, sir! I'll always do exactly as ordered, sir!"

Oh, to be a five-star general with half a million boys like Conrad Whitman MacKenzie at your disposal.

Besides his gung ho attitude, Conrad proved he had a little something upstairs as well. He scored high on his aptitude tests, causing his superiors to think they might have officer material on their hands, perhaps a second lieutenant willing to lead his platoon all the way to hell and back.

At the end of boot camp he reported to his commanding officer. "So, Marine," his CO grumbled in his best and lowest leatherneck voice, "they tell me you got guts, brains, and steady aim. You ready to face the enemy, son?"

Conrad stood board straight in his crisp new uniform. "Yes, sir! Absolutely ready and able, sir!"

"I've taken a good look at your record, son, and I think the engineers might be the right place for you. Plenty of need for good engineers out in the Pacific theater."

"Yes, sir! I'd prefer the infantry, sir!"

"Infantry, huh? You're ready to ship out, are you, Marine?"

"Yes, sir! More than ready, sir!"

"Have an itching to kill a few of the slanty-eyed little bastards, huh?"

"More than an itching, sir!"

The CO sighed and studied Conrad's file. "I could get my ass strung up in a sling for putting a senator's kid in the field, soldier."

"I'd hate to see that happen, sir!"

"Good. Then how does a nice, cozy desk job sound, say, over in sunny Honolulu, maybe attached to some pompous ass navy admiral?"

"Yes, sir! Whatever you say, sir! I'd prefer to fight the enemy at the front, sir!"

So off Conrad went for infantry training at Camp Lejeune in North Carolina. On coastal landscape along the New River, battered and bulldozed to simulate islands in the South Pacific, Conrad learned the true calling of the United States Marine Corps: direct frontal assault.

There on the sandy beaches of North Carolina, the direct frontal assault seemed almost fun. Conrad and his Marine Corps buddies would scramble from a ship into an amphibious landing craft, either a Higgins boat or one of the newfangled beach rammers, an LCP (landing craft, personnel) or an LCM (landing craft, mechanized). They would then proceed directly into the face of the enemy. The moment their landing craft hit the beach, those marines would storm ashore, shouting and cursing and sprinting for the ramparts. And since the enemy shot only blanks, no one got hurt and everyone had a grand time. The officers tried to instill an air of reality into the situation, but usually with little result. It was difficult there in the sweet spring of Carolina to simulate bloody corpses and wounded soldiers screaming in agony.

Conrad completed infantry training in May of 1943. He received a three-day leave. Back in Washington he paraded before family and friends in his crisp Marine Corps blues. He looked every bit the soldier: tall, trim, ramrod straight, proud. His mother pampered him with all his favorite foods. His father took him up on the Hill to show him off to his Senate chums. His high school friends stared at him with envy. And his pretty, perky little Sally covered him with kisses. And when they found themselves alone, she carefully unbuttoned his blues, pulled them off his muscular frame, and hung them neatly on a hanger. She then offered herself willingly to her own personal god of war. Conrad penetrated Miss Colt with such depth and with such force that tears came to her eyes, but she refused to scream; she simply held on for dear life and prayed he would finish before she perished.

Only Ulysses saw through the facade. "You don't kid me, boy, not for one goddamn second. The marines are nothing but a bunch of thugs, hired assassins, brainwashed by their superiors to shoot or get shot, kill or be killed. Big fucking deal. You're a pawn and a witless moron in my book, boy, nothing more."

And with those words of encouragement ringing in his ears, Conrad boarded a troop train bound for California. After a brief layover in San Diego, he shipped out on a troop transport ship bound for Hawaii. At least the rumors among the enlisted men sang of Hawaii and points west. In truth, those young marines had no idea where they were headed or what they would be called on to do once they got there. The corps preferred to keep its fighting men lean, mean, and totally in the dark about their fates.

Nevertheless, on July 4, 1943, his ship pulled into Pearl Harbor. Conrad felt as though he had finally reached the war. But the battles were still a long way off, thousands of miles across the wide green Pacific. He may have reached that famous port where the war against imperial Japan had begun, but Pearl was now as safe from enemy attack as Wichita or Indianapolis.

Over the next four months Conrad found out that a marine spends an enormous amount of his time hanging around, waiting for orders, writing and reading letters, speculating with his buddies about where and when they might get their chance to join the fray. For young, gung ho marines like Conrad who had still not encountered the enemy, the hours and days and weeks of close-order drill seemed like an incredible waste of time and energy.

"Do the dumb bastards in charge want to win this war or not?" was the oft heard question at mess and in the barracks at the end of the day.

"Are we going to spend the whole war marching in circles and shooting at hay bales?"

"I didn't come halfway around the world to get a suntan, for chrissakes."

"Goddamn war'll be over before we get our chance."

Fresh rumors of major battles filtered through the ranks every few days. Where they originated or who started them, no one ever knew. This corporal heard it from that corporal who heard it from a supply sergeant who heard it from a second lieutenant who heard it from a captain on the rear admiral's staff. Usually the rumor just petered out, and another one quickly took its place. Conrad wrote to his father and told him the war in the Pacific was being run by a bunch of lazy imbeciles. But he told his sweet Sally war was hell and that without his thoughts of her he would never be able to keep up the good fight.

Finally, in early November, orders came through that his regiment would be shipping out within twenty-four hours. Conrad had heard similar orders several times before, but this time a flurry of activity followed. And sure enough, the following afternoon, aboard a brand-spanking-new steel gray APA troop transport, his regiment steamed out of Pearl and headed west into the setting sun.

Their ship formed part of an enormous armada. Everywhere Conrad looked he saw evidence of the United States Navy. For as far as he could see in every direction there were carriers and cruisers, battleships and destroyers.

And as the days passed and they sailed farther west, the fleet continued to grow. Conrad and his buddies wondered, with so many ships and so many troops, why couldn't they simply sail into Tokyo Harbor and bomb the emperor and his military machine back to the Stone Age.

Surrounded by all that firepower, those young marines, not one of whom had ever been wounded or seen a man shot, felt invincible.

Early one morning, before dawn, Conrad awoke on his hard, narrow bunk to the sound of the big guns roaring and aircraft buzzing overhead. Oblivious of the strategies of the generals and the admirals, young MacKenzie had no idea where he was or that the battle for Tarawa atoll in the Gilbert Islands had begun. Throughout that day and most of the next, all Conrad and his fellow marines aboard that APA could do was watch, wait, and wonder. Their ship lay at anchor several miles offshore. From there the battle looked and sounded much like a massive Fourth of July fireworks display. From their long-range vantage point, death and destruction seemed to have nothing whatsoever to do with the explosions and brilliant flashes of light.

Late in the afternoon, on the second day of fighting, that APA hoisted its anchor and drew closer to the battle. Conrad could suddenly see the island, a small speck of land called Betio, surrounded by a ring of beautiful green-and-blue coral. The intensity of the noise increased. Conrad was not sure, but he thought he heard men screaming. For the first time since joining the corps, he began to feel fear. His heart raced. His hands trembled. Sweat poured off his brow and down his face. He felt an overwhelming desire to throw up. So he did. Right onto the steel deck of that APA. He was not the only one.

Then he heard his company commander barking orders. "Over the side, Marines! Let's move it! Be orderly! Orderly now! By platoon! We got a battle to fight, a war to win!"

Conrad's head began to pound. The noise! And the smoke! He could barely see fifteen feet ahead. He looked around for a place to hide.

His platoon leader grabbed his arm. "Let's go, MacKenzie! Over the side! Keep your eyes open and your head down, and with a little luck we'll all live through this shit!"

Conrad nodded. He knew what to do. He'd been well trained. He scrambled over the side, his sixty-pound pack and his M-1 rifle slung over his shoulders, down a rope ladder, and into a crowded LCI (landing craft, infantry). Most of the guys in his platoon had already arrived. They hunkered down and peered over the gunwales as the battle raged around them. Conrad did the same. He forced himself to stop shaking. Up ahead, through the smoke, he saw another LCI shove off and head for shore. Several of his buddies, including a few guys he'd been with since boot camp, turned and gave a thumbs-up. Conrad returned the sign. He felt a little better, a little stronger. Then his LCI shoved off and started for the island. Together the two small boats steered for the beach several hundred yards in the distance.

Conrad kept his eyes open and his head down and successfully managed not to defecate in his pants. Others were not so successful. But no one said a word or pointed a finger. A whole new reality had suddenly descended upon those young marines. Conrad kept belching and dry heaving, and he couldn't stop shivering even though he was practically right smack on the equator and the temperature was well over one hundred and ten degrees Fahrenheit.

"Heads down, eyes open!" the sergeant kept shouting. "Our job is simple: reinforce the beachhead and stay alive! We don't need no heroes out here today!"

Conrad had his eyes open all right, wide open, big as baseballs. So he saw very clearly that other LCI take a direct hit. One second the LCI steamed steadily through the smoke, and the next second a Jap mortar shell blew it sky high. Not fifty feet away that small ship carrying at least a dozen of his buddies exploded into a million pieces. Conrad saw bodies fly into the air. Limbs became separated from torsos and heads from necks. He heard screaming and soon enough realized some of that screaming issued from his own mouth.

Chaos ensued. Those young, green marines had no idea how to respond. Some went into the water to try to help their buddies. But their buddies were all dead. Their arms and legs floated on the water. Corporals and sergeants and second lieutenants tried to maintain order, but the noise and smoke and confusion dominated the action that afternoon. By the time Conrad finally reached what the planners had designated Green Beach on the north shore of Betio Island, more than half his platoon had either been killed or wounded.

Welcome to the war, Private MacKenzie.

Conrad survived the bloody battle for Tarawa. But his desire to fight and kill the enemy, for so many months his overriding emotion, had suddenly been sucked right out of his chest, right out of his psyche. All he wanted to do was go home and bury his face between Sally's small but inviting breasts. He wanted to go home so bad it hurt. But home was more than two years and ten thousand miles away.

Another long wait settled in after the successful campaign to take the Gilbert and Marshall islands. But this time Conrad enjoyed the boredom and the routine of the close-order drills. He would never again complain about the lack of action.

Several times a week he wrote to Sally, and more than anything else he looked forward to receiving letters from her. She wrote to him every day, sometimes twice a day, but often weeks would pass without any mail delivery. Then a whole stack would arrive at once. Carefully Conrad would sort out the letters according to date before beginning to read. Sally talked about all the things going on back in the States, about how much she loved him, about everything they would do together once the war ended and he came home. One letter sounded much like the next, but Conrad consumed her words as though they were verses from Scripture. He knew if he could just survive the war, he'd go home, marry Sally, and never worry about anything ever again.

Then he caught the dengue fever and for more than a month he didn't give a damn about the war or Sally or home or anything else. One bite from an infected mosquito and all Conrad wanted to do was lie down and die. He almost did die. During most of January and all of February 1944, young MacKenzie rarely managed to climb out of bed. Dengue fever, far more debilitating than malaria, brought tens of thousands of U.S. Marines to their knees during the war in the South Pacific. Though rarely fatal, full recovery from this bone-crushing fever took several weeks of complete bed rest. Conrad ran a temperature of one hundred and five degrees in a climate where the mercury frequently rose to well over one hundred degrees and the humidity hovered almost constantly around one hundred percent.

The fever made his bones ache and his joints swell. He felt as though he had been beaten unmercifully with a steel switch. Then his skin broke out from head to toe with bloody and painful rashes. For days on end he lay in bed shaking and sweating and moaning. At that time there were no drugs to combat the dengue fever, so the doctors could offer him little more than aspirin and maybe a few words of sympathy.

When he entered the corps Conrad had tipped the scales at one hundred and seventy pounds, a solid chunk of muscular marine. After finally recovering from the fever, he had slipped to one hundred and forty-six pounds. His cheeks were gaunt, his eyes hollow. His uniform looked like something that belonged on another man. But he could feed himself and walk to the latrine, so the doctors pronounced him cured and sent him back to the war. By the middle of March he was back with his outfit, back close to the front.

Within months, in rapid succession, the marines, with help from the army, invaded the Marianas. Bloody battles engulfed Guam, Tinian, and Saipan. Marines died like flies. Conrad MacKenzie was not among them. Because he barely had the strength to stand for more than a few minutes at a time, he had been assigned to a Marine Corps colonel in charge of directing communications between the various companies engaged in battle. So Conrad, safely aboard a navy cruiser, spent his days peering at the battle through a pair of binoculars while passing orders through a two-way radio.

By the time Guam fell to the Allies in the middle of August 1944, Conrad had regained his strength and most of his lost weight. He had also regained some of his fighting spirit. More than anything he still wanted to survive the war and head for home, but he could no longer stand at a distance and watch his fellow marines die at the hands of those dirty Jap bastards. So after a long and difficult battle inside his own head, Conrad went to see his company commander.

"Request immediate transfer to a fighting platoon, sir."

"What's the matter, MacKenzie? Not enough excitement in communications? You want to go out and get your balls blown off?"

Conrad didn't have any rational answers to the captain's questions, but something made him keep pushing until he found himself reassigned to K Company, First Marine Division. One week after joining the company, on September 15, 1944, his platoon invaded Peleliu at the southern end of the Palau Islands. The marines were told just hours before the invasion that it would be a walk in the park, a piece of cake. For several days the navy had been bombing the island, and it appeared most of the Jap resistance had either been killed, wounded, or sent in retreat. So it came as quite a surprise when the battle to take the small island of Peleliu turned into one of the roughest, toughest, bloodiest fights of the entire war.

Conrad made his direct frontal assault in the second wave, as part of a reinforcing effort. His platoon managed to get ashore with only a spattering of resistance. But scattered across the coral landscape were dozens of dead and dying marines. The lieutenant kept ordering his men forward but Conrad couldn't take his eyes off the burned and bleeding bodies. A bevy of naval corpsmen combed the scene, offering water and syringes of morphine to those still alive. But there were so many dead. Some had fallen less than an hour earlier, but already in all that heat and humidity the flies and maggots had arrived to feed.

For days and then weeks K Company battled the Japs on the beaches and in the foothills of Peleliu. The enemy had not been knocked out by the navy, not by a long shot. They had simply gone underground into caves and tunnels dug deep beneath the volcanic island. They would pop out, fire a few rounds, wound and kill a few marines, then slip away, back into their holes. At night Conrad could hear the Japs beneath the hard ground where he tried, mostly without success, to sleep. He could hear them whispering, smell their rice cooking, even occasionally see the smoke from their fires rising out of the earth. They were like animals hidden away in their dens, out of sight; they would come out only to kill.

On Peleliu, madness fell upon more than a few rock-solid marines. They fired wildly into the darkness and even at their own shadows. They began to kick and stab and shoot the dead bodies of the enemy.

"Insanity," Conrad wrote Sally, "utter insanity. I cannot believe what is happening. Are we men? Can we really call ourselves human beings? Earlier today I pointed my rifle at a Jap soldier and fired several shots until he fell over, dead. When I went to get a closer look at him, I saw how young he was, younger than me, just a boy. Why did I shoot him? So he wouldn't shoot me, I know. But why did he want to shoot me? So I wouldn't shoot him, I know. But what if the two of us sat down and just agreed not to shoot? The thing is, I then shot him again, right between the eyes. Twice."

Private Conrad MacKenzie never mailed that letter to his sweetheart. It was still on his person the next afternoon when the corpsmen carried him off the beachhead and settled him into an LCP already overloaded with wounded men.

By the time victory on Peleliu was assured, over twelve hundred marines had died and close to five thousand had been wounded. And even before the battle ended, more than a few high-ranking officers in both the navy and the marines speculated that the island probably could have been ignored, cut off from Japan and starved out, bypassed on the long drive to retake the Philippines.

This speculation did little to comfort Private Conrad Whitman MacKenzie. He received his wound while performing perhaps his one heroic act of the war. His platoon had moved forward into the foothills of the Umurbrogol Mountains. For several hours they were pinned down by a Jap mortar emplacement dug into a cliff three or four hundred feet up the steep coral slope. The platoon leader finally ordered Conrad and PFC Joshua Tyler to make a flanking maneuver up and around the Jap mortar position. "Get above those bastards," he ordered, "and drop a shitload of grenades on the sons of bitches."

Shaking in their boots but trying to act like marines, the two young leathernecks slipped into the brush and started up the mountain. They crawled on hands and knees, drawing blood as they cut themselves on the hard volcanic rocks and the razor-sharp vegetation.

"This is fucking sick," Conrad grumbled as he wrapped a dirty cloth around his bleeding fingers. "We should be home sucking down beers and farting and listening to the World Series on the radio."

Josh Tyler swallowed hard, nodded, and said nothing.

Another hour passed before they finally climbed beyond the mortar emplacement dug into the cliff. They took a few minutes to drink some water and catch their breath.

"Okay, Josh," asked Conrad, "you ready for this?"

Josh, sweating and shaking, nodded.

"All right, then," said Conrad, "we might as well go the hell ahead and do it. You wanna be Warren Spahn or Dizzy Dean?"

Josh smiled and shrugged. "I'll be Spahn. You be Dean."

Conrad nodded. And then, together, at exactly the same moment, they jumped up and hurled half a dozen grenades down onto the three Japs operating the mortar. The grenades exploded. The three Japs flew into the air, their body parts flying in all directions.

Conrad and Josh let out a cheer. But immediately a rain of bullets descended upon them from another Jap battery higher up on the mountain.

Josh took a hit in the back, then another in the arm. His M-1 flew out of his hand. He fell to the ground, bleeding and screaming. Conrad, his adrenaline pumping, began to run down the side of the mountain. But then he stopped, and without really knowing why, he raced back up the hill, straight into that barrage of bullets. He lifted Josh Tyler off the ground and threw the wounded marine over his shoulder.

Down the hill Conrad fled, the bullets whizzing past his ears. Ahead he saw the guys in his platoon. They cheered him on. He ran as fast as he could with a hundred-and-sixty-pound man on his back. And he almost made it. Just before he reached safety a bullet ripped through his shoulder blade. He stumbled forward. Josh went flying. Then another bullet tore through his boot and shattered his ankle. He started falling. A long moment passed before he smashed his head against a piece of coral and knocked himself cold.

February 9, 1985
High Street House

The day before yesterday Pop left the valley. Pop rarely leaves the valley. Something big has to happen for Pop to venture out of the Blue Mountains. He's lived in the valley for forty years, and I've heard folks say, "Hell will freeze over before Conrad MacKenzie leaves his precious island."

Pop went to Washington with Sanders. The Tamaqua Valley Dam and Development Project has started to heat up again. They went down to ask some questions and hopefully get some answers. I wanted to go with them, but Pop told me to stay behind and look out for Mama and Dawn and Alice. He also told me to hightail it out to MacKenzie and check on things if we had a big snowfall. Well, the night before last the valley caught a foot and a half of fresh powder. So yesterday morning, right after breakfast, Dawn and I carried our skis down to the lake. We strapped those planks to our boots and set off across the frozen, snow-covered surface. Dawn moved out in front. Her skis made two perfect trails for me to follow through the deep powder. We skied along, not talking, just gliding through the clear cold morning.

Before too much time had passed we skied into the channel separating MacKenzie Island from Tamarack and right up onto the Tylers' front lawn. The thick limbs of the evergreens sagged under the weight of the snow. Some of the smaller limbs had cracked and fallen to the ground. We cut through the pine grove and came in behind the Tylers' boathouse. The old plank building looked like it had weathered the storm pretty well.

Dawn's grandfather, Joshua Tyler, built the first house on Tamarack Island back in 1948, not long after he and Pop got back from the war in the Pacific. I never knew Josh, being that he died in a lumbering accident a few years before I was born. Pop rarely mentions Josh, but Mama's told me he was without a doubt the best friend Pop ever had.

Dawn unfastened her skis and went into the house to make sure everything was in order while I skied around back to check for damage. A few oak saplings had blown down against the back porch, but otherwise everything looked in good repair.

Back out front I found Dawn coming through the front door. "Everything okay?" I asked.

She nodded and clutched her arms. "Yeah, except it's about twenty below zero in there."

"Come on," I said, "let's go over and get a fire started."

We skied down the hill and across the channel. We entered Loon Cove and I got my first look at the Great House since Thanksgiving. It sure looked lonely sitting there all by itself. The snow had drifted across the front porch and right up against the front door.

"Come on, Willy, let's check the boathouse before we go inside."

"Right." I followed her around the side of the house and through the stand of birches all bent over clear to the ground from the weight of the snow. The boathouse sits in a well-protected nook in the southeast corner of Loon Cove, so it rarely receives any damage, even from the wildest winter storms. But this time there was a broken window. Dawn spotted it first. She pointed to the second floor, to the room where Ulysses used to live.

"That window got cracked back in the fall," I said, "when a sparrow flew into it by accident. I guess the wind finished it off."

"We'd better patch it so the weather can't get in."

"Sure," I said, knowing that's exactly what Pop would want me to do.

"While you take care of that," said Dawn, "I'll go up to the house and get the fire started."

"Okay," I said. "Good idea."

But as soon as she skied off I wished she'd stayed. I don't know exactly why. Something to do with that broken window. Something to do with the wind. Something to do with Ulysses. More though, I think, to do with Pop and Sanders down in Washington. I don't know.

I wasn't sure then, I'm not sure now. I stood there on the dock for a few minutes listening to the pilings creak under the weight of the snow and the pull of the ice. I didn't have much desire to go inside.

But finally I did. I crept into the boathouse. It felt strange. Eerie. And unbelievably cold. Deep-down cold. Ice cold. Colder even than outside. And dark. Like dusk. Something in there I didn't like. Something but what? In the summer the boathouse feels entirely different. Warmer, of course, but something else as well, something more. In the summer I hear the water lapping against the boats, I see the barn swallows darting in and out, I smell the fresh varnish and the gasoline and the oil. In the summer, on rainy days, I sometimes spend hours in the boathouse polishing the chrome and the teak on the old antique wooden boats. Just sit there polishing and thinking it over. Just thinking, letting my thoughts wander. Yesterday my thoughts wandered also, but I didn't much like where they wandered to. I just wanted to get out of there. The boats were all covered and suspended from the ceiling. The sails and oars and motors had all been stowed away till spring. The birds had all flown south. Ulysses had been put to rest the summer before last. There was nothing there for me now. Nothing. Still, I had a job to do. I found a hammer, a saw, a handful of nails, and a piece of plywood. I went slowly up the stairs, into his old bedroom. For just a second I thought I saw him lying there, smiling at me. "We're going to hell in a basket, Willy my boy," he mumbled, "you'll have to make your move." Before I could ask him what move I had to make, he disappeared and on the floor beside his bed I saw the broken glass and a pile of windswept snow. I pushed the debris into a corner. I felt a little better then, a little more at ease with something to do. I measured the broken window and cut a piece of plywood. I set the plywood in the frame and nailed it securely into place. A job finished and well done. I would have something to tell Pop when he got back from Washington.

I looked around the room for Ulysses but he was long gone, so I went downstairs and put away the tools. Then I went back outside and took a deep breath. I'd gotten spooked in there, but now I felt a whole lot better. I put my skis on and skied around to the front of the house. Dawn had already swept the snow away from the front door. And I could see smoke beginning to drift out of the chimney. Dawn hadn't spooked; she'd just done what needed doing, strong as an ox, same as always.

I leaned my skis against the house, right beside hers, kicked the snow off my boots and pants, and went inside. I could hear the fire crackling in the living room. As soon as I stepped into the room I saw Dawn sitting in front of the fire. She heard me come in. "Everything okay?" she asked.

"Sure," I said. "I got the window all patched up."

We sat close and very near the fire. The warm, bright flames shot up the flue. I wanted to crawl in among the embers, curl up, and take a long nap. Dawn said she might want to join me. "But first," she said, "let's eat. I'm starving." She unpacked the sandwiches and the apple pie and the thermos filled with steaming hot chicken soup.

We dug in and didn't stop until almost all the food was gone. I put another log on the fire. It didn't take long for it to burst into flame. It's bone-dry oak I helped Pop cut and split last spring.

Dawn leaned back against the sofa we'd drawn up in front of the fire. She gazed into the flames, smiled, then closed her eyes. I wanted to go over, sit beside her, and close my eyes too. But I couldn't. Not right away. First I had something I needed to say. I'd been putting it off ever since coming through the front door, but it just wouldn't stay put any longer.

"For the last three years," I said, "everyone in the valley's been telling us not to worry about this dam. But I worry about it all the time. I worry about it sometimes till it darn near makes me sick."

Dawn stopped smiling but her eyes stayed closed. "You're a worrier, Willy, always have been."

"Maybe so," I said, "but what'll we do? I mean, if it really happens."

She opened her eyes and looked straight at me. "We'll do whatever we have to do."

"Like what?"

"Like fighting for what's ours. This is our home. We're not about to just let them take it."

"You mean that?"

"Of course I do. What do you think? You're not the only one who loves this valley."

I stared at her. My mouth fell open. I always had the feeling she was stronger than me, tougher, and now I had proof.

She stood, walked away from the fire, and went upstairs. I wondered why but didn't ask. I put another log on the fire and stirred the embers with the poker. Dawn came back carrying a heavy load of blankets. She dropped them on the floor in front of the sofa and went back upstairs. I didn't want to just be sitting there when she got back, so I went out through the kitchen to the back porch. As soon as I got ten feet from the fire I felt the cold. It was no good that far from the fire. I picked up as many logs as I could carry and started back for the living room. I found Dawn spreading those blankets in front of the fire. I set the logs next to the fireplace and thought about what might happen next.

Dawn took off her boots, her down parka, and her wool sweater. I did the same. Dawn slid in between the layers of blankets. She looked calm and comfortable. I was not any of those things. But after a moment I pulled back the bed of blankets and slid in beside her. My legs, actually my pants, rubbed against her pants. I tensed up and pulled them away. Dawn smiled. That helped. She kissed me softly on the mouth. I kissed her back. We pressed our bodies together. Our lips grew curious and active. We touched each other's ears and eyes and lips. And then, slowly, as the temperature under those blankets began to rise, we began to pull off our clothes: the wool pants came first, then the flannel shirts and the turtlenecks. And all of a sudden we lay there side by side, both of us dressed in bright red union suits buttoned up to the collar. The union suits made us laugh. And I knew right then at that moment that Dawn and I were about to do what we had been wanting to do, trying to do, afraid to do, for a pretty long time, a year or more at least.

I have a notion I shouldn't say too much here. What happened between Dawn and me was personal and very private. I feel kind of strange even thinking about it, much less writing about it. We didn't really know what to do, or what to expect. We made a few mistakes, but just like all the hundreds of others things we've done together over the years, we kept at it until we got it right.

And when I was inside her, and so excited I thought I would explode, she held me very still and said, "You see, Willy, we'll always be together. No matter what happens you and I will be together."

My insides stirred and erupted and finally exploded. Dawn held me together. I pushed and strained and in no time at all my body went slack. I thought for just a second I might be dead.

Not too long after, Dawn fell asleep against my chest. I watched her sleep for a long time. I felt safe, no longer spooked. When the flame began to die I carefully slipped out from under the blankets and added two thick logs to the fire.

The room grew dim. The short winter day grew old. In less than an hour I knew it would be dark. No way would we have time to put the house in order and ski back to town before nightfall. So without making a sound I crept into the kitchen and closed the door. I turned on the two-way radio and tried to keep from shivering.

It took a few minutes, but soon I reached Mama at the house on High Street. I told her we would have to spend the night. I expected her to get angry but all she said was, "You're old enough to know best now, Willy." Then she thanked me for calling and told me to make sure I kept Dawn warm and dry.

I assured her I would.

"Then I'll see you in the morning."

"Yes," I said, "in the morning."

I turned off the radio, fetched more logs from the back porch, and went quietly back into the living room. Dawn was still fast asleep. I stacked the logs, stoked the fire, then crawled under the blankets beside her. Very softly I told her not to worry, I would not let the fire go out.

8:26 A.M.
JANUARY 20, 2001
MACKENZIE ISLAND
THE INAUGURATION OF THE FORTY-FOURTH PRESIDENT OF THE UNITED STATES

No doubt Willy is over at the Great House seething because I shared with you the details of his first tryst with the lovely young Dawn. I simply could not resist his beautiful rendering of the setting and the atmosphere. I hope he will forgive me for violating his privacy. Unfortunately, the private life of the president of the United States quickly becomes part of the public's never-ending curiosity. Maybe there was a time in our history when the private life of a public person was not scrutinized by his or her fans or constituents, but no longer. We want to hear, need to hear, feel we have the right to hear the most intimate details about our movie stars, our professional athletes, and, of course, our elected officials. It is part of the price one pays for power and prestige.

But enough apologies. It is almost eight-thirty, eastern standard time, just three and a half hours until Willy takes the oath. A steady snow falls from a low gray sky. Here in the boathouse we have finally driven the temperature up to a balmy sixty-five degrees, but outside, brother, look out; it is, as my father used to say, "colder than the angry hand of the Lord." Not a wisp of wind blows, but step out of doors for just a minute and you feel the marrow in your bones begin to freeze. The National Weather Center says we can expect more of the same throughout the morning and early afternoon: large accumulations of snow and steadily falling temperatures.

Inside the Great House the MacKenzies stir. I can see Willy and Sanders and Conrad on the prowl, roaming from room to room, moving furniture, probably in preparation for the party to follow the ceremony. No inaugural ball for this president. He claims the country is far too broke for a ball, that a small party with close friends will do just fine.

Through the kitchen window I can see Emily and Alice measuring and mixing and checking the oven. Young Emily, the president-elect's little girl, sits at the kitchen table. She is either drawing or writing, hard to tell from here. We will have to scope her through a high-powered lens and fill you in later with the particulars of her musings.

If I didn't know better, I might think the MacKenzies were just getting ready to have a few friends over for supper. I wouldn't for a moment think they were about to become the most powerful and influential political family in the country. Just goes to show how appearances can be deceiving.

So with everything running smoothly here on MacKenzie Island, let us venture back to the South Pacific and see how Conrad and Josh made out after their encounter with the Japanese on Peleliu Island.

* * * * * *

Conrad Whitman MacKenzie slept on a brand-new hospital bed in a brand-new navy hospital on the island of Guam about fifteen hundred miles due south of Tokyo. It was Christmas Day 1944, more than two months since Conrad had gotten his shoulder blown open and his ankle shattered by a flurry of Japanese bullets during the battle to take Peleliu Island.

The marine in the next bunk reached over and shook young MacKenzie awake. "Wake up, Connie," he said, "the brass is coming by to pin some medals on our chests."

Conrad rolled over, grimaced at the pain in his shoulder still on the mend, and smiled at his fellow marine. "What do you say we hide from the sons of bitches, Josh? Maybe under the beds. Make the bastards crawl around on the floor looking for us."

Joshua Tyler laughed but replied, "The hell with that, Connie. They're giving you the Navy Cross for saving my hide."

"That's bunk, Josh, and we both know it. Any other guy would get maybe a bronze star for doing what I did. They're only giving me the cross because my old man's a senator and these lifers can smell brownie points a mile away."

"Say what you want, Connie, but if it were up to me, I'd get you the Congressional Medal of Honor presented by FDR himself. Without you I'd've been food for the maggots."

"Yeah," said Conrad, "I'm a regular goddamn hero."

For the past two and a half months Conrad and Josh had lived side by side, recuperating from their injuries. Since they had little to do between meals and physical therapy, the two marines had traded all the important tales about their childhoods. Josh knew all about Sally Colt, and Conrad knew all about Josh's girl, Mary Ann Parks. Josh had grown up in Baltimore. His father was a carpenter, and the family had just enough money to scrape by, never any extra. He could not believe Conrad had been to Europe and the White House and had attended private school and personally knew Babe Ruth. But the fact that they had grown up on opposite sides of the tracks mattered not at all; these two young men had far more important concerns in common: their love of baseball, for one (Josh had nicknamed Conrad "Connie" for the great Philadelphia manager Connie Mack), and the fact that they had both joined the United States Marine Corps on their seventeenth birthdays. This, they both agreed, was the dumbest move they had ever made.

So Conrad dragged himself out of bed and got himself cleaned up. An hour or so later a towering Marine Corps colonel strode into the hospital ward and pinned a purple heart on Josh and both a purple heart and the Navy Cross on Conrad. And even though earlier he'd sounded somewhat cynical about the whole affair, young MacKenzie beamed with pride when that colonel read the commendation for bravery and courage above and beyond the call of duty.

By the end of February 1945, Josh and Conrad were back in uniform. Rumors had been circulating for weeks that they and thousands of other wounded marines would be sent back to the States and discharged.

But the final drive for Tokyo had begun, and the top brass wanted every able-bodied soldier ready for action.

By the time Josh and Conrad reached Iwo Jima, the terrible battle for that small volcanic island had drawn to a close. But not before four thousand marines had died in less than a month of fighting. Barely pausing to catch its breath, the Marine Corps moved west across the Pacific for the Japanese island of Okinawa. The American people and their politicians were impatient for victory. The war suddenly seemed to have gone on for too long. There was no time left to stop and count the casualties.

For three months the battle on Okinawa raged. Josh and Conrad spent all of April aboard a navy destroyer. Early one morning they watched a Jap kamikaze pilot crash-land his fighter plane into a nearby battleship. The ship exploded, burst into flames, and sank. Half the sailors on board perished. Josh and Conrad helped pull the survivors, many of them ablaze with burning oil, from the fiery sea. Many of the sailors had their skin burned off right down to the bone.

That night Josh and Conrad lay below deck on their hard, narrow bunks. They could hear the wounded sailors screaming and groaning and begging for morphine.

In mid-May their company received orders to go ashore. The beachhead had been secured, so the amphibious landing, the direct frontal assault, went off without anyone getting shot. But soon enough they found themselves in the thick of the fray against an enemy that had gone stark raving mad. Not only had the Japanese become suicidal, but they seemed hell-bent on fighting to the last man, woman, and child.

Over the next three weeks Josh and Conrad fought practically around the clock, twenty-four hours a day. They found little time to eat, less time to sleep. The Japs just kept coming, a dauntless army of ants; kill one and two more took the corpse's place. Everywhere he went, mostly on his belly through mire and mud, Conrad saw Japanese bodies rotting and swelling in the late spring heat. The putrid stench of death and decay permeated the air.

The fighting wore on, random and chaotic. Orders filtered through the ranks, but by the time those orders reached the grunts in the field, they had become incoherent, meaningless. The bottom line: Do anything necessary to stay alive. To accomplish this goal Conrad discarded the last dregs of his civility. At one point he thrust the bayonet attached to his M-1 rifle through the chest of an old man masquerading as a Japanese soldier and brandishing nothing more than a sharpened bamboo stick for a weapon. Blood spurted from the old man's chest as he slumped to the ground, dead. Conrad bayoneted him several more times, just to be sure.

Hell on earth.

Finally, with more than half their platoon dead or badly wounded, Josh and Conrad and the others who could still walk were sent to the rear for a much needed rest. They shaved and showered and ate hot meals for the first time since hitting the beaches of Okinawa. They prayed and slept on dry cots and read letters from home. And even though those marines did not know it at the time, for them the fighting had finally finished. The war would drag on for a few more months, but Conrad and Josh and the rest of their platoon would not fire another shot.

In late June Okinawa finally fell to the Allies. The imperial navy and the imperial air force had become all but extinct. Every morning B-29's took off from airfields on Saipan and Tinian to bomb the Japanese mainland. Slowly but surely these bombing raids demolished the great cities of the empire. But still the Japanese military leaders refused to capitulate. So the Allied commanders had no choice but to prepare for an all-out invasion of Nippon.

"We lived through Okinawa," Conrad told Josh, "but I tell you no way will we survive a street fight in downtown Tokyo. We're as good as dead. We'll never see home again."

Conrad had plenty of reason to sound skeptical. For a young man not yet twenty years old, he had seen his share of horrors. But the show was not over, not by any means. Had the war ended for Conrad right there on Okinawa, had he been sent back to the States immediately after the Japanese surrendered to MacArthur aboard the USS *Missouri* on September 2, 1945, maybe, just maybe, he would have found a way to shake off the insanity and suffering he had witnessed. He had been wounded, laid up with jungle fever, seen men blown to bits, worn the blood of the enemy on his hands and face, listened to dying men scream for their mothers and for Jesus Christ, carried the smell of burning flesh in his nostrils, fired his M-1 point-blank into the face of a young man he did not even know, and on and on, the endless lunacy of war . . . but still, had it ended there he might have gone home a hero with his head held high, maybe run for Congress or taken over the helm at MacKenzie Shipping. Surely he would have succeeded at one socially responsible endeavor or another. But Conrad MacKenzie, and his new pal Joshua Tyler as well, had a few more sights to see before heading back to the land of liberty and the lives they had forever left behind.

On August 6, 1945, at 8:15 on a very warm and cloudless summer morning, Little Boy fell through the bomb bay doors of the B-29 bomber *Enola Gay* and exploded a thousand feet or so above the Japanese city of Hiroshima. Just one rather large bomb, but in no time at all Hiroshima lay in ruins. Just one bomb, but it flattened or incinerated virtually the entire city. And it killed, blinded, or maimed practically every single resident of that city. Just one bomb, but oh what a bomb it was.

When word of this strange and powerful bomb reached the boys on Okinawa, a great cheer rose through the ranks. And when three days later they learned another bomb had wiped out the Japanese city of Nagasaki, they cheered even louder. The fact that two entire cities and a few hundred thousand civilians had been wiped off the face of the earth mattered not one hoot to these soldiers who had been through hell and wanted only to lay down their arms and go home to their friends and families. To them the bombs meant only one thing: Japanese surrender, Japanese capitulation. And surrender meant survival. It meant the emperor would finally be forced to call it quits. It meant there would be no invasion of Nippon, no hand-to-hand fighting in the streets of Tokyo.

For reasons never made clear, Marine Corps Privates Conrad MacKenzie and Joshua Tyler made up part of General Douglas MacArthur's Allied Army for the Occupation of Postwar Japan. These two young men should have been rotated back to the States, but soon after the surrender they found themselves steaming into Tokyo Bay aboard a navy cruiser. For the next four months they lived among the defeated enemy before orders sending them home finally came through.

Conrad could not believe the condition of the Japanese capital. Not a single battle had been fought in or near the city, and yet entire neighborhoods had been destroyed, reduced to ugly piles of rubble. Six months of high-altitude bombing followed by countless incendiary attacks had obliterated and burned Tokyo practically to the ground. Where there had been homes and office buildings and factories, there was now only ash and cinders and broken glass.

At first assigned to supervise a cleanup effort of the streets in the downtown area of the city, suddenly and without explanation Conrad was reassigned to a Marine Corps major general sent from Washington to investigate the damage to the country's infrastructure. Major General Gus Brandon shook Conrad's hand and said, "Saw your father recently, son. Hell of a nice fella, your old man. Sends his best. Hopes to see you stateside soon."

Conrad nodded and managed a curt thank-you.

The general and the private then exchanged a few pleasantries before Brandon said, "I think we could use another driver. Can you recommend someone?"

So that's how Conrad and Josh hooked up for the grand tour of Nippon. The two young marines got to see firsthand the decimation of urban Japan. Tokyo, Yokohama, Osaka: they saw the damage inflicted upon these cities by the B-29 superbombers first from the air, then from the front seat of a battered navy jeep. They saw buildings toppled, bridges crushed, water and sewage systems bombed into rubble. Everywhere they went they found the Japanese people working like dogs, slaving from sunup to sundown, pouring their energy into repairing and rebuilding their homes and their shops and their lives. And as that navy jeep sped past, the defeated would pause from their labor long enough to bow in respect to the victors.

"They got grit!" the major general liked to shout from the back seat of the jeep. "You gotta give 'em that, they got moxie!"

Josh and Conrad nodded but said nothing. For days they had been able to do little more than stare at the damage and at the pitiful attempts to bring it under control. But nothing they saw on the initial phase of their tour prepared them for what they found farther south when their small navy reconnaissance plane circled the city of Hiroshima.

For several minutes no one on board that plane, not even the major general, who had barely batted an eye on their other stops, uttered a word. All they could do was peer out those small dusty windows and gape at the extraordinary sight below.

"One bomb," asked Conrad, finally, "one bomb did this?"

"No way," muttered Josh. "Not a chance." And then, "There really used to be a city down there?"

From the air Hiroshima looked like nothing more than a black and flattened arena of scorched earth. Virtually every single structure had either disintegrated during the atomic blast or been burned to the ground in the terrible fires that followed.

Down on the ground they found the level of destruction far more severe than in the other areas they had visited. Efforts to reclaim the city had thus far proved futile. The survivors of Hiroshima were in no shape physically or mentally to begin the rebuilding process. Many of them simply wandered through the rubble looking frightened and disoriented as they searched for their homes, their belongings, their loved ones.

The infrastructure of the city had been entirely destroyed by the bomb, so Major General Brandon found little of interest for his survey. He wrote this in his notebook: "Hiroshima, an excursion to the Inferno." Then he turned his attention to other matters. More from a morbid curiosity than from any official duties, Brandon decided to visit some of the area hospitals on the outskirts of the ruined city.

"I've heard," he shouted from the back seat of the speeding jeep, "that these atom bombs have inflicted some unbelievable wounds, unlike any shit we've ever seen before. Let's have a look."

So Josh and Conrad, like sweepstakes winners to purgatory, got a tour of the Hiroshima area hospitals. What a treat. It drove those two young marines a little closer to the edge.

In those hospitals outside the devastated city, they found the victims. They saw suffering far worse than they had seen out on the field of battle. Women and babies, children and old people, lay scattered about the wards in various states of pain and delirium. Burns, black and oozing a nasty yellow pus, covered the faces and arms and legs of many of the patients. Others appeared fine and healthy on the outside, but inside their organs failed while their blood boiled from the effects of radioactive fallout. Almost everyone was blind.

The visits became more than Conrad could bear. After seeing a young woman about the same age as Sally but with her hair falling out in clumps and her breasts burned off her chest and her eyes plucked from her skull, he raced outside and threw up. Even during the battles on Tarawa and Peleliu and Okinawa he had not seen such terrible injuries.

Conrad sat out on the front stoop of the hospital, and for all the world to see, that marine put his head in his hands and began to cry. The dam quickly broke, and the tears flowed in a deluge.

"On your feet, soldier!" ordered the major general. "Dry that shit off your face! That's the goddamn enemy in there. The enemy got what it deserved."

Private MacKenzie struggled to his feet and saluted. "Yes, sir, exactly what the enemy deserved, sir." But that night, in bed, Conrad began to cry again. This was not the same gung ho marine who had reported to boot camp some three years earlier.

Josh put his arms around his buddy's shoulders. "Go ahead, Connie," he said, "let it out. A few tears is the least we can do for these poor bastards."

On March 1, 1946, Conrad Whitman MacKenzie, honorably discharged from the United States Marine Corps, walked into his parents' house in Georgetown. A throng of family and friends welcomed him home. They were oh so glad to see him. Too bad they had little or no knowledge of the horrors he had witnessed. They knew only that Conrad had survived the war and that he looked strong and steady in his Marine Corps blues.

His mother hugged him. His father slapped him on the back. His old high school chums shook his hand. And sweet Sally, whole and healthy, threw her arms around his neck and kissed him on the lips. He looked back at all these people and wondered for just a moment who they were and what they wanted.

And on June 1, 1946, after doing almost nothing for three months but sleep and eat and stare out the window at the wide and muddy Potomac, Conrad married Sally at the same church in Georgetown where Lawrence had married Rebecca twenty-one years earlier. The marriage was, to a very great extent, Sally's idea. Neither her parents nor Conrad's parents were particularly excited about the prospect, but they decided not to stand in the young couple's way.

The fact that Conrad proved a study in ambivalence was lost on all of them. "Sure," he told Sally. "You want to get married? Okay. What the hell? Makes no difference to me."

Sally assured him it made a great deal of difference to her, so Conrad stood up in front of the altar and mouthed the words "I do" without hardly recognizing the sound of his own voice. Josh Tyler stood up there with him as his best man. Without Josh at his side, Conrad might not have made it. More than once Josh had to keep Conrad from turning around and just wandering off, down the aisle of the church and out into the street.

Conrad wanted to honeymoon on MacKenzie Island but Sally insisted on a grand tour of Europe. So off they sailed for Southampton. For the first week they followed Sally's carefully prepared itinerary: the English countryside, Stratford-on-Avon, Kent, and Oxfordshire. But when they reached London, the itinerary began to fall apart. Conrad did not want to see Buckingham Palace or the Tower of London or Big Ben. He wanted to investigate those sections of the city still in ruins from the Luftwaffe bombing raids of 1940 and 1941.

And from there he had no desire to see Paris or Venice or Rome. No, he insisted they travel to Hamburg and Dresden and Berlin and Warsaw, to all those European cities that the psychopaths had bombed and burned during the war.

Sally did not understand her new husband's fetish. "Conrad," she demanded, "what is going on? What's the matter with you? Why do you want to see all this devastation? Why can't we go see the Sistine Chapel and the Eiffel Tower?"

Conrad looked at his bride and shrugged. "I don't know, Sally. Right now I can't really say for sure."

"What does that mean?" Mrs. MacKenzie asked. "When will you be able to say? All you do all the time is brood. My God, Conrad, we're on our honeymoon."

True, Conrad may have been on his honeymoon, but nevertheless the young man found it almost impossible to perform sexually. When he had first gotten home from the war he had ravaged Sally two and three times a day. He went at her like a wild animal. And just as she had done before the war, Sally bucked up under the assault, knowing that in time her marine would settle down. He had settled down all right, settled down and gone limp. At night, in bed, after touring the rubble, she would kiss him and stroke him and whisper dirty words in his ear. He would mostly grimace and cringe and then close his eyes and turn away.

"Was it that bad?" she would ask. "Was the war really that terrible?"

He would shrug and maybe answer, "Worse." Nothing more.

Late that summer, on their way home, the honeymoon winding down, somewhere out on the stormy Atlantic, Sally finally managed to arouse Conrad. She did not waste time; she put his erection immediately to work. Their convergence, however, did not last long. After only a few seconds Conrad stalled and sputtered and shot his load. But their intercourse lasted long enough for the union of sperm and egg, thus resulting in the conception of our president-elect's older brother, Sanders Colt MacKenzie.

The young and already troubled couple moved to New York City, took an apartment on Riverside Drive not far from the headquarters of MacKenzie Shipping. Conrad went to work for Ulysses. U.S. was eighty-one years old but still worked twelve or fourteen hours a day six days a week. The war had done wonders for MacKenzie Shipping, and it looked as though the postwar economy would be both strong and vibrant.

"Plenty of money out there," U.S. told his grandson. "We've got our share, but we could always grab for more. What do you say?"

Conrad shrugged and sighed and rubbed his temples.

Ulysses wanted Conrad to work in the office, to learn the fundamentals of charters and leases, of contracts and negotiations. But Conrad had other ideas.

"I want to start at the bottom," he told his grandfather, "and work my way up."

"What do you mean?"

"On board ship. I want to work as a deckhand and learn the business from the bottom rung of the ladder."

"I knew it," Ulysses growled at his grandson. "I knew that goddamn war'd scrambled your brain." But he gave Conrad the job he wanted.

For the next eight months Conrad worked on a freighter plying the waters up and down the eastern seaboard. He spent only a few days each month at home with his new wife. Every time he arrived home he saw the bulge in Sally's stomach looming larger.

"This isn't what I had in mind," Sally would complain, "when I married you. I wanted us to be together, to be a family. Why can't you take a regular job and come home at night like other men?"

Conrad, as usual, did not have an answer. He simply shrugged his shoulders, rubbed his temples, and stared at the fuzzy images on their brand-new black-and-white television set.

On May 14, 1947, after a long and excruciating labor, Sally delivered their son. She had to handle the event all alone because Conrad was down in Miami offloading bananas and ducking invisible bullets flying by his head.

He got back to New York a week and a half later. He took one look at the boy and said to his wife, "We're moving to the island."

"What island?"

"MacKenzie Island."

"No we're not."

"Yes we are."

They argued for over an hour before Sally went into the bedroom and cried herself to sleep. Conrad called Josh Tyler down in Baltimore. "I'm moving up to the island, Josh. Want to join me?"

The transition from military to civilian life had not been easy for Josh, either. Like his buddy, Josh had come home, gotten married, and gone to work. But he suffered from terrible nightmares and horrendous headaches. So after thinking it over for a few minutes, he told Conrad, "If Mary Ann agrees to come, I'll be there, Connie. At least for the summer. After that, well, we'll just have to see."

"Right," Conrad said, "we'll just have to see. One day at a time and all that shit."

Early the next morning Conrad walked into his grandfather's office. "I'm quitting," he announced. "I don't want to work in the shipping business anymore."

Ulysses called his grandson every foul and derogatory name in the book. For the rest of the morning they shouted back and forth. Conrad refused to give an inch.

"So then what the hell are you going to do?"

"I'm moving up to the island."

"MacKenzie Island?"

"That's right."

"Why the hell would you want to move up there?"

Conrad thought about it. "Because it's quiet," he answered. "And because it's safe."

June 7, 1986
Washington, D.C.

We reached Washington late last night, came by train. By we I mean Pop and Mama and Sanders and Alice and Dawn and me. We're staying in a house near the Potomac not far from where Pop grew up. On the way down here I asked Pop for the millionth time what would happen to MacKenzie Island if the Tamaqua Valley Dam became a reality.

"Hell, Willy," he said, "MacKenzie Island's the safest place on earth."

"Yeah?"

"Absolutely. I ought to know. It's been watching over me most of my adult life."

I hope Pop's right. If they build this dam there won't even be any MacKenzie Island.

It's just about seven o'clock. Probably time to wake everyone up. The march starts at eight o'clock sharp, and I know Pop and Sanders have an important meeting at nine. They're meeting with some congressmen and senators about the dam. I wanted to go with them, and Pop was just about to give me the green light when Mama stepped in and reminded me I'd be marching with the Indians and no way was she about to let me miss that.

June 9, 1986
Washington, D.C.

Been away from the journal for a couple days, but I'm finally back. We've been rushing around the capital and I haven't had the time to write a word. I need to remember to take things slower and easier, not to pile too much into any one day.

The newspapers claimed more than half a million people showed up for the march. Looked like a billion to me. I'd never seen so many people in one place before.

EARTHCARE: A MARCH ON WASHINGTON FOR THE PRESERVATION OF OUR ECOSYSTEM. That's the name the people who planned it gave to their three-day environmental event.

The day before yesterday we gathered outside the U.S. Capitol at eight in the morning. For the next two hours folks just kept pouring into the area. By train, by bus, by car, by bike, and on foot they just kept coming. It took some time but we finally managed to divide up into almost orderly columns of marchers. There were men with their sons, women with their babies, old folks and young folks, white folks and black folks and red folks.

Together we marched almost due east across the Mall, past the National Art Gallery and the Air and Space Museum and the Museum of American History. We must've been fifty or maybe even a hundred abreast, row after row of folks waving banners and holding up signs that read: EARTH FIRST, MAN SECOND and SAVE THE PLANET and PROTECT THE INNOCENT and LET'S FIX IT BEFORE IT BREAKS and DO A GOOD DEED: LOP THE HEAD OFF A POLLUTER TODAY!

Dawn and Mama and Alice and I marched with members of the Mohawk tribe. Some of them I knew from the valley, from the annual ceremonies held at the sacred burial grounds on the south shore of MacKenzie. But many of the Mohawk had come from as far away as Michigan and Minnesota. And Indians from other tribes had come all the way from Oregon and North Dakota and New Mexico. Many of the Indians wore their traditional tribal costumes. I saw plenty of beads and feathers and deerskin during the march. A few of the younger warriors even marched wearing full headdress. I asked Mama about it and she said the war bonnets were a symbol of protest.

"A protest against what?" I asked.

"Murder," she said. "Murder and treachery and land plundering."

"Who did all that?"

"No one if not the federal government of the United States."

That left me with something to think about.

We marched all the way to the Washington Monument, then turned north to gather on the Ellipse, a great sweep of lawn across from the White House. A large wooden reviewing stand had been erected at the far side of the Ellipse. I could see folks milling around on the stand, getting ready to make speeches. It must have been close to noon. The sun beat down on us from straight up overhead. I was glad I had a hat to keep that sun off my face. But Dawn didn't have a hat so I gave her mine. She burns a lot easier than I do.

First some woman with long, red hair and a high voice stepped up to the microphone and talked for almost half an hour about global warming. I forget her name but someone said she was a famous movie star. I wouldn't know about that. I've only been to the movies a time or two.

Next this tall guy who stars in some TV sitcom spoke for a few minutes about recycling. I didn't recognize him, either, but then, we don't have a TV. Once in a while we go over to Wilson's Hotel to watch the World Series. Pop likes baseball, especially the New York Yankees.

All these TV stars and sports heroes and politicians droned on for most of the afternoon. At first they got plenty of applause with cheering and whistling, but then folks in the audience started to wilt under that high hot sun. (Hotter than fire here in Washington. Don't know how folks stand it.) Pretty soon some polite clapping was all anyone could muster. Until, that is, my uncle got up to speak.

I call him my uncle but that might be an exaggeration. His name is Tecumseh Brant and he's a direct descendant of the great Mohawk chief Joseph Brant. Mama and I are descended from Joseph Brant also, so somehow Tecumseh and I must be related. I've known Tecumseh my entire life. He's an old man now, some say the oldest living Mohawk, although no one knows for sure.

He's no bigger around than a willow switch and not a whole lot higher than a dining room table, but that afternoon he blocked out the sun with his scrawny little body. During the few brief minutes he spoke, not one of those half million folks in the audience missed a word he said. His voice barely rose above a whisper, but every word he uttered came through as loud and clear as thunder.

"Maybe," he said, "Revelations was right: 'Foul and evil sores for men who worship the beast; blood into the rivers and seas, killing every living thing beneath the water; men scorched by the power of the sun and then assembled at a place to be called Armageddon.' Yes, maybe so."

He paused to let his words settle. Tecumseh, that little old Indian from the Blue Mountains, had the undivided attention of half a million folks.

"What I have to tell you today," he continued, "is a message from the distant past. My people have lived on this continent for a thousand generations. Each generation has communicated to the next generation the information necessary to create and sustain life. The stories and teachings fill a dozen lifetimes, but I will not bore you with the endless philosophical musings of the once mighty Mohawk. No, today it will be enough for us gathered here to stay with the basics. Today I will tell you only about the earth and the air and the water.

"For a million years, for a thousand generations, the purity of this continent's earth, air, and water fed and nurtured my people. One generation after another learned to worship and respect these three vital elements. Everywhere my people roamed, everywhere they settled, they found fertile earth and clean air and clean water. Never did our mothers and fathers allow us to take these elements for granted. From an early age we understood what would happen if these elements turned against us.

"The Mohawk, since the beginning of time, have battled many difficult and deadly hardships: famine, invasion, disease, war. But the earth and the air and the water," and for the first time since he began, Tecumseh's voice rose up as he held high his frail arms and clenched his withered fists, "the earth and the air and the water, the earth and the air and the water—these three elements have provided us with sustenance and hope!"

He grew quiet again, paused for most of a minute. Not one of us stirred or even reached for a deep breath. We knew the old Indian was not finished.

"And now," he began again, "you know what I will say next, what I must tell you before I part the great capital of this great but nevertheless troubled land. A million years, a thousand generations: an almost monotonous eclipse of time. But now, in less than one hundred years, in less time than it has taken this old man to live out a single lifetime, the once fertile earth screams in pain from overuse and chemical contamination, the once clean air hangs foul and infected with disease-carrying toxins, and the once clear water runs filthy with poisons and pollutants.

"How much can we endure? What terrible effects will another hundred years have on these elements if we stay the present course? How will the next generation spread its wings and take flight? How will the babies learn to smile? I tell you I have much fear; fear for us, yes, for every one of us, but even more fear for the earth and the air and the water, and for all living things on this tiny planet."

Tecumseh's voice trailed off at the end. I could barely hear his final words. He grew silent then, and for several moments every single one of us in that vast audience stood frozen even under that boiling hot summer sun. I don't know what anyone else saw or thought or felt during that thirty or so seconds of complete silence, but I saw a dead and ravaged earth floating through space. No more life on earth than the astronomers have found on Pluto or Neptune or anywhere else in the Great Nebula.

Then, as the scene in space faded to black, that crowd erupted. It exploded. Quite a sight to hear half a million people yelling and applauding and cheering all at once.

8:43 A.M.
JANUARY 20, 2001
MACKENZIE ISLAND
THE INAUGURATION OF THE FORTY-FOURTH PRESIDENT OF THE UNITED STATES

Take a look at this. My God! MacKenzie Island invaded by Indians. Through the large front windows of the boathouse, out across Loon Cove, I see as many as thirty Indians, excuse me, Native Americans, coming across Lake Katydeeray.

They must be Mohawk. They have no doubt traveled from their reservation on the western shore of the lake, the reservation purchased for them by Conrad Whitman MacKenzie back in the mid-nineties. They wear snowshoes and parkas as they make their way across the ice and snow, through this storm that has quickly turned into a blizzard. But I doubt they have plans to invade; they have surely been invited to attend the inauguration.

Anyway, Willy was absolutely right. The reaction to Tecumseh Brant's speech during that environmental march on Washington was quite a sight indeed. I know. I was there, just back from El Salvador, where I'd been working on a network news story about some recently murdered American nuns. The crowd went wild with enthusiasm.

What interests me is the fact that for as long as Willy's been in the public eye he has been writing and talking about the fundamental elements of earth, air, and water. We see now where it all originated. But perhaps the most fascinating aspect of that June 9, 1986, journal entry is the way it so completely juxtaposes with the entries he made in the winter of 1997 during his far more famous visit to our nation's capital. Unbelievable what a difference a decade makes. . . .

We have some news out of Washington. Chief Justice O'Connor's refusal to participate in the swearing-in ceremony has many people inside the Beltway speculating on who will administer the oath of office to the president-elect. No one has stood up and volunteered for the job.

Also, the grapevine runs amok with rumors of unusual military movements and meetings at the White House between President Montgomery and leaders of Congress. An assemblage of some two hundred constitutional lawyers has gathered up on Capitol Hill. They have no doubt been given the chore of finding a way to keep Willy from his elected post.

The exact whereabouts and condition of that train carrying diplomats and reporters remains a mystery. The only thing I know for sure is that my crew and I continue to be the only journalists here on MacKenzie Island, the only source for live coverage of this presidential inauguration. So stay tuned, and as more information becomes available we will pass it along to you.

Right now those Mohawk are leaning their snowshoes against the back porch and knocking the snow off their parkas. And there's Conrad MacKenzie, welcoming his guests, inviting them inside, out of the cold and the icy wind.

By early July 1947, Conrad and Josh had brought their families up to MacKenzie Island to escape the cold realities of civilian life in postwar America. They moved into the Great House. Conrad and Sally occupied the enormous master bedroom on the second floor with its floor-to-ceiling windows overlooking the lake. The infant Sanders slept in a brass crib in a corner of the bedroom. Years later he would claim to remember those early days in that room with his mother, who sat for hours on the wide windowsill staring out at the lake while her silent, brooding husband wandered aimlessly through the island's woodlands.

Josh Tyler and his new bride, Mary Ann Parks, occupied the bedroom across the hall. Like Josh, Mary Ann had grown up in Baltimore, part of a working-class family that never had quite enough money. That beautiful island home in the middle of the Blue Mountains was like paradise for Mary Ann. She loved it as much as Sally despised it. From the first the two women did not get on well. Sally, it could be said, was a snob. She only spoke to Mary Ann to criticize or condescend. Mary Ann did all the cooking and cleaning. And after Conrad taught her to operate the launch, she also went to town to do the shopping. Right away, with her smile and good cheer, she made friends with everyone in Cedar Bluffs.

Sally, a frown frozen upon her face, made no friends at all. Every night before bed Sally would have the same conversation with Conrad.

"Just how long do you plan on keeping us on this godforsaken island?"

"I like this godforsaken island."

"Well, I don't."

"Well, I do."

"Dammit," Sally would shout, "I won't stay!"

"You'll stay or you'll go," Conrad would reply. "That's up to you."

In the middle of August, tragic news reached the island. Mary Ann brought it back with her from the general store in Cedar Bluffs. It had come over the wireless. Sally's mother and her father, who was back at the helm of the family munitions business since the coming of peace, were out on Long Island at the grand opening of a brand-new Colt firearms factory. No one knew for sure exactly what happened, but an explosion ripped through the factory during the grand opening ceremonies and the Colts wound up victims of their own success.

Conrad accompanied his wife and son to the funerals in New York City. He hung around the Big Apple for several days afterward while his wife and her sisters mourned and wept and divvied up the family fortune. Sally, it was soon determined, suddenly had a net worth of almost three million dollars.

"Conrad," she shouted, a big smile plastered on her face, "I'm rich!"

"It's time to go back," said Conrad.

Sally frowned. "To the island?"

"Yes."

"Forget it, I'm not going back." The money, it seems, had lit a fire under Sally's feet.

"What do you mean, you're not going back?"

"I mean I'm not going back to that desolate island. Not today. Not tomorrow. Maybe not ever."

"And what about the kid? What about Sanders?"

"He's not going back either."

"We'll see about that."

"Conrad," said Sally, "listen to me. I love you and I want more than anything for us to be together. But this war thing has made you crazy, and until you set it right I—"

"This *war thing*? What's that supposed to mean?"

"I just mean . . ."

But Conrad did not wait for her answer. He turned away and went back to the island.

"Where's Sally?" asked Josh.

Conrad just looked at his friend and shrugged.

Conrad's truly reclusive phase can be dated from his and Sally's separation. This phase lasted, with varying degrees of intensity, for the next twenty years, really until the onset of his relationship with Emily Brant in October of 1966. Critics of the MacKenzies claim, however, that Conrad's splendid isolation continues to this day. You will have to make up your own mind regarding his and his family's ties or lack thereof to the outside world.

Before the ice arrived that first winter, Josh and Mary Ann moved over to Cedar Bluffs. Mary Ann was due to give birth before the coming of spring, so they rented a small house on Water Street and Josh went to work felling trees for a lumber company in North Creek.

Conrad made the decision to winter on MacKenzie. No white man had ever done that before as far as anyone in the Tamaqua Valley could remember. Too bad his preparations proved inadequate. By the first of the year he had almost frozen to death from a severe shortage of firewood. Josh crossed the frozen lake and walked into the Great House on New Year's Day only to find his war buddy curled up in a corner shivering from the intense cold and a high fever. He hefted Conrad over his shoulder and hauled him all the way across the ice to Cedar Bluffs.

"I owe you one," Conrad said after the doctors thawed him out and cut off the top third of his left pinky because of frostbite.

"No you don't," said Josh. "Now we're even."

Then, in late February, Josh found Conrad lying unconscious on the middle of the living room floor. Once more he hauled his buddy across the ice to town. The doctor said Conrad's system had shut down because of an extreme lack of basic nutrients. Conrad, it seems, was not getting enough decent food to eat. If Josh hadn't come out to check on him, young MacKenzie probably would have starved to death—a rather ironic scenario for the sole grandson of one of the nation's richest men.

"Now I definitely owe you one," said Conrad.

"Yeah," said Josh, "now you owe me one."

The very next day Mary Ann gave birth to a baby boy. His parents named him James because they loved that part of the Bible in the Epistle of James where it said, "And the fruit of righteousness is sown in peace of them that make peace." They vowed to live in peace and to fight for peace in the boy's lifetime and never to call him Jim or Jimmy, always James.

The following year Conrad was far better equipped to handle the ruthless severity of a Blue Mountain winter. Over the summer he had befriended a group of Mohawk who came to the south shore of the island to visit the sacred burial grounds. Tecumseh Brant was the leader of these Mohawk.

"The Great Spirit," Tecumseh, already an old man, told Conrad, "gave us summer to prepare for winter. Those who sit idle in summer die in winter."

"That makes sense," said Conrad.

"Study the animals," Tecumseh told Conrad. "Those that cannot migrate spend the warm months preparing for the cold months. They store food and build shelter."

"I already have shelter."

"We have seen your shelter, paleface. It could easily hold all the Mohawk who dwell in this valley. You are only one man, MacKenzie. Think small, think functional."

So Conrad set about building himself a small cabin on the eastern side of the island. He chose the sight for its accessibility to fresh water, its protection from the northwest winds, and the abundance of nearby oak trees. By the fall of 1948, with Josh's help, he had erected his one-room log cabin complete with roof and fireplace, and laid in enough firewood to hopefully keep himself warm until spring. He continued to have problems with his diet during that second winter, but nevertheless he fared much better than he had the first.

The following summer Conrad planted and raised a vegetable garden. He learned how to can and store food. He dug a root cellar and filled it with potatoes and turnips and carrots. His third winter passed with nothing more than a bout or two of food poisoning and a mild case of influenza.

"This is the way to live," he told Josh. "Softly, silently, and with all the self-sufficiency we can muster."

In 1950 Conrad convinced Ulysses to sell Tamarack Island to Josh Tyler for one hundred dollars down and one hundred dollars a year for twenty years.

"Hell," said Ulysses, "I might just as well give it to him."

"He won't take it if you give it to him," said Conrad. "Too proud for that."

"Still," said Ulysses, "that crummy little island must be worth more than two grand."

"Probably so," countered Conrad, "but that's all Josh can afford."

So Ulysses sold Josh the island. And a year later, on his eighty-sixth birthday, U.S. sold MacKenzie Shipping as well, lock, stock, and barrel. "What the hell?" he grumbled. "I'm sick and tired of running the whole damn show myself, and there doesn't seem to be another MacKenzie alive interested in taking the helm. Besides, I got some Greeks willing to pay market value."

Estimated purchase price: two hundred and sixteen million dollars.

And there was Conrad MacKenzie living out in the woods in a one-room shack, eating boiled potatoes and raw carrots from Christmas till Easter.

And if you like the sound of that irony, try this one on for size: The winter after he sold the family business, U. S. MacKenzie lived in that one-room shack with his grandson. Well, maybe not the whole winter, but for almost three long and frigid weeks.

They spent their time cutting and hauling firewood and playing checkers and gin rummy for money until one day Ulysses said, "I'm too damn old for this, boy. I'm going down to Florida and see if I can hunt me up some young suntanned pussy."

Before he left he told Conrad, "I'm deeding you the island. Upon my death—if, that is, I ever die—MacKenzie Island will go straight to you. Lawrence doesn't want it. He hasn't spent a hundred days here his entire life. You'll also get what I've buried on the island. Every penny of it. No one knows exactly how much there is, not even me, but goddammit, there must be millions, tens of millions. Save it for a rainy day, or just buy yourself some eatable chow. For chrissakes, boy, these stinking turnips ain't fit for a hog."

Conrad assured his grandfather he would take good care of the island and the money, and then he hauled Ulysses over to Cedar Bluffs in the homemade snowmobile he had put together from some old cross-country skis, a worn-out leather settee, and a motor and drive train from a John Deere tractor that had years ago seen its best days.

"By the way, boy," U.S. announced just before boarding the southbound train, "I still say you're wasting your life away up here amongst these bohunks and rednecks. You should be out there in the world getting your hands dirty, breaking some legs, making your mark. But if there's one thing I've learned, it's to stay clear of another man's business. Each man's got to pursue what he's got to pursue."

Conrad nodded and shook his grandfather's hand, then waved goodbye as the train rolled out of town. And who suddenly appeared at Connie's shoulder? None other than his beautiful but estranged wife. Sally had arrived quite unexpectedly on the northbound express. Together they walked over to Wilson's Hotel.

"How's the boy?"

"Sanders is fine, Conrad. I have him in private school now down in New York."

"So you're still living in the city?"

"Yes."

"You're welcome to come back anytime."

"I'm never coming back here to live, Conrad. You know that."

They sat in the shadows in a corner of the hotel bar. Conrad nodded.

They endured a long silence. Finally Sally said, "There's a reason why I've come."

Conrad waited.

"Seeing you once or twice a year, for a few days at a time. Well, it just doesn't work. I can't do it anymore."

Conrad sighed. "I guess we haven't really had the best—"

"I've decided to file for divorce."

"Divorce?" The word seemed to shake him.

"Yes, Conrad, divorce. I'm sorry but you seem absolutely resolute about continuing your insane mission to live like an animal." Sally's voice began to rise as she worked her way through the remarks she had been rehearsing for the past several weeks. "I don't understand why you're doing this. Maybe you need professional help. I'm seeing a psychiatrist. She's excellent. Maybe she could help you work out your problems. Because, Conrad, I tell you, this has to stop! Things must change! You can't live up here in the woods forever."

The few other patrons in the bar had their ears pointed at this young woman in the fur coat and the diamond earrings who seemed on the verge of losing control.

Conrad put his hand over her hand. Calmly and quietly he made his reply. "Thanks for the concern, Sally. Really. I know I've messed things up for us. But believe me, I didn't do it on purpose. Things happen. Right now I just like to get up in the morning and work my tail off till it's time to go to bed. That way I can sleep at night without the nightmares, mostly."

Sally took several deep breaths to settle herself. "I don't even know what you mean when you talk, Conrad. I don't even know who you are."

Conrad nodded. "Understood," he said. "And that's why there'll be no arguments from me if a divorce is the route you want to go. Just take care of the details, send me the papers, and I'll sign my name."

Sally began to cry. Conrad held his wife's hand.

"What about Sanders?" she asked finally.

"I'd like to see the boy up here with me. This is where I think he belongs. The future's right here, Sally. The rest is craziness. But you see things differently, and I know you're his mother. So just let him know I'm alive, let him know what I'm doing, let him know I care, and maybe sometime down the road he'll tell you he wants to come up to the island to visit his old man for a while. If he does, let him come."

Conrad suddenly looked exhausted. He had not offered up so many words at once in years. It had taken a considerable effort. But he felt good about it—so good, in fact, that he booked the best room in the hotel, the suite on the third floor overlooking the lake, and ordered a bottle of champagne. He and Sally drank the champagne, and then, like old times, she took off his clothes and carefully laid them over a chair. They made love that winter night for the last time. Sally had tears in her eyes. Conrad gently wiped those tears away. He had never before been so tender with her.

Conrad felt a powerful urge to go back to his old life. All night long he lay awake thinking it over. But in the morning, before dawn, with his wife still sound asleep, Conrad slipped out of bed and pulled on his wool pants, leather boots, flannel shirt, wool sweater, and his wool mackinaw. He took one last look at Sally before he opened the door and crept out into the hallway. He went down the stairs and across the empty lobby. He opened the front door and stepped outside. The air was perfectly still and incredibly cold. It caught in his lungs. Almost imperceptibly, he shivered. He began to march, down Main Street to Water Street to the public wharf where he had beached his homemade snowmobile. He pulled out the choke and started the engine. The sound of that machine shattered the morning silence. Many of the residents of Cedar Bluffs woke with a start. Those who took the time to crawl out of bed and glance out the window saw through the shadows that crazy Conrad MacKenzie accelerating across the frozen lake like some specter from another world.

A thousand miles and yet another world away, Lawrence Van Rensselaer MacKenzie lay sound asleep in his Georgetown brownstone. He had a few months earlier been elected to his sixth full term in the United States Senate. Thirty years he had served in that legislative body, but this, he and his wife, Rebecca, had decided, would be his last term. He would not run again, no matter what events transpired. He would go out a winner, having never suffered defeat his entire political career. In another six years he would retire at the age of sixty-four. After that he and Rebecca would travel the world first class, visiting foreign capitals and dining with heads of state. That was their plan. But as so often happens, as we shall see, a simple twist of fate beyond their control or comprehension threw their plan to the dogs.

Lawrence and Rebecca, as those of us with children can easily imagine, were sick at heart over the plight of their son, Conrad. Like Sally, they could not understand his motives. Oh, they knew the war had messed with his head. They knew he had seen death and destruction. But abandoning his wife and son, living in a shack in the woods, cutting himself off from family and friends, refusing to participate in society—all of these actions made no sense at all to the young man's parents. Larry and Becky were basically shallow and rather simple people, perhaps a tad manipulative, certainly not intellectual or emotional giants. They did not have the depth of character to fathom their boy's pain. They believed, if they actually believed anything, in going with the flow, rolling with life's punches.

A few months before the November elections in 1952, Larry and Becky made the calculated decision to have the senator return to the Grand Old Party. The MacKenzies foresaw the country's conservative swing to the Right and the stars rising over General Dwight, so they decided to act rather than see the senator suffer his first political setback.

"Yes," he answered his critics, "I turned my back on the Republicans during the latter stages of the Great Depression and during the war, but now I have returned. I see clearly the path we must follow for growth and prosperity, and I feel certain Dwight David Eisenhower and the Republican party will blaze that path! I return to the party of my birth hell-bent on seeing America rise to the top!"

It worked. The Democrats came up with some bozo with all kinds of skeletons in his closet, and Senator Lawrence MacKenzie easily held on to his Senate seat. And all through the middle fifties, while his son taught himself the virtues of solitude and self-reliance, Larry languished in the comforts of his elected office. He cared less than ever about the day-to-day affairs plaguing the nation. Civil rights, McCarthyism, poverty, nuclear proliferation—these issues played little on the mind of Senator MacKenzie. He was far too busy with cocktail parties and black-tie dinners. Probably his most difficult task during his final term was keeping Vice President Richard Milhous Nixon at bay.

Everyone in Washington knew Nixon cared about only two things:

Nixon and, of course, succeeding Eisenhower as the next president of the United States. The presidency consumed the young man from California every second of every day. He spent a great deal of his time winning friends and influencing people. Early in his political career Nixon had tapped into Senator MacKenzie. Not only was MacKenzie an ongoing presence in the Senate, but his old man had millions. Nixon's passion for power and money made Larry a temptation he could not resist. The Trickster cornered Larry every chance he got, never failing to inquire about the good senator's family, especially the aging Ulysses.

Lawrence rarely mentioned his son in public during the postwar years. Conrad, we might conclude, was an embarrassment to the aging statesman. But the father did not completely abandon his son. He made several attempts in the 1950s to visit Conrad up on the island. He hated the long trip into the wilderness and the boat ride across the lake and most of all plodding through the woods to that smoky log cabin, where he found it practically impossible to believe his boy, who he had once assumed would achieve wealth, power, and perhaps even greatness, lived. Nevertheless, at least twice a year for six or eight years, he made the trek from D.C. to the Blue Mountains.

"How are you, Conrad?"

"Fine, Dad. Excellent."

This was in early September of 1958. Conrad had long wavy hair by this time and a full, well-trimmed beard. His voice had grown deep and husky from all that crisp mountain air. He had thick, muscular arms and tremendous shoulders from his daily dose of ten or twelve hours of hard physical labor. His eyes were clear and bright, steady and calm.

Still, the senator had a hard time making eye contact with his son. "That's good."

"What about you, Dad? How are you?"

"Oh, you know, can't complain."

"And Mom? And Patricia?"

"They're fine, Conrad. They send their best." Lawrence, wearing handmade Italian leather wingtips, kicked at the dirt outside the cabin.

"So how's things in Washington, Dad? Still busy passing bills and making bombs?"

The senator rolled his shoulders, tried to work a kink out of his neck. His son's dig had gone unnoticed. "Your mother wants you at home, Conrad. We all miss you very much."

"I miss you too, Dad. But I am home. MacKenzie's been home now for more than a decade. This is as far as I plan to go."

"But Conrad, why? I don't get it. I don't understand. There's so much else out there . . . so much more for you . . . to accomplish . . . to discover." The senator's words came only with difficulty.

"Spend a year out here with me, Dad. You'll be amazed the things you'll discover."

The senator tried to concentrate on what was happening. All he could think about was the effort needed to keep his wingtips clean during the long walk back through the woods. "I just hate to see you up here wasting your life."

Conrad smiled. "Funny, isn't it, Dad? I feel the same way about you."

For just a moment the senator's eyes looked puzzled. "What do you mean?"

"Nothing, Dad. Not a thing. Just thinking out loud is all."

Lawrence actually looked his son in the eye. Several seconds passed. Conrad moved to embrace his father, but Larry recovered and backed away before physical contact could be made.

Too bad. They didn't know it at the time, but it was their last opportunity.

Three weeks later, just a few months before he would retire from the United States Senate, Lawrence traveled south to Miami with Dick Nixon for a Republican party fund-raiser. At the vice president's persistent request, Ulysses Simpson Grant MacKenzie, enjoying the good life in the Sunshine State, joined the duo and several hundred other prominent Floridians at a five-hundred-dollar-per-plate luncheon.

Nixon sat between the MacKenzies. He did his best to make hay with the old robber baron, resorting mostly to barbs and accusations against the enemy, those damn commies.

But U.S. was having none of it. "The Russians are exactly the same as us, Dick, only poorer. Best damn thing we could do is just get along with 'em."

The Trickster narrowed his eyes. "Get along with them? Come now, Mr. MacKenzie, you don't mean that?"

"The hell I don't. Won't accomplish a goddamn thing but misery getting into a fight with those sons of bitches."

"But Mr. MacKenzie," insisted the vice president, "the Russians threaten the very fabric of American life. I sometimes think we should attack the bastards with everything we've got before they decide to do the same thing to us."

Ulysses growled. "Do me a favor, will you, Dick?"

Nixon smirked. "Anything, Mr. MacKenzie. Just name it."

"Shut the hell up while I finish my five-hundred-dollar-piece of chicken. And don't waste your time or mine hoping to get me to contribute to the Dicky Nixon for President fund because I ain't givin' you one stinking goddamn dime."

Nixon attempted a response, but the senator elbowed him in the side and the VP grew silent.

After the meal the threesome climbed into the back seat of an open limousine for the short ride to their fancy digs at the Fontainebleau Hotel. A small crowd had gathered along the route. Larry and Dick waved and smiled. U.S. shook his head and muttered profanities under his breath.

Right about then the shot rang out. It was, of course, meant for Nixon, but it whistled past his ear and slammed into the side of Senator MacKenzie's head. The senator fell against his father, blood spurting out of the wound onto the old boy's seersucker jacket.

"Son of a bitch," shouted Ulysses as he tried to plug up the hole with his finger, "son of a mothering bitch!"

The limo raced south to Mercy General Hospital just off Route 1, but too late. Senator Lawrence MacKenzie was dead, stone dead.

May 18, 1987

Yesterday, at one o'clock sharp, Dawn and Pop and I pulled up to the governor's mansion on the banks of the Onondaga River in the heart of the state capital. One of the governor's lackeys led us inside and for over an hour we waited in this lounge area. It was like the waiting room at the dentist's office: the old magazines and the potted plants and the Muzak coming from some speakers hidden in the ceiling. On the walls were photographs taken around the state. We recognized one of Lake Katydeeray taken not too far from MacKenzie.

Dawn and I didn't mind the wait, but Pop became more and more irritated as the afternoon slipped away. "Goddamn politicians," he mumbled. And then, "Man makes a meeting with me for one o'clock, I expect to see him at one o'clock."

The governor's secretary twice came in to apologize for the governor's tardiness. She explained that a hearing on the new budget had gone longer than anticipated. She offered Pop coffee and Dawn and me sodas, but Pop said no, so we did too.

Finally, about half-past two, Governor Montgomery entered the room in a very big hurry. He crossed directly to Pop and held out his hand. "Mr. MacKenzie! Sir! Awfully sorry I'm late. Couldn't be helped. Damn legislature talks more than a women's coffee klatch. Enough to drive a grown man to drink."

All the while he talked the governor had this wide grin on his face and I found myself grinning also, at least until I glanced over at Pop and saw a pretty fair scowl etched into his brow.

Pop introduced Dawn and me. The governor acted like never before in his entire life had he been so glad to meet two people. I was glad to meet him too, although maybe a little less after what Dawn whispered to me as we followed him and Pop into another room, "What a phony."

I wanted to ask her why she thought the governor was a phony, but we headed straight for his office. It was all decked out with real leather furniture and this massive oak desk and more photographs of the state covering the walls and a huge picture window overlooking the Onondaga River.

The governor told us to make ourselves comfortable. He was tall and slim and wearing a crisp blue suit. He looked pretty young, about the same age as Sanders. I had only seen him once before in person, over in Cedar Bluffs when he came to town looking for votes before the last election. "Another sexist white male," Mama called him that day. "And probably a racist as well."

"So, Mr. MacKenzie, sir, what exactly can I do for you today?"

Pop, as always, got right to the point. "As you undoubtedly know, Governor, I'm here to discuss a small project you've proposed for the Tamaqua River."

I could tell right off from the tone of Pop's voice that he hadn't left the valley and come all the way to the capital to mince words or make small talk.

"A project I've proposed?"

"Let's not play games, Governor. We've been hearing about this dam up in our neck of the woods for the past several years. We've done our homework. We know the Army Corps of Engineers came into the valley and made a feasibility study. For a long time, really until just recently, we assumed the feds were the ones interested in developing the valley. But now we find out the project originated right here at home soon after you took office back in eighty-two."

The governor listened while he leaned against that massive oak desk. He kept his arms folded loosely across his chest. "I suppose, Mr. MacKenzie, that you are referring to the flood control project and wilderness recreation area under consideration for the Tamaqua River Valley?"

"You suppose right, Governor."

"Then I will tell you quite frankly that yes, I did have a hand in the creation of that project. And I will also tell you that I continue to pursue the idea with pride and commitment. The Army Corps of Engineers was brought in to survey the area and to make recommendations. This was done out of necessity. A project such as this is enormously expensive. No way could the state afford to do it unless we came up with federal dollars to help pay the bills."

"I don't give a damn about your federal dollars. I want to know why you've proposed this project in the first place."

Governor Montgomery didn't flinch, didn't move a muscle. He glanced down at his manicured fingernails and said, "The Tamaqua River Valley Dam and Development Project, Mr. MacKenzie, offers the people of this great state a wide assortment of benefits."

"Such as?"

"Such as flood control. For decades certain communities in the valley and tens of thousands of acres of farmlands have been victimized by rising water. The proposed dam could easily—"

"That's crap, Governor. I've lived in the Tamaqua River Valley now for forty years, since 1947, and only once in four decades has there been more than minimal damage from that river overflowing its banks."

Again the governor surveyed his fingernails. "Obviously, Mr. MacKenzie, we have a difference of opinion on what constitutes minimal damage."

"Maybe so, but I still say this project stinks of political skullduggery. Be nice, wouldn't it, to have the biggest dam east of the Mississippi on your résumé? I can see you out there on the banks of the Tamaqua surrounded by peons and earth-moving equipment. You'll have your hard hat at a roguish angle as the television cameras zoom in for a close-up of the governor-who-would-be-president. You'll hold forth on man's conquest of nature and on the thousands of jobs your little dam has created. It'll be quite a show, Governor. I just hope I never have to see it."

Governor Montgomery didn't miss a beat. In fact, I saw the very slight hint of a smile on his smooth, handsome face. "Can I assume, Mr. MacKenzie, that you plan to oppose the Tamaqua River Valley Dam and Development Project?"

"Tooth and nail," said Pop. "Tooth and nail."

"That's fine, sir," said the governor, nice as can be, "I have no problem with that. I enjoy a good fight. That's why I went into politics. The rough and tumble and all that. But let me ask you this: Don't you think your position in this matter might be colored by the fact that MacKenzie Island lies right smack in the middle of the action?"

"Damn straight that colors my position. MacKenzie Island will be fifty feet or more underwater if this boondoggle you propose goes through."

Once more with the fingernails, then, "I see. Then let me give you a word of advice, sir. As our battle rages, as we trade blows, try to keep the self-interest stuff to a minimum. It doesn't play well in the media or with the masses. I can already see the headline: FILTHY RICH RECLUSE REFUSES TO BOW TO PROGRESS. They'll eat you alive, Mr. MacKenzie."

Pop glared at the governor, then he glanced over at me. He pointed a finger at the door. "You and Dawn wait outside, Willy. I'll be right out."

Reluctantly, we went. Before we did the governor shook our hands and gave us full-color copies of his official, autographed photo. "Thanks for coming by. And have a great summer."

As soon as he closed the door we pressed our ears against it.

"You son of a bitch," we heard Pop say, "I should knock you down. You want a fight, well, you're in for one now."

I thought I heard something like an index finger thumping hard against a man's chest, but I couldn't be sure.

"Easy, Mr. MacKenzie," we heard Montgomery say. "Remember, I'm the governor of this great state."

Then another thump, followed by, "I don't care if you're the king of jolly old fucking England."

At that point the governor actually laughed. "Why don't you use some of those zillions I hear you have stashed away, MacKenzie, and buy yourself another island someplace safe and far away?"

And then, yes, I'm sure of it, absolutely sure, I heard the sound of a MacKenzie right jab making solid contact with the left cheek of our honorable governor, Anderson Johnson Montgomery, and then the governor falling back against his massive oak desk and crashing to the floor.

A moment later Pop swung open the door. Dawn and I jumped back. Before we had time to check on the governor's condition, Pop took each of us by the arm and marched us down that long hallway and out of the governor's mansion into the bright, late afternoon sunshine.

Oh, yeah, quite a day.

9:02 A.M.
JANUARY 20, 2001
MACKENZIE ISLAND
THE INAUGURATION OF THE FORTY-FOURTH PRESIDENT OF THE UNITED STATES

Quite a day indeed. It's not every day a young man gets to see, or in this case hear, his father deck a high-ranking public official of the state. Such an event definitely would have left an impression on me. The trouble is: Did the incident really take place as Willy described it in his journal? Did Conrad MacKenzie in fact knock Governor Montgomery to the floor on May 17, 1987?

Conrad has refused to comment on the matter, saying only that the private affairs between men should remain private. But President Montgomery flatly denies the assault ever happened. He recalls the meeting between himself and Mr. MacKenzie. He vaguely recalls having words with Mr. MacKenzie about the Tamaqua Valley Dam Project. He even claims Conrad threatened to take a swing, but he insists not a single blow was struck.

So can we assume that Willy's journal entry of May 18, 1987, is, at least in part, a twisting of the truth, perhaps even a total fabrication? Is this the first clear evidence that Willy easily and routinely mixes fact and fiction, that he may even have trouble distinguishing between one and the other? Troubling questions about the man poised to take command of the ship of state.

Here on MacKenzie Island we are being inundated with the white stuff. The snow is piling up at an alarming rate: more than an inch every fifteen minutes. Never in my life have I seen snow fall like this.

Nevertheless, friends and family continue to arrive. These Blue Mountain folk are tough as nails. Outside the weather has turned absolutely vicious. Not only has the temperature plummeted to twelve degrees Fahrenheit, but now the winds have started to swirl and howl. But still they keep coming, these rugged and independent types who inhabit the Blues. Henry Bender and his parents arrived a few minutes ago on their cross-country skis. The Wilsons of Wilson's Hotel snowshoed in right behind the Benders. More local families arrive all the time. We understand most of the valley has been invited.

Interviews with the guests have been in short supply. This is a pretty tight-lipped and tight-knit group. If they bother to acknowledge our presence at all, it is usually only to scowl or mouth some slur better not repeated in the company of children. We come, of course, with two strikes against us: we work for the press and we hail from outside the valley.

Still, I look at these people and grow downright soft inside. It must be some deep-seated romantic root long dormant in my immigrant genes. Look at them: plodding across the lake, trudging through this wall of snow, their bodies bent against the wind. Let your mind wander and you can easily conjure up visions of Pilgrims and pioneers, all those square-jawed, hard-hearted Europeans who came across the Atlantic to have a go at the wilderness.

Sure, I know what happened after too many of us arrived. I know the revisionist history. We raped the virgin forests, subdued the wild beasts, crushed and killed the natives under our iron heel. All of that is a story now often told. But in these simple people of Cedar Bluffs I see back before all the raping and pillaging and murdering began. I see the remnants of a people who wanted only to escape a life of enforced ritual and religious suppression and forge a destiny more closely akin to their own individualistic desires. I might be going overboard here, sounding the call of nostalgia, but if you want to see some authentic Americans, just open your eyes and take a look at these folks braving the elements to attend the inauguration of the twenty-first century's first true populist.

These are Willy's people, the men and women who voted him into the highest office in the land. These are the people who listened when he said we had to slash the bureaucracy to the bone, whittle the behemoth down to size. These are the people who believed when he said big business and big government and big media had formed a secret alliance to keep the groping multitudes in the dark. These are the people who cheered and stamped their feet when Willy said the time had come for the citizens of this great country to take responsibility for their own lives again.

So here they are, gathering to see their boy take the oath.

But they still have a while to wait: three hours by my count. And maybe more if the rumors of delay turn to reality. We will just have to wait and see. And while we wait we might as well go back and check on the MacKenzie clan as the 1950s draw to a close.

* * * * * * *

They never found out who fired the shot that killed Senator Lawrence MacKenzie. The investigation lasted a year or more, but in the end they determined that Vice President Nixon had enemies of every race, creed, color, and political bent, and without some hard evidence it would be impossible to finger the assassin. Certain Cubans, Russians, and Bulgarians were prime suspects. So were some well-known hit men for the Cosa Nostra. Several African-Americans prominent in the civil rights movement were investigated by the FBI. All this came out years later, with the passage of the Freedom of Information Act, when we learned that Mr. Hoover had investigated not only blacks and Italians and communists in the attempted assassination of the VP, but several high-ranking Democrats as well. Nevertheless, the killer, or killers, got away, as the saying goes, with murder.

Not because he was any great shakes as a statesman or because he had accomplished even one extraordinary feat during his long tenure as a United States senator, but more because of the violent way in which he died and because Ulysses S. Grant MacKenzie made such a ruckus, Lawrence Van Rensselaer MacKenzie lay in state in the Capitol Rotunda. An honor normally bestowed only upon esteemed presidents and great military leaders, Larry lay at rest beneath the enormous dome in his flag-draped coffin during the first two days of October 1958. On the evening of the second he was transported to Union Station and carried by train and boat to MacKenzie Island, where he was buried in the family plot on the fifth of October.

Never had MacKenzie Island welcomed so many dignitaries at one time. Nixon was on hand, out of respect for the deceased, but also because the man knew how to exploit a political opportunity. President Eisenhower didn't make the trip, but Senator John Kennedy was there with his lovely bride. We have a photograph of the future president and his wife standing outside the boathouse admiring the MacKenzie collection of fine wooden boats. In the photo the leaves on the far side of Loon Cove have turned their autumn hue. Bright reds and vibrant yellows fill the background. The Kennedys look young and happy and very rich.

Several journalists tried to interview Conrad MacKenzie that day; none succeeded. The only comment that comes down to us, and we have no way of knowing if Conrad actually uttered these words or if some zealous reporter just wanted to increase his chances of reaching the morning editions, is this: "My father stood for nothing and died for nothing."

Throughout the day Conrad stood stoically beside his family. He held his mother's hand while she wept, dried her tears with his handkerchief. He protected his sister when the probing eyes of the press ventured too close. Conrad and Patricia did not often see one another, probably only half a dozen times since the war, but they carried the same blood, and for the MacKenzies that alone would always be a powerful force. Patricia lived a conventional life: a beautiful home in the suburbs, a husband who practiced medicine, and two young children who could ride horses and play musical instruments and converse in French. Patricia donated large amounts of her time and large quantities of her inheritance to various charities. She was a fine, upstanding citizen who rarely uttered a bad word about anyone.

On that day in early October, Patricia's brother could also be seen comforting his ex-wife, Sally, who had come north for the funeral with their eleven-year-old son, Sanders. Pictures exist of the threesome standing over Lawrence's grave, looking very much like a happy family temporarily in a state of mourning.

It would probably be safe to say that Conrad became the head of the MacKenzie clan that day they stuck his father in the ground. Not that old Ulysses had suddenly vanished from the scene. On the contrary, he was still alive and kicking, literally. In fact, probably the high point of the day came when U.S. met with a reporter from *The New York Times.* Dave Megan his name was, a young but already well-known political correspondent. His encounter with Ulysses came after the dirt had been thrown on Larry's casket, after the drinks and hors d'oeuvres had been served and consumed, after the VP and his army of Secret Service agents had returned to the mainland.

"Excuse me, Mr. MacKenzie," Dave Megan said to the aging robber baron, "some people claim you haven't paid a nickel of income tax in more than eighteen years. Would you care to comment on this accusation?"

U.S. stood alone at the end of the dock. In his old age he had started to shrink. Arthritis had forced a pretty good bend in his back. His hands were gnarled and he used a hickory stick for balance. He watched the sun falling behind the mountains to the west.

Witnesses claim when he turned around to face his questioner, the old boy had a tear running down his cheek.

"Yeah," he answered, his voice still firm and steady, "I got something to say."

Ulysses gestured Dave Megan closer. Dave had probably expected nothing but a rebuff from the old man. But Ulysses motioned for Dave to come right out to the end of the dock. So Dave did. Ulysses put his arm around the young reporter's shoulder. He led Dave to the edge of the dock. He pointed to those beautiful Blue Mountains awash in evening sunlight. And then, while Dave studied the scene and considered his great good fortune to have an audience with one of the country's wealthiest and most famous industrialists, old U.S. took a quick step back and gave young Dave a swift kick in the behind. It must have been quite a blow, for the reporter went sailing into the air before plunging into the rather chilly waters of Lake Katydeeray.

And a second later, ninety-three-year-old U. S. MacKenzie cast aside his hickory stick and dived in after his prey. The old boy attempted to hold the young man's face beneath the surface long enough to inflict death. Only the quick reflexes of Conrad brought the situation under control. He sprinted across the dock, plunged into the water, and pried his grandfather's hands off Dave Megan's face. CPR and mouth-to-mouth resuscitation were administered, and before too long that reporter from *The New York Times* was brought back to life.

* * *

The local magistrate had no choice but to charge Ulysses with assault and battery, as well as attempted manslaughter. More than thirty people had seen him shove Megan into the lake, then jump in and attempt to drown the reporter.

The *Times* hired the best lawyers money could buy. They went after Ulysses with all their might and muscle. The newspaper had a vendetta against U.S. stretching back over half a century. During the old muck-raker days, Ulysses had often lambasted *Times* chairman and publisher Adolph Simon Ochs for his negative depiction of the country's bankers, railroad men, and industrialists. On several occasions he had referred to Mr. Ochs as "that powerful little Jew."

Adolph had never forgotten. Neither had his son-in-law, Arthur Hays Sulzberger, who became publisher in 1935 and was still in that position when Ulysses shoved Dave Megan into the drink.

The *Times* covered the story with endless articles and editorials. Ulysses was painted in a most unflattering light. Shady business dealings he had been involved with back at the turn of the century were dug up and run on page one. Potshots were taken at other family members as well. The dead senator was painted as a fool, as a man who had run for office simply for the prestige of holding office. True enough, you might say, but still a low blow to the solar plexus of a man no longer around to defend himself. The *Times* labeled Conrad MacKenzie "the Hermit Heir" and never once mentioned the fact that he had given three years of his life in the service and defense of his country.

The feud between the MacKenzies and the *Times* continues to this day. Arthur Ochs Sulzberger, Jr., runs the show now. And as all of you who read that paper know, the *Times* did everything in its power to keep Willy MacKenzie from winning the White House. Most journalists agree that the *Times* coverage of the candidate was spiteful, malicious, and often erroneous. But really, who cares? So few people read the *Times* or any other newspaper, for that matter. The print medium long ago thrilled in its finest hour. Most Americans can't even read anymore.

The charge of attempted manslaughter was dropped, but Ulysses still had to stand trial for assault and battery. The trial was held in the small county courtroom up in North Creek. There was nowhere near enough room for all the spectators and reporters who wanted to watch the proceedings that began on an unusually hot and humid day in late June of 1959. Even with all the windows wide open, the temperature in the courtroom soared over eighty degrees. Ulysses, surrounded by his defense team, sat there sweating and fanning himself with a legal pad.

The trial dragged on for over a week. The entire history of U. S. MacKenzie went into the record. The heat grew worse. The humidity rose to levels never before encountered in the Tamaqua River Valley. The court stenographer passed out, fell right out of his chair onto the floor. They brought in a new stenographer and proceeded. Ulysses slumped in his chair. A few times he actually fell asleep. His attorney would wake him only if he began to snore.

On the ninth day of testimony, with the defense ready to wrap up, Conrad was called to the stand. He was the last witness for the defense, a character witness who sat up there and praised his grandfather's generosity and wisdom.

The defense rested and the prosecutor rose to cross-examine. He had only two questions for young MacKenzie. "Did you or did you not dive into the water on the day in question to separate Ulysses MacKenzie and David Megan?"

Conrad looked over at his grandfather. Never in his life had Conrad seen the old man looking so small and frail and vulnerable. "Yes," Conrad answered softly, "I did."

"And did you or did you not," asked the prosecutor, "have to forcibly restrain your grandfather, Mr. Ulysses MacKenzie, from drowning Mr. David Megan?"

Conrad took a long time to answer. His eyes wandered around the room. The answer, of course, was yes, but young MacKenzie could not bring himself to say it.

Judge Orrin Stuart, who owed his appointment to the man on trial, reminded Conrad that he was under oath and obligated to answer. But before Conrad had to utter another word, U.S. began to shake and twitch. All eyes turned upon him. The shaking and twitching grew more intense. He began to drool. His eyes rolled around in his head. His whole body shook. Then, suddenly, he grew perfectly rigid. For three full seconds Ulysses froze up with his arms all twisted and his eyes all buggered out. A second later he fell out of his chair and slammed his head first on the defense table and then on the hard wooden floor of the courtroom.

* * *

Ulysses had suffered a stroke. The heat and the humidity and the stress had finally done him in. They rushed him to the hospital, and for the next several days he remained in critical condition, just barely clinging to life. Then, miraculously, he came around and demanded to know if the jury had reached a verdict.

"It's all over," Conrad told his grandfather. "Judge Stuart ruled that you are no longer fit to stand trial. All charges have been dropped."

Ulysses let out a hoot and ordered a bottle of Scotch brought to his room. "I knew we'd beat those bastards," he said in celebration. "Better send Orrin a box of Cuban cigars and a case of his favorite beverage. He's an excellent judge and a first-class Scotsman."

The *Times*, in one of its lowest moments, suggested in an editorial the following day that the stroke suffered by U. S. MacKenzie had been feigned to avoid a guilty verdict.

Any truth to that accusation? Let's just say the old warrior believed firmly in victory at any cost. Although upon his release from the hospital, Ulysses definitely slowed down. He did not resume his active life-style. Conrad hauled him out to the island and installed him in the large master bedroom he'd built for himself back at the turn of the century. A full-time nurse was hired to care for him. For seven years Ulysses lived up in that bedroom. But do not think for a moment that Ulysses faced seven years of exile and solitude. He had his grandson. He had his nurse. He had his colleagues and business competitors, who occasionally ventured out to the island to spend a few days sitting on the front porch, reminiscing, smoking cigars, and yakking it up while they drank themselves into a stupor.

And he had his concubines. Let us not forget his concubines. He would fly the young beauties up from Miami for a week or two of wholesome and healthful exercise. Incredibly, the nonagenarian remained quite virile right up through his one-hundredth birthday.

Sometime during his grandfather's stint up in that master bedroom, Conrad moved out of his one-room cabin and back into the Great House. The circumstances surrounding this move have never been made clear. And so, as often happens when dealing with Conrad, we must resort to speculation. He probably moved out of that cabin simply because he was sick of living in a hovel without running water. Period. He had paid his dues, served his self-imposed sentence. Twelve years or more in that one-room shack were more than enough for any man.

Other possibilities do exist, however. Ulysses, for one. Conrad had a difficult time with his grandfather's nurses. Most of them grew bored after a few months on the island. And the ones who could handle the boredom usually could not handle Ulysses. He was forever pawing at them, trying to pull them into his bed. And they had to put up with the young ladies who came to entertain. Those poor RNs would venture upstairs to the master bedroom to give U.S. his pills and a sponge bath, and there he'd be, naked as a jaybird and diddling some young thing in the doggie position.

But perhaps the ultimate reason Conrad withdrew from the cabin was his son. Soon after Grandfather Larry's funeral, Sanders began asking his mother if he could spend his summer vacations on MacKenzie with his father. Sally at first refused, telling Sanders he was too young and that his father was too busy. But Sanders persisted. He wrote his father several letters asking him if a short visit might be possible.

Conrad didn't write back. He took the train down to New York City and knocked on the door of his ex-wife's penthouse apartment on Park Avenue. Sally was quite shocked to see him.

"I'm here," Conrad said, "to tell Sanders he's welcome on MacKenzie Island whenever he wants for as long as he wants. It's his island as much as mine."

The boy, fourteen at the time, listened from his bedroom. Before his mother could say a word he raced out to the front door, pulling up short right in front of his father. "I'd like to go now, sir, if I could?"

The following morning father and son took the train north to Cedar Bluffs. Conrad let Sanders pilot the launch out to the island. That summer the boy spent just two weeks on MacKenzie. He was shy and nervous, and he missed his mother and his friends. Also, he did not much like the one-room cabin in the woods. It was dark and damp and filled with daddy longlegs and giant black ants.

So the next summer Sanders lived in the Great House with his father and his great-grandfather. He stayed a month. He fished and swam and sailed with James Tyler. He came back on his Thanksgiving break, and again during spring break. And the following summer he arrived the day after school let out and didn't go home until the day before school was set to resume again in September.

So whatever the reason, by the mid-sixties Conrad had permanently installed himself and his few meager possessions in the enormous stone-and-timber house on Loon Cove. His cabin he abandoned to the whims of nature. Nothing remains on the site but the stone chimney and a few small piles of rubble.

Across the channel, on Tamarack, the Tylers were thriving. Josh had built his family the two-story wood-frame house that still stands on the small island today. He designed and built the house himself over the course of several long hot summers. Conrad helped him with all the jobs requiring an extra pair of hands—the roof beams and timber joists and floor supports—but for the most part Josh labored alone. He never rushed, never pushed, never cut a board or drove a nail until he'd checked and double-checked his plan. And for this reason, when the house was finally finished, it fit together perfectly. Every wall was square, every door and window level, every floorboard and piece of molding fitted and nailed to never squeak, shrink, or buckle. It was a simple, straightforward house, nothing fancy or exotic about its design, but it was a thing of beauty, and everyone who saw it knew it would last forever.

"I hope it'll last at least that long," said Josh. "I expect my kids and my kids' kids and my kids' kids' kids to eat and sleep and play in this house."

Besides their oldest, James, Josh and Mary Ann had over the years added two daughters to their brood. Jessica had been born in 1949 and Janice in 1953. The family continued to live on Tamarack during the warm months and in Cedar Bluffs during the winter. They were a happy, close-knit family. And well liked by everyone in the valley. They got on so well with one another and with everyone else that you'd be bored to tears if we had to talk about them for very long.

By the time Kennedy licked Nixon and moved into the White House, Josh was the owner-operator of the Cedar Bluffs Lumber Mill. No written records of their agreement exist, but it's common knowledge in the valley that Conrad financed Josh's venture in the lumber business. Throughout the late forties and early fifties, Josh had cut trees for a living. It was seasonal, back-breaking work with absolutely no hope for advancement. Still, Josh labored without complaint. He thought he was the luckiest guy alive to live in the Blue Mountains with the woman he loved, his three kids, and the best buddy a man could ever have.

"Smartest move I ever made," he told Conrad at least once a month, "leaving Baltimore and following you up here."

The mill prospered. Josh finished the house on Tamarack and bought a house in Cedar Bluffs. He served on the town council and volunteered for the fire department. He donated lumber for the new school and helped construct the new community center down on Water Street. And whenever a local organization, from the Presbyterian church to the PTA to the Boy Scouts, needed funds, Josh always came forward with a check. What people didn't know was that a great deal of this financial generosity came anonymously through Conrad.

Most folks in Cedar Bluffs did not know what to make of young MacKenzie. He was by all accounts the local eccentric. Weeks would pass when no one would lay eyes on him. Then he would appear in town, drink a beer or two at the bar in Wilson's Hotel, maybe stop by Joe's Barbershop for a shave and a trim, buy some supplies at the general store, then disappear again without having offered more than a nod and a "how do you do."

Conrad preferred to work through Josh. He financed the sawmill at a time when several of the fathers in town were unemployed. The mill made jobs. And without anyone knowing, MacKenzie money paid for most of the new school, the new fire engine, the new fire boat, the new ambulance, and the new baseball field up off High Street.

"I don't get it, Connie," Josh asked, "why don't you want them to know?"

"What's the difference, Josh? It's just money. Money I didn't even earn. I'm just watching over it for a while."

"Even so. People should know how generous you are."

"I'm not generous. Ulysses built this town for his own exploitation and amusement. I'm just giving something back."

So when the town needed a new municipal building to house its two-man police force, meeting hall, and free public library, Conrad came up with a brilliant idea.

"You know that land for sale on the northwest side of the lake?" he asked Josh.

"The land Cy Compton inherited from his father?"

"Right."

"Sure I know it. If I didn't have Tamarack, I'd buy it myself. That's a beautiful piece of real estate."

"Well, we're going to buy it, take down the trees we need to build the new Town Hall, then donate the land as a park for all Cedar Bluffs residents."

Josh liked the idea right off. "We can even fell the trees ourselves," he said. "We can float them across the lake to the mill and not spend a nickel for cutting or hauling."

"Exactly my thinking, Josh."

It was the summer of 1965. LBJ occupied the Oval Office. The war in Vietnam poised ready to escalate out of control. Civil unrest swept the nation. But in the Tamaqua River Valley all was quiet and harmonious.

Throughout that summer, whenever they found time, Conrad and Josh worked to bring down the towering pines and pin oaks and mountain maples on the old Compton spread on the northwest shore of Katydeeray. James and Sanders often came along to help.

One Sunday evening late in August, just a few days before Sanders was due to leave to begin his college career at Columbia, the two MacKenzies and the two Tylers worked to clear the last few trees on the high ground overlooking the lake. They labored to get one last giant yellow pine cut and down to the water's edge for transport across the lake to the mill. The days had started to grow shorter and the sun was fast disappearing behind the Blue Mountains.

"The hell with it," said Josh. "We'll get 'er next time out."

But Conrad and Sanders were already halfway through the trunk with their big crosscut saw. Even in those days Conrad refused to use power equipment.

"Plenty of light left, Josh," called Conrad. "This won't take any time at all."

Josh nodded and notched the tree with his ax so that it would fall across the steep slope running down to the lake. Conrad and Sanders finished the cut. They all stood back as the huge tree teetered on its severed base. At first it fell in slow motion, as though making a decision, but soon enough it picked up momentum, cut through the air, and crashed to the forest floor with a mighty sigh and a cloud of dust.

Darkness came quickly as they worked to clear the limbs so they could roll the fallen giant down to the water. It was difficult work because of the steep pitch of the land.

Josh paused long enough to see the sun had disappeared behind the mountains. "I think maybe we better stake it where it is," he said. "No use getting ahead of ourselves."

In the gathering dusk Josh did not notice that the others had not heard his call to cease work. He turned away and started down the slope. He wanted to make sure the other logs were properly secured and would not float away during the night.

Conrad and Sanders and James continued to hack away at the limbs and branches of the fallen pine. Had they heard Josh's order, they would have driven a series of stakes into the ground to keep the tree from rolling. But they hadn't heard, so they continued to cut more limbs away. Before Josh was halfway down to the lake they had the pine ready to roll.

Conrad told the boys to stand aside as he maneuvered the log with a peavey. He glanced around for Josh. "Where's your old man?" he called to James.

James and Sanders looked around. In the dim, dusky light they did not see him.

"Gimme a hand here, boys!" shouted Conrad. "Quick! This bastard's fast getting away from me!"

Indeed it was. The weight of that big pine was too much for them to handle, the pitch of the slope too severe. The log began to roll, slowly at first, very slowly, as they buttressed their peavies and their weight against it. But it was no good. All that mass wanted to go downhill. In a very big hurry. Straight into the darkness.

Conrad and Sanders and James strained and slipped and finally had to scramble out of the way before the log rolled over them.

"Josh!" Conrad shouted.

"Dad!" James screamed.

"Mr. Tyler!" Sanders yelled at the top of his lungs.

The log was loose. It rolled down that slope, picking up speed with every revolution.

Josh could hear it but he couldn't see it. At first, for a moment, he froze, then he began to run. He figured he might be able to reach the safety of the lake. But the avalanche grew closer and closer. He thought about the last time he had run downhill to save his life: that day on Peleliu in the middle of the South Pacific. He had not thought about that day for years.

Two hundred yards up the slope, swallowed by the darkness, Conrad and Sanders and James continued to shout. But the sound of that huge runaway pine easily overwhelmed their voices. They grew silent and listened for some sign.

It came soon enough.

Above the roar of that rolling timber they heard Josh scream: "Connn-nnniiieee!" And then the log again, rolling, then splashing into the shallow water at the edge of the lake. And then silence. Perfect silence.

9:16 A.M.
JANUARY 20, 2001
MACKENZIE ISLAND
THE INAUGURATION OF THE FORTY-FOURTH PRESIDENT OF THE UNITED STATES

Two quick updates:

We have just received a report stating that the train carrying foreign diplomats, dignitaries, and journalists north to the inauguration has turned back. The blizzard sweeping through the Blue Mountains is the official explanation for this retreat, but some have already speculated that an armed wing of the military forced the engineer to head south.

I cannot discount these speculators. Certain very powerful people in this country do not want Willy MacKenzie to assume the presidency. They would like nothing better than to prevent him from taking the oath of office.

Speculation aside, this means I, Jack Steel, will remain the sole media representative here on MacKenzie Island throughout the rest of inauguration morning. Perhaps a few other journalists will manage to reach this snowy enclave, but right now it looks as though I will carry the majority of the load.

Also, a few minutes ago we saw the president-elect and his father conferring with Henry Bender out on the back porch of the Great House. When their conference ended, Henry strapped on his cross-country skis and headed across Loon Cove. I wondered where he was going in the middle of this terrible storm; somewhere pretty important. So I asked for a volunteer willing to pursue young Bender. Both my interns wanted to take on the challenge. I chose Patsy Squire, a twenty-one-year-old journalism student who competes in triathlons in her spare time. She's young and fit and full of vim and vigor. We found her a pair of cross-country skis, handed her a personal communicator so she could stay in touch, and sent her on her way.

So where do I think Henry Bender might be going? Up to the North Creek home of retired Judge Orrin Stuart. My intuition tells me the MacKenzies need a judge to administer the oath of office. Who better to administer that oath than their old family friend?

Will the oath be binding if Judge Stuart swears in Willy as the forty-fourth president of the United States? I'm not absolutely sure. We will check into it and let you know.

Right now I'd like to return to the journals. The Tamaqua Valley Dam and Development Project is becoming Willy's primary focus as we head into the late eighties. He makes mention of it in almost every entry. In the one to follow we will take a swing down to D.C. with Willy, Dawn, and Sanders. Not only is this one of Willy's first encounters with the partisan political system, but it also provides us with more insight into the dynamics of the relationship between young Mr. MacKenzie and Miss Tyler.

January 14, 1989
Washington, D.C.

I just switched off the morning news. The newsman said last night was the coldest night in Washington in forty years: four degrees below zero. In the middle of the night the police found an elderly couple and their two-year-old granddaughter frozen to death in a tenement over on K Street, just three and a half blocks from the White House. They showed the frozen bodies being carried out of the apartment.

Dawn and Sanders and I arrived here in Washington late yesterday afternoon. We came down from Cedar Bluffs on the train. They're still asleep; tuckered out from the long ride I guess.

I'll have to wake them up pretty soon. It's after seven already and at nine Sanders has to appear before the Senate Committee on Interior and Insular Affairs.

Looking out our eighth-floor hotel window, I can see Pennsylvania Avenue all spruced up for next week's inauguration bash. In just a few days the country's forty-first president, George Herbert Walker Bush, will take the oath of office. Dawn and Sanders and I will be gone by then. Too bad, I would've enjoyed the show.

January 15, 1989
Washington, D.C.

Yesterday morning, after breakfast, we took the elevator down to the lobby and went out through the revolving glass doors. The bite in the air reminded me of home. But all the cars and people and noise were a quick reminder that we were a long way from the islands. We walked down Pennsylvania Avenue to the U.S. Capitol. The rotunda was crawling with tourists.

A security guard told us where to go. We walked up this way, over that way, down this set of stairs, up that set of stairs, and all the while I kept thinking how my grandfather had spent most of his adult life working in this building. Finally we wound up outside the room where they hold hearings for the Senate Committee on Interior and Insular Affairs.

The committee room was large and warm and paneled with wood that looked like teak. There were no windows. A young man, not much older than Dawn and me, with a pudgy face and bulging in a gray polyester suit, greeted Sanders by name. They shook hands, then stepped out into the hallway. Dawn and I found seats near the front. About half the chairs in the room were occupied. More people arrived all the time. In the back of the room a television crew prepared to film the hearing.

"I wonder what they're doing here?" asked Dawn.

Before I could come up with an answer, the senators on the committee began to arrive. One by one they sat in their plush leather armchairs at the front of the room. Senator Zachary Moore entered the committee room last. Moore is one of the two senators from our home state. He's tall and broad with thick, wavy hair. He's chairman of the Senate Committee on Interior and Insular Affairs. He banged his gavel and the hearing began.

The first witness was called and sworn in. His name was John

Fry. He worked for the Army Corps of Engineers as an environmental expert. For half an hour the senators questioned Mr. Fry about the feasibility of the proposed Tamaqua Valley Dam and Development Project. It was clear right off that Fry thought the dam was an excellent idea.

It didn't take long to figure out which senators favored the project and which ones opposed it. We could tell by the questions they asked, even by the tone of their voices. It seemed like we had some pretty good guys on our side, especially Senator Ray Andrews from Oregon. He kept saying the country had enough dams, and that the time had come to leave the landscape alone.

Senator Zachary Moore, however, was definitely in favor of the project. In fact, he has long been one of the dam's key supporters in Congress.

Sanders had told us as much on the way down. "Moore's in Montgomery's camp. If Montgomery says jump, Moore jumps. Next year's a reelection year for Moore, and with Montgomery so popular back home, the senator wants to make sure he's on the governor's good side."

"Even if the senator believes the dam is a bad idea?"

"This is politics, Willy. What the senator believes has absolutely nothing to do with what he does."

The hearing wore on all morning and into the afternoon with scientists and engineers and just plain folks taking the stand. Sanders didn't get called until well after lunch.

Senator Moore began the questioning. "Mr. MacKenzie, thank you for taking the time to come and talk with us. You reside in the Tamaqua Valley, is that correct?"

"Yes sir."

"On MacKenzie Island in the middle of Lake Katydeeray?"

"Yes."

"Is it correct that you write and publish a periodical called the American Observer?"

"That's correct, yes."

"I understand your periodical has national distribution and that your circulation is almost one hundred thousand per issue."

"I believe we're close to that number."

"It must be a profitable enterprise."

"We are a nonprofit organization. All revenue after operating expenses is donated to various environmental organizations."

"Including the organization put together by you and your family to prevent construction of the Tamaqua Valley Dam and Development Project?"

Sanders hesitated, then, "Well, as a matter of fact, yes."

"So you are not a particularly objective witness in this scenario?"

"No, I suppose not, but—"

Senator Moore held up his hand. "Let me ask you this, Mr. MacKenzie: Is it true you write, edit, and publish the American Observer right from your home on MacKenzie Island?"

Sanders paused, then shifted in his seat. "Yes, it is, but—"

"And from your sanctuary on MacKenzie Island you write your tales of woe about the dangers of industrialization and modernization, about the terrible consequences of change and progress."

"Is that a question, Senator?"

"A question, a comment, a statement of fact. Whatever."

"Excuse me, Senator Moore." It was Senator Andrews from Oregon. He looked pretty pissed off.

Senator Moore glared down the committee table at his colleague. "Yes, Senator, what is it?"

"Would the honorable senator yield the floor?"

"I really don't see why—"

"Excuse me, Senator Moore," said Senator Andrews, "but Mr. MacKenzie was invited here so that we might find out more about life in the Tamaqua River Valley. Badgering the witness about his—"

"I was not badgering the witness."

"It sounded like badgering to me."

"I don't give a damn how it sounded. I was not badgering the witness. Now, if I may finish my questioning, I will promptly yield to the honorable senator from Oregon."

I nudged Dawn in the side. This all sounded strange and confusing to me, watching grown men in business suits arguing like a couple of school kids. I didn't expect to see behavior like this from two United States senators. "What's going on?"

Dawn shook her head. "I don't know. I think they're just posturing for the television cameras."

Moore turned his attention back to Sanders. "I'm not here to badger you, Mr. MacKenzie. I'm just here to suggest that perhaps your motives in this matter are not entirely selfless. Perhaps your opposition to the Tamaqua Valley Dam is based not on any sound ecological reasoning, but on the simple fact that if this project goes through, it will infringe upon your lifestyle."

The conference room grew quiet. The only sound I heard was the whirr of the TV cameras.

It took several seconds for Sanders to respond. "Senator, I reject your suggestion. No one wants their life thrown into disarray by circumstances beyond their control, but my opposition to this project goes far beyond mere selfishness. I believe—"

"Mr. MacKenzie, surely you understand how desperately the Tamaqua Valley needs economic stimulation. Unemployment in your area is twice the national average. This project will put people to work. How would your neighbors feel, Mr. MacKenzie, if they knew you were down here fighting to take away jobs and opportunities that might benefit them and their children?"

Sanders took a deep breath. He paused a moment, then shifted forward in his seat. "I think they would probably pat me on the back. But if you can refrain from interrupting, perhaps I can explain my reasons for opposing the Tamaqua Valley Dam and Development Project."

Moore actually smiled. I wanted to bust him one right in the chops. "That's exactly what I'd like you to do, Mr. MacKenzie. We are here, after all, to discuss the pros and cons of this proposition."

"You say that, Senator, yet you seem bent on silencing the opposition before we even take the stand. I am here today to pronounce this dam you propose building both unwanted and unnecessary."

"Our studies indicate otherwise, Mr. MacKenzie."

"You can make studies indicate anything you want them to indicate."

"Perhaps, Mr. MacKenzie. But I would suggest that the thousands of new jobs, as well as flood control, hydroelectric power, and freshwater reserves for our downstate areas, offer pretty powerful evidence to support this project."

"Thousands of jobs, Senator Moore? Try hundreds. And most of those temporary positions during construction. Flood control? I'd like an objective engineer to study your data. Very few places along the Tamaqua River overflow even during spring thaw. Hydroelectric power? That's a whole other issue. You can't upset the ecological balance of a vast river valley simply to generate a few megawatts of electricity. And fresh water? We both know there are far cheaper and more efficient ways to insure the water supply to our urban areas."

Once again the committee room grew silent. Senator Moore adjusted his tie and cleared his throat. "I still suggest your opposition to this project stems from the reality that MacKenzie Island will wind up fifty feet underwater if the Tamaqua Valley Dam is completed."

"And I reject your suggestion. There's more at stake here than MacKenzie Island. This dam will create horrendous environmental problems for the Tamaqua Valley and the Blue Mountain region in years to come. It will also destroy three towns, dozens of businesses, hundreds of small farms, nearly fifteen hundred homes, and an entire Indian reservation. Almost seven thousand people will be displaced."

Senator Moore stared out at Sanders, then shifted his gaze to a pile of papers on his left.

I felt a smile spreading across my face. Sanders got off to a slow start but now it looked like he might get the last word.

Senator Moore riffled through his papers. Most of a minute passed. And then, "Is it true, Mr. MacKenzie, that you were dishonorably discharged from the United States Army after failing to carry out the direct order of a superior officer?"

Sanders looked stunned. He tilted his head and asked, "Excuse me?"

"During the war in Vietnam you received a direct order to fire upon the enemy. You refused to carry out that order. In fact, you threw down your rifle and retreated to safety. For your actions you were court-martialed and eventually discharged without honor from the military. Is this or is this not true, Mr. MacKenzie?"

I waited for Sanders to respond, to say something in his own defense. Several seconds passed. All the blood had drained out of his face. I saw his mouth open, but nothing came out.

The TV cameras continued to roll, catching every sight and sound.

Senator Andrews rose to his feet. "This is ludicrous, absolutely ludicrous. Dredging up a man's military record at a simple fact-finding committee hearing. This is totally out of line."

"Sit down, Senator Andrews," demanded Moore, the committee chairman. "I want Mr. MacKenzie to answer the question."

But before Sanders could respond, another voice, firm and very angry, echoed through the room.

"You, sir, are a fraud. A fraud and a hypocrite!"

I turned to my right and there stood Dawn, pointing at Senator

Moore, shaking her finger at him, shouting loud and clear for all to hear.

"A fraud and a hypocrite," she repeated, "with the manners of a wild boar. I thought senators were gentlemen who treated people with dignity and respect. But you, sir, are a United States senator in title only. In reality you are nothing but the pawn of Governor Anderson Montgomery and the powerful construction interests poised to reap excessive profits from this project that everyone recognizes as pure pork barrel politics."

Moore glanced around the room for help. But his aides had gone impotent under Dawn's verbal barrage. She crossed to Sanders and helped him to his feet. "Come on, Sanders," she said. "We don't have to put up with this circus." Dawn gave Moore the evil eye, then she and Sanders turned and headed for the exit. I fell in behind them.

We walked in sort of a daze through the wide corridors of the Capitol. It took some time but finally we found our way outside. The sky had turned gray. It felt like snow. We paused a moment on the Capitol steps and looked west across the Mall. I shivered, turned up my collar, and pushed my hands deep into the pockets of my mackinaw.

Dawn huddled between Sanders and me. The three of us stood very close. After a few moments we started to move. We marched down the steps and out onto the Mall. Sanders took long, loping strides. I wanted to tell him to slow down but didn't. He needed to get it out of his system.

We didn't stop until we walked clear across the Mall, crossed U.S. Route 1, and climbed the small frozen knoll to the Washington Monument. Sanders stopped. He stared up at the tall, white obelisk and said, "Look at that goddamn thing. It's fucking obscene."

I wasn't sure what he meant, and I don't think Dawn knew, either, but we both knew he was angry and confused about what happened back in that committee room, so we just nodded and kept quiet.

After a minute or so we started walking again, marching might be a better word for it. We marched straight for the Lincoln Memorial, but at the last minute we veered off and headed for the memorial to all the soldiers who died in Vietnam. The Vietnam Memorial is a massive black granite wall listing all the names of the Americans who died there. And man oh man were there a lot of names, more than fifty thousand. The number of names took my breath clean away.

The first few flakes of snow fell from the sky. It was late in the afternoon but so dark it might as well have been midnight. The air was perfectly still, and unbelievably cold. It felt so different from the last time we were here a few years ago for the environmental rally. It was summer then, and so fiery hot.

We were the only ones out there, just Dawn and Sanders and me. We stood and stared at that granite wall. I could see Sanders reading the names, looking for friends who had lost their lives.

A tear ran down his face. Then another. And another. Suddenly I felt a tear, warm and wet, run down my face too.

Dawn stepped between us. She put her arms around our waists. "Come on," she said, "let's get out of the cold."

Sanders and I nodded. We didn't resist when she led us away from the wall. We walked for quite a spell without talking.

"Tomorrow morning, early," said Dawn as we walked past the White House on our way back to the hotel, "we'll leave this wretched place and head for home."

9:26 A.M.
JANUARY 20, 2001
MACKENZIE ISLAND
THE INAUGURATION OF THE FORTY-FOURTH PRESIDENT OF THE UNITED STATES

I've seen the tape of Dawn Tyler standing up in that Senate committee room and calling Zack Moore a fraud and a hypocrite, then accusing him of being a pawn to the power brokers. Classic footage. Television Hall of Fame stuff.

That footage, however, exists only by chance. C-SPAN had its cameras in the committee room that day because there was so little activity up on Capitol Hill. George Bush's inauguration was less than a week away, so congressional business had pretty much ground to a halt. Still, C-SPAN had to air something, so the Senate crew went over to the Committee on Interior and Insular Affairs. And right there lies the beauty of being a journalist on the beat: rare and exceptional events sometimes occur at the most unexpected moments.

Take my first big break. It happened almost ten years ago now, the spring of 1992. I had finally managed to land myself a network spot, but I groveled somewhere below the low man on the totem pole. Mostly I covered for guys on vacation. Occasionally they sent me to some faraway burg to cover a kid buried alive in an abandoned well or a tornado that had wreaked havoc on a trailer park or some wacko who had blown away a dozen people at a fast-food joint. I was lucky to get my mug on the tube a dozen times a year. National political correspondent with a nightly ninety-second spot loomed in my future as nothing more than a dream.

But then came L.A. By chance, I was there on holiday with my wife and kids. Disneyland, Universal Studios, Rodeo Drive, the whole bit. Then one morning I got a call at the hotel from my boss back in New York. The jury was about to return a verdict on the cops who had beaten up motorist Rodney King. You remember: the black guy who got dragged from his car by the white cops who proceeded to practically beat him to death. Somebody caught the entire incident on videotape and the whole country went into an uproar.

My boss wanted to know if I could get out to the Simi Valley courthouse and file a report on the jury's verdict. I assured him I could. I rented a car and drove out to the valley, out beyond the Santa Monica Mountains northwest of the city. And the rest, well, is history. My history.

The acquittal of those cops, you may recall, led to some pretty severe civil unrest. For three days L.A. burned. And I was there, on the street, center stage. I was in your living room, day and night, bringing you live footage, describing the violence and the mayhem, the looting and the burning. Right on camera I got hit in the head with a brick thrown by an unruly teenager. Blood streamed down my cheek but I went right on filing my report. I knew, ladies and gentlemen, that my time had come, that a great future lay ahead. No way was a brick and some blood going to put Jack Steel out of action.

And on the third day, with calm finally beginning to return to the city, I uttered my famous cliché, the line that rocked the video world. I stood at the corner of Atlantic and Whittaker in East Los Angeles surrounded by overturned cars, looted stores, and smoldering apartment buildings. I hadn't slept in almost sixty hours, had probably consumed four gallons of coffee and an entire bottle of prescription amphetamines. My anchor back in New York asked me to describe my personal feelings after three days in the middle of the riots.

I stroked the stubble on my chin and stared into the camera lens. "Look," I said, and then I paused just long enough to make an impact, "I hate to call a spade a spade, but dammit, these people are cutting off their noses to spite their faces."

Well, let me tell you, the calls immediately began lighting up the studio switchboard. When I used the phrase *these people,* I certainly meant the black community in East L.A. I never denied that. But I was not calling black people "spades" when I said, "I hate to call a spade a spade." That was just an expression my father, God rest his soul, occasionally let slip when he wanted to let you know a kernel of truth would soon spill from his lips.

Nevertheless, my utterance caused quite a commotion. Black leaders around the country demanded I apologize. I wound up on all the talk shows, sat side by side with many of those same black leaders. They found out I was not a white racist; no, I was just a guy who had mumbled the wrong expression during a time of great emotional stress.

So you see, the disaster that swept through Los Angeles in the spring of 1992 was the catalyst for my first great career advancement. Like surgeons, undertakers, and tow-truck drivers, we journalists sometimes rely on the misfortunes of others to succeed in our ambitions.

But enough about me. Guests continue to arrive here on MacKenzie Island. The Great House looks well occupied. I can see Blue Mountain folk standing around, talking it over, sipping coffee and crunching biscuits. I just caught a glimpse of Willy chatting with his neighbors. He looks relaxed, an easy smile on his face—no small chore for the man soon to become the single most powerful human being on the planet.

That runaway yellow pine had crushed Josh Tyler to death. By the time Conrad reached him, he was already gone. The whole valley mourned, Conrad most of all. He wanted to bury his friend in the family graveyard, but Mary Ann had a different idea.

"I want to bury him here on Tamarack," she said. "He loved this little island, especially that bit of high ground looking out to the west."

Conrad nodded. He had to hold back his tears. And then he tried for the hundredth time since that terrible day to explain, to apologize, to make amends.

Mary Ann took his hands. "It was an accident, Connie, a tragic accident. I don't want you blaming yourself."

"He told us to quit, warned us daylight was fading. I should've listened. I—"

Mary Ann put her finger to his lips. "That's enough, Connie. You gave him twenty years. Twenty years he wouldn't have had without you."

Conrad remembered Peleliu. The memory made him shudder. He put his arms around his best friend's widow and held tight until the memory lapsed.

They buried Josh Tyler on the first of September 1965. And the very next day, for the first time in almost twenty years, Conrad found himself not only alone but lonely. Desperately lonely. The emotion settled deeper inside his chest a few days later when Sanders left the island to begin his college career at Columbia University. Conrad put up a brave front. He slapped his son on the back, shook his hand, and waved so long as the train pulled away from Cedar Bluffs station. But when he got back to the island he sat down on the front porch and barely moved for most of the next week. All those years alone, and yet suddenly the prospect of another whole day to fill sent shivers of fear and dread down his spine.

Matters grew worse as summer turned to fall and the first cold winds blew down off the Blue Mountains. One afternoon in October he crossed the channel to Tamarack and walked up the slope to the Tylers' house. He found Mary Ann putting summer clothes in suitcases.

"I guess it's getting to be that time again," he said.

She did not look at him. "Yes."

"I can't believe another summer has come to an end already."

She glanced at him and sighed.

A moment passed and Conrad asked, "When do you plan on moving over to town?"

She hesitated long enough for him to add, "I don't want you worrying about the island. I can close up the house and get the boats out of the water and—"

"Connie."

"Yeah?"

Mary Ann turned and met his eyes. "I've decided to take the kids to Florida."

"Florida?" Conrad looked confused. "Why?"

"Because my sister lives there, and because I'm sick of the ice and the snow and the cold, and because . . ." A tear rolled out of her eye. She wiped it away. "And because I miss him and I just need to get away from here, for a while, for a few months. We'll be back come spring."

By the end of the month Mary Ann and her three kids had packed up and headed south for the Sunshine State. Conrad felt more alone than ever. And in the middle of November, on a cold and rainy afternoon, Ulysses suffered another stroke. One hundred years young, the old buzzard was purportedly diddling a twenty-year-old hooker who charged five hundred dollars per orgasm when the blood stopped flowing to his brain. She screamed for the nurse, who screamed for Conrad, who carried his grandfather down to the launch and rushed him across the lake through the rain to Cedar Bluffs, where the ambulance waited with its siren wailing.

Ulysses lived, but this time he paid a price. When finally he came around he had only a vague notion who he was and no idea at all who Conrad was. Conrad had no choice but to place Ulysses in the Cedar Bluffs nursing home so the old boy could receive proper, twenty-four-hour-a-day health care.

Winter came early to the valley. Six inches of snow fell on Thanksgiving. When Conrad woke up and looked out the window at the snow, he actually broke down and cried. He missed his family. He missed Ulysses. He missed Sally and Sanders. He missed Josh and Mary Ann. MacKenzie Island felt like a drifting planet a million miles from nowhere. Conrad felt like he wanted to die. He could think of no reason at all to live.

Over the next month his gloom deepened. He slept twelve or fourteen hours a day. He ate his food out of cans and boxes, never bothering to heat it up or put it on a plate. Every day seemed to go on forever. An hour took an eternity to pass. And when finally it did pass there was another one, exactly the same, waiting to take its place.

Conrad considered closing up the house and moving to town for the winter. He thought about traveling, maybe to Europe or Africa, or maybe all the way around the world, taking the same route U.S. had taken some forty years earlier. But the idea of all that movement, all that energy, all those strangers, made him edgy and extremely tired. He went back to bed. He slept for most of another day, and when he awoke he decided the island was his fate. He would deal head on with the gloom, stare it down, and hope that eventually his depression would lift.

Christmas Eve might have been his low point. Never much of a drinker since he had moved to the island, Conrad nevertheless almost drank himself to death that night. He began with a bottle of his grandfather's fine French cognac. The cognac gave way to a few pulls on a bottle of fifty-year-old port. Then he started in on a bottle of Scotch. For years Ulysses had been trying to get his grandson to acquire a taste for the stuff, but always Conrad had thought even the finest single malts tasted like kerosene. Not that Christmas Eve. As he sucked the last few drops out of the bottle, Conrad spun around on his heels and crash-landed on the middle of the living room floor. He awoke several times during the night, but only long enough to throw up onto the hot embers glowing in the fireplace.

Late on Christmas morning (on what he thought was his fortieth birthday) Conrad finally managed to get to his feet. The smell in the living room and on his breath made him retch. He raced to the front door and threw up again in the snow. His head pounded. His back ached. His hands shook.

He pulled on his boots and mackinaw and began to walk. The air was cold and crisp and very still. He walked south along the shore. His head began to clear. He rinsed out his mouth with several handfuls of snow. The sun warmed his face. Before it seemed like any time at all had passed, Conrad found himself near the southern tip of the island. He could not remember the last time he had visited that part of MacKenzie. This, he knew, was Mohawk land, and out of respect he had rarely trespassed.

But today, he decided, he would.

He wanted to circumnavigate the island, and the only way to do so was to pass through the sacred burial grounds of the Mohawk. He told himself to tread lightly, to leave nothing behind but his boot prints in the snow. He knew no living Mohawk would be on the island this day. They normally visited the burial grounds only in late spring and early fall.

So he pressed on. As he rounded the southern tip of the island the quiet winter day grew even quieter. Years earlier Tecumseh Brant had told Conrad that the silence of those woods and meadows was why the Mohawk had first interred their dead there. "A special place," he had said, "protected from the harsh north winds and touched by the soul of the Great Spirit."

Conrad stopped to listen to the silence and to scoop another handful of snow into his mouth. The silence, which he suddenly realized nature had created, gave him hope. And at that exact moment he looked up and saw her. She stood alone in the clearing about a hundred feet from the lake shore. He knew she stood in the middle of the sacred burial grounds. The sun reflected off a string of shiny beads she wore around her neck. He told himself to turn away, to keep moving, to leave her in peace. But he didn't move. He stayed put. He wondered who she was, why she had come, if she was alone. She stood without moving, her eyes upon the frozen lake. Conrad could not tell if she had noticed him or not.

He took a step toward her. Then another step. And another. As he grew closer he saw the long braid of beautiful brown hair hanging over her shoulder. He saw she was young, possibly still a teenager, definitely a Mohawk, tall and slender. She did not move a muscle, seemed barely to draw a breath. Her face, Conrad thought, was perfect, like something chiseled by a master sculptor from some rare and exotic stone.

He tried to back off but found himself taking another step forward. He crossed the clearing and stood not more than ten feet from her before she turned and met his eyes. There was no fear or alarm there, he noticed, only a very slight hint of annoyance.

"Excuse me," he said, his voice like a clap of thunder amid all that quiet, "I just wanted to make sure you were all right."

"Thank you," she answered in a voice that somehow kept the silence intact. "I'm fine."

"My name's MacKenzie," he said after a moment because the silence suddenly made him uncomfortable, "Conrad MacKenzie."

"Yes," she said, her eyes fixed on his, "I know."

He wanted to ask how she knew, but instead, "Well, as long as you're all right, I'll just be on my way."

"I'm leaving also," she said. "I only came to pay my respects."

Conrad nodded. He was not sure what to say. He wanted to put his arms around her waist and hug her to his chest. She seemed to him all at once beautiful and vulnerable and incredibly powerful. "I didn't expect to find anyone here on Christmas," Conrad said, but right away he wished he hadn't.

She narrowed her eyes. "Christmas is just another day," she said, "on someone else's calendar."

"I didn't mean . . ." But he didn't know what he meant, so he grew quiet. Again the silence interrupted. After a few moments he asked, "Do you live . . ." But he could not finish, so he simply raised his hand and pointed up the valley.

"Yes," she answered, and her eyes fell closed for just an instant, "on the reservation."

He felt stupid and ashamed, decided to say nothing more. Most of a minute passed.

"My name is Emily," she told him, "Emily Brant."

He caught his breath. Had her voice softened? "I know Tecumseh Brant," he said. "Are you related?"

She nodded.

"I owe a great debt of gratitude to Tecumseh Brant. He taught me how to survive. . . . He is a very wise man." Conrad thought he sounded foolish and probably condescending as well. It had been years since he had spoken to a woman he did not know, especially a woman to whom he found himself physically attracted.

Emily smiled, but only briefly. "I can see by the shine in your eyes," she said, "that you would like to visit me."

His thoughts detected, Conrad frowned.

Emily smiled again, more easily this time. "So do. Come to the reservation."

Conrad wondered what showed in his eyes. Before he could ask she said, "Now you will have to excuse me. I must go. The family will be gathering." Then she turned and walked away across the clearing.

Conrad thought for sure he saw her sprout wings and fly off across the lake toward the distant peaks of the Blue Mountains.

By the beginning of the twentieth century, by the time Wassanamee had been renamed MacKenzie, the Six Nations of the Iroquois had been almost entirely decimated by the endless wave of Europeans washing up on the shores of the Atlantic. The Iroquois managed to survive, but only as splintered factions occupying small reservations in the northeastern states and Canada. No longer able to travel freely or live as their ancestors had lived, these small remnants of a once mighty people battled constantly against apathy, alcoholism, and bitterness.

The Mohawk of the Blue Mountains lived on a reservation north of MacKenzie Island, farther up the Tamaqua River Valley, in a swale of land susceptible to erosion and flooding and terrible swarms of mosquitoes and black flies. It was land the state had granted the Mohawk after it became clear white settlers found it unfit for agriculture or animal husbandry.

The land was swampy and not particularly fertile. Some years the land did not provide enough food and the Mohawk were forced to leave the reservation and do menial labor among the whites. This went against their traditions and caused even more apathy, alcoholism, and bitterness. They had been taught the earth would provide them with everything they needed to live and prosper and bear new generations. Year after year this teaching proved false. The tribe tore itself in half. Many of the members decided to abandon the old ways and give in to the ways of the white man. They continued to live on the reservation, but more and more they took jobs as masons and carpenters and high-rise steel workers.

It took Conrad several weeks to gather the courage to visit the reservation. He wanted to go the very next day, and his desire only increased as the new year arrived and the intense cold of January settled over the valley.

Finally, near the middle of February, he could no longer wait. He snowshoed across the lake to Cedar Bluffs. He walked up to Frank Bender's garage on High Street and asked Frank if he could borrow his pickup truck for a few hours.

Frank handed Conrad the keys without a word. Frank liked Conrad. He liked any man who kept his own counsel and stayed out of other people's business.

The Mohawk reservation lay on the west side of the Tamaqua River. Conrad had to drive the eight miles up to the North Creek, cross the covered bridge, then head north again along the winding dirt-and-gravel road that followed the Tamaqua through a series of tight, hairpin turns. It was slow going with the turns and the snow and the ice; took him nearly an hour.

Conrad had been to the reservation years ago, back when he was still a boy. Ulysses had taken him there when he had business with the chiefs. For some reason Conrad remembered teepees and run-down huts and dirt streets. So when he drove into the main settlement and found a small, pleasant village of paved roads and single-story wood-frame houses and brick storefronts, he was mildly surprised.

"Yes," he inquired at the filling station, "I'm looking for Emily Brant."

The young Indian who filled the tank and checked the oil looked at him with a mixture of curiosity and suspicion. "First street on the left." He pointed. "Third house on the right."

The house looked like many of the others: square and squat with a small front porch facing the street. Conrad parked along the street, climbed onto the porch, and rang the bell. An old lady with gray hair and a wrinkled face pulled open the door.

"My name's MacKenzie," said Conrad. "I'm looking for Emily."

The old lady's voice came through soft, almost a whisper, but absolutely clear.

Too bad Conrad couldn't understand a word of it. "Excuse me?"

"Another who does not speak Mohawk?"

Conrad shrugged. "Sorry."

"You are looking for the Keeper of the Fire?"

"I am looking for Emily," said Conrad. "Emily Brant."

Emily appeared in the doorway. She whispered something to her grandmother. The old lady scowled at Conrad, turned, and shuffled back into the house.

"My Mohawk name," explained Emily. "Keeper of the Fire."

Conrad nodded. He tried not to look nervous or confused.

"Come in," said Emily. "I've been expecting you."

Conrad visited Emily several times a week for the rest of the winter. Mostly they sat in the tiny living room on a wooden bench covered with a padded quilt. Occasionally they were left alone, but usually Emily's mother or father or grandmother, or one of her brothers or sisters, or an aunt or uncle, sat with them. These chaperones rarely spoke, but they had excellent powers of concentration. They could sit and stare for hours without uttering a word.

Conrad didn't care; he kept borrowing Frank Bender's pickup and driving out to the reservation anyway. And in the spring, after the weather warmed and the ice and snow melted, Conrad used one of the old wooden speedboats to reach the reservation. In just over an hour he could make the trip across Katydeeray and up the Tamaqua to where the Mohawk had a boat landing. All through the summer and fall of sixty-six, Conrad made that trip as many as five times a week. And when winter returned he didn't borrow Frank Bender's pickup anymore; he went down to Seven Points and bought himself a brand-new four-wheel-drive Jeep.

Theirs was definitely an old-fashioned courtship. At first they only held hands. A month passed before he kissed her. The weather and the change of seasons were their primary topics of conversation. But day by day their trust in one another grew. Little by little, one small secret at a time, they divulged themselves, allowed the person inside to rise to the surface.

More than a year after they first met, in late April of 1967, Emily visited the Great House on MacKenzie Island for the first time. They arrived in the launch. Conrad helped Emily out of the boat. They were both nervous. They walked around the grounds for a few minutes, looking at the early daffodils and the old cedars. But a chilly breeze blew off the lake so they climbed the front porch and went inside. Conrad led Emily on a slow tour of the house. He wanted her to be impressed, but the expression on her face never changed.

As they wandered through that endless maze of bedrooms, all of those beds could not be ignored. They finally sat down, kissed, and then leaned back. Emily felt Conrad's full weight on her, but after another long and passionate kiss, they struggled to their feet.

Back down in the living room, Emily asked, "Does your grandfather not live here?"

"Ulysses?"

"Yes. In every room I felt his presence, but I did not see him. We have always been told that the white man who bought Wassanamee from our people had grown extremely old but still lived here on the island in this house. I expected to see him."

"He's still alive," said Conrad. "Over a hundred years old. But he lives in the nursing home now over in Cedar Bluffs."

"A nursing home?" Emily frowned.

"He had a stroke. Winter before last. He can't do anything for himself. Hardly even knows he's alive."

"How do you know what he knows? He should not be in a nursing home. He should be here, on Wassanamee. This is where he belongs. Here, with you."

Conrad thought about the four generations of Brants who lived in that small house on the reservation. "I can't take care of him."

"Of course you can."

Conrad felt frustrated. He had finally convinced Emily to visit MacKenzie so he could show her his home and ask her the question he had been waiting to ask her for more than a year. But now she wanted only to talk about Ulysses: Ulysses, who looked at Conrad with a blank stare whenever Conrad went over to the nursing home to visit; Ulysses, who needed a nurse to feed him and clean him; Ulysses, who still drew breath but nevertheless seemed more dead than alive.

"Your grandfather," said Emily, "holds power over this house and this island. He needs to be here, now and always, forever, to help keep the spirits of evil at bay."

"I don't understand," said Conrad. "I thought the Mohawk hated my grandfather."

"You are right, Conrad MacKenzie, you do not understand. Something far greater than man or Mohawk brought your grandfather to this island."

"Yeah," said Conrad, "greed."

"You see only the human side. There is another side to the wind as well. A mythical, magical side."

They stood in the living room, close enough to touch. Conrad thought he heard Ulysses out on the front porch, playing "Scotland the Brave" on his bagpipes.

"The answer to your question, Conrad," said Emily, "is yes."

Conrad looked confused. He waited for an explanation.

"I will marry you and be your wife. But I have one condition."

Conrad stared at Emily in disbelief. "How did you know I wanted—"

"Men are more obvious than clouds on a rainy day," answered Emily. "And white men more obvious still."

In spite of himself, Conrad smiled. It was that power and beauty and vulnerability that made him want her. "Okay, so what is your condition?"

"That your grandfather return to the island and inhabit this house."

* * *

Their wedding occurred on a warm and cloudless day on the first of June 1967. The ceremony, a simple exchange of vows they had written themselves, took place on the top step of the front porch of the Great House with more than one hundred guests spread out across that sweep of lawn. Emily's entire family was there, as were many other Mohawk. For them this was a marriage between the Indians and the whites as much as between a man and a woman. For the old-timers especially, this marriage meant the Mohawk once more had a claim on Wassanamee.

Conrad's family was there: his mother, his sister, and his son. In fact, Sanders was Conrad's best man. And of course Ulysses, who watched the event with a wide if somewhat detached smile on his face from a custom-made wooden wheelchair. Conrad had to admit the old boy seemed in much better spirits since he'd come back to the island.

The Tylers were there, recently returned from Florida for another summer. Young James Tyler introduced Conrad to his brand-new bride, a pretty blond Floridian named Sandra. Mary Ann told Conrad that Emily was the most beautiful woman she had ever seen. Conrad embraced his best friend's widow while he worked to hold back the tears.

9:43 A.M.
JANUARY 20, 2001
MACKENZIE ISLAND
THE INAUGURATION OF THE FORTY-FOURTH PRESIDENT OF THE UNITED STATES

Ladies and gentlemen, it has been brought to my attention that the network is unhappy with my digressions. They tell me this is not the appropriate forum for me to comment upon my own life and career. My apologies.

That said, I would like to offer up a morsel of Native American anthropology. One of the dominant characteristics of the Iroquois, preceding even the creation of their federation, was, and still is, the role of women in the social hierarchy. The Mohawk, as well as the other Iroquois tribes, have long based their lineage on a matriarchy. No one cares who your father was; it's your mother who matters.

Emily Brant grew up in a society that admired and venerated women. Mohawk women raised the children, grew the crops, ran the household, and ultimately decided the direction their community would take. Mohawk males were taught from an early age to respect the intelligence and the intuition of women. For this reason they could defer to a woman without suffering a crisis of masculine ego.

Emily Brant MacKenzie has certainly had an enormous impact on her son, on his thinking and his attitudes about the world. Willy MacKenzie has always, in his short life, or so it would seem, yielded to the whims of women, especially the whims of his mother and wife. Many people have wondered what effect this might have on the nation once Willy takes over the reins of power. Some think it will have a positive influence on how the government is run, on what gets done. But others feel Willy has no backbone, no moxie, that he may be incapable of making the tough and painful decisions that will certainly dominate his presidency.

But let's not dwell on the problems we will face in the near future. Let's go back to a happier time. We just witnessed the wedding of Willy's parents. Now let's jump ahead a few years and watch as Willy and Dawn exchange the matrimonial vows.

* * * * * * *

June 5, 1990

I'm getting married today. In just a few hours. Which might explain why it's not even four o'clock in the morning yet and already I'm wide awake. But it wasn't the wedding that woke me up. It was that damn dream again, the one wherein Katydeeray starts rising and keeps rising until it rises right up over our heads. Makes me crazy when I have that dream, and I have it at least three, four times a week. I'm hoping once Dawn and I start sleeping side by side every night, the damn dream will quit bugging me.

June 6, 1990

Yesterday, the big day, went something like this: I pulled on jeans and a sweatshirt, slipped down the back stairs, and out the back door. I found my Blue Mountain guideboat tied up next to the launch. I could see her in the fading moonlight.

The guideboat was a wedding present from Pop. He bought her from Al Wilder up in North Creek and had her completely restored. She's sixteen feet from stem to stern, made from nothing but hardwoods and brass screws and a dozen or more coats of marine lacquer. She was originally built back before Ulysses bought MacKenzie, back before railroads worked their way into the Blue Mountains, back when men who wanted to explore the Blues did so with a guide and a special boat like mine that they could portage from one lake or stream to another. A Blue Mountain guideboat can be rowed from midship or paddled like a canoe from the stern. It's not exactly lightweight but the way it's balanced makes it relatively easy to carry with the aid of a neck yoke. Over the next few weeks I suspect I'll be carrying her quite a lot. Dawn and I plan on spending our honeymoon exploring the whole northwest corner of the Blues with our new boat, and even though there's a lot of water up in that neck of the woods, there's plenty of land and a lot of shallow streams as well.

Anyway, I rowed the guideboat across the channel and around the south side of Tamarack to our new dock. The first faint traces of dawn showed me the silhouette of our stone foundation. It sits right on top of the site of our old lean-to. I needed a bit of imagination but I could see our new house rising off that foundation, two and a half stories of windows and clapboards and bright red shutters.

Probably be two years before Dawn and I finish the house. We want to build the whole thing ourselves, just the way Dawn's grandfather Josh built the only other house on Tamarack all by himself. We'll do it one stone, one board, one nail at a time. Seems to me that's about the only satisfying way to do most anything.

Once in a while Dawn and I still have arguments about whether or not building a house on Tamarack really makes any sense, what with the ongoing efforts of the government to build a dam downriver and flood the valley. I'm the pessimist, always fearing the worst. Dawn believes in taking it as it comes, fighting one battle at a time. Right now the Tamaqua Valley Dam and Development Project is on the back burner since the economy's in rotten shape and there's no money to feed the poor or house the homeless, much less build billion-dollar dams. Still, I worry.

I went ashore, mixed up a batch of mortar, and commenced laying stones. It was slow going since I'm a journeyman mason at best, but also because I kept thinking about being a married man by the end of the afternoon. The whole idea of it gave me a case of the jitters.

I managed to lay a few stones, then I settled back to watch the sun sneak up from behind those Blue Mountain hills. I wondered if maybe Dawn would come out to help for a couple hours but figured she probably wouldn't, what with it being her wedding day and all.

The sun was up high by the time I washed up the tools, stepped into the guideboat, and rowed back to MacKenzie. From out on the lake I could see the front lawn already swarming with activity. The caterers had arrived. So had the band. I saw the musicians tuning their instruments. I also saw folks setting up tables and arranging flowers and tying ribbons around the dogwoods and the azalea bushes. Weddings are a pretty big deal in the valley; an excellent excuse to throw a party.

I let the guideboat drift and just watched. Mama came through the screen door and out onto the front porch. She checked things over with a critical eye, then started telling people exactly what she wanted them to do. Pop came through the front door a minute or two later, sized up the situation, and beat a hasty retreat.

I rowed through the channel and into Loon Cove. And sure enough, there was Pop slipping out the back door, along the path to the boathouse, and up the boathouse steps to the second floor, where he likes to go to read and be alone and think things over.

I tied up the guideboat and made a beeline for the back porch. No one spotted me. I shaved, showered, and struggled into my rented tuxedo complete with tails. Only time I suspect I'll ever wear one of those.

"Willy! Are you up there?"

"Yes, ma'am."

"Well, come on down. Your guests are arriving."

I took a deep breath and went down the front stairs. Through the big picture window in the living room I saw them coming: family, friends, and neighbors. This was the before-the-vows-party—an old Tamaqua Valley tradition. The only one not invited is the bride.

They had all come to see me. One by one they wandered up, shook my hand, wished me all the best. A few offered advice, especially the old-timers.

"Be gentle, my boy, but tough."

"Give 'em their way just once, Willy, and they'll demand it the rest of your days."

"Marital bliss is simple, son: the louder she gets, the quieter you get."

And then our local pastor, the Reverend Michael Sayer, came up and put his arm around my shoulder and asked me if, perhaps, I would like to reconsider the wording of the wedding vows that Dawn and I had written ourselves.

Politely, I told him no way.

Someone offered me a shot of bourbon. I don't often take a drink but this time I figured maybe I could use one. There wasn't really a whole lot for me to do but stand around, make nice, and await the arrival of the main event.

After another bit of sour mash and a few more words of wisdom from the locals, the ceremony began. I took my place between Sanders and the pastor on the top step of the front porch, the same place where Mama married Pop almost exactly twenty-three years ago. The guests gathered on the long sweep of lawn between the house and the lake. Some of them stood, others sat in the freshly mowed grass, a few had brought their own folding chairs. We're not real formal here in the valley.

The band struck up the traditional wedding march.

And suddenly the launch, at a low idle, rolled out of the channel, Pop at the helm. Dawn and her father stood directly behind Pop. Dawn looked as good as I've ever seen her look in a dress so white you might've thought she was an angel.

Pop eased the launch across the channel and docked against a temporary bulkhead built just for the occasion. With help from her bridesmaids, Dawn stepped out of the launch and right up onto the lawn. Grasping her father's arm, she came through the crowd. Along the way she waved and smiled at her friends.

Her long white train spread out behind her. It took a few minutes but soon enough Dawn and her father reached the porch. She gave me a wink.

A huge grin washed across my face. "Wanna get married?" I whispered.

She thought about it, shrugged, and said, "Might as well. Nothing else to do."

The pastor took control by clearing his throat and falling back on the old familiar lines, "We are gathered here today in this beautiful setting to join this man and this woman in holy matrimony . . ."

Dawn and I listened carefully to his words, but when the time came to exchange vows, we took over. We held hands and looked one another in the eye.

"Willy," Dawn asked, loudly so our guests could hear, "do you promise to love me as best you can for as long as you can no matter what happens?"

I nodded and said, "I do. Absolutely."

"Good."

"Dawn," I asked, "do you promise to love me as best you can for as long as you can no matter what happens?"

She smiled and nodded and said, "I do."

"Good."

And then the pastor, unsure of all this, declared, "I now pronounce you husband and wife."

We kissed long and hard.

Then the band set the mood with a slow wrap-your-arms-around-me number called "The Light in Your Eye." Dawn and I stepped out for the first dance. The crowd closed in around us. Halfway through the song I gestured to the bandleader to pick up the tempo. We kicked off our shoes. The champagne corks popped. The party began.

Dawn and I took the first half dozen dances together before my new father-in-law cut in for a waltz with the bride. I took the opportunity to slip away. I went up through the crowd, around the back of the house, and down the path to Loon Cove. I went into the boathouse where earlier I had stowed our camping gear. I carried the gear out to the Blue Mountain guideboat. I figured there was no use messing with details once the time came to leave.

I rejoined the party. The dancing kept up all afternoon and into the evening. It only slowed down long enough for us to eat. Dinner was served at long tables set up all over the front yard. The champagne corks continued to pop.

Sanders, my brother and best man, offered the first toast. He stood and shouted, "To Dawn! May she find a moment's peace living with a man with an obsession to write!"

Everyone laughed. I'm not quite sure how folks found out, but my journal and my passion for writing have become pretty common knowledge up and down the valley. It also seems like everyone from North Creek to Seven Points knows I'll be working for the American Observer once Dawn and I get back from our honeymoon. It's tough to keep things secret in a small community like ours. Pop told me a long time ago you have to guard your privacy as though it were a fortress of gold.

Then more toasts from family and friends.

"To a long and bountiful life together!"

"To happiness!"

"To harmony!"

"To the river!"

"To the valley!"

"To the Blue Mountains!"

I counted thirty-four toasts before I decided to stop counting. Between the sour mash and the champagne I possessed only a fraction of my mental skills anyway. So I just sat back, took a listen, and kept on smiling.

The drinking and eating and dancing went on well into the night. The sun went down and the moon came up and still the folks of Tamaqua Valley filled the front yard.

Dawn and I decided to break loose. I lifted her into my arms and carried her all the way out to the boathouse. Upstairs, in the room where Ulysses lived, I helped her out of her wedding dress. We hung it in the closet and covered it with plastic for posterity.

We pulled on jeans and cotton sweaters and went back out into the night. Under the stars and the light of the moon we climbed into the guideboat and rowed out of the cove. We passed by the front lawn and waved good-bye to our guests. Only a handful of them saw us disappear into the darkness.

I rowed the guideboat across Katydeeray to the western shore. Our campsite was already laid out. I had come over the day before yesterday and pitched the tent, knowing we would never get away before dusk.

We carried our gear ashore and crawled into the tent. We unrolled our double sleeping bag, took off our clothes, and, finally, embraced. The night was warm and still. I heard a whippoorwill, then a noisy screech owl. The length of Dawn's naked body pressed against mine had never felt so fine. I decided right then and there that I was the happiest guy on the planet. And when her lips touched mine and I slipped so easily inside, I knew for sure I was the luckiest.

9:52 A.M.
JANUARY 20, 2001
MACKENZIE ISLAND
THE INAUGURATION OF THE FORTY-FOURTH PRESIDENT OF THE UNITED STATES

Weddings, births, and deaths. We're getting a pretty good dose of life's three big ceremonial events in this narrative history of the MacKenzie clan.

What I find interesting about Willy and Dawn's wedding is young Willy's naiveté. First off: the money. In his journal he says a wedding was always a good excuse for the people of the Tamaqua Valley to throw a party. But did he really think anyone else in the valley could afford to hire a caterer or bring in a live band? No way. I checked some statistics. A decade ago the average income in the Blue Mountains hovered right around the poverty line. Most families received some kind of public assistance. Not so the MacKenzies. They had plenty of cash. Probably more than their fair share. And yet Willy barely seemed to know the stuff existed, or that his family had truckloads of cash, tens of millions of dollars squirreled away for weddings, rainy days, and presidential elections.

And second: the Blue Mountain folk themselves. In that last entry Willy talked about his friends and neighbors coming to his wedding. True enough. But what those folks wanted most of all was the chance to get an up close look at MacKenzie Island, its eccentric owner, its famous Great House, its gardens and orchards, all those antique wooden boats. A majority of valley residents had never set foot on MacKenzie Island until that wedding day. Sure, they wanted to glimpse the bride and groom, maybe sip some expensive French champagne, but more than that they wanted to gawk at the valley's most famous family. Willy believed then, and I think probably he still believes now, that he's just like his friends and neighbors: nothing but a regular Joe. But they have always known he comes from a different cut of cloth. He grew up insulated, unaware that his friends and neighbors gossiped incessantly about those strange and filthy-rich MacKenzies living in splendid isolation out on MacKenzie Island.

And now those friends and neighbors have gathered once again. At high noon, in just a couple of hours, if things go as planned, a MacKenzie will be sworn in as our forty-fourth chief executive. But we still have a few hurdles left to cross. We still need a judge to administer the oath. We still have threats from the military and from the bureaucrats in D.C. who want to crush these proceedings before they begin. We still have the worst snowstorm in forty years to hit the Tamaqua Valley. And most important, we still have to cover the last three and a half decades of the twentieth century so that we all might better understand the circumstances that have brought Willy MacKenzie and his family to this place at this moment in history.

★ ★ ★ ★ ★ ★ ★

Conrad Whitman MacKenzie and his beautiful twenty-one-year-old Mohawk bride, Emily Brant MacKenzie, took their honeymoon in, of all places, London, England. It was Emily's idea. As a schoolchild, she had seen pictures of Parliament Square and Big Ben and the river Thames in one of her textbooks, and ever since she had dreamed of visiting the city where, she said, "the white man had conspired to destroy the red man."

This was nothing like Conrad's last honeymoon to the Land of the Rose. His interest in bombed-out buildings had waned. The newlyweds toured the city arm in arm, pausing often to hug and kiss and have their picture taken by strangers in front of Westminster Abbey. They toured the Tower of London, St. Paul's Cathedral, and Queen Mary's Gardens in Regent's Park. They watched the changing of the guard at Buckingham Palace. They shopped for rain jackets and fine chocolates at Harrods. They took a boat ride down the Thames to Hampton Court. They watched a Royal Shakespeare Theatre performance of *As You Like It.*

Then one morning they woke up and Emily said the time had come to go to Scotland to see where Conrad's ancestors had lived before they immigrated to America. Reluctantly, Conrad agreed to make the journey.

They flew north to Edinburgh, hired a car, and headed west. Conrad knew from listening to the tales of Ulysses that the MacKenzie clan had lived in the Highlands, near Fort William. It took some time, several days, in fact, and a lot more questions than Conrad wanted to ask, but finally they found the old MacKenzie homestead. District records showed that a century earlier, Conrad's great-great-grandfather, Thomas MacKenzie, had owned nearly two thousand acres west and north of Ben Nevis. Sheep had dominated the landscape then, as they undoubtedly still do now.

The MacKenzie clan, however, had moved on by the time Conrad and Emily arrived. They had all headed for America or New Zealand or the south of England. But Conrad found the present owner, a little Irishman named O'Donnell, and received permission to roam over the rolling foothills.

"My great-grandfather," Conrad told his wife, "Benjamin MacKenzie, didn't want to herd sheep for a living. He had a hankering to live in the city and work at a desk."

A bit of fog rolled in off Loch Linnhe and pressed up against the west face of Ben Nevis. Visibility vanished. They could see no farther than their new spouse. A cold drizzle fell.

"He wound up in New York City," Conrad said after he raised a wide umbrella over his wife's head. "Went to work for a man named Vanderbilt. Later on he had his own shipping company. Did pretty well, I understand."

The drizzle stopped and the fog lifted as quickly as it had come. The early summer sun squinted through some high gray clouds.

"Ulysses," asked Emily, "is Benjamin's son?"

"Yes."

"And what became of Benjamin? Did he live as long as Ulysses has lived?"

Conrad took a moment to answer. He shook his head. "Benjamin killed himself. When still a fairly young man he chained an anchor to his leg and jumped into the East River."

Emily sighed and let it settle. She took a long look at those rolling hills. "He should have stayed," she said finally, "here, on the land. Never leave the land."

A few days later, homesick and tired of traveling, the newlyweds flew home. They reached MacKenzie Island on July 4, 1967.

Conrad went immediately upstairs to check on Ulysses. A new nurse had been hired but Conrad had worried during his absence that U.S. might not be receiving adequate care. His concerns had been in vain. Nurse Tully was a skilled and compassionate professional. She would look after Ulysses for the next sixteen years, until his death on August 19, 1983.

Ulysses and Nurse Tully lived in the Great House for only another two months. Soon after the newlyweds arrived home, U.S. began experiencing vivid memories from his past. These memories were like nightmares except that he experienced them while wide awake. A psychologist determined that he was reliving all the terrible things he had done to people during his most zealous years of capitalist exploitation. All his screaming and shouting were efforts to exorcise these memories.

Conrad put up with the screaming and shouting until the middle of August, when he convinced Emily to let him renovate the rooms over the boathouse. On the first of September they moved Ulysses into the freshly painted bedroom overlooking Loon Cove. That night Conrad and Emily wandered through the Great House naked, mesmerized by all the peace and quiet. They made love on the sofa in the living room. And again, not long before dawn, between the sheets of their soft down mattress. Simple arithmetic would tell us that was quite possibly the night Conrad and Emily conceived our president-elect, Mr. William Conrad Brant MacKenzie.

He was born nine months later, June 5, 1968, without complications, at two o'clock in the afternoon at the small hospital in Cedar Bluffs.

Two and a half months earlier, at a hospital outside Tampa, Florida, another significant birth had occurred. Dawn Tyler, daughter of James and Sandra Tyler, had entered the world on the ides of March.

Dawn and Willy met, without even knowing it, for the very first time, on June 8, 1968, the same day Emily brought Willy home from the hospital. The Tylers had come north earlier that week to summer on Tamarack. They put the two infants on a blanket on the floor, and immediately they rolled into one another's arms. And all through that summer, according to family legend, every time Willy cried, all his mother had to do was put Dawn somewhere close by and little Willy would instantly grow silent. Right from the start she was his security blanket, his safe haven, his alter ego.

The next big event for the MacKenzie clan came on Willy's first birthday, when his big brother married Alice Warren at a small chapel on the campus of Columbia University. Sanders and Alice had just earned their undergraduate degrees in comparative literature. Even though they both smoked marijuana and drank wine and had experimented with LSD, Sanders and Alice were essentially serious people of a liberal bent who mourned the memories of King and the Kennedy brothers, who opposed the war in Vietnam, and who marched in support of civil rights for all Americans.

To appease Alice's parents, a rather conservative middle-class couple from New Canaan, Connecticut, the bride and groom served up a traditional Christian wedding complete with the proper vows and a long white gown. But the moment the reception ended, Sanders and Alice broke loose. The newlyweds spent the summer growing their hair, making love in unusual and often awkward positions, smoking grass, marching against the war, and generally denigrating the status quo. In August they made their way to a small farm in upstate New York, where for three days they tripped on acid, wandered around naked in the rain, and listened to live rock and roll music.

After Woodstock they returned to the city to begin graduate school. Alice moved on to NYU, but Sanders continued at Columbia. Their academic lives rolled peacefully along until the end of November, when that old family friend, Dicky Nixon, who had by this time finally ascended to the presidency, signed into law the first draft lottery since World War

Two. The military, you see, needed fresh bodies for its police action in southeast Asia.

And how did Sanders MacKenzie fare when they pulled his name out of the Selective Service hat? He drew lucky number seven, a number so low that his local draft board sent him a Merry Christmas card.

The news arrived via the United States Postal Service. The letter informed Mr. Sanders MacKenzie that his Uncle Sam would be honored if he would participate, body and soul, in the United States military establishment.

On Christmas Eve Sanders rode the train north to Cedar Bluffs. He found his father at the MacKenzie house on High Street. Conrad sat before a roaring fire bouncing wee Willy on his knee. The toddler laughed and laughed, not a care in the world.

Sanders handed the induction notice to his father. "If you were me," he asked, "what would you do?"

Conrad read the letter. Twice. As he read it the second time, his own military experience, long dormant, surfaced and spread across his thoughts. The pain and the anger showed on his face. His reply came swiftly. "If those bastards sent me this," he told his son, "I'd tell them to shove it up their collective ass."

Pretty good advice, but maybe a tad too confrontational.

All over the country young men were burning their draft cards, feigning physical ailments, and deserting to Canada. Sanders mulled over his choices. In the end he decided to inform his local draft board that he was philosophically opposed to bearing arms; he wanted to register as a conscientious objector. This was his constitutional right, but the process proved slow and tedious. It demanded his full attention. He quickly realized c.o. status was not something you simply requested; you had to go out and earn it. The military didn't want too many conscientious objectors wandering around the countryside spreading dissent. People might start thinking war was a poor substitute for patriotism.

Religion had long been the primary means of acquiring c.o. status. Quakers, Amish, Mennonites, and other sects had been exempted from military service because of their religious beliefs. But becoming a conscientious objector solely on philosophical grounds was a relatively modern phenomenon. Sanders had to submit an application and an essay to the Selective Service board explaining why he opposed bearing arms against enemies of the United States. The essay he wrote ground on for almost thirty pages. He included quotes from Gandhi, Martin Luther King, and John Lennon. Perhaps it was the sheer abundance of his effort, but whatever the reason, Selective Service stamped its approval on his written request and invited him to participate in the next step: a personal appearance before his local board.

Sanders lived in Manhattan, so it was there he made his appearance. Most people think a draft board is made up of rather rigid military types with medals hanging off their uniforms. But in fact, civilians of all creeds and political beliefs sit on these boards. Residents of a community can be appointed to their local draft board the same as they can be appointed to a local planning board or utilities board or any other government board at the municipal level.

Sanders, his hair cut neat and short, and wearing a brand-new solid blue suit, stood before the board and spoke with passion about the horrors and the evils of war. He told the three men and four women sitting on the board that he loathed all wars, but the war in southeast Asia he found especially abhorrent.

"It is not," he said, "that I fear becoming another casualty in this long, bloody conflict. It is that I believe every single American who has died in Vietnam has died in vain, for nothing more than the petty egos of those who run the American industrial-military-political complex. I will not bear arms against a people who have been invaded by the corrupt political policies of the United States. I believe the war in Vietnam is a sham as well as a national disgrace."

Sanders had no way of knowing, but the Manhattan draft board had been infiltrated by several ultra-left-wingers who despised the war as much as young Mr. MacKenzie. The board deliberated for less than an hour before announcing its decision. They decided to reclassify Sanders 1-A-O (conscientious objector available for noncombatant service).

Sanders and Alice celebrated his new military status by ingesting a couple tabs of lysergic acid. During that acid trip Sanders reputedly gave the following response after someone asked him what he told the draft board: "I told them whatever I had to tell them to stay out of the freaking jungle."

Over the next several months it looked as though Sanders would indeed be spared the long and frightening trip from the Big Apple to southeast Asia. The war, everyone insisted, was finally drawing to a close. Nixon had announced the gradual withdrawal of combat troops. Several thousand had already been sent home. Kissinger and Le Duc Tho worked overtime in Paris to hash out a peace treaty acceptable to all sides. Military inductions decreased.

"It's all over," Sanders told Alice in the spring of 1970, just one week before the incident at Kent State. "I'll never get called up now."

The power of positive thinking has its limitations. By the end of that summer young MacKenzie was a raw recruit over at the Fort Dix army base in the Pine Barrens of south-central New Jersey. He went through basic training with all the other skin-headed grunts. The only difference was that he had to peel potatoes and clean the latrines while the other guys learned how to operate and discharge their firearms.

After basic the army sent Sanders to Fort Sam Houston in San Antonio, Texas, to train him as a field medic. He found out that his 1-A-O status meant the army couldn't force him to carry a weapon, but they sure as hell could send him into battle with a bag of gauze pads and some syringes dripping with morphine.

Sanders followed with no small amount of interest the ongoing efforts of the politicians to bring an end to the war. He read the papers, but he also began to appeal to a higher authority. One of his superior officers has told us he occasionally saw young MacKenzie praying at the foot of his bunk.

But not even the Almighty could stop this one. The war to stop the spread of communism dragged on into the winter and spring of 1971. And even though the total number of troops in Vietnam was steadily being reduced, fresh bodies shipped out daily to replace those whose tours had ended.

In late March, his medical training complete, Medic Sanders MacKenzie received his new orders. Destination: Saigon, South Vietnam.

Because of leave and various bureaucratic delays, June arrived before Sanders reached Saigon. He had expected to find death and despair and destruction on every street corner. But in fact, at that time, Saigon was a reasonably safe and secure city. An unarmed soldier could wander the streets even in the middle of the night and be in less danger than he would in certain tough neighborhoods of New York City.

The first four months of his tour passed without Sanders seeing the enemy or hearing a single shot fired. He worked an eight-hour shift at the local army hospital, but virtually all of the cases he treated were of a noncombat nature. He treated men for syphilis and gonorrhea. He iced down black eyes and taped up broken ribs, usually the result of drunken brawls between various branches of the military. He treated drug overdoses, lots and lots of drug overdoses. Opium and heroin, you may have heard, were widely available on the streets of Saigon.

Sanders would gladly have passed his tour of duty doling out penicillin and treating drug addicts by day, smoking hashish and listening to rock and roll tunes by night, but unfortunately the war interrupted his routine. In late September of 1971, Sanders made up part of a company that moved north out of Saigon to Bien-hoa. Their job was to go in and bring out the wounded. They reached the city some twenty miles up the highway from Saigon without incident. A brigade attached to the First Cavalry Division protected Bien-hoa from Viet Cong attacks coming out of Cambodia.

Immediately upon arriving in the city, Sanders faced his first combat wounds: stomachs blown wide open, hands and feet blown off, eyes blown out of their sockets. Young MacKenzie looked on in horror. More than once he threw up; twice he passed out from the blood and the stench.

It took two days to patch up the wounded and prepare them for transport back to the hospitals in Saigon. During those two days a constant barrage of small-arms fire echoed in and around the city. At night Sanders could hear the enemy shouting obscenities in broken English and screaming at the top of their lungs that soon the Yankees would die.

Sanders begged God to let him live.

On the morning of the third day the convoy received orders to head south out of the city, back to Saigon. Sanders rode in the back of a troop transport truck. He tended to the needs of half a dozen soldiers suffering with gunshot wounds.

The ambush attacked the convoy just beyond the city limits. It came without warning. A flurry of bullets ripped through the heavy canvas protecting the back of the truck. Several of the wounded soldiers were struck in the neck and shoulders. Sanders felt blood running down his face. He screamed. He thought he'd been hit. He thought for sure he was about to die. But the blood belonged to another man, a wounded man, a dying man.

A corporal appeared at the back of the truck. He took charge. He ordered all able-bodied soldiers to get out and prepare to face the enemy.

Sanders, soaking wet with sweat and close to shock, scrambled out of the truck. He looked around for a place to hide, a place to run.

The convoy ground to a halt. Viet Cong fanned out on both sides of the road. The only way out was back.

The noise and the smoke and the screams of the wounded soldiers caused young Sanders MacKenzie literally to shake in his combat boots.

Rifles were distributed to anyone who could still aim and shoot.

Sanders shook his head when presented with the M-16. "No," he insisted, "no! I don't have to take a weapon. I have c.o. status."

An officer, a captain, stepped up to Sanders and thrust the rifle against the young medic's chest. "I don't give a goddamn what kind of fucking status you have, soldier! We're fighting for our bloody lives here. You can damn well fire a few rounds at these slanty-eyed gooks!"

Sanders refused to take the gun.

The captain forced it into his hands. "Take it, goddammit. Take it and fire it!"

Sanders grabbed the rifle but immediately threw it to the ground. And then, the fear and the panic etched into his face, he turned and sprinted full speed back to the relative safety of the city the convoy had just left.

10:02 A.M.
JANUARY 20, 2001
MACKENZIE ISLAND
THE INAUGURATION OF THE FORTY-FOURTH PRESIDENT OF THE UNITED STATES

This incident involving Sanders is the same one mentioned by Senator Zachary Moore during that Senate committee hearing on the Tamaqua River Valley Dam and Development Project. We are all sophisticated enough to know that the senator was out to destroy Sanders's credibility when he brought up young MacKenzie's Vietnam experience. But the truth is, the senator's version of events offered only half the story. What actually took place, as you have just seen, was even more shocking. Not only did Sanders refuse to take the rifle, as Moore indicated, but he then threw the weapon to the ground and fled in the face of the enemy.

I realize this is not real comfortable material. Not for you and not for us. No one enjoys insinuating another man is a coward. But the United States Army's official investigation into the matter does not leave much room for interpretation. It states quite clearly that Medic Sanders MacKenzie, in a cowardly act unbecoming a soldier of the United States military, deserted his post. Period.

Nevertheless, we understand the president-elect is both annoyed and angry about the way we have portrayed his brother. In fact, here comes Willy now.

WILLY MACKENZIE: What the hell's the matter with you, Jack?! Calling Sanders a coward! What kind of crap are you spreading now?

JACK STEEL: Calm down, Mr. President. I never called your brother a coward. I was simply reporting the facts. That's my job.

W.M.: Don't tell me to calm down, you son of a bitch! You know damn well there's another side to that story.

J.S.: And what side is that, Mr. President? That Sanders claims he wasn't the only one who ran? That he insists the whole company freaked out and just about every single soldier fled back down the road to Bien-hoa?

W.M.: Exactly.

J.S.: Sorry, Willy, it doesn't wash. The army held an inquest, and the story Sanders told didn't hold up when the others were questioned.

W.M.: They needed a scapegoat, Steel. And Sanders was it.

J.S.: I'm sorry you can't take the truth, Mr. President.

W.M.: You wouldn't know the truth, Steel, if it fell out of the sky and hit you right smack in the face.

J.S.: Sir, I think I will choose to disregard that remark.

W.M.: Disregard anything you want, Steel, but you still twist the truth to suit your needs. Right now, for reasons I haven't quite figured out, you want to make my brother look like a coward. All morning long, one generation at a time, you've taken your best shots at the MacKenzies. Your style is very refined, very subtle. You seem almost to envy us. You stop just short of lavishing praise upon us. But I see now that little by little, one minor incident at a time, you are setting us up, getting ready to pull us down, drag us through the mud.

J.S.: You give me too much credit, Mr. President. Not only would I never do such a thing, but even if I wanted to, I seriously doubt I have the power or the savvy or the brains to bring it off.

W.M.: Don't hand me that drivel. You have the power, Steel.

And you're plenty savvy, a regular used-car salesman. You've been selling me a bill of goods for years now. And I'm sick of it. So back off. You hear me? Back off and leave my family alone or next time I'll come storming in here with my mouth shut and my fists flying.

J.S.: Is that a threat, Mr. President?

W.M.: No, Steel, it's not a threat. It's just the way things are gonna be.

And as quickly as he came, Willy goes. Out the boathouse door, through the snow, up the porch stairs, and into the kitchen of the Great House.

I really don't know what to say. I certainly didn't mean to upset him. They gave me a job to tell the story of the MacKenzie clan on inauguration morning. I've simply been doing my best to get that story told.

I suppose the time has come to move this process forward. The morning grows late. I had planned at this point to serve up some rather elegant and romantic journal entries written in the year following Willy's marriage to Dawn. His prose during that time was full of Blue Mountain superlatives and lofty descriptions of sunsets and full moons and storm clouds racing across the evening sky. Prose written by a young man deeply in love. But maybe we should bypass those sentiments, skip them altogether. Maybe we should jump ahead to his rather ominous journal entry of October 3, 1992, some two years and four months after his marriage.

And from here on out I promise to keep this live broadcast focused on the facts alone. It certainly has not been my intention to ridicule Willy MacKenzie or any member of his family.

* * * * * * *

October 3, 1992
Tamarack

It's been a while since I made an entry in the journal. More than two weeks now. That's one of my longer droughts since I started writing this thing thirteen or fourteen years ago.

I should mark this entry with a star. It's the first time I've written in the journal here in our new house on Tamarack. We moved in yesterday, exactly two and a half years since the day we started building the foundation. There are still floors to sand and doors to hang and trim to paint, but Dawn and I decided the time had come. We didn't want to wait until next spring. After all that's happened we definitely needed a change of environment.

She's taking a nap in the next room, so I thought this would be a good time to catch up on a few things. Probably I should be working on that election piece for the American Observer, but I'm sure it'll wait. The three candidates ain't going anywhere.

I have good news and bad news. All the news is just sort of tangled up together, just about like my thoughts right now, so I guess I'll try to put things down more or less as they happened.

Back on the morning of September 23rd, the earth-moving equipment moved into the valley. Even out here on the islands we could hear those giant machines rumbling along the old north-south highway. Sure, we knew they were coming, we'd been warned, but that didn't keep the reality from being a cold slap in the face.

Dawn and I cleaned up our paintbrushes, hopped into the Gar Runabout, and sped across the lake. We reached Cedar Bluffs just as that convoy of dump trucks, bulldozers, track hoes, and front end loaders rumbled through town. Most folks, people I've known my whole life, stood out on the sidewalks with their mouths hanging open as that long stream of oversize vehicles snaked through our narrow streets. You might've thought a funeral procession moved through Cedar Bluffs. We all stood there looking more than a little powerless.

That night another meeting was held on MacKenzie Island to discuss what to do. Almost every single adult resident of the valley sat or stood in my parents' living room. Up until that meeting the Tamaqua Valley Dam and Development Project had always been at least partly an abstraction. It had never been more than a plan on a piece of paper, words in the politicians' mouths. Now, suddenly, all that had changed. Completion of the huge dam might've been two years or more away, but the arrival of those machines offered us at least the beginning of the end.

Pop and Sanders updated everyone on the various lawsuits we had pending against the state and federal governments to try to bring a halt to the project.

"Damn lawyers," growled Frank Bender. "They ain't gonna do

us any good. Those government bastards got a dozen Ivy League lawyers for every one we got."

"You're right, Frank," said Pop, "they probably do. But we have to keep trying."

A pretty good argument broke out then about whether or not we had the right lawyers for the job. Some folks wanted to hire new ones. Other folks, like Pop, wanted to stick with the ones we had: these slick hotshots from New York City. All along everyone knew Pop would have the final say since he was footing the bill, most of it anyway, but that didn't keep folks from arguing.

In the middle of the argument I noticed Mama had disappeared. I glanced out the window and saw her coming across the front lawn. She had Tecumseh Brant at her side. Several other Mohawks followed close behind.

The front door swung open. The Mohawks stepped into the foyer. The moment they appeared in the archway leading to the living room, all those arguing voices grew silent.

Mama had her say. "Our friend and neighbor, Tecumseh Brant, would like to speak to us about the situation in the valley."

Everyone knew of Tecumseh, he had long ago become a living legend in the valley, but I could tell by a quick look around the room that only a few of those folks had ever actually laid eyes on him. Over a hundred years old, he'd shrunk down to the size of a dwarf. But that voice still boomed the moment he opened his mouth.

"As you know," he began, "the Mohawk living in the Tamaqua Valley will lose their home if this dam is built. In this fight we are all equal. The Mohawk, however, have been through struggles like this before. Our people know what it means to be displaced. Your government has inflicted mass migration upon us many times in the past two hundred years. I know the pain and suffering displacement brings, and I would not wish it upon my worst enemy. So I have come here today to suggest we combine our meager forces in a unified display of civil disobedience."

Civil disobedience. It sounded like a good idea to me.

After a couple hours of discussion, everyone agreed to give it a try.

And that night, after we got home, Dawn and I continued the discussion. It pretty quickly turned into an argument. I didn't want her to go; I wanted her to stay home. "Most of the valley's going," I kept insisting. "One less won't make any difference."

"No way am I staying out of this fight, Willy."

"You're seven and a half months pregnant," I reminded her. "For two months the doctor's been telling you to rest more, to stay off your feet, to relax."

"I'm perfectly healthy. It's not going to kill me or this baby to sit for a few hours along the banks of the Tamaqua." Stubborn to the core.

Still, that was the plan. A mass sit-in. A peaceful demonstration. We'd march down to the river and sit right smack in the middle of where those enormous earth-moving machines were scheduled to begin moving the earth.

The next morning, just after dawn, more than a thousand residents of Tamaqua Valley gathered at the site of the new dam a few miles southwest of Seven Points. A dirt road had already been pushed through the woods from the highway down to the river. We marched along the dirt road, Indians and whites, men and women, young folks and old folks.

But almost immediately after we reached the river, our plan began to break down. We were not well trained in the principles of civil disobedience. So when the construction workers who had come to devastate our valley taunted us with name calling and petty threats, we retaliated with verbal abuse of our own. And when they lofted rocks into our ranks, we picked up stones off the riverbank and began a counterattack.

"Do not be provoked," shouted Tecumseh Brant, but many in our small army already had their dander up and their arsenals ready. Steady and ugly streams of profanity sliced through the cool, early morning air. Small stones once lobbed turned into larger stones thrown with menace and an intent to injure.

Just as events began to swirl out of control, the media arrived. We had called them the night before, the local newspapers and the cable TV station in Seven Points, to attract some added publicity for our plight.

Our ranks began to close. The distance between their side and our side grew smaller and tighter. Soon we stood face to face. Pushing and shoving erupted on top of that steep and slippery riverbank. Threats were thrown, then fists and more stones.

I tried to lead Dawn away from the fray, but too late.

As we retreated along the embankment, a random stone, thrown by whom we will probably never know, struck Dawn on the side of the head. Her hand slipped from mine. She lost her footing. I reached out to grab her, but no good. I had to watch helplessly as she tumbled head over heels down that steep embankment. She came to rest in a shallow eddy at the river's edge.

"Dawn!!!"

I screamed so loud the swearing and fighting came to an abrupt halt. I slipped and slid down the embankment to her side. I carefully lifted her head out of the water. She did not respond. Her eyes did not open. Over her right eye a large bump began to swell.

I must've gone into shock because the next thing I remember with any clarity is riding in the back of the ambulance and hearing the siren wail and seeing Dawn stretched out with her eyes closed, and Dawn's mom, and the first-aid guy holding a compress on Dawn's forehead. I started to ask if she was still alive but didn't. Then we reached the hospital in Seven Points and they rushed Dawn inside and for more than an hour I sat out in the waiting room, anticipating the worst and hoping for the best.

The doctor, a young woman who I swear had a tear in her eye, finally came into the waiting room where Dawn's mom and I sat holding hands.

A moment passed before a brief smile showed on the doctor's face. "She'll be fine," said the young doctor, and my heart began to beat again, even though I still feared the tear that had by now dried on her cheek.

"She has a few cuts and bruises, and a rather nasty bump on her head. But the X-rays show only a minor concussion. A few days rest and physically she'll be as good as new."

Physically? What did she mean, physically? I was afraid to ask.

Dawn's mom wasn't. "What do you mean, physically?"

"Emotionally," said the young female doctor in a very soft voice, "emotionally she may need some time to recover."

I guess so. Or maybe she'll never recover. Probably neither of us will ever recover.

We knew it was a girl. The tests had told us so. Right away Dawn had said, "We'll name this one Sandra for my mom and the next one we'll name Emily for your mom."

"What if the next one's not a girl?" I wanted to know.

"We'll have nothing but girls, Willy MacKenzie. Half a dozen or more. Tall, beautiful girls with brains who'll take care of us when we get old and maybe save the planet along the way."

There are so many obstacles out there we cannot control.

Dawn stayed in the hospital for three days. I told her about the miscarriage as soon as the doctor told me I could. She didn't say so, but I could tell she already knew. We cried a lot then, and we're still crying a lot now. When Dawn's not crying she's usually sleeping, or pretending to sleep.

I haven't said to her, "I told you so, I told you to stay home, I told you to rest and take care of the baby." Hopefully I never will. I also haven't told her what I try not to even think about myself: that if one of them had to die, I am selfishly thankful it was not Dawn. That sounds horrible, I know, but if Dawn died, I feel pretty sure I'd shrivel up and die also.

The cameraman for the cable TV station down in Seven Points had his camera pointed at Dawn as she took her spill down the embankment and into the Tamaqua River. That night the video aired on the local evening news. The next morning a picture of me holding Dawn in my arms along the riverbank appeared in newspapers across the country. And that night the video of Dawn's fall aired coast to coast on the network news. Journalists from all over the country swarmed into the valley. I refused to talk to them; and no way would I allow them anywhere near Dawn.

Nevertheless, their stories swung the tide, at least temporarily, in our favor. The Tamaqua Valley Dam and Development Project has been put on hold. There will be investigations to determine exactly what caused our child's death. And there will be further review of the overall feasibility of the project. So you might say our civil disobedience paid off. But Dawn and I will never be convinced of that. As far as we are concerned, Sandra was the first, and let us all hope the last, victim of this insane plan to flood the valley and destroy our homes.

10:10 A.M.
JANUARY 20, 2001
MACKENZIE ISLAND
THE INAUGURATION OF THE FORTY-FOURTH PRESIDENT OF THE UNITED STATES

I was among the journalists who swarmed into the valley the day after Dawn lost the baby. That's right, it was my first major assignment after the L.A. riots. At the time I had never heard of Willy MacKenzie or MacKenzie Island or the Tamaqua River Valley or the Tamaqua Valley Dam and Development Project.

All that was about to change.

I toured the valley. I interviewed valley residents and construction workers who had been present during the incident. All parties held firm to the belief that the other side had started the trouble, caused the commotion. How unusual.

Fred Lorry, my cameraman, and I went out to have a look at where the accident had taken place. I stood in front of those giant bulldozers and track hoes, silent and idle since the project had been halted, and gave my impressions of the event while Fred rolled the film. Like almost every other reporter covering the story, I took the human-interest angle. The valley residents played the good guys trying to protect their little corner of America. The construction workers played the bad guys, the thugs carrying out the dirty work for their greedy and evil bosses, played by various fat cat contractors and politicians from Washington and the state capital.

With the camera rolling, I scrambled down that steep embankment.

I stood on the spot where Dawn Tyler MacKenzie had come to rest after her fall. I told my audience that right here was where Dawn and Willy's baby had been lost.

Then, sensing the weight of the moment, I once again called a spade a spade. "This tragedy," I said as the camera closed in, "is the result of election-year politics. For ten years the Tamaqua Valley Dam and Development Project has been studied and debated on the state and federal level. No one has been in a hurry to make a final decision one way or the other. But now, suddenly, with Election Day drawing near, the project is approved and pushed ahead at breakneck speed. President Bush and Governor Montgomery, both up for reelection and lagging behind in the polls, undoubtedly sensed political gain if they could move the plan forward. The president and the governor could point to the dam and tell us how they were creating jobs and resurrecting pride, putting America back to work. However," I added, "there are many who contend that this mess has political payoff written all over it."

It did, too. Bush and Montgomery were both in deep trouble politically. Unemployment was up. Government debt, up. New taxes, up. The economy was in a shambles. The voters were angry and demanding change. You could say election year 1992 was a lot like election year 2000, only then things weren't half as bad as they are now. They might've looked bad at the time, but hindsight tells us the issues of ninety-two were nothing but small potatoes compared to the mess we find ourselves in now.

What I'd said out on the banks of the Tamaqua River was true: for more than a decade the dam project had simmered on the back burner. A few politicians and special-interest groups had worked to make the dam a reality. Another small group, men like Conrad and Sanders MacKenzie, had worked to scrap the project. But a vast majority of people around the country did not even know the dam project existed. Then the president, during a campaign swing through the state, with Governor Montgomery standing at his side, gave the project the green light, and a few weeks later those dump trucks and bulldozers and track hoes rolled into the valley to begin the initial phase of construction. Less than twenty-four hours after their arrival, tragedy struck.

It was a big story but not a huge story. It diverted attention away from the presidential campaign, but it certainly did not swing the election to any particular candidate. Two or three days in the headlines, and then Dawn and Willy and their precious valley gave way to other more pressing stories: hurricane relief in Florida, civil war in Yugoslavia, starvation in Somalia, Clinton the draft dodger, Bush the closet womanizer, Perot the spoiler.

Behind the scenes, however, after all the journalists, including me, had left the valley to pursue other stories, the struggle and the intrigue among the primary players persisted. The project had been slowed but not stopped. And now, after years of speculation and accusation, charges and countercharges, I think I have the true story, the full story, the facts and figures. But let's not get ahead of ourselves. We still have an hour and forty-five minutes until the swearing-in ceremony is scheduled to begin. . . .

A couple of important announcements. First and foremost: All incoming communications have ceased. We are still transmitting but we are no longer receiving. We have not heard from our bureaus in Washington or New York for almost half an hour. Nor have we heard from any of our reporters around the country. Nothing is getting through. We have no idea why.

This breakdown in communication might simply be the work of Mother Nature. We are, after all, out on an isolated island on a very cold January morning surrounded by blizzardlike conditions. Nearly two feet of snow has fallen in just the last few hours. These conditions could create transmission problems. But among ourselves, there has been some speculation that this communication breakdown might be the work of forces who would like to see Willy MacKenzie's presidency brought to a grinding halt. There are certainly people out there who see the end of an era drawing near and who might not relinquish power without a fight.

Our one link to the outside world remains Patsy Squire, our young cub who volunteered to track Henry Bender when he left MacKenzie Island. We armed Patsy with a communication device, and just a few minutes ago she filed her first report. As I suspected, Henry went straight up to the North Creek home of Judge Orrin Stuart. Bender immediately brought the judge up to speed on the situation here on the island. The judge, sitting in his favorite rocking chair, smoking his corncob pipe while watching a video of *How the West Was Won*, thought things over for a minute or two, then decided he could and would administer the oath. But at age eighty-seven, bent almost double with rheumatoid arthritis, Judge Stuart doesn't get around real well. The last we heard, Bender was trying to rig up an old horse-drawn sleigh to haul the judge out of North Creek and down here to the island. The whole thing could take some time.

So this might be a good time to get back to the MacKenzie family chronicles. I don't want to bring Willy's wrath down on me again, but we need to talk about Sanders for just a few more minutes. After that I will focus exclusively on the life of the president-elect. In fact, I intend to let his own words do most of the telling.

* * * * * * *

On September 29, 1971, Sanders MacKenzie was court-martialed for disobeying the direct order of a superior officer and for deserting his post during a time of war. He was found guilty and given a dishonorable discharge from the United States Army.

Young MacKenzie was lucky they didn't throw him in the brig for several years, maybe even put him in front of a firing squad. Don't laugh; at another point in history they might have shot Sanders for desertion. But with the war so unpopular at home, the military decided to avoid any unnecessary controversy. So they stripped Sanders of his rank, flew him back to the States, and told him to get lost.

Sanders, troubled and bitter over his Vietnam experience, drifted for a year or two with little or no direction. He went back to graduate school in the fall of 1972 but dropped out after one semester. He worked for a while in a bookstore in the East Village. He wrote articles for some left-wing underground rag in Soho. But he seems to have spent most of his time hanging around smoking grass, drinking wine, and bitching about the state of the Union.

In early 1973 he read an article somewhere about some guy who had walked around the world. He decided to walk across America. He convinced Alice to go along, all the way from New York to San Francisco.

"We'll see the land," he said, "meet the people. Find out what's really going on."

Reluctantly, Alice agreed. They set out on a warm and sunny day in early May.

In their lightweight hiking boots, they walked all the way to Chicago, Illinois, more than a thousand miles. The distance took them several months to cover. They made anywhere from ten to thirty miles a day.

The Watergate fiasco unfolded as they ambled through Jersey and Pennsylvania, Ohio and Indiana. Sanders asked everyone they met about the break-in. "Do you think the president knew?" he asked. "Do you think Nixon was involved?"

Sanders hated Nixon. He blamed him for his grandfather's death and for his own troubles in Vietnam. So he was mighty glad when a vast majority of the people he asked answered yes to his two questions. Almost everyone believed Nixon's hands were dirty dirty dirty.

"We've walked far enough," Sanders told Alice just a few days before Christmas. "It's time to go home and get to work."

"Good," said Alice. "It's getting cold, and my feet hurt."

Sanders had decided, out there on the road, to become a political activist. But in order to become one he knew he needed capital.

So once again on Christmas Eve, this time with Alice at his side, he rode the train north to Cedar Bluffs. They spent the holiday with Conrad and Emily and five-year-old Willy at the house on High Street. At some point after the gifts had been opened and the feast of wild turkey with all the trimmings consumed, Sanders found a moment alone with his father. "I've got an idea I'd like to talk to you about, Pop."

But right then the phone rang. It was the Tylers calling from Florida to wish everyone a very Merry Christmas. Mary Ann talked to Emily and Sanders talked to James and Alice talked to Sandra, but by far the longest conversation took place between the five-year-olds, Dawn and little Willy. They talked for at least half an hour. None of the adults knew what the two youngsters talked about for so long, but they'd learned from experience not to fight it; letting Dawn and Willy talk kept the peace while the families were at opposite ends of the East Coast.

Later that night, after the others had gone up to bed, Sanders and

Conrad continued their conversation in front of the fireplace. "So," Conrad asked, "what's your idea?"

Sanders told his father he wanted to start a magazine.

"What kind of magazine?"

"A magazine," said Sanders, "dedicated to exposing corruption on all fronts: political, military, environmental, corporate. Anywhere it exists we'll go after it."

Conrad thought it over. He knew his son wanted money. "So what do you plan to call this magazine?"

"The *American Observer*," answered Sanders. *"Citizen's Watchdog."*

The next day Conrad agreed to finance the effort. He was lukewarm on the idea; it irritated his isolationist attitudes; but he decided it would give his son something useful to do.

Money, of course, was no object. The MacKenzies had plenty of money: enough to start their own country or build their own army, certainly enough to launch a new periodical.

Their checkbook swollen, Sanders and Alice went straight to work. They rented a fifth-floor loft down on Astor Place in Greenwich Village. They bought furniture and typewriters and filing cabinets. They hired editorial assistants and a small sales force. By the late spring of 1974, they went to press with their first issue.

In many respects the *American Observer* was old-fashioned muckraker journalism, right out of the school of Lincoln Steffens and Upton Sinclair. The MacKenzies, you might say, had come full circle. Seventy-five years earlier Ulysses had fought tooth and nail with the liberal do-gooders who had worked to suffocate and regulate the way he did business. Now his own great-grandson had joined the enemy. U.S., a hundred and nine years old, probably would have kicked Sanders in the arse for his treasonous behavior, but the old boy lived out in the depths of left field, out beyond the bleacher seats, oblivious to the ebb and flow of the modern world.

When asked about his magazine, Sanders would reply, "Our job is to tell the other side of the story: the side the fat cats and the power brokers suppress; the side you don't read about in the mainstream magazines and newspapers. We don't give a damn what side they take; we just slip in and automatically take the other side."

It would be difficult to pigeonhole the *Observer* or its editorial position. The accepted labels: liberal v. conservative, right-wing v. left-wing, Democrat v. Republican—these labels did not stick then, and quite frankly they do not stick now. Sanders and Alice wandered all over the map with their writings, apparently more for the impact of offering a conflicting point of view than for any deep-seated political or even moral convictions.

The same, of course, has been said about Willy MacKenzie, candidate for president and, now, president-elect. Since entering the political arena, Willy has often seemed more interested in stirring up turmoil and belittling the status quo than in defining his own political beliefs.

You might read one article in the *Observer* and conclude the editors were highbrow, eastern liberal types. They were, after all, positively zealous in their condemnation of the war in Vietnam. And Watergate, well, that was their pet project. Sanders was never at a loss for words when it came time to denounce Nixon and his troika of German henchmen: Kissinger, Haldeman, and Erlichman. "*Das drei Nazis*," he called them.

But not long after Nixon took the royal tumble on August 9, 1974, Sanders began to change his tune. And this is what we mean about it being virtually impossible to label these MacKenzies from a definitive political point of view. In the fall of seventy-four, an editorial in the *Observer* suggested that Nixon's Watergate crimes paled in comparison to stunts pulled by past presidents. Sanders wrote, "By bringing Richard Nixon to his knees, *The Washington Post*, *The New York Times*, and the news departments of the three major television networks have demonstrated once and for all who wields the ultimate power in this country. Make no mistake, America is ruled by the kingpins of the Fourth Estate."

That was the first, but certainly not the last, swipe Sanders would take at the mainstream press. He, and later his little brother, would over the years point their fingers and blame us for most if not all of our social, political, and psychic ills.

It took two years of determined hard work, but with the help of a good sales team, an excellent layout man who gave the magazine a slick but classy appearance, and wheelbarrows full of MacKenzie money for advertising, the *American Observer* found a small but loyal readership. And month by month, issue by issue, that readership grew.

In the summer of 1976, soon after the nation's bicentennial celebration, after two and a half years on Astor Place, Sanders and Alice decided they needed a change. They were sick and tired of the rat race in the city. They felt their sensitivities fading. Too much stimulus. Too many cocktail parties. Too much noise and confusion. And far too many people. So they did what they had been talking about doing since their college days at Columbia: they made the decision to move to the valley. Six to eight weeks a year on MacKenzie was not enough; they wanted to live and work in the Blue Mountains full-time. They hired a managing editor, sold their apartment on the Upper West Side, put their affairs in order, and moved north.

10:21 A.M.
JANUARY 20, 2001
MACKENZIE ISLAND
THE INAUGURATION OF THE FORTY-FOURTH PRESIDENT OF THE UNITED STATES

And who do you think was there to greet Sanders and Alice when they pulled up to the dock on MacKenzie Island? Why, young Willy MacKenzie, of course. He was a spry and eager eight-year-old that summer, with wild eyes and bare feet. He thought his big brother coming to live on the island was just about the best thing that had ever happened.

But who exactly was this stripling, this William Conrad Brant MacKenzie?

We have taken in-depth looks at the important men in Willy's life: his great-grandfather, his grandfather, his father, and now his brother. But what about young Willy? What do we really know about his early days? We have read a few of his early journal entries, learned a thing or two, I suppose, about his thoughts and feelings and ambitions. I think we know he was a curious and sensitive child with a keen imagination and a desire to please both family and friends. But what else do we know? What kind of a boy was our president-elect?

Since his election last November, I have done a fair amount of digging, conducted more than a few interviews, and I can only conclude that there was nothing all that extraordinary about his early years. Nothing, I don't think, to suggest he would one day be chosen to lead this great country into the twenty-first century.

Growing up where he did on that island hinterland might hold a certain mystery and awe and even romance for many of us, but, in fact, Willy was, if we can believe those who reared him and educated him, a decidedly normal and well-adjusted child. Average might be the best word to describe the youngster.

Here's what his own mother told me in an interview:

> EMILY MACKENZIE: Willy took forever to walk. He just didn't seem anxious to go anywhere. For years he was perfectly willing to let me tote him from one end of the earth to the other. But his mouth, now that was something else again. He starting moving his mouth and forming words at a very early age. It shocked us how he could complete entire sentences long before his second birthday. And once he started there was no slowing him down.

And here's what his second-grade teacher, Mrs. Muriel Meade, remembers about little Willy MacKenzie:

> MURIEL MEADE: Willy loved to tell stories. We had a story-telling hour twice a week. Willy would take up the whole hour if I let him. He loved to tell stories about the Indians, probably because he was part Mohawk. And also stories about his famous grandfather, might have been his great-grandfather, Ulysses. I remember him telling us his grandfather was one hundred and eleven years old and every morning the two of them would sit in front of the window and listen to the loons and then they would spread their wings and fly over the mountains. Willy had a fantastic imagination. I think he got it from his mother, who, quite honestly, was kind of a standoffish woman. But he was a sweet boy, Willy. I don't know how good a president he'll be, but he was a very sweet boy.

A very sweet boy. You would be hard-pressed to find anyone in the valley who knew Willy during his youth who would disagree with that simple assessment. He had a carefree and easy smile, good manners, and a very pleasant disposition. He did not seem at all taken with the fact that he was a MacKenzie or that his family had enough cash to buy the entire valley. Folks liked having young Willy around, even if he did talk a blue streak.

Here's Max Potts, Willy's fifth-grade teacher:

> MAX POTTS: Most subjects didn't interest Willy much. He had no use at all for science or mathematics. He liked art class some, even though he wasn't very good at it. And he loved music class, especially when we sang. He had kind of a high, shrieky voice, but he sure loved to project it. I guess if asked, I'd just have to say Willy was a nice young fella, never caused a teaspoon of trouble.

I could give you half a dozen more quotes from various teachers right up through high school and college, but basically they would all reflect this same point of view: Willy was an unexceptional student, but a very nice guy, "a true gentleman," his tenth-grade typing teacher, Grace Vollmer, told me, "a pleasure to have in my classroom."

He was not, however, a particularly good typist. Willy took typing thinking it might help him in his career choice. During his sophomore year, 1983/84, Willy typed virtually all of his journal entries. Terrible stuff. Littered with typos. You need training as a cryptographer to decipher it. Then one day he just gave it up, stuck that typewriter in the closet, and went back to using a fountain pen. And that's what he's used ever since. Never, so far as I know, has he written a single sentence on a word processor or a personal computer.

His personal writing habits aside, I think it would be safe to say that Willy was a friendly, fair-haired lad who got on well with parents, peers, and authority figures. And so we must look elsewhere to unravel the mysteries of this young island dweller who would one day shake to its core the old and brittle bones of the American political establishment. Personally, I think we need look no farther than Tamarack Island and the pretty, dark-haired girl who dwelt there. I think she is the key to the man Willy MacKenzie became.

We have already discussed Willy's early and complete devotion to Dawn. And we have seen it clearly demonstrated in his journals. Whenever possible it would seem the two of them were together. When the Tylers occupied the house on Tamarack, usually from April or May until

October or November, Dawn and Willy saw each other almost every day. Often Dawn spent the night on MacKenzie or Willy spent the night on Tamarack. Their mothers, Emily and Sandra, encouraged the relationship. The MacKenzies and Tylers were as close as kin, Willy and Dawn like brother and sister. Their moms wanted it this way. They knew that island life, for youngsters as well as for adults, could be a lonely life. A good friend and ally was the best defense against loneliness.

So Willy and Dawn grew up best friends, no question about that, but they had other friends as well. The valley teemed with young couples with young children in the 1970s. Disillusioned with war and politics, the generation who came of age in the 1960s escaped the cities and the suburbs to try their hand at a simpler and more honest lifestyle. They wanted to raise their kids where the air was clean and the streets safe. MacKenzie Island often hosted a dozen or more children on a warm summer's afternoon.

I have managed to locate several of these youngsters who have since grown into adulthood. Some left the valley and the Blue Mountains behind, but others stayed to raise families of their own.

Here is Susan Gallagher on her childhood friends:

> SUSAN GALLAGHER: Oh, sure, they were devoted to one another. Right from the word get-go. But I'd have to say Willy much more than Dawn. Willy was obsessive about it, like an addict or something. Dawn was much more high-spirited and adventurous. And independent. She always had to do things her way. Usually Willy just went along with her. He never caused a ruckus. Dawn was kind of like his hero. We used to make fun of him about it. I remember the way he used to mope around when she went to Florida for the winter. I don't know, it's strange, if you'd told me then that one day one of them would be president, I'd've said it would be Dawn. Definitely Dawn. I would've seen Willy more as the husband of the first female president.

Several others offer a similar story. Everyone seems to agree Dawn was the stronger and more potent personality in the relationship, the one who set the tone and determined how things would be done. Of course, these memories come from people twenty years or more removed from the actual events. Over all that time the truth sometimes tends to dissolve into a liquid mass of attitudes and predispositions.

Henry Bender, for example, offers a rather different scenario. Here's what he told me soon after Willy won the election last November.

> HENRY BENDER: Willy was the best. He was the fastest, bravest, smartest kid in the whole valley. He was my best buddy. Still is, I'd have to say. But that's not to say I was his best buddy. His best buddy was Dawn. And hers him. They were a couple peas in a pod, those two. No two ways about that. They just sort of moved around like one person. They could finish each other's sentences, and they always knew what the other one was thinking. Luckily, for me anyway, Dawn went south for a few months in the winter, so that gave me and Willy a chance to pal around together. And we did too, even though I knew he was mostly waiting for her to get back.

Fastest kid in the valley? Bravest kid? I don't know. Maybe. But Willy was definitely not the smartest. That honor would surely have gone to Dawn. She was valedictorian of their high school class. Semester after semester, year after year, both at schools in Cedar Bluffs and in Florida, Dawn proved an exemplary, straight A student. But she was no little Miss Goody Two-Shoes who brought the teacher an apple every morning. Quite the contrary. She argued with her instructors over every fact and figure. She never accepted a word they said without a full and proper explanation. From what I have heard, I would say this lovely and rather petite young lady who looked harmless enough had something of a rebel streak coursing through her veins.

It started with little things. In the seventh or eighth grade she formed a committee at her grammar school in Florida to change the dress code, which did not allow students to wear blue jeans or denim jackets.

"This is ridiculous," she told the principal and the board of education. "Half my clothes are made of denim. Denim is comfortable and practical. Why should my parents have to buy me new clothes just because you have some irrational phobia about Levi's?"

They banned the dress code.

A year or two later Dawn made her first appearance as an environmental activist. She must have been fourteen or fifteen at the time. I think it was the last winter she spent in Florida with her parents. Her cause concerned the vanishing habitat of some large marine turtles that had recently been placed on the endangered species list.

It seems a bunch of these turtles lived along a canal near the Tylers' home south of Sarasota. Dawn often visited the turtles and gave them food. Then she learned that a new housing development would be built along the canal. The day before the workers arrived with their axes and chain saws to begin clearing the palmettos and scrub pines, Dawn went down to the Town Hall to try to find out what would become of the turtles. The clerks and bureaucrats at Town Hall had no idea what she was talking about. They told her not to worry about the turtles. They assured her the turtles would be just fine.

Dawn, always skeptical of authority, did not believe them.

So the next morning, when the workers arrived to begin clearing the land, Dawn and twenty or thirty of her classmates had formed a human ring around the area where the turtles nested and lived. They held hands and refused to move.

The workers called the cops. The cops came. The head cop told the kids, "Okay, fun is fun, but it's time to move along now. Let the men get to work."

Dawn refused to move along. She said they were staying until something was done about the turtles.

The cops, small-town types who did not want any part of trouble with a bunch of teenage girls, decided to call in the mayor. The mayor was a kindly older woman with a love of all things wild, including endangered sea turtles, so right away she sided with Dawn. Before those axes and chain saws bit into a single palmetto or scrub pine, every single one of those turtles had been safely moved to an equally hospitable habitat.

I think we can safely say Dawn, from the very beginning, had her hand in efforts to keep the Tamaqua River Valley Dam and Development Project from ever becoming a reality. She, much more so than Willy, took an active role in the ongoing campaign to keep the valley dam free.

Willy was the worrier in the relationship, the one who relentlessly feared the worst and believed in fate. He would tell you that if a dam was destined to cross the Tamaqua River, all the fighting and protesting in the world would not alter that fact. Dawn, on the other hand, was the optimist and the doer in the relationship, the one who constantly hoped for the best and believed in free will. She had a very refined sense of right and wrong. She would tell you that a dam on the Tamaqua River was wrong, and then, as we shall soon see, she would do everything in her power to prevent the construction of that dam.

April 3, 1994

Yesterday the ice finally let go. Today we returned to the islands. Tomorrow, early, I plan to start writing my first book. Already have a title picked out: <u>FULL MOON OVER KATYDEERAY</u>. Actually, if I'm honest, Dawn came up with the title.

I've been thinking about this book for a while, over a year now, and I think it's time to apply pen to paper. I want to make it kind of a modern-day <u>Walden</u>, meaning I want to talk about living a simple life, a natural life, a life close to the earth. Only it won't be all serious skulls-and-crossbones stuff; I want to inject some humor into the story also. I might even offer some advice on how we might make the earth a better and cleaner place to live. We'll see. I'm not much of an advice giver. But not to worry, I have plenty of time to mull it over.

Dawn thinks I have a pretty good idea for a book. So does Sanders. This morning he and I had our first rendezvous of the new season out on the front porch.

"Pretty rough winter," I said.

He nodded. "All over now."

"Yup."

"We had bluebirds on the feeder this morning," he said.

"A good sign," I said.

"The willows along Looking Glass Cove have started blooming."

"Soon we'll be awash in green."

He nodded again, and then we just stood there for a few minutes, thinking it over, thinking about what will soon rumble into the Blues.

I looked north, up the valley. "Think we'll be able to hear 'em once they start blasting?"

Sanders stroked his chin. He took his time. "The site's quite a ways off," he said finally, "but yeah, I suspect we will."

Then we grew quiet again but I wanted to fill up that quiet, so I said, "I've decided to start working on my book."

He looked at me and smiled. "You've been saying that since last fall, Willy."

"But this time I mean it."

"Well hell," he said, "that's good. High time, too. Far as I'm concerned we can't have enough reading material out there about the land, about the environment."

"Think I'll be able to sell it?"

"Why not?"

I nodded, and then we both stood there, thinking no doubt about the same damn thing: the newly redesigned and reapproved Tamaqua Valley Dam and Development Project. A project slated to begin construction as early as next week.

"So," Sanders asked, "where's Dawn?"

"Where do you think? Up at the site."

"Another demonstration planned for today?"

"Today and every day."

He could hear the edge in my voice. "Between Emily and Dawn they've put together a regular army of passive resistors."

"I guess so," I said. And then, "Just seems to me it's time to put it to rest. It's a done deal."

Sanders laughed and slapped me on the back. "Don't say that, Willy. Never underestimate the power of a determined woman."

Well, Dawn's a determined woman all right. No one will get an argument from me on that. She told me six months after we lost the baby, six months of mostly moping around feeling sorry for ourselves, that the time had come to commence living and making life again. We set to work that very evening, pledging not to stop until we completed the job.

Let's see, that was March of '93, just about a year ago. No luck yet, but Dawn says all we have to do is keep trying. Fine by me. I'd just as soon lie naked with Dawn as draw breath. Trouble is, all this protesting against the new dam keeps her busy night and day.

August 28, 1994

Dawn and Mama were arrested again yesterday afternoon. They only held them until Pop and I went up to North Creek and posted bail. How many times does that make now? Three? Four? How many more times to come? No way the project will be finished for another year or two. Maybe if things get really out of hand, I'll just leave her in jail; for her own good you understand, I'll refuse to post bail.

At least there was no demonstrating today. Sunday's a day of rest for all concerned. The trucks stop trucking. The dozers stop dozing. The dynamiters stop dynamiting. And the demonstrators, thank God, stop demonstrating.

This morning, after Dawn woke up, we went across the lake and cut some firewood for the cold months ahead. We have a permit to cut dead oak on the government's land along the western shore of the lake. But if things go according to plan, by next spring most of that government land will be MacKenzie land. And just as soon as it becomes MacKenzie land it'll become Mohawk land. We'll keep our fingers crossed it all works out.

If it does work out, maybe Dawn and Mama will quit their demonstrations at the dam site and at the state Capitol Building and at the governor's mansion, and life around here can get back to normal. Last week they sat outside Governor Montgomery's office from sunup till sundown, chanting in Mohawk and demanding he close down the dam project. Finally he had them carted off the premises by the state police. Now I hate that son of a bitch Montgomery as much as the next Tamaqua Valley resident, but I almost can't blame the guy for doing what he did. I mean, how can you get any work done with two women screaming outside your window?

Anyway, it's all confusion and chaos around here, and sometimes I get tired to the bone just thinking about it. I try to keep occupied by working on my book. It's been five months now since I started it. I enjoy working on it, makes me forget, at least for a while, about all this other craziness. Another six months and I should pretty well have it finished. Every month Sanders prints a chapter or two in the American Observer. More than ever now the magazine concentrates its contents on environmental issues. With the planet, its resources, and its atmosphere in such terrible shape, all the other political, economic, and social issues have lost some of their urgency.

Right around the middle of the morning Dawn finally crawled out of bed. She came out yawning and rubbing her eyes.

"Have a good sleep?" I asked.

She stretched her arms up over her head. "I needed a few extra hours."

She crossed the front porch of our house here on the northwestern shore of Tamarack. I sat on the top step, sharpening my ax. She sat beside me and we had a hug.

After a few moments Dawn said, "Let me wash up, get dressed, and throw something together for lunch. Then we can get started."

"No hurry," I told her as she disappeared back into the house.

We took the Gar Runabout across to the western shore of Katydeeray. It was a fine late summer morning, just a little bit cool and perfectly clear. The first faint stirrings of autumn lingered in the air.

We went ashore, and Dawn warmed up her fiddle while I made the first cuts into the trunk of a pretty fair-size white oak. We didn't speak. Just the fiddle, sounding sweet, and the whack, whack, whack of the ax. I stopped after a time to put an edge back on the blade. Even the sharpest edge wears dull with use. It's easy enough to keep an unused ax clean and sharp.

I listened to the bluegrass pouring from Dawn's fiddle as I put grinding stone to steel. The sound of the violin floated through the forest. Black-capped chickadees and tufted titmice broke into song. A scarlet tanager and a plump robin redbreast joined the orchestra. A wilderness concert. A greenwood symphony. The movement rose and fell, then rose again to a resounding crescendo. Even the high-strung gray squirrels stopped to listen. But suddenly, overhead, a red-shouldered hawk appeared, his talons spread, his eyes narrowed. He dived. The singers scrambled for cover. The violin fell off to a whisper, and again, the whack, whack, whack of the ax.

Dawn spread our picnic lunch of cold chicken, fruit, and nuts. We ate, then took a nap on our old handmade cotton quilt. Then, again, with the ax.

Dusk started to settle as I worked my way through one last white oak. Long shadows reached across the lake. Dawn sat at the water's edge, watching and waiting and listening. She had been very quiet and pensive all afternoon, not a word about the dam, hardly a word about anything at all.

I asked her what was on her mind, but she only smiled at me and said, "You, Willy MacKenzie, you are the only thing on my mind."

Exactly what she knew I wanted to hear. But I knew there was something more.

"What else?" I asked.

She thought about it. "The baby."

"Sandra?" I asked, softly.

"No," she answered, "Emily."

"Do you think she'll ever happen?"

"As soon as that tree falls we'll find out."

I took a few more whacks. The trunk began to crack. "Tim-brrr!" I shouted. The oak started to topple. Nothing could stop her now. Nothing . . . I watched for a moment, then cleared out of the way. The forest filled with the thunder of breaking branches. Down through the still evening air the oak fell, almost floated, bewildered yet enraged, falling with incredible force until it collided with the forest floor. Then, not a sound. We listened, for a time, to the silence.

Another day I knew I would return to cut and split the oak. But right then, in the failing light, Dawn and I embraced. The early evening air had turned cool, but not so cold that we could not remove our clothes and lie naked on the cotton quilt.

I kissed her lightly on the face and lips. I moved slowly and gently. Tenderly.

But Dawn wanted none of that. "Now, Willy," she practically shouted. "Now!"

10:36 A.M.
JANUARY 20, 2001
MACKENZIE ISLAND
THE INAUGURATION OF THE FORTY-FOURTH PRESIDENT OF THE UNITED STATES

Let's slow down here and take a look at some of the developments Willy just referred to in that last journal entry. We can begin with a close inspection of our Tamaqua Valley map.

Check the location of Lake Katydeeray, Cedar Bluffs, and MacKenzie Island. South of the lake, along the south branch of the Tamaqua River, you will find a small triangle representing the original site of the Tamaqua Valley Dam. This is where valley residents first demonstrated in the fall of ninety-two and where Dawn tumbled down that embankment and consequently lost her and Willy's first baby.

Because of this tragedy, you will remember, construction on the project was halted. What you might not know is that less than a week later that site was entirely abandoned. But had the dam been built along the south branch of the Tamaqua, water levels above the dam would have risen, as Willy had so often feared during his youth, by as much as one hundred feet. Lake Katydeeray would have doubled in size and depth, and the entire island of Tamarack and all but the highest ground on MacKenzie would have wound up underwater.

Also taken out by the dam would have been the entire town of Seven Points, most of Cedar Bluffs, and a large portion of North Creek. More than six hundred families in the valley would have lost their homes. And let us not forget the Mohawk. Their reservation, lying in the wet lowlands, would have gone the way of Tamarack: completely submerged.

Now, if you shift your eyes to the top portion of the valley map, you will find another triangle along the north branch of the Tamaqua River about three and one half miles above North Creek. This triangle represents the location of the Tamaqua Valley Dam as it exists today. This dam is smaller than the one originally proposed, but it is nevertheless a formidable structure that has changed forever the appearance of the valley above the site.

Below the site, including North Creek, Cedar Bluffs, Lake Katydeeray, and the islands of MacKenzie and Tamarack, things have stayed pretty much the same. Water levels may rise and fall depending upon how much volume the engineers allow to flow through the enormous sluice gates, but all in all life goes on as before.

Well, almost.

The question is: Why, after so many years of study and debate, did the location of the dam suddenly change?

At the time, you may recall, if this particular conflict caught your interest, we were told that a reexamination of the engineering reports indicated a more logical site for the dam existed above North Creek. I will not bring to bear all the technical data heaped upon us for this decision; it's nothing but a lot of double talk and mumbo-jumbo anyway. What is important is that one day the government set out to build a dam in the southern tier of the Tamaqua Valley, and just a few days later they canceled that dam and announced plans to build another dam in the northern tier of the Tamaqua Valley.

The question is, why?

Our president (for another hour or so, anyway), Mr. Anderson Montgomery, was still the governor of the Work and Prosper State at the time the dam site was moved from the south branch of the Tamaqua to the north branch. And as Willy's journals have clearly stated, the governor was the point man for the dam project. He saw the Tamaqua Valley Dam and Development Project as a bright and shining feather in his political cap, as a catalyst for national office. And indeed, he used the project to his advantage during his run for the Oval Office in 1996. He used pictures of the dam in his advertisements to present himself as a man who could get the big jobs done. And just as Conrad MacKenzie had predicted that afternoon in the governor's office way back in May of eighty-seven, candidate Montgomery often appeared on television high above the dam wearing his hard hat at a roguish angle and studying blueprints with the designers and engineers.

And now here is where things turn interesting.

We know, of course, that Conrad MacKenzie opposed construction of the Tamaqua Valley Dam. And I think it would be safe to say his opposition was fueled primarily by the very possible and probably inevitable inundation of MacKenzie Island. We can't really blame the guy for trying to save his land. But what the public has never known until today, until right now, is that Conrad MacKenzie was directly responsible for the Tamaqua Valley Dam being built above North Creek rather than below Lake Katydeeray.

It's true. Let's take a look.

A day or two after his daughter-in-law lost her baby, Conrad went down to the state capital for another meeting with Governor Montgomery. He pretty much barged into the man's office. A rather worn and very scratchy tape recording of their meeting exists. Recently I managed to obtain, through sources who would prefer to remain anonymous, a copy of that tape. I would like to play it for you now. But let me warn you in advance, this recording contains language that may be unsuitable for children.

"Thank you, Sally," we hear Governor Montgomery tell his secretary, "I think Mr. MacKenzie and I have everything we need. Hold my calls."

We hear the door close. Presumably Conrad and Governor Montgomery are alone. Just a second or two of silence before their conversation begins.

MACKENZIE: It's time to settle the score, you son of a bitch.

MONTGOMERY: Conrad, I can't tell you how sorry I am about your granddaughter. It was an accident, pure and simple.

MACKENZIE: You shut down that construction site, Montgomery, and get the hell out of my valley or I swear to God I'll bury your ass. I'll find women who'll claim you raped them, men who'll say you butt-fucked them, little boys and girls who'll cry and whisper you fondled their private parts. Get the hell out my valley or you'll have a tough time getting elected to the litter commission.

MONTGOMERY: I assure you, Conrad, you're coming in loud and clear. But try to understand my predicament here. This project is out of my hands. The feds are involved now, the Army Corps of Engineers. Millions of dollars, tens of millions of dollars, have been allocated to push this thing forward. I don't think I could stop it if I tried.

MACKENZIE: You damn well better try.

MONTGOMERY: (pause) It might take some cash.

MACKENZIE: How much cash?

MONTGOMERY: Difficult to say. A million or more, at least. Although maybe less if we suggest an alternative site. Perhaps somewhere north of MacKenzie Island. Perhaps—

MACKENZIE: Look, asshole, you need money to block this thing, I'll find you some money. But hear me good when I tell you if one goddamn drop of water from your stinking goddamn dam ever gets on my island or on any of the members of my family—

Then, without another word, Conrad is heard slamming his fist on the governor's desk, striding across the room, throwing open the door, and marching out.

We can only imagine what transpired in the days ahead. A new location for the Tamaqua Valley Dam is proof enough that something transpired. Exactly how much money changed hands cannot be verified since MacKenzie family finances have long been a source of mystery. What we do know is that Anderson Montgomery entered the 1996 presidential race with a rather substantial war chest.

* * * * * * *

In April of 1994, construction began on the Tamaqua Valley Dam. And construction proceeded despite the best efforts of Emily and Dawn

MacKenzie to bring it to a halt through their legal maneuvers and their demonstrations. The islands of MacKenzie and Tamarack may have been safe, but the two women nevertheless continued to protest. They insisted the dam would cause terrible and irreversible environmental damage to the northern tier of the valley, and they knew for certain the dam would leave the Mohawk without a home.

The site for the dam might have been moved north, out of harm's way, at least as far as the MacKenzies and most Tamaqua Valley residents were concerned, but it had not been moved far enough north to protect the Mohawk and their reservation. It soon became clear that their farms and villages would be underwater once the dam went into full operation. In the fall of 1994 the Mohawk were given a court order to vacate their reservation within one year. But the question remained: Where would they go?

Two choices had been offered, but both choices demanded relocation one hundred miles or more from the valley. The Mohawk found themselves faced with the same situation their fathers and grandfathers and great-grandfathers had been faced with ever since white men had started landing on the shores of this vast continent.

So they fought back the only way they could: they joined the demonstrations. Some days the entire Mohawk community, along with Dawn and Emily and a few other valley residents, picketed the construction site. And occasionally, if the day's news was slow, one of the local TV stations would send a reporter and a camera crew out to film the protesters. But for the most part they demonstrated out of the public's eye, beyond the public's awareness.

By the early months of 1995, with Dawn's second pregnancy beginning to show and with construction all but stopped because of ice and winter weather, the demonstrators shifted their cause to the state house and the governor's mansion. Dawn and Emily would occasionally even spend the night in the capital if events ran overtime or if they had something planned for early the following morning.

Willy, it seems, did not wholeheartedly support his wife's efforts. He wanted her home and at his side. During this time he was essentially a man torn between his own self-interests and the well-being of others. Fully aware of his Indian blood, he occasionally joined his wife and mother on the picket line. But he preferred to wage his battles with his fountain pen from the comfort of his study, whereas his wife favored direct participation in the process.

At home, Dawn's zealous quest to halt the construction project proved a constant source of conflict for the normally happy couple. Especially as her pregnancy progressed.

"Don't you think you should stay home and rest?" Willy asked more than once. "You're almost six months pregnant and it's below freezing outside."

"I'll stay home and rest," Dawn replied, "when we get this project completely shut down and canceled."

"What if you can't get it shut down? What if you can't get it canceled? What if they finish the project? What if the dam opens? Then what, Dawn? Then what?"

Dawn pulled on her fur-lined boots and down parka and headed for the door. "It won't open, Willy. Do you hear me? It'll never open. Never."

"But what if it does?"

"It won't," she insisted. "It can't. I won't let it."

"Leave her be," advised Conrad. "If it was you out there protesting, you wouldn't want her telling you not to do it. Just let her be, boy. It's the only way."

"But you can't be happy with Mama out there day after day."

"I might not be happy about it, but I know she has to help her people. Your mother's a strong, stubborn, independent woman. A lot like your wife. Telling them not to do something just gives them more incentive to keep doing it."

Willy frowned, nodded, settled back in his chair, and sipped his coffee.

It was the middle of April 1995. Spring had once again returned to the valley.

"Besides," said Conrad, "that small land sale we've been working on looks like it could happen any day now."

"You've heard some news?"

"Yup. And I think it's pretty much a done deal."

That small land sale amounted to some twenty-five hundred acres, which, it has been speculated, Conrad paid five hundred bucks an acre for, or a tidy sum of one point two-five million dollars.

"And do you think," Willy asked, "the Mohawk will live on that land?"

"They'd be crazy not to," answered Conrad. "It's prime real estate. Much prettier and more fertile than that swamp they're living in now."

In early June of ninety-five, the day after Willy's twenty-seventh birthday, Dawn gave birth without complications. As planned, they named the baby Emily after Willy's mother. Dawn had, by necessity, slowed down considerably during the last month of her pregnancy. And after Emily's arrival, she slowed practically to a stop. Little Emily made her mother forget all about the Tamaqua River Valley Dam and Development Project. Dawn spent that summer and fall out on the islands, rocking and nursing and loving her baby.

Willy alternately thanked God and the Great Spirit for the safe return of his wife and the healthy birth of his daughter. He could hardly believe his great good fortune.

Emily proved an even earlier riser than her papa. She often rose before the sun showed itself above the eastern peaks of the Blue Mountains. Willy would lift the tiny baby into his arms and rock her out on the front porch while Dawn caught up on her sleep. In the aftenoon Willy would work with Sanders and Alice on the latest edition of the *American Observer*. Another presidential race was already beginning to heat up, and they wanted to make sure the environment was near the top of every candidate's agenda.

And late at night, after his wife and daughter had gone up to bed, Willy would work on his manuscript. By this time he had finished the first draft of *Full Moon Over Katydeeray*, but he had gone back to revise and edit. A perfectionist about his prose, he wanted to make sure he had every word just the way he wanted it.

In early October Willy stuffed a copy of the completed manuscript into a large manila envelope, crossed his fingers, and mailed it to an old friend of Alice's who worked as a literary agent down in Manhattan. Sanders and Alice and Dawn and Conrad and Emily and several other valley residents had read the manuscript. They all agreed it would be a big success.

And believe it or not, Alice's old friend, Beatrice Quincy, thought so too. She called Willy on the telephone the second she finished reading the manuscript. "It's funny and creative and profound, and full of useful information. And it reads like a dream. If I can't sell this one, Willy MacKenzie, even with the book market in the worst shape it's been in for twenty years, I'll quit my job, give up my rent-controlled apartment in the East Eighties, and move to Buffalo."

Ms. Beatrice Quincy, Queenie to her friends, made eight copies of the manuscript and sent them all over town to some of her favorite nonfiction editors. All but one expressed interest after reading just a few chapters.

Queenie called Willy. "We'll have to hold an auction. Any trouble with that?"

"No," said Willy, who couldn't quite believe everything was happening so fast. He had expected to wait months, maybe a year or more, to hear any positive news. "Just sell it to someone who really likes it a lot."

"Good Lord," shouted Queenie, "an innocent! This might even be fun."

The auction reached six figures before the winner called in the final bid. Willy received a one-hundred-and-twenty-five-thousand-dollar advance, plus a guaranteed advertising budget of another fifty grand, plus a nationwide, ten-city publicity tour.

Queenie called Willy with the news. He was very excited but said, "I'm not so sure about the tour. I don't very often leave the valley."

"Don't worry yourself about that just now," said Queenie. "The book won't be published until next fall. Between now and then we'll work out all the details."

10:49 A.M.
JANUARY 20, 2001
MACKENZIE ISLAND
THE INAUGURATION OF THE FORTY-FOURTH PRESIDENT OF THE UNITED STATES

Ah yes, the details. How quickly the details can slip away. How quickly our perfect little worlds can fall apart.

From here on out, folks, unless proper communications are restored, it looks like we're on our own. That last bit about Willy's book contract marks the end of the preproduction profiles relating to the president-elect and the other members of the MacKenzie clan. We already had that piece in the can when the incoming audio-video suddenly went dead on us about forty-five minutes ago. But since our signal still appears to be transmitting, I think we should press on, carry this broadcast to its logical conclusion. So sit back and relax. I know the rest of this story as well as any man alive. . . .

The winter and spring of 1996 were undoubtedly some of the happiest times of Willy's life. His wife was back from the protest trail. His baby was strong and growing by leaps and bounds. His book was sailing through the publishing process. His precious islands were safe and secure. The land sale had gone through, and the Mohawk had a new and better home just across the lake on Katydeeray's western shore. The *American Observer* had achieved a secure and prominent place among the nation's more influential periodicals. Life up in the Blue Mountains was pretty close to swell.

But then, inevitably, the good times began to slip away.

In the early summer of 1996 Dawn renewed her protests against the Tamaqua Valley Dam and Development Project. The move coincided with the release of an independent study that indicated two or three species of fish would be threatened by the new dam. The spawning habits of two types of trout and the landlocked Atlantic salmon, the study claimed, would be drastically altered, resulting in mass deaths and even extinction for one of the species of trout.

This news brought a wave of national publicity, but the coverage proved short-lived what with the economy in ruins, the federal government teetering on the brink of bankruptcy, and the vast majority of people primarily worried about their own financial extinction.

But the study infuriated Dawn. And so soon after Emily's first birthday, she left Willy in charge of the baby and headed back to the now nearly finished Tamaqua Valley Dam. Her motives for this have been a steady source of discourse. Most pundits have pointed to this study about the fish, but personally, I don't buy it. I think Dawn needed to prove herself. For so long she had vowed to close down the project, to keep the dam from opening. Suddenly it looked as though she would fail.

Yes, more than forty families were still being displaced by the dam, and Dawn no doubt protested in their behalf. And certainly she had strong feelings about those fish and about the thousands of acres that would be laid to waste as the water levels rose. Nevertheless, she must have known her efforts would be in vain. Virtually everyone else involved in the protests, including her mother-in-law, had backed off, accepted the Tamaqua Valley Dam and Development Project into their lives.

I know this is pure speculation on my part, but perhaps Dawn's desire to jump back into the fray had more to do with her competitive relationship with Willy than with any profound need to halt a multimillion-dollar water project. Perhaps Willy's success as a writer caused in Dawn a feeling of inferiority. Perhaps she began protesting again to show that she too could do important and useful things.

Whatever her motives, throughout the summer of ninety-six Dawn demonstrated. And more often than not, she demonstrated alone. Hour after hour, day after day, she stood at the edge of the construction site up on the north branch of the Tamaqua River, holding up various signs in opposition to the dam and to Governor Montgomery, who was by then in the midst of a rough-and-tumble dogfight for his party's presidential nomination.

When a reporter ventured out to the site to have a word with her, Dawn inevitably offered up the same spiel. "This dam never should've been built," she said, her voice rising. "This dam serves no one except the petty and corrupt political ambitions of one man: Governor Anderson Montgomery! I stand here in protest because I was taught America is a democracy. I stand here to preserve my democratic principles and my democratic rights. Every time we give an inch to these greedy, selfish, power-hungry politicians who wish to control us, we lose a yard of our liberty and a mile of our self-esteem."

It sounded good, and it played well both in print and on the tube, but for most Americans it was just more pop entertainment. We got a mild charge out of watching this lovely but nearly hysterical young lady bad-mouth the hotshot governor with the blow-dry haircut who wanted more than anything in the world to be the next president of the United States.

And by the middle of that summer, Governor Montgomery had indeed moved a little closer to 1600 Pennsylvania Avenue. At his party's political convention, after a lengthy and bitter floor fight, he won the nomination to run for president in the November elections.

One of his first public appearances after the convention was at the formal opening of the Tamaqua River Valley Dam and Development Project. The ceremony was set for Saturday, September 7, 1996. Governor Montgomery was scheduled to deliver a few remarks, then open the sluice gates of the new dam, allowing the first cascade of water to roar over the edge.

Just two days before the ceremony, Thursday the fifth, the candidate's advance team rolled into the valley. They drove out to the dam site, and do you know what they found? They found Ms. MacKenzie dressed as the Grim Reaper and holding up a large sign that read ANDERSON MONTGOMERY: SNAKE, LIAR, LAND PLUNDERER, MURDERER.

Those boys practically peed in their pants, then they collected themselves and swung into action. By evening they had taken care of Dawn

Tyler MacKenzie. They ordered the state police to arrest her for trespassing and for inciting a riot. By dusk they had Dawn safely stowed away in the North Creek jail.

Up until that day Willy MacKenzie's life had been pretty much a carefree romp. Sure, there had been, as we have seen, a few rough spots, but all in all a fairly smooth ride.

Everything was about to change.

September 6, 1996
North Creek Jail

Yesterday they arrested Dawn for interfering with the grand opening of the Tamaqua Valley Dam. They brought her here to the North Creek jail, where Pop and I spent most of the night trying to get her released. Finally, close to midnight, I convinced Judge Stuart to let me take Dawn's place.

"We have a one-year-old daughter," I told the judge.

"Yes," said Judge Stuart, "I know. How is Emily?"

"She's fine. But she needs her mother."

"All right," he said, "I'll let her go, but only if you promise me she'll behave herself."

"I promise, Judge."

"As you well know, Willy, Governor Montgomery is coming to the valley on Saturday, and he called me personally to make sure we had this situation under control."

"No problem, Judge," I said with all the surety I could muster. "She'll behave."

So now I'm in and Dawn's out, and I really don't have any idea what she might do. I should've left her in here, at least until after this sleazeball Montgomery skips town, but she begged me to help her get released.

"I just want to see Emily," she kept insisting. "I don't even plan to go to the demonstration on Saturday. I couldn't care less."

That I found hard to believe. But it's a done deal now.

The demonstration is planned for tomorrow afternoon out at the dam site. Montgomery will be there to put the whole business into operation. I don't know, Dawn says she won't go, but sitting here now, I feel pretty damn stupid. I should've left her here in this cell to cool her heels.

Oh, well. Water over the dam, so to speak. Judge Stuart said he'll probably let me out tomorrow at noon anyway, so I'll just have to keep an eye on her.

I guess the good news is that in a few days the whole thing will be over. The dam will open and the construction workers will go home, and if we're lucky, maybe Dawn will come home too.

And then early next month the book comes out. That should be pretty exciting. I mean, it's not every day your first book hits the bookstores. Already, because of the advance publicity, I'm receiving letters and telegrams from people around the country who want me to come and address their nature clubs and environmental groups and Audubon societies. Even the mayor of New York City sent me a letter. It seems some rare owl has been sighted in Central Park and he'd like me to come down there and verify the sighting. Probably I'll go, if Dawn'll come. My agent thinks I should do it. Good publicity and all that. But that's a ways off. First let's get through this weekend.

September 9, 1996
Tamarack

I'm going to do this. I don't care if it kills me; I'm going to get this down. I need to get this out....

Sheriff Young swung open the jailhouse door just before noon on Saturday. "Judge Stuart called and said to let you go, Willy. You're a free man."

I thanked the sheriff and went out into the bright, late summer afternoon. Before I could take a deep breath, some TV reporter stuck his microphone in my face. "So, Willy," he said to me as if we were old chums, "today's the big day. We hear your wife's got some fireworks planned. Care to comment?"

I scowled at him. But at the same time I felt something like fear scurry down my spine. "What are you talking about? Who even mentioned my wife to you?"

He shrugged and looked bored. "Hey, listen, what do I know? Probably just talk filtering through the grapevine."

I pushed him aside and walked out into the street. A steady stream of traffic poured north out of town, all headed for the Big Event up at the dam. A limousine passed, its headlights flashing. Through the darkened windows I saw Governor Anderson Montgomery smiling and waving. To whom? The guy might win every single town across America in his presidential bid, but no way will he win even one vote here in the valley. I was surprised he had the gall to even show his face around these parts.

Henry Bender pulled up beside me in his pickup. "Hey, Willy, you're out of the slammer."

I smiled and nodded and climbed into the pickup. "Seen Dawn?"

"Last night."

"She say anything?"

"Just that she might or might not come to the demonstration today."

I shrugged.

We worked our way through the traffic. But about a mile south of the dam the traffic slowed to a crawl and then to a complete stop, so we pulled onto the shoulder and started walking.

"Never seen a crowd this size in the valley before," said Henry.

I nodded but said nothing. I felt like I had a grapefruit stuck in my throat and another one stuck in my chest and another one stuck in my gut. I didn't know exactly why, but I was as tense as a band of steel, as if I were plugged into an electrical outlet.

We left the highway and followed the crowd down a narrow, dusty road. The whole damn valley's dusty. It's been one hot, dry, dusty summer. Hottest, driest, dustiest goddamn summer of my entire fucking life.

After walking for about a quarter of a mile, we came into a wide clearing. The new dam loomed dead ahead behind a high, chain-link fence. Above the dam, the north branch of the Tamaqua had slowly begun to inundate the upper valley.

The crowd split into opposing teams. Their team had come to celebrate the completion of the dam and to toast its grand opening. Our team had come to protest the dam and to demonstrate against the dam's most ardent supporter, Governor Anderson Montgomery.

I saw Montgomery in the distance, the presidential candidate surrounded by peons and Secret Service agents. He stood atop the enormous reinforced concrete wall that had been built to hold back the river. Montgomery fingered a microphone, ready as always to deliver his well-rehearsed rhetoric.

"Willy! Willy, over here!"

I turned and saw my family: Mama and Pop and Sanders and Alice and little Emily sleeping in Mama's arms and Dawn's mother and father and . . . Wait a second.

"Where's Dawn?"

"What?" They all looked puzzled.

"Where," I repeated, "is Dawn?"

"She told us she was going to North Creek to get you. That was hours ago."

A moment of silence fell over us.

Instantly that silence was filled with the booming and amplified voice of Governor Anderson Montgomery. "Ladies and gentlemen, thanks for coming out! Today is a great day! A great day for this valley and this state and this country!"

Cheers and boos rose out of the crowd.

The grapefruits in my throat, chest, and gut grew larger. I could hardly breathe or swallow.

"The Tamaqua Valley Dam," shouted Montgomery, "is grand proof that America can still overcome obstacles and achieve great things!"

"But," said Alice, speaking for all of us, "if she's not with you and she's not with us . . ."

Someone tapped me on the shoulder. I swung around.

"Willy MacKenzie?"

"That's right."

"Jack Steel. ANN."

"ANN?"

"American Network News."

"Yeah? So?"

"There's something you should know."

"To succeed and prosper!" exclaimed the governor, his voice echoing off the distant hills. "To succeed and prosper we need to work together to pursue the common good!"

I turned to this guy Steel. "Look, pal, why don't you back off? I don't have time for your bullshit right now."

"But Mr. MacKenzie," he shouted above Montgomery's blabber, "it's about your wife!"

"My wife! What about my wife?!"

And Montgomery, "This dam is a perfect example of what we can accomplish if we set our hearts and minds to it. And so now, without further ado, I open these sluice gates with pride, and with the full knowledge that discipline, hard work, and determination will always win the day."

"What about my wife?!" I shouted again.

But Montgomery pulled all the right levers and pushed all the right buttons, and those enormous electric sluice gates began to open. The captive waters of the Tamaqua rushed forward. A deafening roar filled the quiet, afternoon air. Everyone turned to watch the tremendous spumes of water cascade over the dam and into the waiting river far below.

I pounded Steel on the chest. "Goddammit!" I shouted into his ear. "What about my wife?!"

He answered but that thunder of water stole his words away.

I shook my head, so he cupped his hands, put his cup around my ear, and shouted, "You'd better follow me, Willy! Now!"

So I did.

At first we walked through the crowd. Then we began to jog. Finally we broke into a run. I pushed friends and enemies aside.

Soon we reached the chain-link fence bordering the dam and overlooking the river a hundred and fifty feet or more below.

Steel pointed.

I followed his finger through the fence and out across the open void. I saw nothing but the river, shallow but rising, and some boulders protruding off the bottom.

"What?" I shouted above the roar. "What is it?!"

He continued to point. "There! Look!"

I squinted, shaded my eyes from the bright sun directly overhead. I struggled to focus. . . . Wait . . . it couldn't be. . . . Impossible. . . . I turned to Steel. "Is it?"

He nodded.

I did not hesitate for a second. I threw myself against the chain-link fence and started to climb. But just as I reached the top, a hand reached up and grabbed my ankle. At first I thought it was Steel, but when I looked down I stared straight into the eyes of an armed security guard. I kicked him as hard as I could full in the face. He released my ankle and grabbed his head. I scrambled over the fence, landing in a heap on the rocky ground beside the dam.

The rush and roar of water made my head spin. I felt dizzy, disoriented. . . .

I shook it loose and sprinted the length of that chain-link fence. At the end of the fence the earth just dropped away, a virtual cliff of clay and stone left ungraded in the all-out effort to finish the dam in time for the governor's run for the White House.

That slimy son of a bitch. He'll pay for this. He'll pay with his life....

I took another look at the river far below. For certain now I knew it was she.

I should have known she might try something insane. I should have left her in jail, safe and sound behind bars....

I checked the river. The water was fast rising.

I attacked the cliff head on. I slipped and slid and slammed my body against the jagged rocks. My knees and elbows began to bleed. But I kept moving, practically rolling, head over heels, a virtual human landslide down that precipitous slope.

While far below, the river continued its steady, incessant rise. And high above, the towering man-made waterfall sent wild and I thought angry plumes of water rushing over its side.

And then I saw her clearly, anchored, or so it seemed, against the watery onslaught by holding firm to a large and very smooth bluish gray boulder.

But why! Why! What did she think she was doing?!

Hold on, Willy. Settle down. Calm yourself....

The water kept rising. Rising! Rising! Terrifying hallucinations raced through my mind ... while I kept rolling downhill, a human cannonball!

The Tamaqua River suddenly looked surreal, like something from a bad dream, from a horrible and endless nightmare. For a second or two I felt pretty sure the whole thing was happening nowhere but inside my head.

"Dawn! Dawn! Dawn!" I shouted, but that wild rush of water snatched away my words and spit them into the stratosphere. Even to me my voice sounded hollow and very far away.

Finally, bloody and bruised, I reached the riverbank. I dived straight into the swirl of water. The current grabbed my body and swept me downstream. I did not struggle against it, for I felt certain it would lead me to Dawn.

But would I be there in time? Would I be too late?

Smooth and massive boulders protruded out of the fast-rising water. I floated past without injury. I saw each stone clearly and unemotionally. But then— Look: what has she done? My God!

Fuck God!

I grabbed hold of her anchor. The water had risen and covered everything below her neck.

"Why?!" I shouted above the water's terror. "Why?!"

She tried to answer but the swollen river rushed past her mouth.

The current worked to sweep me away. I barely hung on to the massive boulder that had taken her prisoner. Or had she taken it prisoner? Either way, their fates were clearly linked by a length of heavy-duty steel anchor chain.

Yes: Dawn, my friend, my lover, my wife, the mother of my child, had chained herself to a rock in the middle of that raging and untamed river. And the waters kept rising!

"I thought I could stop them," she managed to tell me. "I wanted to stop them, Willy. You know I wanted to stop them. I needed to stop them." She paused a moment for air, and then her eyes rolled to the side. "And I had help."

I turned my head to follow her eyes and saw a most unbelievable sight. Over on the far bank of the river a man stood with his TV camera balanced on his shoulder. He was busy capturing all the action.

"I thought," Dawn said with difficulty, "when Montgomery and the others learned I was down here, chained to this rock, they would stop the ceremony, postpone the opening. I thought—" But rising water rushed into her mouth, forcing her to grow silent.

I wondered for just a moment why she had waited until the sluice gates had opened before making her presence known. And then I wondered about that journalist—what was his name?—Steel, who had found me in the crowd. And I wondered about that cameraman on the riverbank....

And now, two mournful days later, I continue to wonder....

But I had little time to wonder then. Reality kept rising. I held my breath and dived. I grappled with that anchor chain. She had it wrapped securely around that boulder. And a brand-new, heavy-duty steel lock bound together the two ends of the chain. I surfaced.

"Where is the key, Dawn!? Where is the key to the lock?"

I had to take her a breath of air before she could answer.

"In my ... my poc ... my pocket."

I dived and thrust my hands into the pockets of her shorts. I searched through every pocket three, four, five times. I found nothing but a small silver spoon she uses to feed Emily.

I surfaced, caught some air, then dived again to search the river bottom for that damn key. Mud and sand. Rocks and water. Too much damn water.

I found nothing. My lungs exploding, I frantically tried to pull the chain away from the boulder. No good. I rushed to the surface.

The river had risen now up and over her mouth. I took her a breath of air. She accepted it with a smile.

Between breaths I hollered and waved frantically at the cameraman. Couldn't he comprehend the severity of our situation? Or did he simply not give a damn? Did he care more about capturing Dawn's desperation on videotape?

I do not know, but finally he abandoned his camera and headed for somewhere, for anywhere.

For help, I prayed.

"I love you, Dawn!"

But she could no longer hear me. The water had risen over her ears. I took her breath, filled her lungs.

Our eyes met. Even underwater tears poured down our cheeks. I kept telling myself this was impossible, no way could this be happening. We were home, on the islands, happy and safe and tickling Emily in the ribs.

That's all I wanted: to see my baby smiling in my wife's arms. That's all I wanted. That's all I want. To hell with all the rest of it....

Fool and stupid bloody idiot that I am, I loosened my grip on the anchor chain and reached up to touch Dawn's face with my fingertips. A gentle touch has always made her feel better, calmer. But this time my touch lasted only an instant. The current tore at my arm and swept me away.

Dammit to hell! I should have hung on to that chain. Why did I let go of that chain?...

The river sucked me violently downstream. I slammed into a rock but felt not even a twinge of pain. I felt separated from my body. Perhaps Dawn felt the same....

Am I to die also? I hope so. Or am I destined to survive this Deluge? Is this just the beginning of my suffering? I think about this now, and I thought about this then. It seems almost funny that I would have had time to ask myself these questions. And also to remind myself that I was a useless and impotent piece of protoplasm, a wet and worthless piece of shit....

Time passed. I fought my way to the riverbank. I waded ashore. I sprinted back upriver to where Dawn lay trapped beneath the surface. People ran toward us now from all directions. And high overhead I saw that powerful and deadly stream of water had finally ceased rushing through those sluice gates, over that reinforced concrete wall. The valley was once more silent as I dived back into the river.

In no time at all I was at her side. I took a deep breath and slipped below the surface.

But too late. She floated in a state of dreams, angelic and asleep. She had no more need for air, no more needs at all.

I watched her for a long time. She watched me, too, until I reached up and gently closed her eyes.

She looked perfectly beautiful, perfectly serene. I pressed my face against her cheek until I realized we both had other worlds to conquer.

Then I kissed her blue lips and floated away—far, far away. . . .

11:03 A.M.
JANUARY 20, 2001
MACKENZIE ISLAND
THE INAUGURATION OF THE FORTY-FOURTH PRESIDENT OF THE UNITED STATES

Powerful, touching, emotional stuff.

I am amazed Willy had the presence of mind to capture the essence of that tragic event just two days after it took place. Further evidence, I suppose, that writing has always been a potent catharsis for our president-elect.

As Willy indicated, I was there. I bore witness. Although, I must admit, I arrived late on the scene after being restrained by that security guard posted at the chain-link fence. But I saw Willy in the water. And I saw his brother and Henry Bender go into the water and haul him out. I saw Conrad and James Tyler wade into that swollen river with a pair of steel cutters as long as my legs. I saw them cut Dawn loose from that chain and bring her lifeless body ashore.

Willy wrote about her death on the ninth of September, and the following day, at dawn on the tenth, they buried Dawn on Tamarack Island right beside her grandfather Joshua. Most of the valley showed up for the funeral. Quite a few outsiders as well. I was there, and I can tell you this: Not a single dry eye could be found on that entire island.

Willy cried, but more than anything else he seemed lost in a state of shock. I tried talking to him, but he didn't hear a word I said. I could just as well have been talking to a ghost. His face looked sad and angry and crazy and confused all at once.

I have seen enough horrors to know that I looked into the eyes of a man who had some very tough times ahead. Dawn's sudden departure, and the terrible circumstances surrounding her demise, had scrambled Willy's psyche, pushed him into a place he probably never thought he would have to visit. I had the impression he would need some time, a month or more, at least, over at the local psychiatric hospital. Little did I know the whole country would soon become Willy MacKenzie's bughouse.

Yes, just two days after the fact, Willy had enough control to describe the terrible events surrounding his wife's death. But that control soon waned. The shock, you might say, wore off, and the reality of the situation quickly began to wear him down and drive him crazy.

* * * * * *

September 12, 1996
Tamarack

Dawn: the arrival of day, or the departure of night? Or: Where have you gone, sweetheart, and how do I struggle on through this meaningless wasteland some fools call life?

Let Willy think. Willy, yes, that's me.... Where should I begin this requiem, this eulogy for the person I loved and even liked? At the beginning? But how can I? Beginnings do not, cannot, exist in a round universe. Beginnings are merely moments manufactured by our minds to reduce the pain of a past gone sour. Like Genesis: God created woman in Her image, and God gave woman man, and God said all creatures on this earth will live equally under the Laws of Nature.... But before, during, and after the Illusion of Genesis, a giant space shovel from planet Spiros swooped down and covered this crazy earth with red clay. Eons passed and still pass.... A couple crawls out from beneath the clay. They seek food, and stimulation for their genitals. In time they learn to kill, forage, and fuck—the nucleus of life on earth.... The Nucleus. The Center. The Conception. The Birth. And ah, yes, the Beginning.

Perhaps I seek a new beginning. Perhaps I <u>must</u> seek a new beginning. After all, Dawn is dead. They killed her during our struggle to save the islands, to save the river, to save the world, our world. She was my wife and my friend. It has been years, many years, since I have had to pass even one full day without her.

But now, suddenly, she is gone forever. Nothing but a memory to those of us who knew her and loved her. Dawn is another victim of this corrupt and overly politicized technological age. One day, friends and neighbors, we will all be victims. Unless, of course, we are first swept into the sea, into the great black abyss where we will either perish or grow gills and slowly lose the power to use our thumbs. Beneath the sea I doubt our brains will be able to do much damage.

Yes, Dawn is dead. We buried her yesterday. Or was it the day before yesterday? What, in the scheme of things, does a day matter anyway?

Near the end I heard her heart beat. It sounded to me like golden trumpets hailing forth a new and far more promising age. What another fool was I. There is no new age, just the same old crap over and over and over again.

For some pathetic reason I live on. Maybe it is a curse for terrible things I have done in past lives, a kind of eternal punishment. Surely it will be hell on earth to get through even a single night without the hope of Dawn. . . .

11:09 A.M.
JANUARY 20, 2001
MACKENZIE ISLAND
THE INAUGURATION OF THE FORTY-FOURTH PRESIDENT OF THE UNITED STATES

Even as Willy slipped over the edge, the great rotation of the planet persisted. On the other side of the Blue Mountains, over in the state capital, the candidate for president of the United States, Anderson Johnson Montgomery, never missed a beat. Monty had no time for tears. The governor, wily and ambitious pol that he was, managed to turn a possible campaign disaster into a political bonanza. In a hastily called press conference in response to nationwide outrage that he might have been somehow indirectly responsible for the tragic death of Dawn Tyler MacKenzie, Monty gave one of his most inspired public performances. Many critics have likened the performance to Dick Nixon's famous Checkers speech.

He called Dawn Tyler MacKenzie "a true and vital champion of democracy." He said she had "democratic spunk" and that she was "the kind of woman I want in my administration, in the very highest levels of my cabinet." His voice cracked and his eyes misted over as he talked about "that terrible, terrible accident on the Tamaqua River." He clenched his hands together and held them out for the whole nation to see.

And then, in that smooth, controlled voice of his that makes us want to believe him, he added, "Tragedies like this can bring us strength, draw us together. In two hundred and twenty-five years as a nation, we have faced countless dangers and adversities. But always, in the end, we have prevailed by pulling together. And so we must now. We must not allow Dawn to die in vain. Let us mourn her passing, and then let us use her memory to make us whole again, whole and strong and healthy."

And the very next day, you might remember, the governor took a dramatic jump in the polls. The American people had bought Monty's act lock, stock, and pork barrel. The man was on a collision course with the Oval Office.

A few days later, Henry Bender invited Willy over to his house and showed him a video of Governor Montgomery's speech. Rumor has it that Willy watched with no expression at all on his face, but when the tape ended he stood up and kicked a huge hole in Henry's TV screen, then mumbled, "I'll kill that stinking son of a bitch. I'll kill him dead."

Dawn's death, and the videotape of Dawn drowning and Willy frantically trying to save her life (which, by the way, aired from coast to coast on the morning and evening news shows for nearly two weeks), did wonders for the sale of Willy's book. The first printing of fifty thousand copies sold out even before the book hit the bookstores. The publisher took out full-page ads in newspapers and magazines all across the country. Reviews of the book sprang up everywhere: in print, on radio, and on the tube. Requests poured into his publisher's office for appearances, interviews, and exclusive photo shoots of the author.

Willy, however, was in no mood to meet the public. The young man could barely crawl out of bed in the morning. His once joyous nature had turned sad and solemn. If he spoke at all, it was usually only to mutter some inane gibberish that even his mother and father could not comprehend. Emily had taken over full-time care of her granddaughter, but all efforts to move Willy back to the Great House on MacKenzie failed. He preferred to wander alone through the house he and Dawn had built on Tamarack. Emily and Sandra and Alice stopped by every day with food, but they had begun to worry what would happen once winter arrived.

"He'll be fine," insisted Conrad. "Leave him be. MacKenzies are tough, resilient. I feel sure he'll work this out. Maybe he'll pass a winter or two on Tamarack. He's always wanted to winter on the islands. Maybe now he will."

But the women did not listen to Conrad's advice. They began a campaign, almost a siege, to get Willy out of the house on Tamarack. They enlisted Sanders and James and Henry Bender in their cause. Every single day, two and three times a day, for nearly six weeks, from the middle of September until the end of October, they visited Willy alone and in small groups. They entertained him with tales of fun and good times traveling around the country, meeting new people, signing copies of his books, being interviewed on TV and radio, seeing places he had never seen before.

At first Willy barely acknowledged their presence. He just sat there and stared out the window at the lake. At times tears would unexpectedly pour down his cheeks.

But his family persisted. They painted vivid mental pictures of a world out there Willy could take by storm. And slowly, very slowly, Willy began to come around. He spoke to his agent, Beatrice Quincy, on the telephone. Queenie told him the book was literally flying out of the bookstores, "and everyone," she said, "just everyone wants to meet you."

Finally, reluctantly, his brain splitting into a million pieces, Willy agreed to go.

On the morning of October 31, 1996, All Hallows' Day, family and friends put him on the southbound train to New York City and wished him Godspeed.

And now, before we examine Willy's journey through Willy's eyes, I will simply ask you to prepare yourself. An air of madness wafts through many of the following passages.

October 31, 1996
New York City

I tried to nap but awoke soon after dusk from a terrible, murderous dream to the sound of kazoos, Jew's harps, and harmonicas tooting, twanging, and humming on the street below. From the dusty window of my third-floor hotel room, I peered through the early evening light. The players with their tinny ten-cent noisemakers called forth a wild assortment of pale and listless men, women, and children. Their army stretched for blocks along the wide boulevard.

A few of the soldiers wore the fashionable garb found only in the finest department store display windows. Others marched in full uniform: faded denim jeans and bright white T-shirts emblazoned with their favorite slogans: SAVE THE WHALES, SAVE THE RAIN FORESTS, SAVE THE DAY. Or that last one may have said: SEIZE THE DAY. It was hard to tell from here. Especially since my eyes only focus lately on the things they want to see.

Still others in that mostly unarmed force came as themselves: as witches and warlocks, as ghouls and goblins and ghosts, as pimps and prostitutes, as baseball players and ballerinas, as businessmen and businesswomen. There was a wizard in the crowd and more than one person wearing a rubber mask bearing an uncanny resemblance to Anderson Montgomery, the man many political prophets claim will be our next president by the time the polls close on Election Day this coming Tuesday.

As the army shuffled through the airless corridors of this foul metropolis, muddy puddles of perspiration formed at their feet. They moved so slowly that finally they did not move at all: pedestrian gridlock. But then a man who looked exactly like ex-President Richard M. Nixon stepped forward to assume command. He raised his arms high over his head, shook his jowls, and offered the international symbol of peace and victory.

And the troops chanted, "Four more years! Four more years!"

Four more years of what? I wondered as the army began to march again, this time around the corner and out of sight....

Across and down the boulevard the bells of a cathedral rang in a new hour. I listened and counted as the tolling continued, but my concentration faded long before time could become a fixed and coherent value.

I fell back upon my damp and musty mattress. And once again I conjured up the final act of that terrible, murderous dream: Dawn and the waters of the Tamaqua River rising, rising, rising up and over her head ... No, no, no!!!

I sprang to my feet. I had to forget that damn dream. That dream could only lead to madness. So I scurried about the room for pants, shirt, and shoes. Down the rickety elevator and through the front door I flew, to forget the facts I have been trying unsuccessfully to turn into fiction.

Through these dangerous corridors I roamed, thinking of the snowy owl and wondering why such a wild, cautious, cold-weather creature would come to this slum of misery and oppression. Of course, I wondered the same about myself.

But then my curiosity acted upon my brain like a hallucination—nothing but a temporary, subordinate illusion to ease oneself in and out of reality. Ah, yes, reality. I stepped off the curb into the waiting limousine.

And whisked away to the cool, gray office of the mayor. I stood and stared at a reproduction of Mr. John Trumbull's <u>The Declaration of Independence</u> when the mayor himself entered the room from a low, narrow door behind his desk. A short, thin, balding politician with a bad complexion, purplish lips, and dishonest eyes, I could not help but wonder if the man had ever been rendered helpless by coitus.

His Honor crossed the plush crimson carpet and shook my hand with great fanfare. "Welcome, Mr. MacKenzie, to the greatest and most exciting city in the world. I'm glad you could find the time to accept my invitation."

"Call me Willy, Mayor."

"Okay, Willy," he said, "call me Mayor." He reached out, put his hand on my shoulder, and led me across the office to a large window overlooking a small park. Soda bottles and beer cans and candy wrappers littered the small patch of brown turf. A homeless man in tattered clothes and soleless shoes rummaged through the refuse. I thought how easily that man could be me.

The mayor saw me frowning at the scene. He thought I was uncomfortable with the litter and the condition of humanity in this bastion of Western civilization. "The dupes at Sanitation," he explained, "are out on strike again. Same old roll call: more money, better benefits, less hours."

"Right," was all I could think to say.

The mayor walked me back to the center of the office. "So, Willy, tell me, how was your trip? I understand you came by train. Everything satisfactory? How's things up in the Blue Mountains?"

Rat-a-tat-tat. My thoughts reeled: They told me to go. Family and friends—they said it would do me good to get away for a while, see some of the country, meet some new people. So I agreed and they arranged my itinerary: book signings and interviews and bullshit like this with assholes like him.

My thoughts spun back. I found the mayor with his hand on my shoulder. "You okay, Willy? You look a little peaked."

I brushed his hand away. "Ease off, Mayor."

"Hey, Willy, what's the problem?"

"You tell me, Mayor. What's this meeting all about?"

"What do you mean, Willy?"

"You know exactly what I mean, Mayor. You invite me down here to observe and to identify this snowy owl even though there are a couple dozen excellent ornithologists between here and the Blue Mountains with the qualifications to do the job. So why don't you just clue me in on your motives. I figure you must be trying to capitalize on all the publicity that has surrounded me these last few months because of my wife Dawn's death and because of the publication of my book, Full Fucking Moon over the Universe."

The mayor frowned. "That's not the title of your book, Willy."

"It is now, pal. I changed it."

"Now, Willy," said the mayor, "calm down. You're young and idealistic. You need to learn to ride the wind, follow the breeze no matter where it blows. You can't count on public opinion staying behind you forever. They're a fickle group—the masses. They'll turn on you"—and he snapped his fingers—"just like that."

"So, you did invite me down here for political reasons?"

"Now, Willy, my boy, I wouldn't go that far," said the mayor in a tone of voice that made me want to slam my fist into his smiling mug. "But certainly we felt that your presence would lend a degree of credibility to our sighting."

"Who's we, Mayor?"

"Well, myself and the two professors of ornithology who head up the Snowy Owl Research Committee."

"Snowy Owl Research Committee! You must be joking?"

"No, Willy, not at all. They have already started writing a book about this rare and unusual event."

"A book! You can't be serious?"

"Quite serious, actually," said the mayor. "I'll be writing the foreword. Or, rather, a ghostwriter will be writing it for me."

"Jesus, a migrating bird strays off course, winds up here in New York City, and already you people are forming committees and writing books. This is totally absurd, absolutely ridic—"

"Ah, here they are now. Good evening, gentlemen."

The mayor crossed the office to greet the two bird professors. And indeed, they both looked like birds. The shorter one looked like an old marsh hawk with his hooked nose, fierce red eyes, and small plump body. The other one looked like a whooping crane. His arms, legs, and shoulders were long and thin and bony. His beady, rust-colored eyes darted about the room.

And then the mayor made the introductions. The cow dung spread so thick and so quick that Trumbull's rendition of democracy turned into Goya's The Third of May executions right before my eyes. Fortunately, an aide's knock on the door ended the flow of phony pleasantries. Our friendly quartet was wanted downstairs.

We hurried down to the lobby to face a firing squad of photographers and reporters. They wanted to know how Willy was. They wanted to know whom I blamed for Dawn's death. They wanted to know if I planned to file suit against the government.

I gritted my teeth. I wanted to tell them I blamed that scumbag Montgomery. I wanted to tell them to hell with lawsuits, "I seek an eye for an eye." But instead I mumbled, "No comment."

Then the mayor placed his hand on my shoulder again, buddy style, but I drooled on His Honor's fingers as the shutters shuttered and the flashes flashed. The mayor laughed and poked me in the ribs, but I knew now it was Hizzoner who wanted to slam his fist into my face.

Around and around our little planet goes, but where it stops no one knows.

Fortunately, the mayor long ago learned the power of diplomacy. So in his very next breath he announced we were off to the park to have a look at the winged visitor from the far north. I tried to make a break out a side door during the hurly-burly, but two agents wearing mirrored sunglasses herded me into the mayor's stretch limo. We sped off: me, the mayor, and the two bird professors. Along the way we had ourselves an intellectual discussion.

I informed the two bird professors that the snowy owl lives primarily in the extreme north, along the frozen tundra, and that the species usually nests on the ground, rarely in trees. "Snowy owls," I continued, "often migrate south in winter, but to find one in this temperate zone, well, I must tell you, I have certain reservations about the accuracy of your observation. And since only a single snowy has been sighted, a male, in the height of breeding season, perhaps the owl has been mistaken for a snowy; perhaps it is an albino barn owl or a light-colored barred owl—both have monkeylike faces similar to the snowy. And hey," I added, "don't feel bad if it turns out not to be a snowy; even a professional can err."

The bird professors glared at me. For some punk from the wild north country to question the validity of their observation irked them no end.

"Sir," began the shorter of the two intellectuals, "the snowy owl is comparable in size to the great horned owl and the great gray owl. The owl we have observed is at least sixty centimeters in height and surely close to four or even five kilograms in weight. Now that, sir, is certainly no barred owl, and your hypothesis that it might be an albino barn owl is simply theoretical poppycock."

I nearly fainted at this academic utterance of profanity, but I managed to arouse myself and inquire if the bird had been calling.

The tall, whooping crane–like professor answered. "Yes, he has kept up an almost constant cry, especially in the evening and at night. Definitely the call of a snowy during breeding season. Quite fascinating, really. I mean, considering there is probably not a female snowy within five hundred kilometers of here."

"Yes," I concurred, "quite fascinating. What does his call sound like?"

The two bird professors answered in unison. "Kre, kre, kre! Kre, kre, kre!"

"Ah," said I, "sounds like a snowy to me."

The bird professors looked smug while they smirked.

"Well," I said, "I can see it's futile for me to argue with experts. I seem to be in the presence of an authority on owl size and another on owl calls. Thank God for the doctoral thesis."

I then turned to the mayor. "What about you, Mayor? You pretty certain you have a snowy owl over in your Central Park?"

The mayor stared out the blue-tinted, bulletproof window waving to no one. "I don't know a goddamn thing about owls."

I gasped. "You don't know anything about owls, Mayor? But I thought your handlers recently dubbed you 'the Big Apple's First True Champion for Environmental Sanity.' Are you telling me, sir, that this label is fictitious, that in reality you don't give a rat's ass about the environment? I'm shocked, Mayor, shocked and dismayed."

"Shut up, you stupid backwoods prick."

"Excuse me, Mayor, was that prick or hick?"

"Prick, boy. As in that thing hanging between your legs."

I blushed with embarrassment. But then, somehow liberated with this newfound knowledge of my true identity, I climbed over the two bird professors and pushed the shiny chrome window button. And when the limo slowed at a traffic light I jumped out the window and fled. Two law enforcement officers in blue uniforms assigned to the mayor's office and riding tall white stallions pursued, but I hurtled a high mesh fence, ducked down a dark alley, and hid behind a discarded carnival scene. Amid broken bumper cars, wheels of fortune, and an empty tunnel of love, I rested and waited for time to pass and memories to float away....

11:18 A.M.
JANUARY 20, 2001
MACKENZIE ISLAND
THE INAUGURATION OF THE FORTY-FOURTH PRESIDENT OF THE UNITED STATES

Hold that thought. I just need to pass along a couple of quick updates before we go straight back to Willy down in the Big Apple.

Almost twenty after eleven now. It's still snowing, a full-blown blizzard. But call the weather balmy and beautiful compared to the major league problems brewing out there in the real world. Just a trickle of information is getting through because of this communication breakdown, but we have just received word via shortwave that Congress will shortly vote on a resolution to make the election of Willy MacKenzie null and void. A vote of this nature had been expected for weeks, but it lost its impetus as Inauguration Day grew near. Members of the House and Senate feared alienating their constituents if they pressed too hard for the removal of President-elect MacKenzie.

Now, or so it would seem, they have changed their minds. With less than an hour before Montgomery's term expires and MacKenzie's term begins, I would think they might be voting even as we speak. There is, after all, if you will excuse the expression, little time left to dance. If Willy takes the oath of office before Congress passes a resolution, he will become the forty-fourth president of the United States, and only successful impeachment proceedings will alter that fact.

On another front: A company of marines attached to the Special Forces has supposedly been observed leaving their base south of the Blue

Mountains. I say "supposedly" because we do not have any confirmation on this mobilization. All of our information is sketchy at best. We have no idea exactly where these well-armed marines might be headed. The Tamaqua River Valley? Lake Katydeeray? MacKenzie Island?

We will just have to wait and see.

Last, all communication with Patsy Squire, our young cub sent to follow Henry Bender on his mission to North Creek to fetch Judge Orrin Stuart, has ceased. At this time we do not know why. Just under twenty minutes ago she reported in to say Henry had the judge ready to travel. She said they would be returning to MacKenzie Island as soon as possible. Her personal communicator worked perfectly, no problems at all. Her voice came through loud and clear. But now, nothing, not a trace. So we have no idea where they are, how they are, or when they will return.

These developments are certainly cause for concern. But since we are powerless to control events, we may as well take this opportunity to dig deeper into the soul of our president-elect. His political persona, buried for nearly thirty years, has finally emerged and is preparing to run wild.

November 4, 1996
New York City

Yesterday morning: rain and solitude. A pretty depressing combination.

I left the hotel, tipped back my head, and tasted the drizzle on my tongue. It had a harsh, bitter flavor. I spit it out, disrobed, and danced down the street. The clouds exploded. My fellow citizens raced for shelter, their heads covered with this morning's newspapers, the copy bleeding black into the collected water along the sidewalk. No one had time to gawk at my nakedness. The rain had them in a tizzy. Modern humans, especially of the urban variety, seem not to like getting caught in the rain. They hate the way it mats their hair and soaks their important papers.

Electrical energy dominated the sky—energy unleashed by the Great Spirit high above the clouds. I stopped dancing and gazed into the gray heavens. But I saw nothing. And heard nothing. The Great Spirit had mercifully neutralized my senses. Yet my thoughts remained my own: undetected and confidential, and blurred only by my own inability to further abandon convention.

I dressed and walked casually up a wide boulevard. Soon I found myself standing in front of a large bookstore. A long line had formed outside the store. I wondered why and so decided to join the line and discover for myself. Fifteen minutes, then half an hour passed. The line did not move a millimeter. People began to grouse and grow impatient.

I had decided to leave and come back later when all of a sudden a young lady inside the store, standing in the huge display window, started waving her arms wildly in my general direction. I looked around but couldn't figure out who or what she was waving at. Then I realized she was waving at me. I pointed to myself and she started grinning and nodding and motioning me to come inside. But I thought not. She was attractive in kind of a pale, scrawny, city way, but I am still a widower in deep mourning.

But I had it all wrong. She came out onto the sidewalk with her boss, and I soon found out that I was the reason why all these people were standing in line. They had come to buy an autographed copy of my book, Full Fucking Moon over the Universe.

"You don't have to wait out here, Mr. MacKenzie," said the store manager, a tall geek with a pointy goatee. "You're the guest of honor."

So in I went, smiling all the way, and was put in the charge of the young lady, who I now saw was pale beyond the death. Her skin was almost transparent. But she seemed to like me. "I just absolutely adored your book," she said. "It's changed my life. I see now that I can make a difference."

"You're an idiot," I wanted to tell her but didn't, "for believing what you read in books. No one can make a difference. The planet's fucked." No, I didn't say that, I'm a good boy. I just smiled and took my seat behind a table stacked high with copies of my opus environmentalus. People gawked at me. I could feel their eyes crawling around on my arms and legs.

"That's him," I heard more than one person say.

That's who? I wondered.

My charge handed me a beautiful black fountain pen. I wanted to plunge the nib into my palm to see if I still bled and felt pain, but the onslaught began. My hand shook violently, but I signed my name, boldly, across the title page. And below my signature, on every book, I scribbled: CARPE DIEM! Seize the Day!

If not me, maybe them.

Most folks wanted me to personalize their book. Like we were old pals. To Mary or Joan or Bob, I wrote as quickly as I could, Keep the Pace! But New York is full of foreigners with strange names. Many had to spell them for me, slowly, so I could get it right: Mulucki, Guillermo, Chentao, Poopsie.

Some folks wanted to talk, get to know me. They wanted to

shower me with praise, then tell me their life story. All in less than a minute.

"I've read your book now twice, Mr. MacKenzie. Willy. Can I call you Willy? I feel like I know you personally. It's just the funniest and wisest book I've ever read. And I want to help, really. Like you say, this is the only earth we've got."

How original.

That one went away and the next one stepped up, leaned way over the table until I could see her rosy nipples. She gave me a toothy smile, handed me her copy of my book, and said, "You're cuter than your picture."

Her perfume slammed into my nose. It smelled like the fuel mixture I use to run the outboards. "Oh," I said, "thank you." I opened the book and scribbled my name as fast as I could.

"To Fiona," she said, breathless.

I wrote in the name and handed her the book. She took the book, then grabbed my hand and squeezed. I felt a tightening in my groin. She slipped me a scrap of paper.

"My address," she whispered, "in the Village. Come anytime, day or night."

Then she sprouted wings and flew away, straight through that display window without causing a crack. I crumpled up the scrap of paper, threw it on the floor, and kicked it into a dusty corner.

The morning passed and pushed slowly into afternoon. The book buyers kept coming. Most proved amiable enough, wanting nothing more than my signature and a smile.

Beatrice Quincy, my agent, showed up for a while and sat close at my side. She's a large, feisty, wild-eyed woman with a mass of red hair. "This is big, Willy," she kept saying, "very big. Could be the biggest book of the year." She spooks me. I was glad when she left.

And the consumers kept consuming. Over three hundred already and no end in sight. I started to feel anxious and slightly claustrophobic, especially after I accidentally opened to the dedication page and saw, in large block letters: TO DAWN, MY ONE AND ONLY.

I wanted to make a run for it, but then, for the first time since I'd arrived, I took a good look at the front of the book. I saw a beautiful painting of the moon rising over our lake, and the title: Full Moon over Katydeeray.

I rose up out of my chair and slammed my fist down against the table. "No!" I shouted. "No! No! No!" I tore off one of the jacket covers and held it up for everyone in the bookstore to see. "This is wrong," I screamed. "Wrong! Wrong! Wrong!"

"Willy," asked my pale assistant, "what is it? What's the matter?"

"The title!" I answered, my voice scaring even me. "This is not the correct title!"

She trembled. "Really? I thought it was. What is the correct—"

"Full Fucking Moon over the Universe!" I shouted. And then I shouted it again. And again. And what the hell? I shouted it one more time. "Full Fucking Moon over the Universe!"

And then, before anyone could calm me down or shoot me full of tranquilizers, I made a mad dash for the exit. I had signed my name enough for one day. Give a man a break. I needed some air, even the foul air of this urban hellhole.

November 6, 1996
New York City

The headline of The New York Times this morning said it all: MONTGOMERY ELECTED!

Good God, how could we be this stupid, this shortsighted? The man is a swine, a lying, conniving swindler. And a murderer to boot. With the most destructive century in the history of mankind drawing to a close, when we so desperately need a secure, stable, and enlightened statesman, we instead elect a megalomaniac starving for power and attention. The bastard doesn't give a damn about this sick and dying planet or about the millions of sick and dying people who have to live here. The bastard only gives a damn about—

Oh, fuck it! We get who we deserve. Why should I raise my blood pressure over it? . . .

Yesterday: another day of rain. I walked the streets, my arms swinging at my sides. I had decided to feel good for a change, to feel fine.

But suddenly a frail, long-legged youngster with a face full of freckles and a crop of orange hair stood before me and asked if I was Willy MacKenzie.

"Who wants to know?"

"The Citizen's Urban Army Against a Technological Holocaust," he answered, although he might have said, "Just a poor homeless kid who hasn't eaten in a week."

He asked me to come with him. Against my better judgment, I agreed. I followed Carrot Top across town to a dilapidated warehouse on a rotting pier sticking out into the polluted waters of the Hudson River.

Inside the warehouse: wrack and ruin. Garbage, most of it rotten and stinking, lay everywhere, enormous piles of crap humans no longer want. And the humans: pathetic specimens, several hundred strong, dressed in rags and lying about listlessly in their own waste. Poor and homeless men, women, and children crushed by the weight of a society on the balls of its ass. How was I to know?

I wanted in the worst way to run away, all the way back to MacKenzie Island. But I didn't. A little voice inside of me these past few days has been telling me to pursue with gusto all fresh and unusual educational opportunities.

Carrot Top pointed to the far end of the warehouse. I looked to where he pointed and saw a tall, homely black woman motioning me to come. I went. I passed through the ranks. Cracked and swollen lips smiled at me, exposing rotten and neglected teeth.

The tall, homely black woman towered over me. She was easily the size of an NBA power forward. Her head was the size of a basketball, her hands like a pair of baseball gloves. Her eyes sparkled like a couple of huge grape gumdrops. She smiled; only a few molars remained.

"Thank you for coming, Mr. MacKenzie. I know you are a busy man." Her voice creaked.

"Busy as a bee," I said.

"Life is not just," she said.

"La-de-da," said I. "What else is new?"

"The people you see here have done nothing to suffer this way."

"One of life's great riddles," I said, "how some folks suffer and other folks thrive."

Those great big gumdrop eyes stared down at me. "We are not bad people, Mr. MacKenzie. We are just people down on our luck who need help."

"Yeah. So? The whole planet's down on its luck lately."

"I've had a premonition, Mr. MacKenzie, a premonition that you have been sent to help us."

"Little old me?" I answered with sarcasm only because I was not yet convinced this was anything more than a whimsy of my imagination.

"Yes," she said, "little old you."

I took a good look at the tall, homely black woman. "Look, lady," I said finally, "I think you have me mixed up with someone else. I just came down here to promote my book. Very self-serving stuff. They gave me a pretty sizable advance, you see, and for that advance it was stipulated in the contract that I'd make some public appearances. Then there was this thing with the mayor."

Have I always been this sarcastic? I don't remember being this sarcastic.

"The mayor is our enemy," said the black giantess. "He treats us with disdain, as if we were no better than sewer rats."

"Yeah, well, he invited me down here to have a look at this owl. In fact, I should be over at the park doing my duty. But anyway, as far as helping you, well, that wasn't in the cards. No one said anything to me about helping the sick and downtrodden, the pissed off and the disenchanted. I'm just a writer, lady, an environmental writer. I sure as hell ain't Mother Teresa."

The tall, homely black woman listened patiently, then said, "Saviors, Mr. MacKenzie, are often the last to know."

"Savior? Lady, you must be putting me on. My itinerary says nada about saving you or anyone else. I figure I'll be lucky to save myself."

"But Mr. MacKenzie, look around you. These are society's rejects and misfits and outcasts. Our ranks are growing daily. Soon we will be larger than the middle class. The middle class is falling into our pot like so many sliced vegetables into the soup. Soon, except for the rich and the powerful, we will be the only class left in this society. What you see before you is the future."

I looked around the huge warehouse and sighed. Unprepared for all this, I decided to hang a little humor on the situation. "You're an awfully serious gal, you know that? Have you ever considered trying out for the New York Knickerbockers?"

"Mr. MacKenzie, a few days ago I saw your picture in the newspaper. I read the article about your life. You have had a good life with many advantages, but you have also lived through a horrible and painful tragedy. What happened to your wife is sad, but also alarming. Like us, Mr. MacKenzie, your wife was a victim. And now you too are a victim. Your world has been shattered by forces beyond your control."

She had a point, so I said, "We're all victims, lady, the second we slip out of the womb."

"Yes, perhaps, but you, because of who you are, a wealthy and well-educated white man, have the power to fight back. When I read that article, I wept, for I knew—"

"You knew nothing, lady. Nothing. Not a damn thing. Life holds no mysteries. We live. We suffer. We tell a few jokes around the campfire. We die."

"Yes," she said, "for sure we die. Which is why I asked you here today. You see, every night for the past seventy-seven nights I have dreamed that today I would face death by guillotine—"

"Guillotine!"

"Yes, guillotine."

I heard a strange sound. It came from out on the end of the pier: WHOOOSH! then steel meeting steel. Then an unoiled pulley, straining, stopping, releasing, and once again WHOOOSH! then steel meeting steel: a sharp, terrifying sound.

The tall, homely black woman stood. "Farewell, Mr. MacKenzie. Perhaps I will see you on the other side."

And with that, she strode across the concrete floor, her long, thin neck held high. I watched her disappear through the door leading to the pier. Her homeless friends did not even look up.

And suddenly—WHOOOSH!—the sound split through time and space, clear and crisp, but then dying all at once with a dull thud, like fingertips striking wood; and then a long, whimsical groan followed by an even longer, thoughtless silence, perhaps an entire second, and finally—SPLASH!—a head separated from its torso and falling into that dark, dirty, and fetid river.

More meaningless death. . . .

Well, let me tell you, I got out of that warehouse and off that pier as fast as my little feet could carry me. And a good thing, too, because I felt sure that homeless band of dirty vagabonds would soon be annihilated from the face of the earth.

I drifted back to the heart of the city. . . .

The air felt cooler after the rain. The streets were filled with people like me, people from out of town, from distant ports. Together we strolled the wide sidewalks lining the broad wet avenues. We wandered aimlessly, mouths wide open, gawking at the sights and sounds. We peered into department store display windows, listened to Salvation Army bands, watched as the hawkers and pimps sold their wares. Quite a show. I relaxed and felt almost human again. But not for long.

Suddenly I found myself studying my reflection in the window of a pastry shop. Time passed. It grew dusky, then dark. My mouth sucked furiously on an imaginary lemon tart. Man's need to make plans, to prepare for the future, to seek light at the end of the tunnel, spewed forth from my pursed lips. My mouth went dry. My fellow travelers stared at me as though I might be a loony, another crazy kook capable of unprovoked acts of extreme violence. They backed off, whispered words like freak, wacko, and weirdo to one another. Then, all at once, like a routed army, they ran for their lives.

I just laughed and asked myself this question: "What am I doing here in this forbidding jungle of fragility?" And I knew the answer lay in the absence of Dawn.

La-La Land slipped its slippers onto my feet. I turned into a lower primate with a caustic sense of humor. Bent over, fingers sweeping the street, I let fly a savage roar, then hailed a passing taxi. "To the nearest natural museum," I commanded.

The driver watched me carefully in his rearview mirror. But not because he thought I might put an end to his sweet sweet life, but because he thought he recognized my mug. He thought his fare might be a celebrity. "Hey," he asked, "don't I know you?"

"I doubt it," I told him. "I'm new in town."

"Yeah, but I know you from somewheres."

"Maybe from that giant billboard high atop Times Square. They got a huge mug shot of me up there advertising my new book."

The driver shrugged. He wasn't a reader. "Maybe, I don't know." Then, "I once drove Don Ho from the Waldorf to Lincoln Center."

"Wow. Really?"

"Cheap son of a bitch. Didn't even gimme a tip."

I didn't, either. At the museum I paid the fare, climbed out the window, and bounded up a long flight of marble stairs.

Inside the museum, a virtual fortress of stuffed animals, I joined an evening tour entering the Hall of Apes. The guide, a woman with a pointed nose and a pointed view, an opponent of Darwin, led us through a sketchy history of evolution. She had this attitude about man suddenly and spontaneously arriving in the Garden of Eden. Something like the Aristotelian view of insect reproduction.

"No, no, no!" I shouted. "Man made God! And before that monkeys made man!"

Before she could respond, I sprinted off along those wide, marble corridors until I found the museum's ornithology collection. It took a few minutes but finally I located the Birds of North America. And soon after that I found the owls. And soon after that, the snowy owls.

But wait a second, there was only one, a female snowy, behind glass, perched upon a blanket of fake snow. Beside her was a nest of pine boughs containing four plastic eggs. And next to the nest, protruding out of the Styrofoam snow—the sharp, vacated point of a mounting peg! "Good God!" The snowy's mate had been plucked from his perch.

I raced out of the museum and stood on the wide portico above the sidewalk. "Kre, kre, kre! Kre, kre, kre!" The distinctive call pierced the still autumn night. I tracked the shrill cry along the street, around the north side of the museum, and directly into Central Park. I had been warned repeatedly to stay out of the park, especially after dark. But damn the rogues and muggers and the murderers, I had to see for myself.

My eyes adjusted slowly to the darkness. I heard again the call. "Kre, kre, kre! Kre, kre, kre!" I scanned the treetops but saw nothing save the leafless branches and the jet black sky. Moments later I heard voices. I crept forward on hands and knees through a wet tangle of rhododendron.

At the edge of a clearing I saw two police officers. They stood talking beneath an enormous American sycamore. One of them said something I couldn't hear, and the other one laughed. Then the owl called again, very close now, almost directly overhead. I looked up, and there—in the upper branches of that old sycamore—a tall, broad snowy owl.

The cops laughed again, then moved off in different directions. I crawled on my belly to the trunk of the sycamore. "Kre, kre, kre! Kre, kre, kre!" Like a frightened cat, I scrambled up the tree. Up and up I climbed, to within five feet of the bird. And still the snowy did not fly away. He just sat there swiveling his head from side to side. Definitely a mature, chalk-white snowy owl, but—

On the ground, new voices: the mayor and his two bird professors! The mayor thanked the cops and sent them away. I clung to the tree and stayed very still. The trio spoke softly, too softly for me to hear. I pulled myself up one more branch and reached for the sharp talons of that snowy owl. "Kre, kre, kre! Kre, kre, kre!" Higher and higher my fingertips reached until finally I grabbed hold of those soft, downy tail feathers. But still nothing, not even a shudder or a squawk. Just another shrill, mechanical call, "Kre, kre, kre! Kre, kre, kre!"

I shook the body but the bird was dead. Stuffed. Stolen, just as I had suspected, from his mounting peg over at the natural history museum. And packed beneath his fine plumage: a tiny tape recorder for sound and a small, battery-operated motor for movement. Very clever, but why? Why? I did not understand. At least not for a second or two.

Then it all came clear. I flung the rigid corpse down at the three conspirators. They screamed like schoolchildren when the lifeless owl shattered at their feet. "Kre, kre, kre! Kre, kre, kre!"

Soon they regained their wits. "It's him!" one of them shouted, "MacKenzie!"

Indeed.

"We have to stop him before he gets to the press."

Down I climbed. And along the way I wondered how these three perfect assholes planned on stopping me. Would they reason with me on an intellectual level? Or would they use physical means? I hoped for the latter. I felt the need for a bit of jousting.

My anticipation grew as I descended. I decided not to wait for them to make their move; I took the offensive. So when I reached the lower branches of that tall and stately sycamore, I swung down upon them, sending the trio sprawling to the hard ground. I then gave each of them a solid kick to the groin area before making good my getaway.

They chased me through the park. I stayed just beyond their reach, taunting them every step of the way with my impression of the snowy owl. "Kre, kre, kre! Kre, kre, kre!"

The mayor, the Big Apple's First True Champion for Environmental Sanity, and his two sidekicks, who wanted so badly to write and publish a book about the snowy owl who had spent the summer and autumn in New York's Central Park, gathered rocks and bottles and rusty pieces of pipe. They hurled their petty arsenal at me, but I ducked and dodged and feigned and faked and repelled their every attack. I proved too much for them. Their soft, middle-age bodies soon grew weary and weak. Long before I was ready to rest, the inept trio collapsed on a park bench as they struggled to fill their lungs with air.

I kicked dirt in the cuffs of their pants and shuffled off for home. Home? Home is where I write in my journal: a dirty, roach-infested hotel with damp walls and a musty bed. I lie upon this bed scribbling these sentences and waiting for dawn.

At dawn I will say farewell to the Big Apple. My itinerary has me visiting the seacoast next, to address some small-town society of enthusiastic environmentalists who are supposedly hell-bent on armed warfare if that's what it takes to get potable water and chemical-free green beans. And after that, the blackpoll warblers. That should be something.

But right now I need to get some sleep. I have not been sleeping well due to my fear of falling back into that terrible, murderous dream. But I have to try. I must. Willy needs his rest. . . .

11:27 A.M.
JANUARY 20, 2001
MACKENZIE ISLAND
THE INAUGURATION OF THE FORTY-FOURTH PRESIDENT OF THE UNITED STATES

So, what do you think? Does Willy sound like a man who has tumbled over the edge? Lost his equilibrium and maybe his mental marbles? Perhaps borrowed a few hits of lysergic acid from his older brother and dropped them on his way down to the Big Apple?

Let's look at the facts. We know, of course, that Dawn's death had struck an enormous blow to Willy's emotional well-being. We know he was on unfamiliar turf down in New York City, far from home and on his own. We know his fragile psyche was exposed to raw and unfiltered stimuli. If we combine these circumstances with his vivid and expansive imagination, I think we can begin to understand the madness behind his prose.

Believe me, I have looked very carefully at these journal entries. And I think explanations exist for even his most bizarre vignettes. That very first scene in the city, for instance, when he sees the people marching along the street dressed in costumes and masks. It all sounds pretty strange, I know, but it was Halloween after all. Willy must have looked out the window of his downtown hotel and seen the famous Greenwich Village Halloween parade passing by. But to a young man riding an emotional roller coaster in that aggravated state of awareness, it must have looked like an insane army of urban outcasts marching home in retreat.

And what about his antics in that midtown bookstore? Well, I don't pretend to know all the particulars, but it's clear Willy did act up a time or two during the many book signings he did, not only in New York City, but across the country. And once or twice, yes, he even got up, ranted and raved about one issue or another, then stormed off without a word of explanation to anyone. But these performances, either spontaneous or premeditated, only heightened public interest in the author and led to even further increases in the sale of his book.

Now whether or not Beatrice Quincy had anything to do with these outbursts, I don't know, but Willy definitely proved his own best PR man. Every strange and eccentric thing the guy did—and trust me, there are plenty of strange and eccentric things to come—created ever more interest in himself and in his work. During this time he became a favorite topic of all the trendy journalists. Hundreds of thousands of words were written about him during those first months after the book's appearance. One of the more memorable lines I remember described him as "a wealthy and reclusive mountain man with a troubled past but with a new and very clear vision for the future."

This vision, I gather, originated in Willy's book. *Full Moon over Katydeeray* took the country by storm. Everyone wanted a copy. Its clear, concise prose, teeming with simple, homespun profundities and witticisms, proved much more than just an environmentalist's plea to take care of the planet. The slim volume became a kind of political manifesto, the world of the twenty-first century according to Willy Mac.

No way had Willy intended his book as such, but once the ball started rolling no one could slow it down. I don't think Willy had a clue people would embrace his message with such diligence. He just thought he'd written a small and lively tale about the joys of living a modest, uncluttered life. Then some professional scribe, writing, I believe, for *Vanity Fair*, described Willy as "a modern-day Lao-tzu," and his book as an "updated version of the Tao-Te Ching."

And away the book went. Tens of thousands of copies took wing and flew off the bookstore shelves.

Let's take a quick look inside, just for fun.

On page 27 of *Full Moon over Katydeeray* Willy, after commenting upon *Homo sapiens*'s inability to communicate honestly and openly with one another, writes: "Put a clothespin on your tongue and a foghorn in your ear."

Okay, fine, not a bad idea. I get the message. But every time I turned around I found this quirky little profundity staring me in the face: on billboards and greeting cards, even on the box of my morning breakfast cereal.

And what about this line from page 88: "Turn off the water, gang, or there won't be any water to turn on tomorrow."

Makes sense to this reporter. Nothing earth-shattering, mind you; I've always made it a practice to turn off the water once I'm done using it. But did Willy mean, as the critics and the analysts now claim, that water equals government expenditures, and unless we bring these expenditures under control we will soon find ourselves with nothing but an empty well?

Personally, I find the analogy a bit strained.

And this line from page 132: "We used to have black bears, musk-rats, and even coyotes here on MacKenzie Island. Not anymore, folks."

Okay, I get it, humans have been tough on Mother Earth. We've done more than our fair share of damage, driving many species to extinction and countless others to the brink. But the critics claim these two brief sentences from page 132 of *Full Moon over Katydeeray* do more to bring man's exploitation of the planet into perspective than do all the countless academic and environmental volumes written on the subject.

Well, if you ask me, all this is a little too much reading between the lines. And Willy certainly has not helped matters, saying only that the words mean what they mean, nothing more and nothing less.

But who knows? Maybe my cynicism is nothing more than veiled envy.

So let's skip the petty analysis of *Full Moon over Katydeeray* and get back to our discussion of Willy's journal.

What about that scene in the warehouse out on the Hudson River? This is a tough one to figure, but I think Willy went out for a walk, came across a band of society's disaffected, and one of them (the tall, homely black woman) managed to get his ear. I doubt very much she died by guillotine, but Willy's rather indifferent reaction to her pleas for help provide us with an interesting insight into his character. We know Willy was brought up to believe a man should take care of his own needs, pursue a life of self-reliance. I think seeing those poor bastards lying around in their own waste on that filthy warehouse floor insulted his sense of individualism. If they wanted help, they could damn well get up and help themselves. This is not to say Willy didn't feel a certain amount of compassion for their plight, but he is, after all, the candidate who called for the complete elimination of the welfare system.

What about the mayor and those two bird professors? The story Willy relates about the snowy owl is essentially true. Two professors of ornithology at the City College of New York did indeed place a stuffed owl up in a tree in Central Park in an effort to attract media attention for a book they were writing on owls. The mayor joined the hoax, presumably in an effort to lure tourists back to his dirty, crumbling, crime-infested metropolis.

I don't know if Willy ever climbed up into that old sycamore and found that stuffed and mechanical snowy, but he definitely uncovered the deception and brought it to the attention of the public. Even *The New York Times* gave him credit for that. So I guess we could say the accuracy and chronology of his accounts may be questionable, but we cannot deny the fact that his rendering of events makes for some excellent and highly unusual reading.

Willy, you might say, writes parables. He uses half-truths and suggestive metaphors to speculate on our motivations as political animals. I'm not a psychologist or a literary critic. I don't pretend to understand all the meanings and symbolism behind his descriptions and digressions. I don't know if he was just practicing the art of creative writing or if he authored events as they actually occurred, even if only in his deluded imagination. I'm not sure it really matters. What matters is the subject of his inquiries and the intensity of his observations.

But enough with the mouth lather. Time to let Willy take the reins.

These next few entries, you might notice, do not provide a specific location. I think the following events took place on Cape Cod. Others believe they occurred out on the eastern end of Long Island. Still others suggest somewhere on the Chesapeake, or even along the Outer Banks off North Carolina. Place, however, does not matter nearly so much here as purpose.

November 21, 1996
Along the Coast

At the moment I cannot recall exactly where I am or how I got here, but I can tell you this: The terrible, murderous dream has ended, at least for the time being. I rest comfortably now at a small inn near the beach, a fine white beach I can see through my open window.

Events here have led me to believe that my arrival was not unexpected. But when first I ventured off the dunes, whale blood covering my hands and knees, I wondered where I was and why I had come. A young man wearing a green uniform greeted me by name and offered me a ride in his 4-wheel drive, all-terrain Jeep Cherokee. A patch on the sleeve of his uniform told me he worked for the National Park Service. An insignia on the door of his Jeep matched the patch. So I accepted his offer of a ride but demanded to know how he knew my name.

He looked at me and smiled, a big, stupid smile. His face was as smooth as driftwood. "They told me."

"Who told you?"

"You know, Willy, the local environmental group."

My memory started to focus but I did not let on. "No," I said, "I don't know. Tell me more."

But before he could answer we pulled into the driveway of the inn. An old and rambling weatherbeaten seaside house with steep gables and a wide front porch stood before me. A huge banner hung off the front porch: WELCOME, WILLY MAC—ECOLOGY BEFORE TECHNOLOGY!

That sounded familiar, so I stepped out of the Jeep and followed the young man down a slate path. I could hear waves breaking on the beach behind the house. But that sound vanished when the front door burst open and a dozen women and almost as many men streamed out of the inn, across the porch, and into the space around me. They buzzed about like bees. Fortunately, they smiled, or I think I would have made a mad dash for the dunes.

The kid from Park Service told them he'd found me out on the Lighthouse Road Beach. I didn't bother to deny or confirm this statement. It didn't seem to matter. The crowd closed in tight on my space. A few of them even touched me with their sweaty palms. They brought their faces close to mine and offered me their heartfelt condolences concerning my wife. More than one of them even said it was an honor to have me visit their town.

"Who are you people?" I asked. "What do you want?"

They did not answer. They led me up onto the porch, where they pushed crackers covered with little yellow blobs of processed cheese food into my hand. All at once they talked at me. I tried to make sense of their chatter but their voices made my head throb. They wanted to know my position on the baby seal situation in Nova Scotia, the black rhino situation in East Africa, the slash-and-burn situation in the Amazon basin, the ozone depletion situation over Antarctica, the spotted owl situation in the Pacific Northwest, and on and on.... I wanted to answer, even tried to answer, but each time I prepared to open my mouth the conversation pressed forward. I couldn't keep up. The chitchat roamed from toxic waste dumps to fluoride in the water supply to the greenhouse effect, far too fast for my thoughts to spin.

Then more crackers and a glass of wine. The wine gave me courage. "Don't you people have anything better to do," I shouted above the hum, "than stand around bitching and moaning?"

Their smiles faded. They moved away, gave me back my space.

I wiped my bloodstained hands on my shirt and continued my assault. "Bitching and moaning while you stuff your faces with coagulated cow fat. Aren't you aware of the irony? Shit, don't you people have dogs to walk or mates to fondle or errands to run?"

Their eyes filled first with shock, then quickly with hate. All that hate made me feel great. I was sick to the bone of being a nice boy.

One of the womenfolk spat at me. One of the menfolk tore down my welcome banner. Then, in unison, they turned on their heels and marched off across the lawn.

"Idolize your lovers," I shouted at them, "not your warriors!" But they didn't hear me. They had gone home to tell their families about the madman from the Blue Mountains.

I heard applause. Across the porch sat a frail old woman in a wooden rocking chair. "That was a fine speech, Willy." She had a small, wrinkled mouth. A patched quilt covered her knees.

"Who are you?"

"I'm Lorelei Constantine, rocking chair woman and keeper of the inn."

"That's fine," I said. "Any chance I might get a room?"

"Of course," she answered. "I have a room ready for you. And already paid for as well."

"By who?"

"By those fine folks you just tore into tiny pieces."

I started to explain, but Lorelei Constantine held up her bony hand. "Fine folks," she said, "but very self-righteous. They haven't learned to let life roll over them like a wave washing onto the beach. You look tired, Willy. You'll find your nice, clean room up on the third floor. Dinner's at seven."

I thanked her, went through the front door, and up the stairs.

And now here I rest, some days later, cozy in my third-floor bedroom with a view of the dunes and the smell of the sea wafting through the windows. Unlike those dark and dreary accommodations in the city, this room fills with sunshine even on cloudy days. I have a firm bed with sweet-smelling sheets and a sturdy desk to record my experiences.

Before dawn I rise, dress, slip out the back door, and walk briskly down to the beach. The air feels cool and tastes salty as I cross the dunes. I find a young couple sprawled in the sand, their bodies close and naked. They stroke each other's tufts of pubic hair. They lose control so quickly, so carelessly, that they think nothing of coming again and again. I peer through the fast-fading darkness at them. They seem to me like animals in the wild. I was once an animal in the wild. No more, no more.

Before they glance up and spot the loony staring down at them from this sandy summit, I slip away and mosey down to the water's edge. The sea rolls. The sun peers over the horizon. Dawn! And the anticipated arrival of the blackpoll warbler. What more could I want? What more could I need?

While I try to answer those questions, I return to my third-floor room at the inn and recall my encounter with the whales.

Yes, the whales.

It all started on the ferry from there to here. Low, heavy clouds swallowed up the sky. Thunder and lightning and heavy seas. Day into night. Light into dark. The ferry rolled, took on water, began to sink. "Abandon ship!" came the call from the bridge. "Abandon ship!"

And so we did. At least I did. I dived, as ordered, into the sea. The cold water grabbed me by the balls and squeezed. I loved it. The icy sensation assured me I was still alive.

I stroked steadily to the west, away from the sinking ferry, toward what I hoped would eventually be some sandy shore. But then, suddenly, my energy vanished. I could barely lift my arms out of the water. My legs hung from my hips like dead branches. Small fishes swam through my chattering teeth and down my throat into my belly. It gave me sustenance.

I rolled over and floated. Time passed. My face, chest, thighs, and kneecaps burned red and raw from that star we call the sun. I thought for sure I'd go insane when out of nowhere a fluorescent yellow life raft drifted past my arm. I reached out and grabbed it and climbed aboard. The raft carried all my favorite fruits: plums, peaches, sweet cherries, apples, and black raspberries. I settled back against the rubber gunwale for a succulent feast.

But the fruit disappeared so quickly that I had to wonder if the slender, inflatable woman sitting in the bow had an open invitation to dine. She looked familiar—too familiar, in fact. I moved over closer to her. We shared the sections of a juicy navel orange. She wore a funny smile on her neoprene face, as though she knew exactly what I was thinking. And I . . . I burst out of my fantasy and found myself still swimming, the sun slipping away, my head reeling, my heart pounding, my stomach growling, my eyes scanning the horizon ahead.

Thousands of nocturnal butterflies descended upon me as I neared the shore. The large, colorful, glowing insects lit upon my shoulders and back. A sliver of moon hung in the night sky. I heard the sound of waves breaking upon the beach. And then, quickly, I rode atop the waves, rushing forward wildly and crashing in a heap on the hard wet sand. I do not know where I found the energy but for most of the night I rode those waves. Finally, at some time not long before dawn, on hands and knees, I crawled away from the sea. The tide receded. The butterflies, which had been circling overhead, now covered me like a blanket, protecting me from the cool ocean breeze.

I slept.

And when I awoke, the butterflies had fled and the whales had arrived. Forty-three of the mammoth ocean mammals lay stranded upon the beach, washed ashore and left by the tide. And all forty-three of them crying: seet, seet, seet . . . seet, seet, seet . . .

Pilot whales—an entire school: males, females, and calves. At six feet from head to toe, I stretched four and a half times across the back of the largest pilot. He did not battle or even budge when I climbed on top of him, using his pectoral fin as a step. His sleek, cylindrical body glistened black and blubbery in the white sand. His head was simply an extension of his body, not pointed or shaped at all, just round and smooth and massive. His thick dorsal fin, just behind the blowhole, curved back and down like a breaking wave. And although his sad lament echoed from deep within his tremendous body, he wore a kind of silly smile across his wide mouth, as though, perhaps, he understood exactly what he and his cohorts were doing.

But me, I understood nothing. I jumped off his back into the shallow water and struggled to drag the giant beast back into the sea. Using every ounce of my physical strength, I pulled and tugged on his great tail fin, but no way could I free the landed brute. And then, with a swish of his flukes, he sent me somersaulting through the air. I landed in a heap somewhere out beyond the breaking waves.

"Why are you doing this?" I screamed. "Why? Why?!!!" A wave broke over my back and nearly snapped me in two. "What are you doing here? What are you trying to prove?"

My mind spun in great circles of confusion. Stars burned out across the heavens. New galaxies formed spontaneously from black holes. I swam ashore. I scurried from whale to whale, demanding an explanation for their mass suicide. But those goddamn pilots just yawned and smiled at me with their big, stupid mouths. I dropped to the sand and wept. What more could I do?

The tide washed in, under the bellies of the forty-three stranded pilot whales, and I thought for sure they would take the opportunity to return to the ocean blue. But no—not one of them made an effort to free his or her body from the wet sand. In fact, they squirmed farther up onto the drier sand, securing their position on the beach-head. I could do nothing, nothing, nothing at all.

Three of the younger calves had ceased breathing. I attempted mouth-to-mouth resuscitation, but their oral openings were far too large. Many of the others gasped for air—a rather harrowing sound from an ocean mammal who normally rises to the surface for air only once in an hour.

I was out of my mind with horror. Were these giant creatures going to die right in front of me? All of the scientific explanations for mass strandings meant nothing with the reality of the whales' demise filling my eyes and ears. No one could have convinced me that these beasts were lost or sick. Nor had their echolocation gone awry. No way. The beach dropped off sharply a few yards off shore. Food was abundant just beyond the shoals. This was a perfect habitat for pilots. So what then? Why were they here? For sure something else was troubling them. Something profound. But what?

And then my thoughts began to focus. I could see the truth in their eyes, hear the truth in their lament: these whales had come to protest, yes, protest. They understood death was a consequence of their action. They understood the finality of their act.

This realization calmed me. I stopped trying to make things right. Things were right. As right as things can be. I just sat there in the sand and quietly joined their vigil.

Time became irrelevant in the presence of purpose. Waiting and dying without problems, only solutions. By destroying Nature, man eventually kills himself. The whales understood this, and so they sacrificed themselves as a means of expressing the severity of the situation to the rest of the animal kingdom. The whales knew man had to be stopped.

And as the hours passed the animals arrived in pairs to pay homage. Large animals and small animals, animals that fly and animals that swim, fast animals and slow animals, animals that swing and animals that slither, dumb animals and smart animals, every variety of animal under the sun—they all gathered on the beach in a thoughtful and moving communion.

I was the sole representative of the human race. My mate had already been sacrificed.

The great male was the last to die. He remained alive long after the other animals had left and the forty-two members of his herd had perished. Together we wondered how it had come to pass that so few could fuck it up for so many. We knew God did not exist except in the minds of men. He winked at me just before his final earthly moment. And I knew he'd accepted me as an individual even though he detested the whole of the human race: those self-proclaimed masters of the Natural Order.

After his death I made a small incision in his back and smeared my body with his blood. Then I left the beach and wandered across the dunes, where, eventually, that young man from Park Service found me and offered me a ride in his 4-wheel drive, all-terrain Jeep Cherokee.

And he wondered why I seemed lost.

December 1, 1996
With the Blackpolls

The time came to say so long to Lorelei Constantine. I didn't want to leave the old woman and the sea behind, but I knew the blackpolls would never wait for me. So here I sit, on a black and starless night, in the high branches of a towering red maple, certain this clear, cool weather will bring the blackpolls to my perch.

While I wait, I imagine their departure from the edge of the timberline in northern Canada: polar air blasting out of the Arctic, crossing the tundra, and spreading through the quiet, coniferous forests of Labrador and Newfoundland. Hundreds, thousands, tens of thousands of blackpoll warblers flying out of the virgin spruces upon the sheets of rapidly warming polar air. A truly unbelievable display of mass migration. And Polaris lighting the way.

I keep this image in my mind as I anticipate the arrival of the blackpolls. And look: here comes the moon! Absolutely full and shining like a just polished silver bowl.

I keep my eyes fixed on the northern sky, my expectations soaring, and there—coming in low and fast—the first line of blackpolls! Only a dozen or so, probably scouts, but surely harbingers of blackpolls to come.

And now, like approaching storm clouds, the great flocks wing across the night sky. I stare in awe at the solidarity of their flight. These birds will fly over the ocean and travel south for thousands of miles in search of warmer temperatures. But first they will need to rest here in preparation for their long migration. They will eat until the weight of their tiny bodies more than doubles. Even then, each bird will weigh less than one ounce! Warblers are not diving birds, so they have to consume enough food to fuel their flight across the seas. They will not eat again until they reach their winter habitat somewhere in the rain forests of Central and South America. If any of those rain forests still stand.

Now the sky is so thick with blackpolls that the moon cannot be seen. The adult males still wear their black-and-white breeding plumage, but soon they will turn a greenish hue like the fledglings and the females. I see a few red-breasted warblers also, and an occasional pair of yellow warblers, but mostly I see blackpolls—the finest flyer and the most ambitious adventurer of all the warblers, perhaps the most courageous creature, ounce for ounce, of all creatures who inhabit the earth.

Questions fill my head as the birds glide in over the treetops: What makes these tiny winged animals journey several thousand miles every spring and autumn? Why do they travel to the edge of the tundra to lay their eggs, then fly south nearly to the equator to pass the chilly winter months? Why not settle in some pleasant woodland somewhere in between and just sit back and watch the seasons slowly pass? Why traverse the seas? What's the point? What's the purpose? From where do these wild migrating instincts originate?

I have no answers but I have this thought: The warbler migrates simply to propagate its species. And it does so without violence or malfeasance. And so I forget my silly questions and just enjoy the show—surely one of Nature's most inspiring.

Midnight and the hours after pass. The large flocks begin to fill the trees. And finally, the birds start to settle in my corner of the forest. The message spreads that insects are plentiful among the red and silver maples. More blackpolls arrive every second. One lands close to my shoulder but scurries away when I exhale. I'm amazed at its size: three of them would fit easily into the palm of my hand.

And now they surround me. They gather on the higher and lower branches, uninhibited and full of energy. Their rapid-fire chatter flies without beginning or end. Could these warblers be talking about me?

Oh, how I wish Dawn could be here now to see this, to hear this, to share this moment. She would talk to them, question them, entice them into telling us about their lives. She would soon have a flock of blackpolls perched upon her shoulder.

I try to charm them as the dark hours pass, but without success. I do not have Dawn's touch.

As morning approaches, the birds begin to settle down. All night long they have celebrated the successful first leg of their journey south, but now the time has come to rest and gather their energy before they begin the long migration over the open sea. Their active, high-pitched lisps rise and fall in a series of gathering crescendos: seet, seet, SEET, SEET, SEET, seet, seet, SEET, SEET, SEET!

Something like the pilot whales, I think, only more of a celebration than a lament. Where there is joy there is also sorrow. All part of the cycle, this journey around time.

11:39 A.M.
JANUARY 20, 2001
MACKENZIE ISLAND
THE INAUGURATION OF THE FORTY-FOURTH PRESIDENT OF THE UNITED STATES

Fascinating stuff. But what does it all mean?

I suppose each of us will have to decide for ourselves what Willy means. They say the outcome of a baseball game means different things to different people. Scientists claim that no two of us collect and process data in exactly the same way. One man's butter knife is another man's murder weapon. One woman's sexy lover is another woman's unfaithful husband. Beached pilot whales for me represent the sentimental grist for the evening news mill. But for Willy these same whales symbolize the wrath humans have inflicted upon the planet. In fact, a case can be made for Willy having a greater empathy for animals than for humans. Just look at his reaction to those whales and those blackpoll warblers, then go back and check his reaction to those poor homeless buggers lying around in that dilapidated warehouse.

This is not a criticism, you understand, merely an observation. . . .

Late that fall, while holed up in Lorelei Constantine's seaside inn, Willy appeared, for the first time, on the cover of a national magazine. His book, *Full Moon over Katydeeray*, had just hit number one on *The New York Times* best-seller list. Unless you lived alone in an igloo up above the Arctic Circle without access to radio or cable TV, you couldn't get through a day without hearing someone mention Willy MacKenzie's name.

And yet, incredibly, not once anywhere in his journals does he ever refer to this sudden and spectacular rise to fame; not one word about his appearance on the cover of *Time*. Not one word. Amazing. It is as though he didn't even know what was going on out there beyond his own private party. And who knows? Maybe the guy didn't know. Or maybe he just didn't give a damn. Maybe he found it all an utter waste of time and energy.

I certainly had my eyes and ears wide open to this latest media phenomenon. Not only had I met the man on an occasion or two, but as a journalist who had been clamoring for two decades to reach some point of prominence in his profession, I was both perplexed and daunted by the way this unknown mystery man had captured the public's attention. So when I saw his picture on the cover of *Time*, I decided to do some digging of my own.

At the time, I lived in Washington, assigned to the Montgomery transition team. Elected in November by the shine of his glistening white teeth, Anderson Montgomery had immediately gone to work preparing his assault on the nation's capital. My job was to cover this assault by keeping an eye on the people who might be asked to serve in his administration. I investigated the lives and backgrounds of possible nominees for secretaries of state and defense. In other words, I sifted for dirt: political, social, sexual. It didn't matter as long as we had something negative to say if and when that particular man or woman's name slipped into the public domain.

I learned then that no one is clean, no one. It's all in the presentation.

All this dirty work ate up my time, but late at night I caught up on the latest material about this fellow MacKenzie. As a seasoned journalist, I could tell that most of the stuff being written about him relied more on the reporter's imagination than on facts. Not that I cared much about the credibility of the information. That's not what interested me. What interested me was the sheer quantity of information. Everyone had boarded the MacKenzie bandwagon. Journalists from TV, print, and radio had all stepped forward to hype Willy and his book.

The reasons why such things happen are difficult to fathom. I think Willy's family had a lot to do with this particular promo job: Ulysses, Lawrence, Conrad; the money, the politics, the legends. It all made for great copy. The word spinners just couldn't resist.

But in all the material I watched and read, I found an enormous hole right where Willy's mouth should have been. Few of these journalists talking and writing about Willy had ever met the man, much less managed to get him to sit down and talk things over. I decided to make that my job. I decided to hit the road and get an exclusive interview with Willy MacKenzie.

And believe me, I tried. All through December and the early part of January I searched high and low for him. And I was not the only one. A whole army of reporters roamed the countryside in pursuit of our elusive prey. But Willy moved so fast that I rarely managed to even catch a glimpse of his face. . . .

Before we return to the journals to find out where Willy was and what he was up to during the weeks preceding Anderson Montgomery's inauguration, a brief update: Patsy Squire remains incommunicado. We still do not know why.

Those U.S. Marines supposedly headed for the Tamaqua Valley may be coming our way, but at the moment no one knows where they are. And members of Congress, we understand from a report just received via shortwave, continue to talk, although thus far no vote on the resolution to roll back Willy's election has been cast. Our legislators continue to procrastinate.

Willy, for his part, has been seen pacing up and down the halls of the Great House. He appears impatient, anxious, heavy with stress. And from an informant we have on the catering staff, we have just learned that Willy has been verbally attacking this reporter. It seems my line about him not being particularly compassionate toward those less fortunate souls in our society did not sit well with the president-elect. Our informant told us Willy slammed his fist down against an oak table upon hearing my remark. He split the table in two, possibly cracked a bone in his hand, and told his family, "I want that son of a bitch off this island!"

Well, folks, we're still here, alive and broadcasting. Better batten down the hatches. We could be in for some rough seas ahead.

December 11, 1996
On the Road

Some time ago, my good pal Henry Bender found me sprawled out on the ground, semiconscious and covered with brown leaves and broken branches. I'd fallen from that towering red maple while observing the blackpoll warblers and recalling the demise of those forty-three pilot whales.

"Are you hurt, Willy?" he asked.

I looked up at him through blurry eyes, didn't right away recognize my old childhood chum. His face looked huge, distorted. Quite frankly, that face scared the bejesus out of me. I sprang off the ground, backed away from his great, bear-size body. Blood drained out of my head, into my toes. I wobbled on the balls of my feet.

"Maybe you should sit down, Willy," he said. "Take 'er easy." He had a high, tender voice, not the voice you would expect to come out of that massive body.

I wondered how such an imposing figure could have such a frail set of vocal cords.

He smiled down at me. "Been looking for you for days, Willy. The whole dang world's been looking for you."

"What do you mean, the whole dang world's been looking for me? Why?"

"Well, maybe not the whole dang world, but a goodly sized portion of it."

That's when I recognized him, realized who stood before me. Tears came to my eyes. I gave Bender a great big bear hug.

Pop and Sanders, I soon found out, had sent him to look out for me, keep me company, guide me from town to town.

"Close to thirty years I've known you, Henry, and let me tell you, you've never looked this good to me before."

Henry smiled.

His smile did not last long. We wandered around in the woods for a couple days before we finally found a way out. The way out led to a gravel country lane not much traveled by man or automobile. Tired and hungry, and not at all sure which direction to take, we took up residence on an old and splintery split-rail fence.

We sat on and rested under that fence for two days and two nights before Bender asked, "Hey, Willy, know any good songs we could sing?"

"Sure, Henry. What do you want to hear?"

"Oh, I don't know," said Henry. "How 'bout something old, something new, something borrowed, something blue?"

So I thought for a minute while Bender searched through his rucksack for his harmonica. He finally found it, one of those giant chrome jobs that could play in two keys. "Ready, Henry?"

"Sure, Willy."

I started right in. "Hang down your head, Tom Dooley, hang down your head and cry. Oh, hang down your head, Tom Dooley, poor boy you're bound to die, poor boy you're bound to die, oh, poor boy you're bound to die."

Henry had the harmonica against his lips, but he hadn't played a note. "Geez, Willy, that was pretty depressing. Don't you know any happy, upbeat tunes?"

"Fuck you, Henry," I said. "Just fuck you."

Henry dropped his head like a dog who had just been scolded. Before I could console him, a car came screaming around the curve. Bender shot off the split-rail fence, hurried across the gravel shoulder of that country lane, and stuck out his thumb. The car, a metallic black sedan, bore down on him. Henry held his ground. I sat there and watched as his eyes grew wider and wider. Less than a second before impact the black sedan swerved, missing Bender by inches. A red, white, and blue beer can shot out of the window of the sedan. It hit Bender in the thigh and fell to the ground. Bender looked at the can, then he squashed it flat with his heavy hiking boots.

"Shit," he mumbled. He shoved his hands into the pockets of his baggy corduroy trousers and returned to the fence.

We did not communicate the remainder of that day.

Early the next morning Bender said in a low voice, "Willy, I'm awful sorry about the mess. It's all my fault."

"I know it's your fault, Henry," I said, "but don't sweat it. So what if we're stuck out here in the middle of nowhere? So what if the rest of humanity continues to engage in meaningful encounters and provocative exchanges? Things could be worse."

Bender hung his head. I'd upset him again. But I felt sort of feisty, touchy after three days along that road with little to do and less to eat. I took a perverse pride in making Bender feel bad. "So you screwed up, Henry. So what? Anyone can get lost in the woods. Or in life, for that matter. Anyone can drift off course. No one ever said you were God Almighty, for chrissakes."

His head dropped even lower. All the joy passed out of his little corner of the universe. Poor Henry. I could see him praying for the appearance of another car.

And finally, hours later, another car did round that wicked curve. It came full throttle. A speeding blur. Bender raced to the side of the road. He stood at the edge of the asphalt, a desperate gleam in his eye, his thick arm stretched out across the roadway like some automated tollgate. The low, sleek Italian sports car, like the black sedan the day before, bore down on him. I thought for a moment I'd have to scream, but the car swept under Henry's arm without losing a single RPM. Henry turned slowly away, rejected and dejected.

"Don't take it so hard, Henry," I said, feeling almost sorry for him. "There wasn't enough room for both of us anyway."

"Yeah, but there might have been enough room for you."

I looked at him. I could see he meant what he said. Bender had been given a mission, and he was fully prepared to complete that mission at any cost. My rendezvous with the ecological elite and the political fat cats down in D.C. was more important to Bender than even his own self-preservation.

Fortunately, after another day or two along that country lane, Henry and I got ourselves a ride. A rusty old rack truck slowed and stopped right in the middle of the road. The truck was loaded with crates full of live chickens. I took one look at those sickly and smelly birds and almost declined to climb aboard. But Bender had already climbed into the cab, so I followed along.

The driver, an old fart with a deeply wrinkled face and a short crop of oily gray hair, held out his hand and smiled with his last couple of teeth. "Drove past you fellers a few days back," he said, "but I was 'fraid to stop. Cain't be too careful these days, what with all the wild-eyed mental patients roamin' the countryside 'cause of all the loony bins bein' closed down for lack of government funds.... You two fellers ain't mental patients, is you?"

Uncertain, I assured him we certainly were not, and off we went. He dropped us in front of the Adamsville General Store in the center of Adamsville. He needed roofing nails and tar paper to repair his coops. I asked him where we could get a hot meal. He pointed down the street to Sally's Luncheonette.

Sally's had pink porcelain walls, pink plastic chairs, and pink Formica tables. Sally wore a white dress and a pink apron. She was in her early forties, must've had a pound of makeup caked onto a face that had years ago seen its best and brightest days. "What'll it be, boys?"

Henry ordered four burgers, two large orders of fries, and a double-thick chocolate malt.

"Skip the malt, Henry," I said. "All that sugar will weird you out."

"Okay. Give me a Coke, a large Coke. No ice."

"Try a glass of milk, Henry." I turned to Sally. "Give him a large glass of milk."

Sally glared at me. "Who are you, this fella's keeper or somethin'?" Then she leaned over close to Bender and stuck her big bazookas right in his line of vision. "What'll you have to drink, big boy?"

I couldn't see Sally's face but I sure could see Bender's. It had turned as red as one of Mama's summer tomatoes. Poor Henry has always been kind of shy around the ladies.

"Milk'll be fine, ma'am," he mumbled.

Sally straightened up, sighed right smack in Henry's face, then turned to me with eyes colder than steel. "What's yours?"

I ordered a cheese sandwich on whole wheat, then we watched Sally shuffle off for the kitchen, the sole of her left shoe flapping as she went.

Bender scratched the dirt out from under his fingernails with a fork. I yawned and glanced out the front window. The chicken farmer walked by. He waved. I waved back. Friends.

A fat slob with a bright red nose wearing a greasy apron came out of the kitchen. The cook. He looked us over. I nodded to him. He grunted and went back to the kitchen. I heard Sally and the fat man laughing. I imagined them doing rude things to our food, so I stood up and told Henry to meet me outside when he'd finished eating.

Before Sally returned with the victuals, I made my exit. I walked up Main Street. I passed a bar, a drug store, a liquor store. Modern Americana.

It was cold and damp, not many folks around: in fact, none at all. I walked into the town square. In the middle of the square stood a tall bronze statue of a soldier carrying a musket and wearing Revolutionary War garb. Pigeonshit covered the soldier from head to toe. The brass plaque at the base of the monument read: W G V R LL N TH F GHT F R L B RTY, J ST C , ND FR D M. G D BL SS M R C .

All the vowels had been chiseled off. And below the inscription was a long list of Adamsville's favorite sons who had died in America's wars, but not one of those names contained a vowel, either.

After long and careful consideration, I deciphered the inscription: WE GAVE OUR ALL IN THE FIGHT FOR LIBERTY, JUSTICE, AND FREEDOM. GOD BLESS AMERICA.

Just as I finished my exercise in cryptography, a pigeon swooped in and dropped a load smack dab on the end of that soldier's nose. The soldier wiped his schnoz, raised his musket, took aim, and pulled the trigger. The mechanism misfired in a puff of black smoke. The pigeon squawked, then flew off before the soldier could reload.

A parade of veterans swept into the square. "Pearl Harbor lives," they chanted. "Never forget Pearl!" They held high a large banner that read FIFTY-FIVE YEARS & COUNTING. And another even larger one that read THE ONLY GOOD JAP IS A DEAD JAP.

I thought about Pop, then I slipped off the square into the residential section of Adamsville. I passed Piney Lane and Meadow View and Willow Way. On the corner of Willow Way and Maple, I stopped to admire an old and spooky-looking stone church. It was protected on all sides by a high wrought-iron fence. With a little force, the front gate creaked open, so I entered the courtyard and had a look around. I climbed the stone steps leading to a pair of massive oak doors. But the doors were locked. A locked church? I had never seen such a thing. The two churches in Cedar Bluffs never lock their doors.

I ventured around back in search of a way inside. I don't know why but I had an almost desperate need for some religion. But all the doors were bolted shut. I peered into the church through dusty but clear-paned windows. A Sunday school class of young Christians was in session. Several obnoxious heretics, however, shot spitballs at their teacher, a bespectacled virgin of thirty-nine who used her holy Bible as a shield against the gooey onslaught. But wait: this could not be, Sunday had come and gone days ago. I blinked three times, then peered through the window again. Ah yes, nothing there but small wooden desks with empty ink wells and, on the front wall, a map of ancient Jerusalem.

But beyond the classroom more dusty windows, and beyond the windows another courtyard, an inner courtyard surrounded by the interior walls of the church.

I cupped my hands around my eyes and pressed my face against the glass. And what a sight I saw! Worn and weathered gravestones, graves open and empty, and the reverend moving among the piles of damp dirt with a shovel in his hands and sweat pouring off his vestments. I closed my eyes and rubbed them thoroughly.

When I opened them I saw the reverend, not six inches from the end of my nose, scowling, his face ablaze. Only a pane of cheap glass separated us. But it was enough to keep the heavens from the hells. His deep-set eyes burned right through me. I shivered. He shouted what sounded to me like obscenities. A preacher spitting curse words?

Out the gate, down the street, and into the town square I fled. Bender dashed into the square from the opposite direction. Like me, he ran like a man pursued.

"Willy, we gotta get outta here! Quick!"

"Right." We looked around, each of us breathing hard.

"This way," he said, and he started toward the church.

"No!" I shouted. "Not that way, you moron, this way," and I headed back toward Sally's.

Bender grabbed me from behind. "No! For crying out loud, not that way!"

"Why not?" But Bender didn't have to answer. At that exact moment, the cook, Sally's fat and greasy cook, came rumbling into the town square with a giant meat cleaver in his right hand. And from the opposite direction came the reverend, still bearing his mud-caked shovel.

Henry and I chose a neutral route out of Adamsville. Mile after mile we ran until we felt sure our pursuers had given up and gone home. We collapsed in a pile of autumn leaves, our breath coming in short, frantic gasps. A large part of the afternoon passed before we spoke.

"Why was that cook chasing you, Henry?" I asked. "Did you try to duck out of that greasy spoon without paying?"

Henry sat against an old oak. His eyes refused to meet mine. I waited for him to answer. "That woman," he said finally, "Sally. She brought me my burgers and fries. She set 'em down in front of me, then mumbled something about dessert. Before I knew it she'd slipped under the table and grabbed my you-know-what. Shocked the heck out of me, Willy, I'll tell you."

I didn't say a word. I knew Henry spoke the truth. He doesn't have the imagination to tell a lie.

"So then she unzips my pants and pulls the thing right out into the open. It was like a steel rod by this time, bigger round than a hickory limb. I thought for sure I'd, you know, unload or something, but then all of a sudden that fat cook came tearing out of the kitchen waving his cleaver and screaming bloody murder that he's gonna chop off my member. I jumped clean out of my chair and bolted for the door. He came right out after me. You saw him, Willy. He wanted to split me in two."

"He did look mildly pissed off, Henry."

"I just hope the fat jerk doesn't hurt Sally."

"Feel kind of responsible for her now, do you?"

Bender bowed his head and nodded. "Maybe a little. . . . You know how it is, Willy."

"Sure, Henry, I know how it is."

We sat quiet for a few minutes, then Henry asked, "Why were you running back there in town, Willy? Who were you running from?"

I looked at him like he was deaf, dumb, and blind, or maybe just plain stupid. "Hell, Henry, I was running from that crazy preacher. The one with the shovel. You saw him."

"Preacher with a shovel?" Henry scratched his chin. "I didn't see any preacher, Willy. I didn't see anyone at all chasing you."

Henry's comment got me thinking about the accuracy of my vision, so after we settled down in our bedrolls for the night and Henry had fallen fast asleep, I slipped out of our camp and back into town. I wanted to have a closer look at that stone church.

Adamsville was quiet. Everyone had retired to their TVs for the evening. I kept to the shadows, avoiding any chance encounters. A block from the church I hopped over a white picket fence and slipped into the backyard of a typical American family. I crawled on my belly through the damp grass to the metal storage shed at the far end of the yard. Light from the TV flowed from a picture window in the living room. I stood up and looked back across the yard, through that window, at the modern-day nuclear family of four that I'll never have eating TV dinners as they watched the tube.

At the exact moment I looked through that picture window, my mug appeared on their television screen. I filled that screen from top to bottom and from side to side, a great big grinning portrait of Willy Brant MacKenzie. Next came a close-up of my book jacket, the one with the full moon rising over Katydeeray. Then a picture of Dawn. I just about freaked out. I almost went right through that picture window, right into those fucking people's living room. I wanted to go in there and slam my fist through their TV screen and then break their legs. But I didn't. I turned away. I left them alone.

I broke into their utility shed instead and stole a hammer and a screwdriver. They had no qualms about invading my life, my privacy; I had no qualms about stealing a couple of tools from them.

The night was cool, almost cold. I could see my breath as I entered the courtyard through the iron gates. As expected, the massive oak doors were locked. I placed the screwdriver against the keyhole and swung the hammer. Several blows later the lock gave way. I cast aside the tools and slipped inside, through the shadowy foyer and into the nave. Plenty of light there. Enough to lead me along my way.

The silence of that autumn night fell away under a barrage of religious oratory. The reverend stood high in his pulpit, delivering his message. "God is at the core of your existence here on earth! God and only God! Remember Him always, and be eternally grateful for His great gift of Life! . . ."

The reverend directed his dark eyes at me. I lowered my own and moved forward in search of a seat. The pews were crowded, a full congregation.

"Be not tempted to go beyond what God has granted you! You are nothing but a limited mortal wallowing in a boiling caldron of sin, deceit, and petty hate! . . ."

My collar began to smolder from his visual attack. I doused it with spittle and dropped a dime into the collection plate.

"The power of God is omnipotent! Do not allow Satan to muddy your path. God is your eyes and ears! Only God can purify your soul! . . ."

I dropped another dime into the plate and moved forward. "Excuse me, sir," I said to an old man in a tweed jacket with suede elbow patches seated on the end of the pew.

"God is your Creator! The master of your universe! . . ."

I felt myself shudder. The old man did not move. "Excuse me," I said again, and I put my hand on his bony shoulder. "May I sit down?"

But the old man did not respond. He could not respond. He could not even move. Not under his own power. The old man in the tweed jacket, you see, was dead, stone dead.

"God holds the power of life over all men, over all mankind! Serve God faithfully, repent your sins, or rest assured that God will exterminate the species we call man! . . ."

The whole stinking congregation was dead! Not a warm body anywhere. Young and old, male and female—all dead! The choir, dead. The organist, dead. The elders, dead. The ushers, dead. I let loose a series of horrible screams. Those old stone walls shook with my terror.

"Fill yourself with God! Fill yourself to the brim and God will lead you away from the precipice, protect you from the evil spells of Satan! . . ."

The reverend's words caromed off the stained-glass windows, reducing my screams to mere whimpers. That entire house of worship went dark, then light, then dark, then light again. Once again I fled from the reverend.

"Only complete absolution will lead to your salvation! . . ."

The dead roared as I reached the doors. Locked! But how and by whom?

I ran down the aisles, my arms flailing, knocking death to the floor, but his voice would not let me alone.

"You must rise out of the abysmal chasm of selfishness and self-pity in which you flounder. You must plead to God for mercy, and for mercy for this earth! For God is the only Truth! . . ."

Ah yes, I stopped and thought, Truth: that ages-old aphrodisiac; that ancient formula for the way things ought to be. The Truth. Right. Fucking A. . . . The absurdity of it all calmed me. I settled down, realized where I was and what I was up against. The light began to shine.

"The only Truth, the only Truth, the only Truth!"

And the congregation began a steady chorus of, "Amen, thank the Lord. Amen! . . ."

I scampered up a circular stairway to a balcony overlooking the scene below. Up there, above it all, I suddenly understood the illusion of Life and the capriciousness of Truth. I stood tall and pointed down at the reverend. "Enough rhetoric, you double-talking dipstick of divinity, you loose-lipped twister of the Trinity! Man invented God.

God did not invent man. Man will extinct mankind. And every other kind. Not God. God's just someone else to blame."

"Blasphemy!" came the response from the rev. "Blasphemy! Capture the heretic!"

Before they could, I slipped through a door leading into a long, narrow hallway with plate-glass walls. Kerosene lamps hung from the ceiling. A strut in my step, I sauntered across the plush, crimson carpet. I felt proud of my ability to handle strange and difficult situations. But then those oil lamps went dead, my limbs grew weak, and the reality of fear crept back into my psyche and settled in the most primitive part of my brain. I stood perfectly still and waited. Time passed. Who knows how much time? I don't know. All I know is that at some point that seemed like the future, those lamps began to flicker, and a thousand powerful lights, as bright as the sun, illuminated my little space on the planet.

The congregation loomed beyond those plate-glass walls. Their faces contained no color but their lips curled up in sort of a wry, awkward smile. I screamed, stood, and ran . . . but slipped in a puddle of my own urine. In slow motion I fell through the air and knocked myself cold. . . .

Early the next morning (a raw, damp morning just a few days ago), the congregation shook me awake and led me into the inner courtyard of the stone church. And there, without hesitation, they filed into their open graves. Water had collected in the bottom of their burial pits, but they accepted this discomfort as their final tribulation before redemption.

When everyone was safe and secure, the reverend appeared wearing nothing but his starched white collar. I was surprised to see he was not circumcised. He gave a brief eulogy in Latin, then he turned to me, and in a thick Scottish brogue he said, "Aye, Willy, me boy, the time has come. I want you to fill in those ditches. Give those bodies back to the earth."

I wondered how he knew my name. But the reverend did not explain. No, he simply loosened his collar and returned from whence he had come, back to the rectory, I assumed.

I took up the shovel and threw the black earth back into the graves with energetic zeal. One by one I filled the pits, covered those ghostly bodies. I thought about Ulysses while I packed the dirt firmly into place by dancing a short jig on top of each burial site. It was fine work. Time passed quickly. A man, I decided, could do worse than be a digger of graves.

As the morning wore on I fought the urge to taste the soil. Finally I could fight it no more. I bent down and scooped up a handful and placed a few clumps on my tongue. It tasted mostly of decayed flowers and tears. And I knew then, for certain, something I had suspected long ago: Death is a far bigger pain in the ass for the living than for the dead. So I spit out the soil, took hold of the shovel, and went back to work, more determined than ever to wreak my revenge. . . .

11:52 A.M.
JANUARY 20, 2001
MACKENZIE ISLAND
THE INAUGURATION OF THE FORTY-FOURTH PRESIDENT OF THE UNITED STATES

Religion. Strange stuff, religion. The great equalizer, my daddy, God rest his soul, always called it. Gets the hair bristling on the backs of normally passive persons' necks.

It's an issue I would like to avoid; one of those no-win situations. But we need to discuss, if only briefly, the role religion has played in our president-elect's life. This role cannot be easily understood or ascertained. Still, I'll give it my best shot.

As a boy, Willy must have been at least mildly confused by the two extreme religious points of view coming from the maternal and the paternal sides of his family. The Mohawk, for instance, like most North American Indian tribes, did not even have a word in their language that meant religion. The word simply does not translate, not as defined in a Judeo-Christian sense: a belief in and reverence for a supernatural being. The Mohawk had no such being. They viewed life itself as a religious experience. Religion was not something they practiced for an hour on Sunday morning. It encompassed every moment of every day. Willy's mother instilled this attitude in her son. She taught him about the Great Spirit, the "Great Mystery," as she liked to call it. This Great Spirit, in a broad sense, was God. And God was Nature. And since man was part of Nature, it followed that he was also part of God. The Mohawk did not separate one from the other. All the elements spun in harmony through the seasonal cycles.

Emily Brant MacKenzie taught her son to respect Nature, to pay homage, as we have seen in the journals, to the Three Sisters, and to the earth, the air, and the water. All the rest of it, she told him, would forever remain shrouded in mystery. The Indians, unlike the Europeans, have never had this overpowering need to explain all the secrets of life. Their culture flourished around mysticism and the continual and open pursuit of one's own imagination. It's clear to me that these great emotional eruptions we have recently witnessed from Willy's imagination stem from his Mohawk upbringing. For years, even decades, Willy may have suppressed these eruptions, but circumstances beyond his control, including the dam spanning the Tamaqua River and the violent death of his wife, finally brought them to the surface.

So what, then, of his Christian upbringing? The MacKenzies, members in good standing of the Church of Scotland in the middle of the nineteenth century, were avid churchgoers: pious zealots, say some. All that changed when they emigrated to America. Their attendance dropped dramatically. Ulysses attended Sunday school as a child in New York City, but as an adult he kept his appearances to a minimum: Christmas and Easter. Senator Lawrence MacKenzie went to church maybe once a month, but only because he did not want his political opponents labeling him a nonreligious man. And Conrad, as far as we can tell, has not been to church a single time since his experiences in the South Pacific during World War Two.

Does this failure to attend church services on a regular basis mean Conrad's son, the next president of the United States, is something less than a fine and upstanding Christian? Difficult question to answer.

Willy, you might be interested to learn, has never been baptized, never taken communion, never been made an official member of any church of any denomination. What might this tell us about his character? And about his moral convictions? And what does it tell us about his days in Adamsville? What was that craziness all about? Was there really an old stone church? A reverend with a shovel in his hand and talk of Satan on his tongue? And what about all those dead folks rising from their graves? Strange events indeed.

Some of you might call Willy's performance in Adamsville sacrilegious. Do I hear calls of blasphemy echoing out there across middle America? Ungodliness? Desecration? Perhaps even a bit of devil worship?

I suppose it boils down to this: Does Willy MacKenzie know what is morally right? Or has this lurid dichotomy between his Indian roots and his European background fractionalized his thinking, made it virtually impossible for him to embrace a set of strong, conventional values with which the American people can feel comfortable?

Troubling questions at this late date, I know, but nevertheless questions that must be raised. Granted, Willy was elected by the people. Not a whole lot of people, mind you, less than twenty-one percent of all citizens eligible to vote, but enough people to carry the day under the recently adopted Twenty-ninth Amendment. But did those people know who they were voting for? Did they know who they were putting in the Oval Office?

Let's just consider the situation for one minute. I think we would all admit we elected Willy out of a sense of frustration. So many years of stagnation and corruption in Congress and in the White House. So much false debate between the two ruling parties. So much debt. So much crime. So much civil unrest. So many voters fed up with the professional pols spewing out the same old rhetoric. The time was ripe for a man like Willy. He was in the right place at the right time when history called. We embraced him and his apparent innocence on pure emotion without even pausing to reflect upon his character.

But enough of my editorializing. What's done is done. In the end we all must draw our own conclusions.

It's closing in fast on high noon. The time has finally come to make Willy MacKenzie our next president. Unfortunately, we still do not have anyone to do the job, to administer the oath of office. Or perhaps I should say fortunately, if you are among those citizens who would like to keep Willy off the grounds of 1600 Pennsylvania Avenue.

Communication remains a problem. Still no word on the whereabouts of Patsy Squire, Henry Bender, or Judge Stuart. Nothing new on those marines, either, or, for that matter, from the halls of Congress.

But this storm, I can tell you, continues to grow worse. Even to get from our location here in the boathouse across the way to the back porch of the Great House would demand a major effort. Not only has almost three feet of fresh snow fallen since we began broadcasting early this morning, but strong, gusty northwest winds blowing off Katydeeray have caused massive snow drifts five and six feet high.

I doubt very much we could leave this island, even in an emergency. And just as unlikely would be anyone managing to reach the island from the mainland.

So what does all this mean for the MacKenzie presidency? Will Willy be inaugurated this afternoon or not? I don't know. I can't really say with any certainty. It doesn't look good. All we can do for now is sit back and delve further into the adventures of Roaming Willy, best-selling author at large.

January 1, 1997
On the Road to Washington

A New Day. A New Year.

I need a new day. I need a new year. I need a new life. This one's turning into a great big pile of shit.

Some folks say I need a new wife. Fuck them.

Maybe I'll make it my life's work to kill that bastard Montgomery, assassinate the son of a bitch, put him out of the country's misery. And so what if I go to jail for my crime? So what if they give me the electric chair or the gas chamber or the lethal dose? It'll be worth it just to rid the planet of the scum who murdered Dawn.

An eye for an eye, a tooth for a tooth, you fuck with me I'm gonna fuck with you; maybe those Bedouins were on to something.

Bender and I travel mostly at night now. It's the old sleep-by-day-so-as-to-keep-out-of-sight routine. Not that I sleep very much no matter what time we put our heads down. Too much going on upstairs. The terrible, murderous dream and all that crap.

For several days now Henry and I have hiked north and east through hills and valleys virtually unspoiled by the invasion of man or his domesticated beasts. Rarely do we see or hear anyone, and when we do, we hit the turf and slip away unnoticed.

The days pass. We have had fine weather, more like late summer than early winter. A bit chilly at night but not even a heavy frost has covered the ground yet. Perhaps soon the earth will not even have winter. I wonder what that would mean? For me? For Dawn? For Emily?

Emily: our little girl. My little girl. I miss her. I should've brought her along. She would've kept me sane, at least kept me in line. She's so young, so perfectly innocent. . . . I was innocent once. . . . She would've seen all this . . . all this responsibility . . . as nothing more than a great big wild adventure. The little thing doesn't even know her old man has flipped his switches. She thinks I'm the greatest. World's Best Dad. I need to remember to call her and wish her a Happy New Year. I'll do it first telephone we find.

"You okay, Willy?" Bender asks.

He asks me that ten or twelve times a day, every day, day after day. I'm getting sick of it. Soon I'll have to send Bender away, back to the valley.

More time passes. Time is now a measure of how far into the distance I can see: the other side of that meadow; the next peak; the next valley; beyond the evergreen forest; across the stream; across that muddy lane. Never very far, really, except on cloudless nights and when the past intrudes. Then I feel like I can see forever, and my whole body starts to shake and rattle like I'm riding in the rusty bed of Henry's old pickup truck.

I take another step. Walk another mile. Settle into a comfortable pace. I try to remember who I am and why I'm here. Tough memories.

I trade barbs with Bender to keep from going completely insane.

"What are you going to be when you grow up, Henry?"

"I'm already grown up, Willy. And you know as well as I do that one day I'll take over my father's garage."

"An honorable profession, Henry, even if I don't think carb adjustments and fixing flat tires will ultimately challenge your sensibilities as a twenty-first-century man."

"What kind of crap you talking now, Willy?"

"Nothing, Henry. Not a damn thing. Just more verbal flatulence."

We walk another mile, whistle another tune. The earth turns a corner, and there hangs our friendly neighborhood moon.

"Are you really going to meet with the president, Willy?"

"That's right, Henry. The president and the president-elect."

"Anderson Montgomery will be there?"

"That's right, Henry, our old foe, A. J. Montgomery. Soon to be our commander in chief."

"At the White House?"

"So they tell me. The Environmental Summit, I believe they've dubbed it."

"And what are you going to say to him?"

"To who? Montgomery?"

"Yeah."

"I suspect I'll say, 'Fuck you, you dirty asshole,' and then I'll shove my index finger in his eye and gouge it out."

"Ouch."

"Just kidding, Henry."

"Don't do anything stupid, Willy. Sanders told me to be sure and tell you not to do anything stupid."

"Hey, don't worry about me, Henry. I'm just a regular guy going through some tough times. We all go through tough times. We just have to buck up and face the music."

January 5, 1997
Still on the Road to Washington

Another day or two passed and suddenly we were close enough to the District of Columbia to see, hear, and feel the bureaucracy at work. No more hills, no more valleys. No more thinking Bender and I were the only survivors left on earth.

We walked along a busy highway with cars and trucks screaming at one another in an endless procession of noise and speed and exhaust.

I screamed at them to slow down, to take it easy, to stop and smell the flowers. They blew their horns and spat out their windows at me in response.

Above us rose a concrete embankment. Painted green. Like grass. Several dozen people occupied the embankment, all of them sitting on old blankets and tattered lawn chairs.

"Look at that," Henry said to me. "Look at all those folks out on this nice winter day enjoying a picnic lunch. It must be a family outing."

"I don't think so, Henry. I hate to ruin the illusion for you but the people you see up there are pimps, panhandlers, drug addicts, and alcoholics."

"You think so?"

"Trust me on this one, Henry."

"Hey, mister," one of them shouted not to me but to my good buddy, "do you have any loose change?"

"Sure," Henry answered, "I think so."

"Don't encourage them, Henry."

"What do you mean, don't encourage them? He asked me if I had any loose change. I told him yes. What's the big deal?"

"Can you spare some of that loose change, mister? I haven't had a morsel of food in weeks."

"Did you hear that, Willy? Poor bastard hasn't eaten in weeks."

"Shit, Henry, he doesn't want food. Look at him, all red-eyed and wired like he's plugged into an electrical generator. He wants a line of coke and a bottle of Thunderbird."

Still, Henry couldn't be stopped. All the years I've known Bender I never knew till that moment that the guy's a natural do-gooder, a regular Good Samaritan.

Not until he gave away every last penny he possessed did I get him back on the straight and narrow. We kept moving down that road. The sights astounded me: bright neon lights, motels with water beds by the hour, malls with four hundred stores and more coming soon, cars waiting on line for fossil fuel while their drivers coughed and cursed and smoked filtered cigarettes.

"I'm starving, Willy."

"You say that six or eight times a day, Henry."

"Well."

We went into a fast-food restaurant to get Henry some much needed nourishment. I gave him the money since he gave all his away, then I headed for the back, for the restroom. I washed my hands, splashed water on my face, and took a good long look at myself in the mirror. Another human being. So what? Big fucking deal.

A boy entered, eleven, maybe twelve years old. He glanced at me, scowled, looked away. He crossed to the crapper, closed and locked the metal door. I heard him unzip his pants and squat on the hard plastic seat. Then silence. Perfect silence. I slipped away. We all need our space to do the things we need to do.

"All filled up again, Henry?"

He belched and nodded and off we went.

Back out on the road for less than another hour before I saw, in the distance, the huge white rotunda atop the United States Capitol.

Henry saved me the trouble of having to tell him to get lost. "I can't take it anymore, Willy. Too much confusion. Too many people. Too much noise. I gotta get out of this place."

"No problem, Henry. I understand."

"Will you be all right?"

"Sure, Henry," I told him, hopefully for the last time, "I'll be fine."

"Why don't you come with me, Willy? We could be back up in the Blues in a few days."

"Listen, Henry, I'd like nothing better than to get back to the valley, but it's not quite time for me to head home yet. I have some unfinished business, some loose ends to tie up."

Henry nodded. We shook hands.

"You take care of yourself, Willy."

"And you too, Henry. You too."

We hugged and slapped each other on the back. Old buddies. For real. I could tell by the tear that rolled out of my eye and down my cheek.

After a second or two Henry turned and started north along the highway.

"See you back in Cedar Bluffs," I shouted, but the traffic noise swallowed up my words before they could reach Henry's ears.

So once again I found myself running solo, playing mental solitaire, mumbling to the breeze; but not really. Tweedledee and Tweedledum danced along beside me. . . .

HIGH NOON
JANUARY 20, 2001
MACKENZIE ISLAND
THE INAUGURATION OF THE FORTY-FOURTH PRESIDENT OF THE UNITED STATES

I hate to interrupt, but we have just seen a most remarkable sight here on MacKenzie Island. It looks like I will have to eat my words. Not long ago I claimed no man could reach MacKenzie Island before this ferocious winter storm abated, but I was wrong wrong wrong.

At first I thought some strange and barbarous apparition had descended upon the island; but no, it was Henry Bender! Looming like some wilderness specter, Bender appeared suddenly out of the whiteness. He came off the frozen cove carrying Judge Orrin Stuart across his shoulder like old St. Nick bearing a hefty sack of holiday gifts.

Incredible!

He trudged through waist-deep snow. One painful step at a time he fought his way to the safety of the Great House. Just before he reached the back porch, the MacKenzies came streaming out to lend a helping hand: Conrad and Sanders and the president-elect. They plowed straight into the drifts. Henry swung the judge off his back and gently handed him over to Willy. Willy turned and headed for the porch.

And then Bender collapsed! Flat out onto the snow. The man must have been exhausted from his superhuman effort. I thought for a moment he might even be dead.

Conrad and Sanders grabbed him under the arms and pulled him to his feet. They literally dragged Bender across the snow, up the steps, and into the house.

Unbelievable!

But the show wasn't over. Just as Conrad MacKenzie closed the back door, another figure appeared out on Loon Cove. It was our own Patsy Squire! She crawled off the cove, tiny balls of snow clinging to her clothes and eyelashes.

We rushed outside and carried her into the boathouse. We wrapped her in blankets and settled her beside the fire. As long as we can stave off hypothermia, I think she'll be fine. But for the time being she's resting quietly, so perhaps we should not press her quite yet for a full report on what happened out there after they left North Creek.

It's twelve o'clock sharp. Time to inaugurate our forty-fourth president. We now have someone on the island who can administer the oath. If, that is, he's strong enough to stand up and do the job. The judge looked pretty feeble to this reporter. That journey from North Creek could easily kill him. We'll check on his condition and let you know. Right now we should head back down to D.C. Willy's just about to enter our nation's capital: a place, I can tell you from personal experience, which has never been quite the same since his visit.

* * * * * * *

January 11, 1997
Washington, D.C.

Time slipped slowly away. While I waited. And wondered. And worried. About my past. My present. My future. Where did I do all these things? In my hotel room high above the political citadel.

I also slipped in and out of that same old dream. That terrible, murderous dream: the waters of the Tamaqua River rising, rising, rising.

"Dawn!" I shouted. "Dawn! Dawn! Dawn!"

"Willy, wake up, it's well past dawn. It's the middle of the afternoon. You're just dreaming."

I opened my eyes and rubbed my lids. "Just dreaming? Who the fuck are you? How did you get in here? Who gave you a key to my room?"

He hovered over me, tall and broad and handsome, too handsome, some might think, for his own good: blue eyes, straight teeth as white as chalk, a smile made in heaven. Or maybe hell. He shoved his hand at me. "Steel, Mr. MacKenzie. Jack Steel."

The voice sounded like the face looked: perfect. Too perfect. All these smooth, smiling angles coming at me. I'd seen this guy somewhere before. But where?

"Yeah. So?"

"We've met before, Willy. Do you mind if I call you Willy?"

I took a closer look at him. Some memory covered with refuse fired off a red light. "Tell you the truth, I do mind. You call me Mr. MacKenzie. At least for the time being."

He just kept smiling. "Okay, Mr. MacKenzie. No problem. Anyway, we've met before. A couple times, in fact. Once out on Tamarack Island at your wife's funeral. I was there but couldn't get close enough to you to express my deepest condolences. So please, accept them now."

Smooth as silk. Like a freshly sanded piece of white oak. This guy wanted something. That was as plain as the part in his blow-dried hair.

"Condolences accepted. Now what do you want?"

"I don't want anything, Willy."

"Deer dip."

"Deer dip?"

"Poppycock."

"Oh. Well. I just want to talk."

"So you do want something?"

"Just to talk."

"You're a reporter, aren't you?"

"I am, yes, but—"

"I knew it. I could tell by that look in your eye. The gaze of a raptor. And by the way your nose sniffs the air. Trying to find the scent of blood. Like a carnivore."

"No, Willy, you've got it wrong. That's not why I'm here. I'm here because I wanted to meet you, get to know you. I'm intrigued by your life and by the sudden rise to stardom you've made these past few months. I want to know you better, Willy. The American people want to know you better."

"Screw you," I said, "and screw them, too. Don't any of you have anything better to do?"

He smiled down at me again. "I've brought you a little present, Willy."

I narrowed my eyes and asked, "What's your name again?"

"Steel," he said, "Jack Steel." Then Jack Steel turned his back on me and crossed to my hotel room door. He opened the door and in stepped a tall, slender, blond bombshell. I mean a real looker: long wavy hair, big beautiful liquid green eyes, full ruby-red lips, a body so curved and smooth I could not ignore the heat lightning in my groin.

"This is my friend Lulu, Willy," said Jack Steel. "She wanted to meet you, too."

Lulu came forward, right up to the edge of the bed. Her large breasts, barely contained by a sheer, low-cut dress, bobbed just inches from my eyelashes. She jiggled them ever so slightly and said, "I read your book, Mr. MacKenzie." Her voice was all air and sex. "I just loved it. It was sooo funny. And sooo wise. You must be a very centered person, very evolved."

I started to ask what that meant, but Jack Steel got his mouth open first. "Gotta run, kids. Ciao. Don't do anything naughty."

Before I could slow him down he was out the door and gone.

Lulu sat on the bed, my bed. I repressed a desire to rip off her flimsy little dress and have my way with her. I could feel Dawn looking down on me, watching me, waiting to see how big a fool I might make of myself.

I smelled something burning so I looked away from Lulu, across the room. A wisp of black smoke curled toward the ceiling. "Why is the carpet smoldering?"

Lulu put her hand on my thigh. "I don't know, Willy. Looks to me like you built a campfire out of the night table."

"A campfire? Why would I build a campfire in my hotel room?" And yet the evidence could not be ignored: charred table legs, embers still glowing orange, the deep pile carpet scorched black, smoke rising to the ceiling.

Lulu shivered. "It's freezing in here, Willy. Why are all the windows open?"

The windows. Right. The missing windows made me remember. I had removed the sealed windows during the night. I'd needed some air and hadn't been able to open the windows, so I'd unscrewed them and pulled them out of their frames. The screws fell twenty-two stories onto the District of Columbia streets below. Soon the room grew cold. So I split up the night table and started a fire.

Lulu moved closer. "Maybe we could cuddle against the chill. I just hate the cold. Don't you hate the cold, Willy?"

I wanted to say, "No, I don't," but the heat lightning flashed in my groin again. I had an overwhelming desire to press my flesh against Lulu's. But I didn't, I held back. I regained control and made a move for the other side of the bed. Lulu followed. Like a cat.

I soon ran out of room. Lulu's paw brushed against my arm. I pulled away and fell off the bed onto the floor. Lulu laughed. But not in a mean way. Just because it's funny when someone falls out of bed.

I felt confused. I stood up, looked around for something to cover my naked body.

"Nice pecs, Willy," said Lulu. "Very well developed."

I started to thank her, but she slipped off that skimpy little dress and all of a sudden we were both stark naked. My penis pointed directly at her like some kind of sexual divining rod.

"Come over here, Willy," she said. "Come to Lulu." Her tongue flicked in and out of her mouth as she beckoned me with the middle finger of her right hand.

I took a step forward. Then a step back. Then a step forward. Back. Forward. Back. And all the time my penis grew longer, like Pinocchio's nose.

And then I heard Dawn whisper in my ear, "She's beautiful, Willy. Gorgeous. But she's as dumb as a stick and nothing but Jack Steel's whore."

I took two giant steps back. Almost stumbled into the red-hot embers. I found my pants and pulled them on. "If Jack Steel wants an exclusive interview with me," I told Lulu in a clear, firm voice, "then you tell Jack Steel that Willy MacKenzie wants something in return."

"But you do get something in return, Willy. You get me."

"Not good enough."

Lulu stared at me in disbelief. These were words she did not often hear. She pouted. She felt bad that I'd rejected her advances.

"Get dressed," I ordered her.

Slowly she pulled on that little dress. It hurt to watch that body go undercover, but I had other fish to fry, other angles to work.

"What's the matter, Willy," she asked spitefully, "you don't like girls?"

I ignored her. "You tell Jack Steel that he gets his exclusive interview with yours truly after I get my eight-by-ten color glossy of our soon-to-be president, Mr. Anderson Johnson Montgomery, in the throes of sexual passion. I want a full-color photo of that son of a bitch screwing a woman, any woman at all, any woman but his wife."

Lulu's mood brightened. She liked this kind of talk. "An eight-by-ten glossy of the president-elect in the act! Oh, Willy, I love your style."

"Good. Then go tell Steel what I want."

"If Jack can't find a photo," said Lulu, her mind active, "maybe I could fashion one for him. I think Monty's kind of cute."

"Fine, Lulu. Whatever turns you on." I showed her to the door. "Now run along."

She smiled and kissed me on the cheek. I flushed crimson, then gave her a shove out into the hallway. I quickly closed and locked the door.

I shaved and showered. The hot, steamy water did nothing to diminish my desire to have sexual intercourse with Lulu. "So what if she's dumb?"

Dawn did not bother to provide me with an answer. So I had to take care of my desires in the only way left.

And when I came out of the shower, temporarily relieved, whom did I find standing in the middle of my hotel room? I found the hotel manager and a couple of his lackeys. One of the lackeys, I found out fast, headed up hotel security. The other lackey specialized in high-rise window repair.

"What the hell is going on in here?" demanded the manager.

I avoided looking at the campfire or the missing windows. "Nothing," I told him. "Just got out of the shower. Plenty of hot water, thank you very much. Excellent water pressure, I might add."

But my compliments, I'm afraid, did not make everything better.

"You've ruined this room!" shouted the manager. "Are you some kind of maniac? A lunatic? A fucking rock and roll star, for chrissakes?"

I tried to explain but even I could not comprehend my explanation.

The manager, needless to say, didn't buy a word of it. "Out!" he shouted. "Pack your bags and get out!"

So I did. I had only one small bag, one of those little plastic jobs with the fake leather handles. It said TAMAQUA VALLEY HIGH SCHOOL across the front of it. I crammed my few personal belongings into the bag and waved good-bye. I rode the elevator, crossed the lobby, and hit the streets.

I strode down Pennsylvania Avenue. The last light of a short winter's day had already started to fade. It was cold. A raw wind blew from the north, from home.

I passed the White House, spit, then crossed the frozen Ellipse and climbed the small knoll to the Washington Monument. Right before my eyes that tall, slender shrine turned into an enormous phallic obelisk.

Spooked by this transference, I slipped inside. The monument was open for business. The guy from National Park Service tried to usher me into the elevator, but I insisted on taking the stairs.

"It's quite a hike," he shouted as I began my ascent, "897 steps to the top."

I didn't care. I needed a physical challenge. I needed to feel my heart pound. So up and up and up I climbed. Faster and faster. When I reached the top I vomited and passed out.

A stern, mechanical voice pulled me awake. It came from a scratchy squawk box overhead. "The monument will close in five minutes, five minutes. It will reopen tomorrow at nine a.m. Please proceed promptly to the elevator. Thank you for your cooperation."

And indeed, everyone did cooperate with the unseen voice. Everyone, that is, but me, wee Willy MacKenzie. I had no desire whatsoever to cooperate with the authorities. So I glanced around for a place to hide.

It looked at first like I would be unable to find a spot to secret myself away, but then, when the Park Service guy turned his back, I spotted a crevice in the shadows up above. I shinned up the fresh-air vent and wedged myself into a dusty and oily corner near the top of the elevator shaft. I moved not a muscle, drew only the most shallow breaths. And then, like I had been doing earlier, I waited. And worried. And wondered what my imagination might tell me to do next.

The elevator descended, carrying the last of the tourists back to planet Earth. The observatory grew quiet. I prepared to exit my cave. But suddenly I heard voices. Two men stepped off the elevator directly below me.

"Hell, Frank, I wish I had your job. You got it made in the shade. Walk around all day wearing that fancy uniform, giving people directions, pointing out important national landmarks. Real cozy job, Frank, my man, real cozy job."

"Believe me, Joe, it gets pretty damn boring sometimes. Pret-tee damn boring."

"Boring! Jesus, Frank. You want boring? Try sweeping up garbage and emptying litter baskets and cleaning out crappers five days a week, eight hours a day. Now that, my man, is boring."

Frank, the one with the uniform, took a quick look around for stragglers. He pointed his flashlight up in my direction but I had become one with the monument.

"All clear, Joe. I'll be heading down. See you tomorrow."

"Right, my man. Tomorrow."

Frank rode the elevator back to the bottom. As soon as he left, Joe turned on his portable radio, cranked up the sound, and began scrubbing the floor with a damp mop. He sang along with an up-tempo tune with a very catchy lyric. "Wooo, get down, get down, get down! Wooo baby, you know you got to get down, get down, get down . . . for love!"

Right. For love. I plugged up my ears and waited for the pain to pass.

Joe spent almost half an hour tidying up the observatory. Finally he finished his cleaning, packed up his gear, and prepared to move out. I watched him step onto the elevator. The second those elevator doors closed, I crept out of my cave.

I could hear the sound of Joe's radio fading as the elevator made its hasty descent. I took a deep breath and stretched my muscles back into shape. The obelisk was mine for the night.

I peered out the just washed windows. All around me lurked the capital, awash in artificial light and glowing with all of its excessive and extravagant symbolism: the monuments and memorials and museums illuminating our Glorious Past; the Capitol Rotunda radiating our vision of the Future; the Presidential Palace blazing with all of our petty, middle-class American Dreams of the Present. And the whole mess so strikingly clean, so brilliantly white.

My nose picked up a strange but familiar scent. It smelled, I don't know, like greed and power and corruption. But no, wait, not quite so pungent. Rather sweet, actually. It oozed, like time, through the thick walls of the obelisk. And then, yes, of course, it came to me: it was the smell of fresh semen.

The noble obelisk, a monument to our Founding Father, our great and beloved general, our first and foremost president: nothing but an enormous marble hard-on symbolizing man's domination of woman and a nation-state's desire to dominate the planet and everyone and everything on it.

But like all lonely men without love, the obelisk had nowhere to stick it without first paying the price. Let's face it: the builders, designers, and worshipers of the obelisk were, are, and always will be powerful men who jerk off into their wastepaper baskets. Frustrated men. Angry, aggressive men who seek power to hide their fears of failure and impotence. Men without women. Men without balls. Men willing to kill, even obliterate the planet, simply to soothe and satisfy their tiny, stinking egos.

All through the night the obelisk beat itself off, beat itself silly.

I found refuge up in my head, where I passed the hours thinking of Dawn and Emily and the peace and quiet of our little islands out on the edge of the planet.

12:11 P.M.
JANUARY 20, 2001
MACKENZIE ISLAND
THE INAUGURATION OF THE FORTY-FOURTH PRESIDENT OF THE UNITED STATES

What do you think, folks? Has the time come to call in the psychoanalysts? Or should we forgo the shrinks and just bring on the boys in the white suits?

Wacky stuff, I know. But don't look to me for explanations or interpretations of this latest journal entry. I don't have a clue. I studied journalism in school, not psychology. The Washington Monument as a gigantic marble penis. The head doctors could have a field day with that one.

I do think we can say with some certainty that Willy was royally ticked off at Anderson Montgomery, so ticked off he wanted to kill the guy. This anger undoubtedly grew out of Willy's firm belief that the former governor was directly responsible for Dawn's death. Monty had been the chief advocate of the Tamaqua River Valley Dam and Development Project. He's the guy who had opened the sluice gates on that fateful day. And let's face facts: it is Dawn's death that lies at the heart of Willy's dementia or psychosis or neurosis or whatever you want to call it.

Lulu, for instance. Lulu did not and does not exist. Lulu was nothing more than a figment of Willy's overwrought imagination. Again, I cannot begin tell you why he did it, but the guy simply made Lulu up.

Look, I might be ambitious to a fault, but I am not amoral. I might be competitive in my drive to reach the top of my profession, but I would never play the pimp just to solicit a stupid interview. Never in my wildest dreams would I resort to such contemptible and unprofessional shenanigans.

Sure, I went to see Willy at his downtown hotel. I won't say which hotel, but I will tell you it stood not a stone's throw from the White House. Willy had a regal suite, one of the finest rooms available in that old Washington establishment, which has, over the years, hosted kings and queens and elected heads of state. If Willy tore out the windows and built a fire in the middle of his room, no one who works there ever admitted as much to me.

But that's neither here nor there. Improper decorum often demands a cover-up.

Anyway, it took me several days to locate Willy. And once I finally did locate him, I still had to get in to see him. No easy chore.

I tried repeatedly to make contact by telephone. Willy refused to accept or to return my calls. So in the end, out of desperation, I had to book a room at that downtown hotel, at five hundred dollars per night, just down the hall from Willy. Then I had to pay the bellhop another five hundred bucks to unlock the door and let me into Willy's suite.

I found Willy in there sleeping and dreaming, in the middle of the afternoon, just as his journal said. But this thing about me offering him some beautiful blond bombshell named Lulu, well, that's simply ludicrous.

But if we leave Lulu out of the picture, most of Willy's account rings true. He proved almost immediately that he is definitely the grandson of Senator Lawrence MacKenzie. Willy put his political moxie on display by coming right out and telling me I would have to come up with a photograph of Anderson Montgomery copulating with a woman other than his wife before he would grant me an interview. He didn't beat around the bush, didn't mince words; nope, he just came out and told me the way things would have to be.

I told him that I never had and never would deal with extortionists. "There's a matter of professional ethics here, Mr. MacKenzie."

"Fine," said Willy. "You don't want to get me the photo, I'll find some word hustler who will. You hacks are a dime a dozen."

I ignored the insult. I hung around for a few minutes, trying to convince him to change his mind, but when he picked up the telephone and started dialing security, I cleared out fast. I didn't need that kind of trouble.

All the way down in the elevator I kept thinking about the thousand bucks I'd just dropped, and how I had dropped it for nothing. And then I realized Willy was right: if not me, someone else would get him that photo. So by the time I reached the lobby—and I admit this to you in complete candor—I had started to wonder where I might get my hands on an eight-by-ten color glossy of President-elect Montgomery in a compromising position.

I knew one had to exist. Everyone knew Montgomery slept around; he hadn't been faithful to his wife for years. But knowledge, especially in this game, is useless without proof. So I left the hotel, went back to my office, and reluctantly began to make a few calls. On the sly, you understand. Off the record. . . .

Something else I should mention. It has to do with the entries in Willy's journal during his stay in Washington. I found it rather odd, and I think you will, too, that not a single time on a single page does he refer to the events that brought him to Washington in the first place.

He stayed for two weeks, from his arrival on the sixth of January to his sudden, and rather unexpected, departure on the twentieth, the day of Anderson Montgomery's presidential inauguration. During this two-week period Willy had two very successful book signings. At one bookstore on Capitol Hill he signed over six hundred copies of his book. And at the other signing on Wisconsin Avenue in Georgetown, not far from where his father had lived as a boy, Willy penned his name another four hundred times. No mention of either signing in the journal.

Willy also gave a standing-room-only reading at Kennedy Center attended by too many dignitaries for this newsman to name. He read for nearly an hour, twice bringing his audience to a standing ovation. Again, not a word about this in the journal.

And the next night, in the Senate reception room of the United States Capitol, more than two dozen Republican and Democratic senators attended a cocktail party given for Willy in honor of his grandfather

Lawrence. At the party several senators asked Willy when he planned to run for political office.

"You can't miss," one of the senators told him. "You have money, connections, charm, youth, and good looks."

Willy just smiled politely and sipped his beer. But once again, not a word in the journal about this affair.

I doubt if anyone at that cocktail party knew Willy had spent the night in the Washington Monument fantasizing about ninety-thousand-ton penises. But it is exactly this ambivalence, this duality, that makes him so interesting, so intoxicating, to the curious mind.

What was going on inside his head that he wouldn't even make a note about these highly public events? After all, they were marks of his success as an author and a MacKenzie. I tell you, even after all the hours I have spent digging into Willy's family and into his own personal past, I don't really feel as though I'm any closer to answering the questions I posed to you early this morning: Who is Willy MacKenzie? And what does he want from us?

Before we continue with Willy's exploits down in the District of Columbia, including the infamous scene that once and for all delivered him onto the political battlefield, let me briefly bring you up to date on the physical condition of our three intrepid travelers.

Our own Patsy Squire suffers from severe hypothermia. Thus far she has been unable to give us any details about what happened after the threesome left the North Creek home of Judge Orrin Stuart.

The judge, we understand, remains secluded in an upstairs bedroom of the Great House, buried beneath a thick pile of down quilts and wool blankets. He has frostbite on the tips of at least three toes, two fingers, his earlobes, and the end of his nose. He shivers uncontrollably. No one knows when he will be able to administer the oath of office to the president-elect. I continue to wonder if he will be able to do so at all. And since the time is now quarter past twelve, the appointed hour has already come and gone. Does this mean the United States of America does not, at this moment in history, have a bona fide, duly elected president?

Our informant on the catering staff tells us that Henry Bender is alive and well and talking a mile a minute. We don't have the particulars yet, but it sounds like a band of men wearing the winter uniforms of the

United States Marines waylaid the trio on the outskirts of North Creek. I am presently trying to get Henry out here so he can give us a full report. If and when I get that interview, we will bring it to you live.

Other than that, we wait. Nothing else we can do. We're here for the duration. Venture outside in this storm and you can't find your hand in front of your face. The snow falls. The wind howls. The day wears on. While history, it would seem, stands perfectly still.

January 17, 1997
Washington, D.C.

I strolled down Pennsylvania Avenue, on my way to the White House, incognito. I wore a false beard and a pair of black plastic eyeglasses with bushy eyebrows.

"Willy, is that you?"

I glanced to my left and saw Jack Steel. "How did you recognize me?"

He ignored my question and came closer, right up into my face. He held up a large manila envelope. "I got it."

"You got what?"

The morning felt warm, almost like spring, even though big, wet drops of snow fell from a low gray sky.

"The photograph," he said. "I got the photograph of Anderson Montgomery. Believe me, it wasn't easy, and it cost me a bundle, but I got it."

I caught a few flakes on my tongue. "Let's see it."

"Not so fast, Willy. First we talk."

"First I get the picture."

"First I get my interview."

"Okay," I said, and I stroked my fake beard, "but you at least have to show it to me. I get to see the goods before I talk."

"You can see it," said Jack Steel, "but you can't touch it. Not yet. Not until you answer my questions."

"You drive a hard bargain, Steel," I said, "but you have a deal. Let's have a look."

And so right out there on Pennsylvania Avenue, less than a block from the White House, with tourists and members of the House of Representatives striding by, Jack Steel pulled the photo out of the envelope. And there he lay: in living color, the next president of the United States, Mr. Anderson Johnson Montgomery, bare-ass naked on some cheap motel room bed and fully inserted inside a luscious blonde.

My God! Lulu!

"Christ, Jack," I asked, incredulous and maybe slightly jealous, "does this babe Lulu do all your dirty work?"

He snickered while I snuck another peek at the erotica. The photographer must've crept into the motel room, focused his lens, and said, "Good evening, Mr. President."

Our soon-to-be commander in chief must've turned his head sideways, his eyes suddenly as big as moons and filled with fear, sweat running off his brow from the physical exertion of his efforts, and— Snap! The flash flashed and the shutter shuttered, forever freezing Monty and his delectable tart Lulu in the throes of illicit passion.

I began to drool, unsure if it was the political damage I might inflict upon Montgomery with the photo or if it was the sight of Lulu's perfectly erect and rosy nipples. She might've been working an angle on President-elect Montgomery, but that had not prevented her from having a good roll in the hay.

Jack gave me one last look, then slipped the photo back into the manila envelope. "Question-and-answer time, Willy."

I wiped my chin. "Okay, what do you want to know?"

"Let's walk a bit, Willy. It might help you relax. You seem incredibly tense."

"I'm on my way to the White House."

"I know," said Jack, "but there's plenty of time for our little chat." He took my arm and led me away from the crowded street corner. We walked across the Mall to where the Great Emancipator sat in eternal judgment before the nation: his gaze steady, his posture perfect, his immortal words carved in stone: "Fourscore and seven years ago our fathers brought forth on this continent a new nation, conceived in liberty, and dedicated to the proposition that all men are created equal ..."

"Manifest bullshit," I mumbled.

"How do you mean, Willy?"

I could tell by the sudden rise in his voice that Jack Steel thought

America was just peachy, not a flea to be found anywhere on the old dog. "I mean Honest Abe meant well, but the guy obviously hadn't studied his history books thoroughly."

"Why do you say that?"

"The Founding Fathers slipped that phrase, 'all men,' into their important decrees, but they failed to mention that they did not include blacks, Native Americans, or women in their freedom package."

Jack considered this and then asked, "Would you consider yourself a patriot, Willy?"

"Is this the interview?"

He looked at me and smiled. He was smooth all right. "Sure, I guess."

"Just wanted to square that up."

"So how do you like the capital, Willy? Ever been here before?"

"I like it just fine, and yes, I've been here before. My father grew up in this town, and my grandfather worked here in the United States Senate for most of his adult life."

"But what about you, Willy? Any ambitions to one day serve here in Washington?"

"Maybe."

"What do you mean, maybe?"

"When I was a kid I wanted to be president."

"And do you still?"

"My great-grandfather Ulysses wanted his son to be president, then later he wanted his grandson, my father, to be president, and after that he wanted me to be president. Claimed he had visions of me sitting in the Oval Office. See, Ulysses thought the MacKenzies had the breeding and the grit and the good sense to run the country."

"So you still harbor at least a small ambition to live in the White House?"

"I didn't say that."

"But you alluded to the fact that—"

"Don't hand me that 'alluded to' bullshit, Steel. I changed my mind. The answer's no, I don't want to be president. I just want to be left alone."

"You might find that difficult, Willy. The masses have embraced you."

"Idiots."

"You're a celebrity now, Willy, public property. Loss of privacy goes with the territory."

I decided the time had come to put an end to my little conversation with this jackass Jack Steel. "Give me the photograph, Jack."

"Not quite yet. You haven't answered all my questions."

"I've answered all the goddamn questions I intend to answer."

"Do you blame Anderson Montgomery for the death of your wife?"

"The son of a bitch killed her, didn't he?"

"But Willy, it was an accident. Certainly the ceremonial opening of the Tamaqua Valley Dam would have stopped had anyone known Dawn was chained to—"

"Don't hand me that naive horse crap, Steel. It doesn't fit your own slick image of yourself."

"But, Willy, really. Why would Anderson Montgomery have intentionally opened those sluice gates if he'd known Dawn was—"

"Because she was noisy. Noisy and aggressive. They don't like noisy, aggressive women."

"Who exactly are they, Willy?"

"Who do you think, jerk-off? The motherfuckers with the power. Now gimme that goddamn photograph."

"Hold your horses, Willy. We made a deal. No photograph until you've lived up to your end of the bargain."

"The hell with deals, Steel. This is America. Deals are made to be broken. Every man for himself."

I reared back and let fly a furious right hook. It caught Jack Steel on the side of the head. The reporter wobbled on the balls of his feet, then hit the frozen turf just beyond the Lincoln Memorial. I reached down to grab the manila envelope, but a gust of wind swooped in and stole it away. I watched it for a moment, then gave chase. The breeze carried it out and over the reflecting pool. I waded into the icy water and snatched it out of midair.

As I came ashore, Jack Steel struggled to his feet. "Goddammit, MacKenzie, gimme back that envelope!"

"Sorry, Jack," I said, "no can do."

He lurched at me, but I sidestepped out of the way.

"Gotta run, Jack. Late for my date at the White House. Write whatever you want about me. Put my remarks in quotes. I don't give a good goddamn. In the end, when all is said and done, we have only ourselves to face anyway."

And with that simple profundity floating on the wind, I fled across the Ellipse and up to the wrought-iron gates surrounding the Presidential Palace.

An armored guard, that is to say a guard clad in armor, stopped me at the palace gate. He wore the presidential seal on his breastplate. "Who goes there?"

"Just me," I answered, "wee Willy MacKenzie."

He placed his gauntlet on my head and squeezed. "Enter, peasant, but beware." He poked me lightly with his lance as I scooted through the gate.

The snow turned to rain as I crossed the palace lawn. I shoved the envelope inside my jacket to keep the precious photo dry. I was ushered inside by a Secret Service agent wearing dark glasses. He led me down a long, bright hallway to the East Room. "The reception," he informed me, "has already begun. The president and the president-elect will be along shortly."

I gave him a quarter and went inside to mingle. The country's conservation and environmental elite stood around in small circles discussing the planet's problems while sipping rum punch. Mostly they looked like a bunch of twits in their tweed jackets and designer hiking boots.

We had all been invited to meet with the outgoing and the incoming presidents so that both men could feed us their arsenal of environmental lies and distortions, tell us just how genuinely committed they were to protecting and preserving the planet. It was really just a fancy political photo-op, a one-hour bullshit session to make the masses think their sovereigns were swell fellas with great big hearts. The presidency has become a fucking joke, and our phony gathering in the East Room the other day is all the proof I need to make that declaration stick. I would've bagged the whole performance, stood outside the wrought-iron gates with the poor and the pitiful and the disaffected, and heckled those sons of bitches, but it was my grand opportunity for an up close and personal with President-elect Montgomery. The two of us had a few things to discuss.

Finally, after two glasses of punch and enough blabber to drown a fish, I spotted the president and the president-elect. Amid great fanfare, they floated through the doors of the East Room. The two men absolutely loathe one another. Not only do they hail from different political parties, but they uttered the most awful things about one another during the campaign. Ugly, ugly, ugly.

Several slick aides followed in their footsteps. They spread through the East Room like a well-developed cancer. The two pols attacked us with wide smiles and firm handshakes. But the president, who just four short years ago looked so young and full of promise, now looked weary and bewildered. I think he had us confused with some other folks. He kept mumbling under his breath about the dirty rotten conservatives they had allowed into the White House just three days before his retirement.

Fortunately, one of his aides took the president aside and whispered in his ear that the men and women gathered in the East Room were not conservatives, sir, but conservationists.

But the president was merely an aside. I had no interest in him. He'll be writing his memoirs in a few days; already has a handsome book contract, I understand. No, I wanted his heir apparent.

I pushed through a crowd of radical green reformers to get close to him. His toothy smile vanished when his eyes roamed my way. I could see Monty was surprised to find me on the grounds. He tried to move off but I quickly moved in. I shoved my hand into his. I crushed the bones in his fingers and palm as best I could. He tried hard not to wince. All around us flashbulbs popped.

"Good afternoon, sir," I said, nice as can be. "Willy MacKenzie. So glad I could be here with you today."

"Yes, Willy," he said, the smile broad but wary, "how are you? Nice to see you again. How's your father?"

My palms sweated and my hands trembled, but I figured, what the hell? we have to do what we have to do. Life demands it. So I pressed on. "Fine, sir, very well. The whole family's fit as fiddles."

"Excellent. Great to hear it."

He tried to move along, on to the next handshake, but I was way ahead of him. "I was wondering, sir, if I might have thirty seconds of your time."

His smile faded. He glanced around the room, trying to catch the eye of one of his aides. "Sure, Willy," he mumbled. "What's on your mind?"

"It might be better if we had a little privacy, sir."

A hint of panic crossed his puffy face. Maybe the bastard thought I had a gun or maybe a Molotov cocktail. Maybe he thought I was going to waste him right there in the East Room. That would be a first.

I led him away from the crowd. The eyes of his aides suddenly burned into my back. There was no time to waste. My mouth opened and started to operate. Words spilled out. "Well, sir, it's like this: The way I see it, well, you're the stinking bastard responsible for my wife's death."

I could see he wanted to call out for help, but at the same time he didn't want to portray any sign of weakness in front of the press, not three days before his inauguration. "Willy, I really don't think—"

"Shut up, asshole," I told the president-elect, and it felt good, very good. So I whipped out the photo and held it up for him to see. "A very nice likeness of you, wouldn't you agree, Mr. President?"

He immediately tried to snatch the photo from my hand.

I pulled it back. "Not so fast, Monty."

"What the hell is this?" he demanded. "What do you want?" Anderson Montgomery tried to sound presidential, but the sweat shimmering on his upper lip gave him away. The man was, well, scared shitless. His face turned bright red. I'll bet his blood pressure was out of sight, off the monitor. Maybe he'll explode, I thought, blow a hole through the top of his head.

"Retribution," I answered. "I want retribution."

Several of his aides began to circle. They sensed trouble. They got paid to sense trouble. They surrounded us.

I smiled at them, and then I put my arm around the president-elect's shoulder and whispered in his ear. "The photo's just the beginning, you dirty scum-sucking fuck weed. I'm gonna get your ass and feed it to the wolves."

Then I backed away and gave his boys another big smile. "So long, fellas," I said. "See you down at the unemployment line."

I sauntered out of the East Room, down the long corridor lined on both sides with portraits of past presidents, and out of the White House into the gray and dreary afternoon. Fearing Monty's aides or a squad of Secret Service agents might follow, I hit the pavement running, and kept running until I could run no more.

12:21 P.M.
JANUARY 20, 2001
MACKENZIE ISLAND
THE INAUGURATION OF THE FORTY-FOURTH PRESIDENT OF THE UNITED STATES

Let me apologize for the president-elect's foul language. He seems to have inherited that rather nasty trait from his great-grandfather Ulysses. There will be more four-letter words in the journal entries to follow, so parents of young children, please beware.

That said, let me once again say that I hate to contradict the president-elect of the United States of America, but, well, certain elements in his account are simply not accurate. Willy and I did have a meeting at the Lincoln Memorial, but it was a prearranged meeting, time and place agreed upon by both of us a day or two in advance. It was a glorious winter day in D.C. with temperatures soaring into the fifties by early afternoon. I do not remember a single drop of rain or snow. Nor do I remember Willy wearing a false beard and plastic eyeglasses with bushy eyebrows. He was clean-shaven with hair combed neatly, wearing gray corduroy slacks, a flannel shirt, and an expensive leather jacket.

We sat on the steps of the memorial for almost an hour. He had agreed to an hour in exchange for the photograph. Yes, I did have the photograph. And yes, the photograph was of President-elect Anderson Montgomery in a compromised position. But the woman's name was not Lulu. Her name, her working name anyway, was, I believe, Clear Blue. Maybe somewhere along the way Willy confused Clear Blue with Lulu. I don't know. The names sound somewhat similar.

So I showed the photograph to Willy before our interview began. He smiled a wicked smile when he saw Montgomery humping a woman other than his wife. My memory serves me well in recalling exactly what Mr. MacKenzie mumbled at the time. "This little number," he said, his finger pointing to the eight-by-ten glossy, "will help me bury that son of a bitch. Bury him and kick dirt on his grave."

I shivered and quickly slipped the photo back into its protective envelope. We chatted then, amiably even, for fifteen or twenty minutes. I told him a little about me: my midwestern rearing, my college days, my early jobs as a journalist, my family. He listened attentively, appeared genuine in his interest, even asked a few polite questions. Then, slowly, tactfully, I began to move the focus of our conversation from me to him.

To digress for a moment: During the course of Willy's last several journal entries, starting with those bizarre events in New York City, I believe we have witnessed the emergence of a young man on the brink of an emotional breakdown. His rendering of events, at least occasionally, suggests someone teetering on the brink of delirium. But at the beginning of our interview, for nearly half an hour, I found Willy quiet but confident, modest but self-assured, and eager to talk about his father, his brother, his grandfather, and even Ulysses. I began to learn then a little of what I have shared with you today. Willy spoke about his family with enthusiasm, warmth, and passion.

But then—and maybe here I was to blame, maybe I tackled the subject too quickly, too eagerly—it just seemed the time had come to turn the conversation to Dawn. But the moment I did, our rapport began to disintegrate. Willy's eyes narrowed and grew hostile as soon as I mentioned her name. He scowled at me, scrunched his head down into his neck. A whole new personality emerged.

"The interview's over," he growled.

I took a step back but made my plea. "Willy, please, a few more minutes. Just a few more questions."

"No!" he snapped, and I had the feeling he might haul off and crack me. But instead of hitting me, he said, "You're a parasite, Steel. Sweet-talking and smooth as butter-cream icing, but still a parasite. A two-bit hack reporter trying to act like my pal so I'll spill my guts. Well fuck you. I'm not letting you or any of your scumbag reporter friends violate the inner sanctum of my family."

The color rose in his cheeks as he verbally assaulted me, but the verbal assault proved unable to temper his displeasure with yours truly. He clocked me then on the side of the head with a roundhouse punch. That punch sent me tumbling down the hard marble stairs of the Lincoln Memorial. The fall knocked me out, if only for a moment, but long enough for Willy to snatch the photo and head for the White House.

He did, in fact, have an invitation to a reception in the East Room that afternoon. More than one hundred prominent writers and scientists active in environmental matters attended that reception. I was not invited, so I cannot confirm or deny Willy's version of events. I do know that Anderson Montgomery, just three days away from becoming the forty-third president of the United States, was at the White House for that reception. And I have every reason to believe that Willy MacKenzie, just three days away from becoming a national cult hero, did indeed give the president-elect a quick look at that lovely snapshot of him penetrating Clear Blue.

Beyond that, your speculations prove as viable as mine.

But let's put all this sexual innuendo aside for the time being. We have just finished setting up a remote over at the Great House, where Henry Bender has kindly agreed to give us a few minutes of his time.

JACK STEEL: Hello, Henry. It's Jack Steel.

HENRY BENDER: Yes, Mr. Steel.

J.S.: Can you hear me all right, Henry?

H.B.: Yes, Mr. Steel, I can hear you fine.

J.S.: Call me Jack, Henry.

H.B.: Okay, Jack.

J.S.: How you feeling, Henry?

H.B.: Pretty good. Maybe a little tired.

J.S.: I'll bet. So tell us, how's the judge?

H.B.: The judge? Well, I'd have to say he's in pretty rough shape.

J.S.: How rough?

H.B.: When I saw him a few minutes ago he was shivering up a storm under a pretty thick pile of wool blankets. But he should be okay just as soon as his body temperature stabilizes and we get some warm liquids in him.

J.S.: So when can we expect him up and around?

H.B.: I don't rightly know the answer to that. I just got a feeling he'll be peeved at me for a long time to come for dragging him out in this weather.

J.S.: I wouldn't worry about that, Henry. He knows you did it for a good cause. Which brings us to the inauguration. As you probably know, we're running a little late. Any idea when Judge Stuart will be able to swear our good friend Willy into office?

H.B.: Like I said, Jack, I don't rightly know.

J.S.: Care to venture a guess? Within the hour?

H.B.: Maybe. Hard to say.

J.S.: Thanks for your decisiveness, Henry. Very reassuring. Now let's turn to another matter. I would like you to tell us what happened after you left Judge Stuart's home in North Creek.

H.B.: Yeah, well, I got the judge strapped into this makeshift sleigh and we started south for Cedar Bluffs. It was slow goin', what with the roads impassable and the snow fallin' so fast I couldn't keep my bearings. And we had that girl, Patsy, with us, the one you'd sent. Never should've done that, Jack. Frail as a willow shoot, that one. How is she?

J.S.: Coming along, Henry, coming along.

H.B.: That's good.

J.S.: So what happened out there?

H.B.: The buggers jumped us, that's what happened. They

must've been laying for us. Eight of them. Commandos wearing winter fatigues. Special Forces toting M-16 assault rifles.

J.S.: Why do you say they were Special Forces? Did they identify themselves?

H.B.: Heck no, they didn't say a word. Just surrounded us, pointed their rifles at us, and made it clear enough that we were their prisoners.

J.S.: So why do you think they were Special Forces?

H.B.: Their winter fatigues gave 'em away. Definitely Special Forces attached to the United States Marines. I've been a military nut for years. I know uniforms.

J.S.: Okay, so they took you prisoner. Then what?

H.B.: Well, a couple of them talked it over, then we started back for North Creek. But after just a few minutes it grew clear to me that these guys were lost and had probably never set foot in the valley before. Finally they had to ask me for help. I thought about telling them to go to grass, but then this plan popped into my head.

J.S.: Plan?

H.B.: Yeah. I agreed to lead us back to North Creek, so they put me out in front. Right away I began to veer us off course. One step at a time I swung us over to the southwest in the direction of the lake. There's some forest about halfway between Cedar Bluffs and North Creek that's as thick as the fur on the back of a Belgian sheepdog. I got us tangled up good in that forest, and what with the storm holding visibility to nil, it wasn't no time at all before those marines started wandering off in every which direction. I grabbed hold of Patsy and Judge Stuart, and the three of us stayed real quiet while panic set in among the troops. Once it did, once those marines started running around in the woods like a bunch of headless chickens, I steered us for the river, and, well, after a heap of a struggle, including damn near freezing to death, we made it back here to the islands.

J.S.: Unbelievable, Henry. You deserve a medal.

H.B.: Nah.

J.S.: And no sign of those marines?

H.B.: No, sir. No sign at all. They may still be wandering around in that forest.

J.S.: Tell me this, Henry, why do you think they did it? Why did they jump you?

H.B.: Geez, Mr. Steel, I mean Jack, for a goodly long time I didn't have a clue. I thought maybe . . .

Henry's voice suddenly trails off. There is a brief silence, then another voice I cannot immediately place. "That's enough, Henry. You've said enough. Go into the kitchen now and get yourself something hot to eat."

J.S.: Henry, hold on a second. What's going on over there? Who's that with you?

CONRAD MACKENZIE: It's me, Steel, Conrad MacKenzie. Henry's said all he's going to say.

J.S.: Conrad! How are you?

C.M.: I'm pissed off, Steel, that's how I am.

J.S.: Conrad, old friend, what's the problem?

C.M.: You figure it out, Steel. You tell me why those stinking sons of Marine Corps bitches jumped Henry and Judge Stuart. You tell me.

J.S.: Well, hell, Conrad, I don't know. I suppose—

C.M.: You suppose, my ass. You stink worse than a pig's sty. It's pretty clear, Steel, that someone didn't want Henry to get back to the island with Judge Stuart. Someone who wanted to postpone this inauguration.

J.S.: You may be right, Conrad. In fact, you probably are right. But I still don't see why you're mad at me. What did I do?

C.M.: You didn't do a damn thing, Steel. No, not you. You're as pure as the snow piling up outside. But answer me this: How did those marines know Henry went up to North Creek? And how did they know he'd gone there specifically to fetch Judge Stuart?

I can't even get my mouth open before Conrad answers for me.

C.M.: I'll tell you how they knew, Steel. They knew because you told them. You and your big goddamn mouth announced it for the whole world to hear. I know that for a fact; heard you blab it with my own ears. But what I'm not too sure about yet is your motives for making this announcement. Either you did it because you are an obnoxious megalomaniac willing to say or do anything for a few ratings points, or you did it because you, like so many other paranoid agents of the status quo, deem it necessary to bring my boy to his knees. If it's the former, I'll break your arms. But if it's the latter, I'll break your arms and legs, pluck out your eyes, and cast you stark naked out into the middle of this storm.

Before Conrad can bombard me with more threats, I think it's best if we cut off the remote. No sense giving voice to a raving lunatic. Better to return to Washington, where Willy is on the fast track to fame and political fortune.

January 20, 1997
Washington, D.C.

The time has come. My time has come. Anderson Montgomery, your time has come. So deliver me from evil, give me my daily bread, and lead me, Lord, into temptation.

These last few days have passed quickly. I have worked hard and done my job well. My most difficult task still lies ahead, but soon, very soon, it will all be over. I look forward to a long and leisurely and much deserved rest.

I had a photo lab down in Georgetown make me one hundred 8-by-10 color glossies of our very-soon-to-be next president balling the lovely Lulu. I paid for the prints with my American Express card, but I had to pay the darkroom technician a thousand bucks cash to keep the contents of the photograph to himself for at least twenty-four hours. By then, everyone will know. The secret will be out. Every citizen from Maine to Maui will have seen Monty's skinny white ass.

After I got the prints back from the lab, I purchased one hundred sturdy manila envelopes. I addressed the envelopes to the one hundred largest newspapers, magazines, and TV stations across the country. Into each envelope I stuffed a photograph and a terse note: "Here's the vile son of a bitch you windbags catapulted into the White House."

I signed each note with a flourish, then mailed the envelopes from the post office over by Union Station. I next went into Union Station, where I bought myself a one-way rail ticket north, which, God willing, I will be using in just a few hours.

These past nights, since my meeting with the president-elect in the East Room, I have kept a low profile. I've been sleeping inside expensive automobiles, limousines mostly, parked in high-class parking garages. During the day, when not working on my mass mailing, I've been roaming through the capital's free museums, museums filled to the brim with American memorabilia: Lindbergh's Spirit of St. Louis, Jefferson's handwritten copy of the Declaration of Independence, J. Edgar Hoover's handcuffs, Archie Bunker's armchair. Swell stuff.

And oh yes, I have also been keeping up with current events. I've been listening to the radio and reading the newspaper, The Washington Post, faithfully, every single day. I consume every last word about the upcoming inauguration. There is no end to my interest. And this morning, just a few minutes ago, in fact, I found what I had been so desperately looking for these past several days: a map of the president's motorcade route. I refer here to the route our brand-spanking-new president, Anderson Johnson Montgomery, will take to the White House soon after he takes the oath of office on the steps of the United States Capitol.

My prayers to the Great Spirit have been answered....

January 21, 2001
On the Run

I tore the map of the motorcade route out of the paper and left the parking garage. I ventured into the heart of the capital and walked the route several times. It was a simple, straightforward route. The new president, after delivering his inaugural address, would climb into the back of an open limousine with his wife and kiddies. They would circle the Capitol Building a time or two, turn right onto First Street, then left onto Pennsylvania Avenue for a direct shot to the Presidential Palace.

I thought I might just be able to throw a monkey wrench into the prez's plan.

I walked the route half a dozen times as the sun pushed into the sky on this short winter's day. The first half of the route proved useless. Much too exposed. No means of escape. Too risky. And no grassy knoll, no high ground. I needed some height to stand above the cheering crowds.

I kept searching. I started down Pennsylvania Avenue, my eyes alert for a clear and advantageous position. Among the marble government buildings, some very real possibilities arose. Perhaps the Labor Department Building. Or the U.S. Courthouse. Maybe from one of the upper floors. Or even up on the roof. Yes, the roof!

My eye suddenly caught what I had been waiting all morning to see. And thank the Great Spirit, for morning would soon give way to noon, to the witching hour. There—along the Mall, the perfect site: the National Gallery of Art. The roof loomed high and flat and just waiting for Willy to take his best shot.

But before I entered the art gallery I needed to make a quick phone call. I dialed and waited for him to answer.

"Steel here."

"Jack, it's Willy MacKenzie."

"Willy! Where the hell've you been? I've been looking all over town for you. We need to talk. I need to see—"

"Shut up, Jack. Shut up and listen. I feel bad about decking you the other day at the Lincoln Memorial, so I've decided to make it up to you."

"Say what?"

"You heard me."

"I guess maybe I did. What do you have in mind?"

"I'm giving you an exclusive here, so just pipe down. Montgomery gets inaugurated at noon, in less than an hour from now."

"Hell, Willy, I know that. The whole country knows that. I was on my way to the show when the phone rang."

"I told you to shut up, Jack. You talk too damn much. I want you to skip the lies and bullshit up on Capitol Hill. Get yourself a camera with some high-speed film and a telephoto lens. Find yourself a cozy spot along Pennsylvania Avenue directly across from the National Gallery of Art."

"National Gallery of Art? I don't get it, Willy. Why?"

"Just do it, goddammit. And make sure you get your ass there before Montgomery's limousine passes."

"Okay, Willy, take it easy, I'll be there. But what about a few more clues? You know, like, what should I look for? Who's gonna do what? And when are they gonna do it?"

"Just be on time, Jack, and you'll have all the answers your grubby little heart desires."

Steel started to babble again but I hung up on him and walked away. It's always best to leave a reporter with a few questions tumbling around in his head. Makes them feel useful.

Now maybe it was just my imagination running amok, but at

least half the people wandering up and down Pennsylvania Avenue looked like either undercover cops or Secret Service agents. And every last one of them seemed to know exactly what I had in mind. No doubt about it; they were all watching me through their mirrored sunglasses, taking note of every move I made.

I thought about canceling my plans for the president, but decided that fate was a far more powerful force than fear.

I climbed the marble stairs, took a quick look over my shoulder, then slipped discreetly into the National Gallery of Art, my brand-new nylon day pack slung over my shoulder. The place was packed with camera-toting tourists staring at sculptures and pictures on the walls. They blocked my path. Valuable minutes ticked away. I calmed myself and slowly made my way through the gallery.

I wanted to scream out, tell the bloody fools to stand aside, inform them of the importance of my mission. But I managed to keep my cool. I ascended a flight of marble stairs and stood beneath the great rotunda held up by a dozen or more black granite columns. I ventured down East Sculpture Hall and into the East Garden Court. A fountain sent plumes of water cascading into the air. I slipped quickly into a gallery of 19th-century French paintings: Cézanne and Monet and Renoir.

My eyes, however, were not on the Impressionist masters. I was far more interested in the partially hidden door over in the far corner of the room. That door, I felt sure, led to the roof.

Then more stress. More trauma. Security guards roamed everywhere. Their eagle eyes burned right into my head. And all the while, the moment of reckoning drew near. I thought for sure it would pass me by.

But no, the Great Spirit intervened once again: out in the East Garden Court this time. A little old lady stumbled and crashed head-first into that watery fountain. I heard her scream. So did the guards. They ran off to lend a hand.

I did not hesitate. I made my move. I crossed the gallery to the partially hidden door. My God, it was locked! Son of a bitch! But a little abracadabra and an ice pick I'd been carrying in my belt to thwart would-be muggers in those high-priced parking garages, and I was through the door and racing up the concrete stairs.

Through another door, and, ah, Harmony and Bliss: exactly what I had in mind. An absolutely ideal site. The perfect roof. Not too high. Not too low. Plenty of visibility up and down Pennsylvania Avenue. Yes, a splendid place to complete my mission, to make my statement. And what a glorious winter day: high white puffy clouds beneath a deep blue sky and a warm sun.

I took a good, long look around. I knew now I had the time. In the distance, up on Capitol Hill, I could hear the masses cheering as the new president wound up his inaugural address, the same old pathetic drivel about how bright and wonderful the future will be with him at the helm. Nothing but a bunch of buzzard turds.

Still, it seemed a shame to ruin the guy's day.

Fuck it. That fucker ruined my whole life.

I planned my escape route: across the roof, over the side, using my length of heavy-duty hemp neatly coiled in my day pack, a sprint across the Mall, around the back of the Capitol, and then a brisk three-minute walk over to Union Station and a train ride to freedom.

I took up my position high above the street. I waited impatiently to impose my will upon the forty-third president of the United States. But what, I wondered, if this guy's the next George Washington or Thomas Jefferson? What if I'm about to spurn greatness?

My thoughts turned to Dawn. And that settled that.

I thought about friends and family, how they all told me to take this journey across America. "It'll do you good," they insisted. "It's just what you need."

Right. I wonder what they'll say when they see the morning papers? Time, they said, heals all. Bullshit. Time heals nothing. Time just drives the pain deeper. No, my only hope is the bittersweet taste of revenge.

I peered over the side and scanned the mob scene below. Americans of every race, creed, color, and fiscal class lined the broad avenue to welcome their new political leader. But where was Jack? "Oh where, oh where does my little Jack roam? Oh where, oh where does he roam?"

There! Across the street, standing on a low marble wall above the sidewalk. He used his left hand to shield his eyes from the sun as he looked upward to the roof of the National Gallery of Art.

I wanted to wave, but decided it would be prudent to remain hidden until crunch time.

And then, finally, crunch time arrived: the presidential procession slowly rounded the corner and headed west on Pennsylvania Avenue. The moment of truth had arrived.

I wondered if I would have the guts to do my familial duty?

The president's long black limo rolled into view. And there he sat, the smug bastard—Dawn's murderer—smiling and waving at the teary-eyed masses. The stupid pigeons who double as citizens in this country are so easily rendered emotionally incontinent.

The wife sat beside the new president: a frail, bony wisp of a woman with a shrill voice. And his kiddies, a couple of asexual teenyboppers. To hell with her. To hell with them.

The crowd cheered. Anderson waved. Willy stood.

I climbed right out to the edge of the marble facade facing the street. I climbed out there for all the world to see. Steady, Willy boy, steady now. Steady as she goes. Patience, my good fellow, patience. Not too fast. Stay calm. Keep yourself in check. Don't be too quick to draw. No need to push. No need to panic. Plenty of time. Easy, Willy, easy.

I let a few more seconds pass to make sure Jack had time to bring me into focus through his telephoto lens. I didn't want any blurry, out-of-focus images of this event. This was a once-in-a-lifetime opportunity. Then a quick check for the president's limo. Right smack down in front of the gallery now, directly below my perch.

Away we go!

I swung around, pulled down my pants, and offered Anderson Montgomery a personal view of my full and shining moon. I hung it out there like Old Glory flying over Fort McHenry. All I needed was a loud and brassy rendition of "The Star Spangled Banner." after all, I was simply invoking my First Amendment right granting every citizen of this great nation freedom of speech and expression.

Oh yes, this afternoon I felt proud to call myself an American.

Even above all the noise and chaos I could hear the shutter on Jack Steel's camera working like crazy. I knew for sure he had captured the moment forever on film. His pictures would surely be worth a thousand words. Probably more.

I took a peek through my legs, between my knees. I saw all those undercover cops and Secret Service agents swing into action. I decided to be on my way. Hanging around that part of town, I realized, could be hazardous to my health.

And that's when a shot rang out. Jesus! Then another. And another. Bullets rained all around me. I could hear them ricocheting off the roof, blasting chinks in the concrete. What did these idiots think? That I planned to shoot the president of the United States with my rear end? What a bunch of fucking morons.

I pulled up my pants and fled across the roof. I uncoiled my rope, secured it to a steel stanchion, and slipped over the side. I dropped to the turf, biting my tongue when I hit the ground. Blood! I spit the red stuff from my mouth as I sprinted across the Mall. But running, I decided, might attract attention, so I slowed to a jog, then a brisk walk. I reached Independence Avenue (a perfect metaphor) and made my way around the east side of the Capitol. My heart raced, my nerves pulsed, perspiration streamed off my brow.

And then, suddenly, I found myself face to face with an officer of the law, a tall and muscular D.C. cop in a crisp blue uniform. We stopped abruptly and studied one another with narrowed eyes. I quickly realized I would be expected to speak first.

I swallowed hard and asked, “What’s all the commotion over on Pennsylvania Avenue?”

The officer actually snickered. “Oh, nothing. Some nut just mooned the president.”

I managed to laugh. “No kidding? Mooned him, huh?”

He nodded his huge head, then took another look at me. “What’s the hurry today, friend? And what happened to your mouth? Looks like someone popped you.”

I wiped the sweat and the blood off my lips. “Oh,” I told him, “no. No one popped me. I bit open a canker sore on my tongue while running to catch a train.”

“A train, huh?”

“Yeah, a train. I’ll be lucky to make it. Seems like I’m always running late.”

Another pretty long look before the officer nodded and said, “Well, if you got a train to catch, you’d better shake a leg.” He turned and ambled off.

I sprinted the rest of the way to Union Station. I reached the platform just as the northbound train began to roll. I climbed aboard and collapsed in the first available seat.

A few minutes later the conductor asked to see my ticket. I handed it over.

He was a slow-moving, slow-talking, amiable sort of fellow, the kind of guy who stays loose and rolls with life’s punches. Sort of like me.

“So,” he asked, “where you headed, friend?”

“Home,” I told him. “I’m heading home.”

12:33 P.M.
JANURY 20, 2001
MACKENZIE ISLAND
THE INAUGURATION OF THE FORTY-FOURTH PRESIDENT OF THE UNITED STATES

Heading home? Willy might have thought, might have hoped, might have prayed, he was heading home, but home still loomed many miles and many months down the road. Winter would pass, and most of spring, before Willy would finally slip unnoticed into the Blue Mountains and make his way across the valley to Katydeeray.

The scenario after he left D.C. went something like this: Willy rode the rails for a day or two, believing he would simply go home to MacKenzie Island and make an effort to get on with his life. But on the morning of January 22, 1997, from the train station in some small northeastern town, telephone records indicate that Willy made a collect call to the family's winter house in Cedar Bluffs. It rang several times before Sanders picked up.

"Hello?"

"Sanders?"

"Willy! Where the hell are you?"

"I don't know exactly."

"What do you mean, you don't know exactly? How can you not know? You're not in jail, are you?"

"No, I'm not in jail. Of course I'm not in jail. Why would I be in jail?"

"Because."

"Because why?"

"Forget it, Willy. Does anyone know where you are?"

"I don't even know where I am. All I know is that I'm on my way home. I just wanted to let you know."

"Coming home might not be such a hot idea, Willy."

"Why not?"

"The valley's crawling with federal authorities and state police."

"Why?"

"Willy, give me a break. You know why."

"Because I shot a moon at Montgomery?"

"Right, Willy, because you shot Monty a moon. But they claim you endangered the life of the president."

"What?"

"You heard me. And now you listen. Pop and I have talked it over and we think the best thing you can do is get lost for a while. Make yourself scarce. Go into hiding. Just for a few months. Until this thing blows over. Until things calm down."

"A few months! Sanders, I want to come home now. I want to see Emily and Mom and Pop and you and Alice. I miss you guys. A few months! Jesus. It's been so long already."

"I know, Willy, but you have to do it. Believe me, it's for your own good, your own safety. The second you hit the valley they'll place you under arrest and maybe send you away for a lot longer than a few months."

Willy protested for another ten or fifteen minutes, but in the end he promised Sanders he'd do as ordered. He'd go undercover, blend into the countryside. And let me tell you, he did a hell of a good job of it. For the next four and a half months no one could find hide nor hair of him. Well, almost no one.

Just about the entire population, for one reason or another, participated in the search for Willy MacKenzie, but nowhere could Willy be found.

President Montgomery had the federal marshals, the FBI, and probably the CIA roaming the streets and hillsides in search of Willy. And why not? The guy had single-handedly turned Monty's coronation into a circus. Montgomery wanted to bring the full weight of his new office to bear upon this renegade who would dare to mock the presidency by exposing himself in public. He wanted to nail Willy's moon to the doors of the Oval Office.

But let's, just for a moment, reconsider the facts. Four years have now passed since the mooning incident. It's easy to forget the details.

For weeks prior to his inauguration, Montgomery had been fending off charges on several controversial fronts. The guy definitely had some image problems long before Willy dropped his drawers. First off were the endless innuendos about his blatant womanizing. But other problems existed as well: the illegal campaign contributions, the suspected drug use as an undergraduate, the motivations behind the Tamaqua River Valley Dam and Development Project, the unsavory characters sometimes seen slipping in and out of the governor's mansion in the middle of the night. All of these issues dogged the president day in and day out. And not only before his inauguration, but long after as well.

Nothing was ever proved, no charges were ever brought against President Montgomery, but the damage hung around his neck like a noose. Getting mooned by Willy MacKenzie only punched another hole in Monty's bubble. You might say Monty had a very tough public relations problem. Especially after the anchormen and the editorialists, whether they agreed with Willy's posterior display or not, claimed that Mr. MacKenzie had mooned Mr. Montgomery as a national protest against a president who had quite possibly been involved in illegal activities and general wrongdoing.

This scenario, coupled with the photo of Monty in the sack with Clear Blue, really did a number on the opening moves of his administration. The guy went from Thoroughbred to pack mule in one brief twenty-four-hour period. It would not be unfair to say that, because of these various developments, Anderson Montgomery spent his four years in office defending his ethics and morality, warding off impeachment proceedings, and otherwise working to stay one step ahead of his own shadow. And all of this while the country foundered, while we fell farther and farther into the economic and environmental abyss.

And so I think it would be safe to say that Montgomery's fall led directly to the meteoric political rise of Willy MacKenzie. Cause and effect. Supply and demand. Ebb and flow.

During the thirty-three seconds that Willy had his pants down and his moon shining over the capital, I snapped off a dozen full-color photographs. Two of the twelve came out perfectly: composition, tone, focus, and angle—all right on the money.

So once again, I'd found myself in the right place at the right time. And no doubt about it: those photos, and the story I wrote to go along with them, shot me to the top of my profession.

The photos helped Willy as well. Already well known by this time for *Full Moon over Katydeeray*, his mooning of the president propelled him into superstardom.

Willy is thin and handsome, a ruddy-looking guy, so editors and producers felt confident putting his face on their magazine covers, newscasts, and entertainment shows. But it was the pictures of his backside that people really wanted to see. On TV screens and magazine pages all over the country, side-by-side photographs of Willy appeared. Anterior and posterior shots cluttered the airwaves and newsstands. *Vanity Fair* slapped Willy's cheeks right smack on the cover with the bold headline FULL MOON RISES OVER A NEW AMERICA.

For weeks the mooning seemed like the one and only subject from coast to coast. No one talked about anything else. Walk into a hotel lobby, a restaurant, a barbershop, a bookstore, a movie house, almost any public place, and you could hear people talking and gesticulating about Willy MacKenzie and what he had done from the roof of the National Gallery of Art.

Opinions differed on the incident, no doubt about that. It was certainly not hailed by all citizens as the Greatest Show on Earth. People came to blows over whether Willy should be crowned or castrated, dubbed a knight or incarcerated for political heresy. Everyone had an opinion. Especially members of the media. We discussed the subject ad nauseam. One highly respected anchorman, unable to keep his emotions in check, described the rooftop performance as "an ugly and grotesque act of subliminal perversion."

A popular newspaper columnist and social wit entitled his piece on the mooning "The Bottom of American Morality." He said, "Insofar as I can tell, after a thorough examination of the photographs in question, a full moon did indeed rise over our nation, in the middle of the afternoon no less, during the inauguration of our forty-third president."

And a widely read political cartoonist turned Willy's derriere into a much sought after guest on the television talk show circuit. In a continuing series of strips spread over several weeks, he had the infamous MacKenzie buttocks interviewed by all the biggest names in TV chitchat: Oprah, Phil, David, Sally Jessy, Arsenio, Jay.

The editors of a leading national newsmagazine characterized the event as "innovative, daring, honest. Four stars for freedom of expression!" The fact that these same editors loathed Anderson Montgomery may or may not have had something to do with their opinion.

But one of the more powerful Sunday morning evangelists, in a rousing sermon from his high-and-mighty pulpit, denounced the mooning as "decadent, destructive, and demeaning. A subversive plot to undermine the principles and foundations of Western democracy."

The White House issued this statement: "The incident in question was a demonstration of behavior that is socially and ethically unacceptable to a majority of Americans. The incident was contrary to the values and the convictions of our civilization. This Administration condemns such flagrant abuse of personal freedom."

Maybe Monty and his team did, but the majority of the American people did not. Within a week of the mooning, a nationwide survey discovered that almost sixty-three percent of the people approved of Willy's public dissent as a means of social commentary. Almost as many people said they hoped to see similar protests in the future.

At the same time, Monty's approval ratings plummeted. Because of all the charges aimed at him, he did not receive the honeymoon normally granted a newly elected president. Then, to add insult to injury, protesters lined up outside the White House, demanding he resign even before he'd warmed the seat of his leather chair in the Oval Office.

And within a week an army of grass-roots supporters ventured forth with the idea that Willy MacKenzie should be president of the United States. Their initial slogan, you might recall, declared: "Willy MacKenzie: The Last Honest Man in America!"

This slogan played well, but later these supporters discovered the now famous slogan, the one cited as perhaps the foremost reason for Willy's election, the one we saw for four years plastered to billboards and buildings, to automobile bumpers and baby carriages, to farm tractors and executive briefcases: "Willy MacKenzie: The Last Innocent Man in America!"

Yup, no doubt about it, a revolution started soon after that moon rose over the nation's capital. And Willy, unwitting subversive, found himself cast in the role of rebel.

But where was Willy? We all wanted to know.

When he failed to surface and meet our needs, when the days slipped away without an appearance on "Good Morning, America" or "Donahue" or "Entertainment Tonight," the legend of William Conrad Brant MacKenzie began to take flight.

Was his disappearance and continued absence a calculated decision? Did he know exactly what he was doing? Was this supposedly naive and innocent youngster manipulating public opinion by keeping himself secreted away?

Difficult questions to answer, even today. I honestly don't know just how cunning Willy might be. It remains one of the great mysteries in his rise to power.

A week passed. A month passed. Six weeks. Eight weeks. No one heard a word from Willy. Some speculated his family, with all the money in the world, had flown him out of the country, perhaps to Scotland or darkest Africa. All kinds of pundits popped up to speculate on Willy's whereabouts. And the more they speculated, the more the legend took root and spread and finally flourished.

So what did I do? I went looking for him. I located the cop who'd seen Willy running across the Mall. He remembered that Willy said he had a train to catch. At Union Station I talked to a ticket agent who said he'd sold Willy a ticket on a northbound train. For weeks I rode the rails. I must have showed Willy's photograph to every engineer and conductor from Washington, D.C., to Bangor, Maine.

Then, finally, during an afternoon when I felt certain I would never find him, I picked up the telephone to call my wife and suddenly my brain whirled with inspiration. Yes, I thought, of course, the telephone!

I quickly made my way to Seven Points, to the regional offices of the Blue Mountain Telephone Company. There I paid off a worker, some lowly clerk who nevertheless had the proper access, and in no time at all I received a copy of the MacKenzies' telephone bill. On that bill was a collect call, I felt sure from Willy, placed the morning of January 22, 1997.

I went to the small town where that collect call had been made. I started asking questions, probing for answers, digging for clues. And little by little, day by day, I came to the conclusion that Willy was still in the country and that he was probably somewhere in his element: out in the wilderness, up in the mountains, hiding, waiting, biding his time, staying scarce, still slipping in and out of reality.

It took time and hard work, but I stayed on his trail. I kept my nose to the ground and my eyes squarely on the prize.

But right now, with Judge Stuart still half-frozen and flat on his back over at the Great House, let's return to Willy's journal so he can tell us where he was and what he was up to after his adventures in Washington.

April 1, 1997
April Fools' Day

The beginning of the end of my cross-country journey was like something from Brothers Grimm: a new name, a false identity, a fresh start, a town never before seen by my eyes, a warm and well-lit room over an old-fashioned barbershop, and a kindly old man with tough, gnarled hands to build me a Blue Mountain guideboat.

No April Fools' joke here. This is all true true true.

Duluth Griffin told me he had a guideboat almost finished; another three or four weeks and the job could be completed. I took one look at that beautiful hardwood hull and shook his hand.

Years ago, as a young man, Duluth Griffin had built nothing but guideboats. He had learned the trade from his father, who had learned the craft of guideboat building from the Mohawk, my people. What more did I need to know?

I paid him in full for the boat, then took a room over Joe's Barbershop to await his completion of the task. I introduced myself around town as Willy Sabattis. Quite a number of folks knew the name. A few old-timers even claimed an acquaintance with my great-grandfather, the preeminent Blue Mountain guide, Mitchell Sabattis. I told them my mother had taken me from the woods while still a babe so that I might receive a proper education. But now I had returned to pursue my real calling in life—that of backcountry woodsman and wilderness guide.

The locals who hang around the barbershop chewing tobacco

and cutting farts bought my story with nary a raised eyebrow. They have other stories on their minds anyway: one in particular. They have this strange fascination with the mooning incident that took place down in our nation's capital a week or so prior to my arrival in their town. They know all the details of the event, and more than anything else they love to discuss those details at great length. They mull over the whole project, yuck it up, then spit some tobacky juice into the brass spittoon resting in the middle of the shop next to the pile of freshly clipped hair.

Even though they seem to hold the mooning incident in high regard, and the moonman as a sort of national spokesman for the disgruntled masses, I keep my identity in my pocket. These boys don't recognize me as the moonman, not with my pants raised and belted, not with my brand-new buzz haircut, my scraggly beard, and my gold frame, rose-colored eyeglasses. And I have decided to keep it that way. To them I'm just another city boy come to the country to find his roots.

But I can tell from their talk that folks around the country are pretty stirred up over what I did on the roof of the National Gallery of Art. I only did it to avenge my dear departed Dawn, to give that bastard Montgomery his comeuppance, but it sounds like I'm a wanted man for that simple act of pulling down my pants. I have by and by come to realize that spooks from the intelligence agencies and the Federal Bureau of Investigation might well be on my trail. They want to nail me for indecent exposure, lewd and obscene public behavior, exhibitionism, and trespassing. I think they even tried to add the charge of threatening the life of the commander in chief. Talk about April Fools' jokes. I was, and continue to be, about as threatening as a wasp in winter.

I find all of these charges absurd, totally ridiculous, but Sanders ordered me to stay undercover, so I figure I best do exactly that. Besides, call it intuition, but I have this deep-down, uneasy feeling that every wacko, weirdo, and patriotic loony-tune who took offense at my rooftop display might be burning to get their hands on me. That's why I decided to get me a guideboat and get as far back into the wilderness as humanly possible.

I feel temporarily safe here in my room over Joe's barbershop. The room smells of hair tonic and old magazines, and whenever Joe gives a shave with the hot towels, the small window over my bureau fogs up. I write Dawn's name over and over in the steam.

Laughter and muted voices reach me from the shop through the hot-air vent. Sometimes I go downstairs and visit with Joe and the boys. They like having an outsider around. It gives them the opportunity to retell their favorite stories: tall tales mostly, but still a fine and pleasant way to pass an afternoon.

Anyway, a few days ago, Duluth Griffin stopped by the barbershop to tell me he'd had a call from a man looking for a wilderness guide. Duluth suggested me. And so next week this fellow's coming to town to discuss with me the possibility of setting up a trip into the backcountry.

The boys in the shop are even more excited than I am. They view my desire to rekindle the glory days of guideboating as a means of renewing their youth. I haven't told them that all I want is some place to hide out from the law and the psychopaths while the smoke clears over the Capitol Rotunda.

April 23, 1997
Out in the Wilds

Early one evening, as the last rays of sunshine streamed through my room, he knocked loudly on my door. He followed his knock directly into my humble abode without bothering to wait for me to grant him permission to enter. That should've given me a clue about the true nature of his character, but I had my guard down in that peaceful little backwater town.

"Willy Sabattis?"

"That's me," I said, my voice a whole lot deeper and different from the one I used as Willy Brant MacKenzie. "At your service."

"Barton Vandermeer. You can call me Bart. This here is Artemus. He may look mean but he's a pussycat. Wouldn't hurt a tick, no sir."

Barton Vandermeer looked very familiar. I felt sure he wore a disguise, just like me.

Artemus did not wear a disguise; didn't need one. He sat quietly at his master's feet. But he nevertheless looked capable of tearing the heart out of a full-grown bull elephant. Artemus had a long, wiry-thin, jet-black body; a long, wiry-thin, jet-black head; and long, wiry-thin, jet-black legs. His huge canines, in contrast, sparkled white. Artemus was a fully matured male Doberman pinscher. He still had his balls. They hung from his groin like a couple of grapefruit. His sire, I would learn later, had been an attack dog on the maximum-security ward at Leavenworth Penitentiary. But when Bart said sit, thank God, Artemus sat.

I asked, "Tell me, Bart, do you plan on bringing Artemus along on the trip?"

Bart slapped me on the back as though we were childhood chums. "Now don't you worry none about Artemus, Willy. He takes commands better'n any man alive. He won't be no trouble at all."

We spent the evening discussing the details of the trip. Bart wanted to get under way as soon as possible. He said he'd been itching to get back to nature for a long, long while. I told him I'd be ready to travel in one week. Bart agreed and we shook hands like a couple of country gentlemen.

After Duluth put the finishing touches on the guideboat, I had her hauled up to Razor Lake to get her used to the water. Razor is the southernmost in a series of deep glacial waterways called the Chain Lakes. Bart wanted to travel north through the Chain, then head deeper into the remote and wild backcountry. Fine with me. The deeper the better. I studied the maps and prepared to shove off.

Our first of many conflicts, however, arose even before we left the shore. It concerned Bart's gear. He had two large rucksacks, a huge military duffel bag, and a couple hundred feet of heavy-duty half-inch manila rope. I told him the guideboat couldn't take all the weight. Well, right away the guy got his dander up, informed me that he was the one financing the trip. He insisted each of the articles was necessary to insure his comfort and enjoyment.

I didn't buy it. I told Bart it was my boat, and if he intended to carry all that gear, then Artemus had to stay behind. Bart pouted. Art whimpered. But I stood firm. Finally, reluctantly, Bart dragged his excess gear into the nearby woods. He moved far enough under the cover of the trees that I could not see him. A few minutes later he emerged carrying the duffel bag and one of the rucksacks. He threw them into the guideboat. "This," he announced, "is as light as I travel."

I said nothing. All I had were the clothes on my back, a couple of extra shirts, a single-barreled Browning semiautomatic shotgun, a fishing pole, and a box of tackle. After Bart and Art got settled, I pushed the boat off the shore, and away we went across Razor Lake in the early afternoon of the first truly warm and sunny day of the new spring.

We shoved off with me paddling from the stern, Bart in the bow, and Artemus stretched out midship. Several times during those first days I accidentally kicked Artemus in the face. Each time I did, he growled at me and prepared to tear off part of my leg. But always, at the last possible moment, Bart ordered him not to attack.

I think the two of them enjoyed the game.

May 19, 1997
Out in the Wilds

Spring. And the earth grows warm. Leaves burst from the long dormant trees. Warblers fill the forest with song. And I sense it all as my paddle passes swiftly and silently through the clear water.

At night the air grows cool but no longer cold, so I sleep peacefully beneath my thin blanket. I no longer dream the terrible, murderous dream, and when I awake early in the morning my thoughts of Dawn are clean and pure and simple.

Too bad I have to put up with Barton Vandermeer and his best buddy, Artemus, canine from the river Styx. It would be paradise out here without them, with this wilderness all to myself. Why didn't I make this part of the journey alone?

Bart brought along a book about the grand old days of guideboating. One night, a week or so ago, by the light of our campfire, he read aloud the chapter on hunting. It described, in vivid detail, the various ways guides used to take deer. Bart's eyes grew wide as he read the passages. He wanted to do some damage first thing in the morning.

So after breakfast we hunted by hounding. Artemus proved very useful as the hound. We put the beast ashore, and Bart commanded him to locate deer and drive them toward the water. Artemus went immediately to work. He disappeared into the brush. Bart and I waited in the guideboat, secluded in a thick clump of reeds. For over an hour we waited. Black flies and mosquitoes the size of hummingbirds turned my face into a mass of sore red blotches.

I sat there swatting and imagining that angry, jet-black Doberman covered with a million of the bloodthirsty winged creatures when suddenly we heard the thunder of hooves. Two young and still spotted does exploded through the brush. They headed straight for us. Artemus pursued, his jaws snapping, his death bark curdling the morning air.

Bart calmly raised the Browning. And just as those two does reached the edge of the water, the shotgun roared twice. Instantly the chests of those two innocent animals blew wide open, throwing blood in every direction.

Bart laughed. Artemus foamed at the mouth.

I waited in the boat with the black flies while Bart and Art took an early lunch.

For three days and three nights we hunted by hounding. Finally, I could take it no more. We sat near the lake surrounded by deer carcasses.

"Bart," I asked, "don't you find this slaughter a bit uncivilized? I mean, we don't use but a fraction of the meat from these animals. The rest just rots and goes to the buzzards. Why kill so many?"

Well, Bart paused for just a second or two, then he sighted me in along the oily barrel of that old Browning. "What are you, Sabattis, one of them stinking bleeding-heart liberals? One of them sissy perverts who'd like nothing better than to take away my rights under the Second Amendment to the United States Constitution?"

I didn't quite know what my political bent had to do with slaughtering deer, but Bart didn't give me the opportunity to ask. He began to rant and rave—not for the first time during our weeks together, and probably not for the last.

"You're not a fucking homo, are you, Sabattis? Where do you stand on the sexual hilltop? Are you a pussy pounder or a dick licker?"

I ignored the question.

Deer blood dribbling off his chin, Barton Vandermeer chuckled and said, "Me, I only swing with the ladies. Any kind of ladies'll do. Diversity's the key. You want great sex, you gotta be diverse. You gotta nail white women, chinks, spics, spades."

"Spades?"

"That's right, Sabattis. Spades. Coons. Colored folks."

"That's ugly, Bart. Truly ugly."

This time he ignored me. "What about you, Sabattis? Huh? You like variety? Or are you one of those guys imprisoned by a single white woman's cold and woolly freezer? I'll bet you're the kind of horse's ass who only dips his stick into one very selective cake pan."

Dawn, my beautiful but very dead white woman, looked at me from the other side. She waited for me to defend her honor.

I stood up and spit in the dirt. "You see that spittle, Bart?"

He nodded.

I ground my heel into it. "Well, imagine it's your face." Then, before he could respond, I turned and walked down to the water.

Fortunately, young Artemus was off in the woods trying to inflict cardiac arrest on one wild animal or another.

May 23, 1997

And so, the days pass. And as they pass it becomes more and more evident that Bart and I do not see eye to eye on a wide range of issues. We have conflicting personalities, incompatible philosophies. You could say we march to different drummers. But mostly I keep quiet because Bart pays me a hundred bucks a day plus expenses. So while he babbles and tries to ruffle my feathers, I just stare at him and try to figure out who he is and where I know him from.

Day by day the tension between us begins to shimmer in the twilight. And slowly but surely I begin to enjoy it, to enjoy the aura of danger. I know, eventually, something will happen. I want something to happen. I need for something to happen.

And while I wait, I rediscover some of the simple pleasures that had once, long ago, made me a happy man, a boy in a grown-up's body: I fish for trout in the swift-moving streams. I cleanse my soul by taking only as many brookies as I can eat. Usually I fish in the middle of the afternoon when Bart and Artemus take naps. It is the best time of the day. I wander off, assemble my simple spinning rod, cast my line into the water, and sit back to listen to the treetops whispering to one another through the light breeze. I catch the scent of sassafras or wild mint or even the delicate fragrance of the miterwort. The smells remind me of home, of Dawn. I watch the clouds pass beneath the sun, throwing shadows randomly over the countryside. I try not to think. But the thoughts keep coming, endlessly, without pause; mostly from the past. The futility of it all puts its hands on my shoulders and presses down and down and down until my body becomes impressed upon the damp earth. But then, high up, in one of those whispering trees, a mockingbird rattles off his repertoire of songs, none of them his own, and I have to smile at the alliance between illusion and reality. Then a red-winged blackbird flies out and over the lake. An orange beetle crawls over my boot and up my pant leg. A gray squirrel scurries across the forest floor. A rainbow trout bites at my line but I quickly pull back before it has a chance to swallow the hook.

Bart and Art dream and snore. While I tarry, absolutely unable to stop making mental images in my dusty attic. Why didn't God fill our heads with music rather than these silly words? Why didn't He fill our hearts with symphonies? Our feet with springs? Our fingertips with tiny golden angel wings?

Sometimes I think God must've been a pretty strange character with a very twisted sense of humor. Either that or human beings were just an accident out of control and He actually intended the warbler to be His special offering to the planet.

I try my best to make my peace. With myself and all the others. I know I have to before I can return home to my family, to my little girl. For the rest of my days I know I will feel sorrow over the loss of Dawn, but still, I have to get on with it; I cannot forever ramble the earth striking down demons and indulging my whims and fantasies.

But then, and this is just today, just moments ago, I realized why Barton Vandermeer looks so damn familiar. Bart is actually Jack Steel, journalist from hell.

I keep this realization, at least for the time being, strictly to myself.

12:46 P.M.
JANUARY 20, 2001
MACKENZIE ISLAND
THE INAUGURATION OF THE FORTY-FOURTH PRESIDENT OF THE UNITED STATES

Of course it was me, Jack Steel. I never tried to act like anyone else. Willy knew it was me right from the moment I walked into his room over Joe's Barbershop. This Barton Vandermeer character is just another figment of Willy's deluded imagination. Ask me to illuminate the reasons why Willy carries on like this and I simply will not be able to offer you any viable explanations. I suppose paranoia, or any of the other mental psychoses, might be the answer.

Here's what happened: After an intensive and exhaustive search, I finally found Willy in that small lake town in the southwestern tier of the Blue Mountains. To complete my search I had to call in markers from fellow journalists and anonymous sources from all over the country. I hated to cash in my hard-earned winnings but I felt the prize warranted it.

And so one clue at a time I pieced together the puzzle until I found Willy's hiding place. As stated, he was living in a small room over Joe's Barbershop, and yes, he was having a man named Duluth Griffin build him a Blue Mountain guideboat.

I went to see him, not yet sure if he would be my man. Even after he had opened his door and invited me into his room, I still wasn't sure. Willy wore a very convincing disguise, and he spoke with an accent nothing at all like the one I remembered from our days together down in Washington, D.C.

But I saw something in his eyes, some faint glimmer of familiarity, and I knew then it could be no one other than William Conrad Brant MacKenzie. I might add that I had no doubts whatsoever that he recognized me right from the first as well, even if he refused to acknowledge our acquaintance.

He shook my hand, almost formally, and said, "The name's Sabattis, Willy Sabattis. I hope I can be of service."

I could see he was not about to budge from this alias, so I backed off, let him have his way. I played along in order to gain proximity to his person.

But as for this pooch named Artemus, well, I can't touch that one. I've never owned a Doberman pinscher. In fact, I've never owned any dog of any breed. To tell you the truth, I don't even like dogs. I find them stupid and much too dependent. I'm afraid, folks, that old Artemus was just another one of Willy's fantasies.

As for the rest of our trip together into the wild backcountry, I found it taxing and very tiring physically, but extremely stimulating, almost intoxicating, mentally. Our first few weeks out proved especially difficult. Young MacKenzie had definitely blown his fuses. His wiring system had gone awry. He trusted nothing and no one. At night, I swear to God, the guy slept with his eyes wide open and his hands clutched around that Browning shotgun.

I just tried to be nice, to put him at ease. Sure, I had an ulterior motive. I was there to pursue a story, uncover the facts, get to know the man better. But I don't see myself as ruthless or uncaring. I'm not even particularly manipulative. I knew Willy was struggling to put his life back together. Hell, I'd been witness to some of the terrible stuff he'd been through.

In the evening he occasionally wrote in his journal. It was then I learned for the first time that he had been keeping a journal for almost twenty years. I wanted in the worst way to get a look at that journal, tried more than once to take a peek, but it proved impossible; Willy guarded those notebooks with his life.

So together we let the days of spring slowly unwind. I slept on the ground for the first time since my youth. I slept badly and usually awoke with an aching back. I ate my bland, watery meals from a cheap aluminum mess kit. Like a bear, I shat in the woods. And all the while, every waking moment, I watched Willy. Young MacKenzie flourished in this primitive environment, became one with nature, another of the wild beasts. I just tried to hold my own and not miss my creature comforts too much. My job, I knew, was to gain Willy's trust, become his confidant, and so I stuffed away my petty gripes and worked toward that end.

Little by little, one careful step at a time, I broke down his defenses. I pulled him ever so cautiously out of his protective shell, until finally he shed his alias altogether, his persona of the redneck wilderness guide Willy Sabattis.

"Welcome back, Mac," I told him.

He said nothing, but he smiled and seemed to draw a sigh of relief. I could see he needed a friend in the worst way.

I let another day or two pass before I congratulated him on his successful mooning of President Montgomery. "A brilliant maneuver," I told him. "Extraordinary timing."

"You really think so?"

"Definitely. A truly unique American political statement. Right up there with the Boston Tea Party."

He nodded and narrowed his eyes and said, "I only did it to him because of what he did to me . . . to us . . . to Dawn. I just wanted to give it to that son of a bitch good, wreck his big day in the limelight."

"Whatever your reasons," I replied, "they worked to perfection. You're the main topic of conversation all over the country. For weeks now you've been dominating the airwaves. Some nights you're the lead story on both the 'Nightly News' and on 'Showbiz Tonight.' You've bridged the gap, Willy, between news and entertainment."

He looked at me and shook his head. "That's something."

I swear, the guy was absolutely unaware of the commotion he'd caused.

"Hell, Willy," I told him, "you might not know it but there's a whole army of royally pissed-off citizens out there banning together with the sole aim of making you the next president of the United States."

"President, huh?"

"Yup, President MacKenzie. How does that sound?"

"Pretty good," he said. "Yeah, I kind of like the sound of it."

I nodded. "Me too."

"It'll never happen though."

"Why not?"

He shrugged. "Just won't."

I ignored his pessimism and asked, "Tell me, Willy, what would you do if you did become president?"

He drifted off, took some time. "I guess," he said finally, "I'd just try to do the right thing."

"Admirable," I told him. "Very commendable."

Over the next several days, even weeks, I tried to solicit his political point of view. But, quite frankly, he didn't seem to have one. Well, that's not entirely true. He definitely believed in safeguarding the environment. And as a strong proponent of individual responsibility, he thought the government was far too involved in our daily lives. Beyond that, I would have to say Willy vacillated on the issues. So our talk turned to other matters: his family, mostly. I learned then more of what I have told you today.

But what I think we should do now is go back and take a look at Willy's version of what happened during those days he and I spent together out in the wilderness. His version may not jibe with my version, but it provides us with more insight into his character and into the subtle nuances of his psyche. It also makes for some extraordinary reading. We best get at it, however, since word from the Great House is that Judge Stuart has been seen out of bed and taking nourishment. We might just have ourselves an inauguration after all.

June 16, 1997
Along the Muscatunk

For several weeks now I've watched him without letting him know I know his true identity. Better to keep our enemies in the dark.

We've moved northwest through the Chain Lakes and up the Musaki River. At the headwaters of the Musaki we portaged over a series of low hills to Hutchinson's Lake, a carry of almost three and a half miles. I made three trips: one with the boat and two with the gear. Steel and Artemus made one trip, then napped in the shade while I worked my ass off.

We crossed Hutchinson's and yesterday entered the Muscatunk River. In the distance, to the north and west, I can see the high peaks of the Blue Mountains: Nuttyback, Ondaga, and Whiteface. But those peaks, like home, still loom a long way in the distance.

July 2, 1997
On the Muscatunk

Summer has arrived here in the Blues. The days have grown long and warm. Yesterday afternoon, for the first time since we set out on this adventure, the sun actually felt hot. It burned the skin. We went ashore to rest in the shade of a tall poplar growing along the riverbank. Jack Steel, alias Barton Vandermeer, and his wild beast lay down and closed their eyes.

I too nodded off, but only for a moment. The terrible, murderous dream slammed into my head and woke me up. And when I opened my eyes I saw the waters of the Muscatunk rising like the waters of the Tamaqua did on the day Dawn died.

But no, the Muscatunk meandered with barely a ripple. Muscatunk means "peaceful" in Mohawk, and I easily understood why. The river meant me no harm.

Still, when I closed my eyes, I saw the Tamaqua River rising. I saw the new dam. I saw Anderson Montgomery standing atop the dam, orating on his own greatness. I saw myself standing among my friends and family. I did not see Dawn. But then I saw a man, a reporter, finding me among the crowd of protesters.... He tells me his name is Jack Steel. He utters Dawn's name, asks me to follow him.... I kept my eyes closed and saw the two of us running. I saw myself climbing a chain-link fence, somersaulting down a steep, rocky embankment. I saw the waters of the Tamaqua River rising, rising. And then I saw Dawn out in the middle of the river. No! I wanted to open my eyes and forget the terrible, murderous dream, but I didn't, I couldn't. I had to see the rest. So I kept my eyes closed and saw myself diving into the raging, swollen current. I saw Dawn struggling to keep her head above the surface. I saw myself at her side, taking her a breath of air. I saw that cameraman over on the far riverbank passively filming the drowning of Dawn. And that's when I saw something I had not seen before in the terrible, murderous dream ... standing beside that cameraman I suddenly saw him ... Jack Steel. Yes, definitely, Jack Steel, standing there telling the cameraman to keep filming, to keep his camera rolling no matter what happens.

My eyes flashed open. And there was Jack Steel again, just across the way, in the shade of the towering poplar tree, sleeping, snoring, his arm around his carnivorous beast.

"Murderer," I mumbled.

Quietly, and oh so cautiously, I rose to my feet. I picked up the Browning semiautomatic shotgun. I took three quick steps and stood over my prey. The beast stirred. I ignored him and tapped the barrel of the shotgun against Jack Steel's chest. Artemus growled.

Jack's eyes opened wide. "Willy!"

"I know who you are."

"You do?"

Was that fear I heard in his voice? Alarm? Apprehension? Trepidation?

"Damn right. I know exactly who you are."

He hesitated a moment, then regained his composure. "Oh, and just who am I, Willy?"

I wanted to say, "You're the stinking son of a bitch who murdered my wife. You're the bastard who let her drown, who let her die." I wanted to blast a hole the size of a window in the middle of his chest, but I couldn't bring myself to pull the trigger. I didn't have the guts.

Maybe, I decided, I just need more time.

July 13, 1997
Bull Moose

We reached the beautiful deep blue waters of Bull Moose last week at dusk, a sliver of silver moon in the eastern sky. To get here we had to cross Greater Lewey Lake, then portage for three tough days through swamp and nettle. But now that we've arrived, I believe the exertions worth the trouble. I believe here, on Bull Moose, I can give Jack Steel, alias Barton Vandermeer, his due.

Bull Moose lies between Piney Ridge and Rising Moon Mountain. A deep, narrow lake, maybe half a mile across at its widest point, it reaches north for almost twenty miles into the central foothills of the Blue Mountains. Not a single road connects Bull Moose to the outside world, and there are no houses or cabins along its banks. This is the heart of the wild backcountry. This is where the loons live.

And last night, while the loons carried on like inmates at some wilderness insane asylum, Jack, alias Bart, moved onto the offensive. By the light of the campfire he looked at me and laughed. His hair had grown long and ragged. He hadn't washed it since before we left on our wilderness trek. He looked like a wild and mangy dog. And then he asked, "Would you consider yourself a religious man, Willy?"

"Not in any formal sense, no."

"Do you believe in God?"

"I believe in the Great Spirit."

"Great Spirit. Shit. I swear to Christ, you're one queer son of a bitch."

"Let's not start this again," I said. "I'm just not up to it."

He stood, crossed to my side of the fire, and stared down at me with the eyes of a cold-blooded killer. Then he really threw me for a loop when out of nowhere he asked, "Tell me, Sabattis, what do you think of this pervert who mooned the president?"

A chill ran through my body. "Pervert who mooned the president? What are you talking about?"

"You know damn well what I'm talking about. I'm talking about the perverted homo who mooned the president back in January. What do you think of him?"

I swallowed hard and managed to mumble, "Well, I dunno. I guess—"

He cut me off and said, "I'll tell you what I think. I think that bastard raped the Stars and Stripes when he exposed his asshole to the nation."

I felt a little queasy, a touch light-headed. "Sorry," I said, "but you've lost me."

"I think that flaming faggot took a great big crap right on Old Glory. I think we oughta hang the homo by his balls and beat him with sticks until he dies."

Loud and chaotic bells started going off in my head. Good God, I thought, here, in my very presence, is the patriotic psychopath I ventured into the wild backcountry to avoid. Son of a bitch. I couldn't help but worry about what he might do next.

But he didn't do anything. He didn't say a word. Didn't make a sound. Just stared at me with those killer eyes. I watched his lips curl up into the slightest smile. His expression said it all.

The night slipped slowly by. The loons partied till dawn. While I pondered my fate. . . .

Morning, and a soft rain fell. I opened my eyes and found Jack, alias Bart, and his best pal, Artemus, absent from camp. A pot of hot coffee sat on a rock beside the smoldering campfire. The guideboat lay upside down on the bank. Everything seemed the same—but no, wait, the Browning—gone. The boys had wandered off with their favorite toy. Or were they lurking behind a tree, watching my every move, preparing to blow off one of my hands or maybe one of my kneecaps? No—I heard the roar of the shotgun far off in the low hills to the west. The boys were just out murdering fawns.

So I slipped on my pants and tore open Jack's rucksack. In the bottom of the sack I found a tiny tape recorder. I pushed the play button and heard my voice: "Sorry, but you've lost me." Then Jack's voice: "I think that flaming faggot took a great big crap right on Old Glory."

Trouble.

I rewound the tape to the beginning and played it back. And there it was: our entire conversation from the night before. That son of a bitch had recorded the whole goddamn thing. The shotgun roared again. Closer this time.

I rummaged in the rucksack and found more tapes. I inserted them one by one into the recorder. All our conversations were on file, every last one, even that first meeting we'd held back in my room over Joe's Barbershop. I also found in his rucksack my complete dossier. My life history. And a lengthy file on Dawn as well, including a long memorandum on how she had fought to prevent the opening of the Tamaqua Valley Dam and Development Project. The memo portrayed her as a political dissident bent on disrupting and even destroying the Establishment.

Dawn?

And in another part of Jack's bag I found detailed maps of the lake region and a book on how to survive alone in the wilderness. The shotgun roared again. Much closer now. Not more than a few hundred yards off.

Time, I knew, to make my move. Time to go on the attack. Time to purge this murdering maniac from this peaceful and pristine planet....

July ?, 1997
Bull Moose

I did what I had to do. But not before quite a struggle....

As I prepared to purge Steel from the planet, his beast caught me by surprise. Artemus came out of nowhere and grabbed my ankle with his enormous jaws. As I tried to shake myself loose, Steel rolled into camp.

"Going somewhere, Willy?" he asked. Jack, alias Bart, stood before me holding the Browning in one hand and two jackrabbits in the other.

I shook my head. "Nope, just getting ready to break camp."

"Not today," he said. "It's starting to rain. Looks like it might rain all day. Today we'll make a pot of rabbit stew. Maybe leave tomorrow. We'll see."

I stood there staring at the dead rabbits and said nothing.

"So why don't you just sit yourself down, Willy," suggested Jack, alias Bart, "and have a cup of coffee."

I decided it might be better to obey. At least for the time being. I sat by the fire and sipped the bitter brew. Artemus stretched out at my feet. I didn't dare shoo him away. The rain fell faster. Jack, alias Bart, skinned and gutted those rabbits and placed them in a pot of boiling water over the fire.

The morning passed without a word. Even the loons grew quiet as the rain increased. Bart stirred the stew with a cedar sapling. The concoction smelled like boiled glue. I sat in the rain and watched the cedar sapling go around and around. There was nothing else for me to do. I was cold and wet; my brain shot only blanks. I could not even conceive of what might happen next.

And then the afternoon passed more or less like the morning, except the rain fell even faster, finally exploding from the sky as though the heavens had once and for all decided to cover every inch of the earth's surface with water. I just sat there and took it. Not until dusk did I make up my mind to keep warm and dry. I stood and moved slowly toward the tarpaulin that served as our makeshift tent.

Artemus stirred and followed.

Jack, alias Bart, watched me with those eyes from across the stew pot and asked, "Where you going, Sabattis?"

"Where does it look like I'm going? I'm going under the tarpaulin to get dry."

"Faggot."

"You know, Bart, or whatever the hell your name is," I said, pulling off my soaking wet sweatshirt, "you are, without a doubt, the biggest asshole I've ever met in my entire life." The sweatshirt covered my head at the moment I finished this insult, so I fully expected to have my chest blown wide open before I could pull it off.

But things didn't happen quite that way. I suppose they rarely do.

I pulled off the sweatshirt, and Jack, alias Bart, still stood there stirring the stew. He hadn't moved a muscle. But then he opened his mouth and threw me for another loop. "Parker's the name, sonny boy. Just Parker. No past. Got it? Good. Intelligence sent me. I figure you must've found the tapes. Thought you should know the score."

I processed this new package of information while I pulled on a dry shirt and tried to keep from soiling my pants. "Parker now, is it? You're a man of many names, Parker."

"Just one from here on out."

"So what happens next?"

"I've been thinking real hard on that, Sabattis. Or should I just call a spade a spade and call you MacKenzie? I figure I should take you in to stand trial, but those bleeding hearts at Justice will do nothing but squeeze your precious apples and turn you loose. Now I ask you, would that be fair after what you pulled?"

I thought it sounded fair enough but decided not to say so.

"No," he said, "you'll have to die out here in the wild. I wanted to hang you from your scrotum and beat you to death with one of those guideboat paddles, but you made me leave my length of rope behind. No matter. We'll find another way of eliminating you. Not to worry, plenty of time."

How much time? I wondered.

The answer came promptly. "Okay, Artemus, on your feet."

Artemus, always alert to the sound of his master's voice, jumped to attention.

"Now, Artemus, rip down the canvas. Rip it down, boy! Rip it down!"

Artemus sprang into action. He tore down the tarpaulin with his mighty jaws, tore it right down to the ground as I stood there shaking visibly from both the cold and the fear. Once again I found myself out in the rain.

"Now, Artemus, rip off the enemy's shirt. Rip it off, boy! . . . No, Artemus, not his chest, just his shirt. . . . Good boy, Artemus. Now the enemy's pants, Artemus. Rip them off, boy! Rip them— Easy, Artemus, don't damage the enemy. Not yet. Good boy. Now rip off . . ."

Moments later I stood naked except for my boots and a few drops of blood spattered across my body. I shook no longer from the cold, the cold had retreated into some primitive part of my brain; I shook now from holy terror.

Parker, alias Jack, alias Bart, laughed and tossed me a bar of soap. It hit me in the abdomen and fell into the mud. "You need a bath, boy. So go on, soap up and wash off. But leave a good lather on that famous redeye of yours."

I obeyed. Couldn't think what else to do. . . . Give up control of your life, and in no time at all, you're fucked.

Parker rubbed the barrel of the Browning with gun oil. He shoved a handful of shells into the chamber and started toward me. "Turn around, boy. Turn around and bend over. I want to see that moon of yours rise and shine now. Come on, boy, one more time before I blow it and you sky high."

Again I did as I was told. And as I turned and bent over, I realized just how easily oppression leads to conformity.

Parker pressed the cold steel barrel of the gun against my buttocks. The sensation cleared my mind. Death seemed suddenly intimate. . . .

I saw Dawn naked and smiling, beckoning me to join her. But then Parker, nothing but a closet queer in macho man's clothing, tossed aside that Browning and thrust his ugly and swollen member against my bare flesh. "Open wide, you Scottish mongrel redskin bitch! Open wide and take what you got coming to you!"

No way! I refused to obey. Death was one thing but sodomy was something else altogether. I tightened up my sphincter muscle like a vise and threw my limbs into action. My elbows reared up and drew back flush into Parker's exposed sack. He doubled over in agony. I swung around in a perfect pirouette and kicked him squarely in the testicles with my steel-toed boots. He squealed like a pig, did Parker, and then he toppled over into the mud.

I dived for the shotgun, hoisted it high into the air, and smashed it across his forehead. Blood flew everywhere. Down went Parker.

But Artemus had mobilized. He leapt at my throat. I pulled the trigger of the Browning. An instant later the top third of the beast's head blew off. That slowed him down. But still he kept coming. I flung the gun at him and made for the guideboat. Just as I jumped aboard, Artemus made one last desperate lunge for my leg. But the beast missed and instead chomped deeply into the forward gunwale. I paddled like mad out onto the Bull Moose with the ravaged animal's bloody mouth clinging to the boat.

Parker appeared at the water's edge in his bloodstained shirt. "Kill, Artemus, kill! Destroy the enemy, Artemus!"

But poor Artemus could do absolutely nothing to harm me. He flailed about in the water like a hooked bass. I rather enjoyed watching him struggle. I quickly purged this joy, however, for I felt it made me too much like them.

Parker fired several shells, but the pellets fell like raindrops into the dark water. I laughed for the first time in weeks as I plotted my revenge. . . .

By midnight, Artemus, exhausted, had calmed down. I had paddled far enough across the lake to make Parker's commands almost inaudible above the laughter of the loons. I spoke constantly in a firm but gentle voice. "I want you to listen carefully, Artemus. I'm your master now. I hold your life in my hands. Do you understand, Artemus? . . . Good. Now do you hear that evil voice in the distance? That is the voice of the enemy. Listen, Artemus, listen well to that voice. That is the enemy, Artemus, the enemy."

From across the lake we could just barely hear Parker, alias Jack, alias Bart, struggling to make himself heard: ". . . kill, kill, kill . . ."

I rubbed Artemus's gouged and bloody snout. "That's exactly what we are going to do, Artie, old pal, old friend, old chum. We are going to kill the enemy. We are going to wipe the enemy off the face of the earth."

For three days and three nights Artemus went through a rigorous reconditioning program. His jaws never eased up on the gunwale. And on the third night, sometime after dusk, I dragged him into the boat. He was elated. He licked my face and pawed my chest while I rubbed his belly. Willy's best friend. And after he settled down, I gave him his orders for the evening and promised him a hearty supper upon completion of his mission.

An hour later I silently rowed the guideboat back across the lake to where I had last spotted Parker earlier in the day. The moon and stars hung invisibly behind heavy clouds. I brought the boat to within a few yards of shore. Artemus sniffed the air. I ordered him into action. He responded immediately.

I waited in the boat, beyond range of the Browning, while Artemus flushed his prey. An hour passed. Two hours. The loons rattled my senses, made me question the soundness of my soul. Their cries made me feel lonely and depressed. Will I ever, I wondered, experience love again? It seemed practically an impossibility.

And then I began to worry: What had happened? Where had that damn dog gone? Had Parker somehow outwitted me? Had he regained the loyalty of the beast? Were they waiting out there together in ambush? Should I make good my escape? No, I decided to stay put, at least until dawn.

But the fireworks started much sooner than that. Artemus flushed Parker out of the forest soon after midnight. I heard them running through the dark woods. The shotgun roared. Artemus cried out in pain. But his barking continued. As did their running. "Down, boy! Down, down! Back, Artemus, back! Heel you stupid beast, heel! I'm not the enemy, Artemus, I'm your master!"

But Artie no longer thought so. I'd saved his life. He thought I was the cat's meow. So he drove Parker down to the lake's edge and then into the cold, dark water, exactly as I had commanded. Yup, that beast had learned well the foul sport of hounding during the many hours he and Parker had traumatized all those wild and innocent whitetails.

"How does it feel, Parker," I shouted into the night, "to be the hunted rather than the hunter?" I didn't wait for an answer. I swung the guideboat into action. Parker swam after the boat. Artemus swam after Parker. I led them on a merry chase out across the Bull Moose. Parker pleaded with me to help him into the boat, to rescue him from the beast.

I just laughed while he begged for mercy, for salvation from his terrible sins. I must say: I played a rather sadistic savior. "Murderers gotta go, Parker or Steel or Vandermeer or whoever you think you are, murderers gotta suffer. Murderers gotta pay the piper, gotta pay with their lives."

"I'm no murderer, Willy. I'm a peace-loving kind of guy."

"Bullshit. You murdered my wife. You murdered Dawn."

"I thought you said Montgomery murdered your wife."

"You and him together. Maybe you most of all."

"I don't know why you say that, Willy. But if you'll help me into the boat, we could talk it over." He tried to climb over the gunwale but I whacked his fingers with the paddle. "Ouch!"

"You set her up, Jack. You knew she was chained to that rock out in the middle of the Tamaqua River. You knew she was out there. You knew she was in danger. The plan, I feel sure, was to get a few pictures of her out on the river before they opened the sluice gates, then you would go and let the appropriate people know the situation. But you decided to hold off notifying anyone until after the gates were open, until after the water had started to run, until after the river had started to rise. What I wonder, you bloodsucking savage son of a bitch, is why? Why did you do it?"

"You got it wrong, Willy, all wrong."

"You could have stopped it. You could have saved her."

"Willy, no, don't think like that. I did the best I could."

"Horseshit."

"No, Willy, you have to believe me. I did the best I could."

"You had your cameraman standing along the riverbank filming as the water rose up and over her head."

"That's what she wanted, Willy. She wanted her protest on videotape for all the world to see."

"But she didn't want to drown, jerk-off. She didn't want to die!"

Desperation spewed from Jack Steel's mouth as Artemus, like some canine shark, drew closer and closer. "Willy, please, listen to me. I never would've done anything to harm her. Dawn's safety was my paramount concern. She came to me that morning and told me what she wanted to do, and I—"

I smashed his fingers again with the paddle.

"Ouch! For chrissakes! That hurts."

"So I was right," I screamed into his ear, "you did know! You were in on the whole damn thing from the very beginning. You knew all along she was chained to that rock."

"Yes . . . I did . . . I knew . . . but I never intended—"

"Shut up, asshole! I get it now. You waited until the gates had opened and the river had started rising because you realized it would make the whole event more exciting, more dramatic. That's why you came and got me instead of going to the proper authorities. You knew I'd race to her side, try to save her life. You set us both up. You miserable murdering bastard. You let her die for the story, for the fucking story!"

"Willy!" he screamed. "Noooo!"

Too late. I raised my paddle high over my head and methodically fractured his hands, his wrists, his elbows, his collarbones. His horrible screams brought forth the loons. Those sleek and wild red-eyed birds bobbed all around us in the dark, placid water. This was a show they had never seen before.

I giggled . . . while Parker, alias Jack, alias Bart, hung from the gunwale by his neck. His arms had been shattered, rendered useless. And then Artemus, injured but still mobile, arrived on the scene and wasted no time ripping open his ex-master's muscular thigh. The sound of the tearing flesh made my skin crawl; my heart skipped a few beats. Parker continued to try to pull himself into the guideboat by flexing the thick muscles of his neck.

It was a sad but comical sight. I laughed but then cried: cried for Parker and for all the rest of the meaningless death in the world. Then I stood up, raised my paddle high into the night air one more time, and brought it crashing down across the top of Parker's head. The skull splintered. Parker seemed to sigh. I suppose, in the end, death is what all of us really yearn for. And then, after no time at all, his body went limp and slid into the murky waters of the Bull Moose.

Artemus tore insanely at the lifeless form of his old master. This attack proved too much for me to bear. And so, in a complex act that

I think demonstrates my desire to regain my mental equilibrium, I reached down into the water, scooped the beast up into my arms, and brought him into the boat. I calmed him, dressed his wounds, then paddled to shore, where I fed him his promised supper. And when he had finished, eaten his fill, we settled down for the night, huddled together against the cold and the dark and the fear.

I did not actually sleep, but I was comforted by the beast's steady breathing and beating heart....

So went the events of yesterday. Or the day before yesterday. Or whenever what happened happened. It was in the past that Parker, alias Jack Steel, alias Barton Vandermeer, died that terrible, brutal death. In the past, that's all I know, all I remember. Does the precise moment of death really make any difference? Parker said he had no past. Now he has no future. Like Dawn.

So call me Fuck It. Willy Fuck It. No past. No future. No nothing. I live in Fuckitsville in the state of New Fuckiton. The time is nearly half-past Fuck It. And today is the Fuck It of Fuck It in the year of someone else's Lord, nineteen hundred and Fuck It.

This morning I carved a notch in my paddle. My first kill. Parker had to die so I could live. But who could live so that Dawn had to die? Violence. Death. Destruction ... We die by water, we die by fire, we die at dawn, we die at dusk, we die in the beginning, we die in the end, we die naked, and we die alone: forgotten, perhaps forgiven.

Who gives a shit?

The time has come for me to head for home. To end this journey. To see some old familiar faces, some friendly smiles.

America has become a violent state, a deranged man's paradise. I am not deranged. I am sane. I just want to deal with some folks who'll see me and say, "Hey, Willy, how's things?" Folks who'll stop by to borrow my ax and stay for supper. Folks who want even less from me than I want from them.

I want to take a spin around the islands in the Gar Runabout. I want to see Mama and Pop. I want to see Sanders and Alice. Most of all I want to hug Emily to my heart. I want to sit out on the end of the dock with her and watch the swallows dive. I want to take a walk up to the graveyard and cry. I want to kiss the soil that protects her soul. I want. I want. I want ...

12:58 P.M.
JANUARY 20, 2001
MACKENZIE ISLAND
THE INAUGURATION OF THE FORTY-FOURTH PRESIDENT OF THE UNITED STATES

Unbelievable. What an imagination! Where does he come up with this stuff? And who's this guy Parker from Intelligence? Parker. Vandermeer. Steel. I suddenly have more identities than a cat has lives.

But I'll tell you one thing, I don't much like being called a sodomite. On the other hand, I don't mind playing the role of Christ. Hey, you heard it straight from Willy's own mouth: I died, he killed me, quite brutally, slammed me over the head with a guideboat paddle, sent me to my watery grave. And yet here I am: resurrected, alive, and doing quite well. Makes you wonder what really happened out there in the wilderness, doesn't it?

Not all that much, if you want to know the truth. Certainly nothing resembling the chaos and insanity just depicted by the man slated, incredibly, to become our forty-fourth president.

Let me see if I can give you a more accurate account of what really happened during those weeks Willy and I spent together out in the wilds. I'll keep it brief since we understand Willy has requested a few minutes of airtime over at the Great House.

We camped and paddled and hiked in the hills. We fished and went swimming once the weather turned warmer. We even used that Browning semiautomatic shotgun a few times: not too often; I don't really like guns, never have. But we used it to shoot a few rabbits, a few birds, I think one or two deer. Only what we could eat. We never hunted just for sport.

We both did a lot of relaxing. And reading. And writing. Willy worked in his journal and I worked on my notes. And yes, I did make tape recordings of many of our conversations. And I did so without Willy's knowledge. But those recordings were just grist for an old journalist's mill. Nothing sinister there. I started taping conversations twenty years ago so I could be sure when I went to do a story that I had my facts straight, that I had my proof documented.

Willy found out about the tapes, and, well, he got kind of bent out of shape about the whole affair. He flew off the handle, went into a rage, accused me of just about every crime under the sun, including participation in Dawn's death.

"Willy," I assured him, "believe me, I had nothing to do with that terrible tragedy. I suffered right along with you. I was on your side then, just as I am on your side now."

It took several days, no, several weeks, before he finally began to trust me. Willy does not wear his emotions on his sleeve, but I saw the relief on his face once the man knew he had a friend.

I suppose Willy and I spent most of our time out there in the wilderness talking. We talked about everything: our hopes, our dreams, our fears, our families.

I tried to get Willy to tell me what he would do if he became president, but as I said a short time ago, I made these inquiries without much success. He mentioned a few things, although even now, almost four years later, I'm not all that sure where Willy MacKenzie stands on many of the important issues.

I think a lot of people who voted for Willy voted for the symbol more than the man. His supporters voted for him not so much for his positions, but because he seemed good and decent and honest, even innocent. He spoke for all of us when he attacked the scoundrels and thieves entrenched in power down in Washington. After so many decades of ineffective, greedy, and corrupt government, Willy smelled like a breath of fresh Blue Mountain air. But what we may have missed along the way was a candidate expressing some very unusual, even radical, political ideas.

"Liberty and responsibility," he told me one day, "that's what I stand for. That's what the Founding Fathers had in mind: individual liberty and personal responsibility. I was brought up to rely on myself, on my family, and on my community."

"But the country's a different place now, Willy. We have almost three hundred million people living between these shores. And more coming all the time. It's not 1787 anymore."

"You're right, Jack," he said, "it's not 1787 anymore. All the more reason why I think we should take these professional politicians like Anderson Montgomery out behind the barn and shoot 'em down like old dogs. Just shoot 'em and leave 'em for the vultures. Then we'll take an ax and chop the federal government down to size, right down to its roots, make it leaner and meaner, the way Jefferson meant it to be."

"Sounds kind of drastic."

"Why? It doesn't take a genius to see that the United States government has failed in its efforts to be all things to all people. The Treasury's flat broke, the economy's in ruins, crime and taxes have run rampant, fear and ridicule have become the national pastimes, the cities look like Third World countries, and the environment, shit, the environment has turned into a three-headed hydra spewing venom at us from the earth, the air, and the water. And still these sleazy politicians tell us we should keep calm, stay the course, reelect them ad infinitum."

Yup, Willy can really roll once he gets started; sounds occasionally like that old warrior, Ulysses Simpson Grant MacKenzie.

I think we can safely say that Willy has no intention of keeping calm or staying the course. He has changes in store, but exactly what those changes might be, even at this late date, remains a mystery. Which is why so many people are running scared; why Congress is voting even as we speak to make Willy's election null and void; why the Supreme Court has failed to recognize his presidency; why more and more people are hoping Willy will do the country a favor and simply call it quits, pack it in rather than proceeding with the oath of office.

"The time has come to rely on ourselves again," he told me near the end of our wilderness sojourn. Time to quit pretending that big government is the only solution to our social, political, and economic ills. All big government has done in the last sixty years is create a nation of crybabies constantly demanding to suck on the swollen federal tit."

Willy talked while I listened, my tape recorder running. I liked what I heard. Some of it anyway. My daddy, God rest his soul, believed in hard work and self-reliance. And I guess, if I think about it, I do too. To a point.

We're sending you over to the Great House now to hear from the president-elect. Rumor has it that Willy will make a brief speech, then, hopefully, he will do the right thing and offer the American people his resignation. The viability of a MacKenzie Presidency is fast dissipating. . . .

The president-elect sits in a leather armchair before a roaring fire in the living room of the Great House. His mother sits beside him. His father and brother stand at opposite ends of the fireplace, their elbows resting on the thick oak mantelpiece. Friends and neighbors, Anglos and Indians, close to a hundred Tamaqua Valley residents, fill the rest of the room.

The one person not present is Judge Orrin Stuart. He must still be bedridden after his difficult journey from North Creek.

The mood in the Great House appears subdued. The MacKenzies look pale and worn-out, even withdrawn, as though they wish only for their long and stressful ordeal to come to an end. A hint of perspiration shows on the president-elect's brow as he prepares to speak. . . .

> WILLY MACKENZIE: Jack Steel thinks I should resign before serving even a single day. I don't know if Steel's right about this, but he's right about a couple other things. He's right that Judge Stuart is in a bad way. No way will the Judge be able to administer the oath of office. He may not survive the night.
>
> Steel is also right when he says that we MacKenzies must be ready for this long and stressful ordeal to end. We are way past ready. If, that is, the ordeal he refers to is his own long and tiresome broadcast.
>
> Steel has sold the American people a bill of goods. For the past seven hours he's done his best to portray the MacKenzies as eccentric, money-grubbing, land-grabbing infidels.
>
> And by twisting and manipulating my private journals, Steel has put into question my patriotism, my ethics, my honesty, even my sanity. If the American people had any empathy left for me at all, I feel certain Jack Steel destroyed that empathy

here today with his cunning and calculated abuse of my own words. Until today no one, not even my late wife, had read my journals. They were my own private thoughts recorded on paper. Now they have been stolen and used against me.

All morning I've sat here hoping and praying to God and the Great Spirit that this inauguration would go forward, and that I might actually get the chance to bring the country together. It appears, however, that my prayers have gone unanswered. Fueled by the ravenous appetite of the press, circumstances beyond my control have interfered with a peaceful transfer of power.

But I cannot sit idly by and allow Jack Steel to further butcher my character. I would now like you to hear something from my journal that I have chosen. I doubt if Steel had the following entry on his agenda. It does not serve his purposes. It shows him for what he is: a liar and a scoundrel. The following was written soon after the two of us reached the valley after our long journey through the Blue Mountains.

No, Jack Steel, alias Barton Vandermeer, alias Parker, was not dead. I had not killed him out on the Bull Moose. I had wanted to kill him, put him out of my misery, but I had not been able to muster the courage to do the job. So I killed him in my journal instead. It helped distill the pain.

* * * * * * *

August 9, 1997
Tamarack

I reached the valley late last week. But I didn't come directly home. I paddled past the islands in my Blue Mountain guideboat and headed for town. Still wearing my disguise as Willy Sabattis, wilderness guide, I wanted to check out the lay of the land, see if those federal marshals Sanders had warned me about had waited all these months for my return. I also wanted to get a room over at

Wilson's Hotel so I could relax, recoup, have myself a shave and a hot bath. I wanted to go home looking presentable.

I left the guideboat down at the town dock and walked up Water Street. It being the height of summer, I saw several unfamiliar faces, visitors to the Blue Mountains. But I also saw a few familiar faces, including my buddy Henry Bender, who didn't recognize me, walked right by without a second glance.

They didn't recognize me at Wilson's Hotel either. I asked for a room, signed the registration book as Willy Sabattis, and took the key from Marty Stowe, the old clerk who's worked the front desk since back before I was born.

"Room 302, Mr. Sabattis," said Marty. "Two flights up, first room on your left. Has a real nice view of the lake."

I thanked him and started up that wide mahogany staircase. But before I hit that first step, Marty Stowe called out to me. "Oh, Mr. Sabattis, I almost forgot, you have a message."

"A message? For me?"

"Yes," said Marty, "from a Mr. Jack Steel. He's in room 304. Just down the hall from you. He'd like to see you at your convenience."

I was not surprised. Steel had left the backcountry a week or so before me. Claimed he had the flu or an inflamed Achilles' tendon, some such nonsense. He'd just lost his nerve is all. He needed a soft bed and a warm meal; he needed civilization.

I reached the third floor and knocked on the door of room 304. And who do you think answered that knock? None other than the beautiful and sensual Ms. Lulu.

"Willy! It's so nice to see you again."

Lulu wore nothing but a sheer silk kimono. When she reached out to give me a hug, the kimono fell open, exposing those perfect breasts and a wonderful patch of blond pubic hair. I immediately felt that burning sensation down in my groin.

"Willy," Jack called from the bed across the room, "you're back! Come on in here. Take a load off. Let me pour you a whiskey." He lay there naked, a tumbler of sour mash resting on his hairy chest.

I stepped into the room, dropped my bag on the floor, and collapsed in the rickety wooden chair near the window. Artemus slept behind the chair. The beast growled and showed his sparkling canines when I sat down.

Jack laughed, handed me a glass of bourbon, and asked me how I'd been.

I sipped the fine Kentucky whiskey, took a look out across the lake, saw the outline of MacKenzie in the distance, and told him I'd never been better.

Lulu came up behind me, put her hands on my shoulders, and began to massage my weary bones. I sighed and let the months of stress and strain melt off my body.

She massaged my shoulders, my neck, my scalp, my face, my chest, my abdomen, my back, and my thighs. I did not put up a struggle. I only remember moaning and groaning and feeling like a pool of water and then, suddenly, dropping off to sleep.

I awoke the next morning in my bed over in room 302. Just as I opened my eyes I saw Lulu slip through the door and out into the hallway. I called her name but she was gone. So I shaved and showered, felt that rush of hot water wash away the sweat and the grime. And while I rubbed myself dry, I happened to glance out the bathroom window. The small window, fogged with steam, overlooked the corner of Main and Water. I noticed a crowd gathering on the street below, so I used my towel to wipe away the steam.

The first thing I saw was a huge banner. It read: WELCOME HOME, WILLY!

There must've been a hundred people down on the street, and more coming. The whole town had turned out, the whole valley.

Jack appeared behind me. "Time to get dressed, Willy, and put in an appearance."

"An appearance? For what?"

"For your fans."

"My fans? But how did they know I was here?"

"I told them. I told them you were back."

I glanced out the window again. Several television cameras lined the street.

"Why?"

Jack stood at my side. "Because, Willy, it's an event. You're an event. This little welcome home party will be seen by a couple hundred million people before dusk falls on another day."

"But why?" I wanted to know. "What's the point?"

"The point's publicity, Willy. Exposure. Good clean positive exposure. If we're going to make you the next president, we've got to create a good clean positive image."

"President?"

"That's right, Willy. And I think we can do it. I really do. The polls say we can do it too. The shitty shape this country's in, barely able to afford a pot to piss in, we might just be able to pull it off. All we'll need is a little luck and carte blanche at the MacKenzie coffers. Believe me, Willy, we might just be able to slip a regular guy like you into the Oval Office while no one's looking."

"You think so?"

"Hey, at least it'll be fun to try."

So I dressed, and down the stairs and across the lobby and out onto the front porch of Wilson's Hotel we went. A cheer rose up out of the crowd as I came through those glass doors.

Then I saw Mama and Pop and Sanders and Alice coming through the crowd. Mama held Emily in her arms. They came up the stairs onto the porch and Emily yelled, "Daddy!" And right away, all at once, I began to laugh and cry. Emily climbed into my arms and I hugged her little body so tight that I thought for a second I might crush her. But she just giggled and kissed me on the face. And then we all embraced, one big happy MacKenzie family.

And that night, it was those emotional pictures of our family reunion that the networks beamed into the homes of tens of millions of American families. The pictures showed me with tears streaming down my face, then thanking everyone for coming out, the whole town, the whole valley.

The networks didn't show the part later when the federal marshals came and placed me under arrest for my antics down in the District of Columbia. I spent that night in the Tamaqua Valley jail, but by morning, after a massive public outcry against my incarceration, Judge Stuart released me on my own recognizance.

There might be a trial, probably not. I don't think Montgomery or anyone else has the balls to press charges. Public opinion runs too high in my favor.

So here I am, home again at last, ready to settle in with my little girl and get on with the tasks at hand. There's been a lot of neglect around here these past several months, so I'll have plenty to keep me busy, to keep me sane.

Jack Steel wants me to run for president, claims the MacKenzies have been preparing for the presidency for four generations, since crossing the Atlantic.

Maybe he's right, I don't know. Sanders likes the idea. So does Mama. She says it's practically my duty to run. She insists I'm the spiritual reincarnation of the great Iroquois peacemaker, Hiawatha. But Pop thinks running for president is a lousy idea. He says if I want to hold public office I should run for mayor of Cedar Bend.

I guess we'll just have to wait and see. Hell, I'm not even thirty years old yet. The United States Constitution says you have to be at least thirty-five years old to be president. I won't be eligible until the elections in 2004. By then everyone will have forgotten about me.

Emily just came into the room. She's still kind of shy around me after my long absence, doesn't quite know yet what to make of her old man.

"What are you doing, Daddy?"

"Nothing, kid. Just sitting here waiting for you."

She pokes around the room a bit: picks up a book, spins our globe of the world, switches my desk lamp off and on and off again.

I grab her and tickle her ribs.

She giggles.

I give her a big wet kiss on the face.

She wipes away the kiss and giggles again. "Can we go out and pick some wildflowers?"

"Sure we can," I tell her. "That's exactly what we can do."

She smiles, just the way her mama used to smile. "Maybe we'll see some butterflies."

"Yeah," I say, remembering, "maybe."

She grabs my hand and away we go.

1:10 P.M.
JANUARY 20, 2001
MACKENZIE ISLAND
THE INAUGURATION OF THE FORTY-FOURTH PRESIDENT OF THE UNITED STATES

Willy's right, I had no intention of including that particular journal entry in our broadcast here today. Time limitations demand a certain amount of editing. As for Lulu and Artemus, well, they may indeed exist. But so what if they do? They have no bearing on the strength and stability of Willy MacKenzie's character or, for that matter, on his ability to function as the forty-fourth president of the United States.

Still, I'm glad Willy took a shot at me. He has been wanting all morning to get a few things off his chest. Hopefully he sees now how insignificant personal conflicts are when stacked against matters of national interest.

Wait a second, what's all this? A mass exodus appears to be taking place over at the Great House. Through the boathouse window I can see those Tamaqua Valley residents streaming out the back door, crossing the porch, and gathering in the yard heaped with snow. Everyone who was inside is now suddenly outside, young and old, Indians and whites, men and women. And they're all bundled up, ready to battle the elements.

And look at this: here comes Willy. And his mother. And his father. And his brother. In fact, Willy's headed this way, straight for the boathouse. He throws open the door. Frigid air and swirling snow follow him into the room.

"We're leaving the island, Steel."

"Leaving the island? Why?"

"Because it's time, that's why. We have a couple extra pairs of skis. If you and your cameraman can handle the cold, you're welcome to tag along."

"Along where, Willy? Where are you going?"

He ignores my question. Instead he holds up two fingers and says, "Two minutes. You got two minutes." And then he's gone, leaving the door wide open as he trudges through the waist-deep drifts.

I had not anticipated anything like this, but . . . but . . . but I guess I'm no good to anyone sitting here. "Let's roll, Fred."

Fred Lorry, my cameraman, and I pull on every stitch of clothing we can find. We cover ourselves with hats, gloves, and extra sweaters. This is no time for vanity.

Henry Bender stamps into the boathouse and hands us each a pair of cross-country ski boots. Mine fit, marginally.

Our skis and poles await us outside, old wooden planks and wooden sticks, warped and battered. We strap on the skis and prepare to leave. No time to ruminate now. This army is ready to move out.

"Any idea where we're going?" I ask several of Willy's friends and neighbors.

They reply with glares and scowls.

We push off. The MacKenzies lead the way. We cut through a stand of evergreens, their heavy branches bent with snow. It is dark beneath the pines, and incredibly cold. Already my feet feel frozen and my boots feel two sizes too small. I hope we don't have far to go.

Soon we clear the trees, shoot down a small but rather steep hill, and ski out onto Loon Cove. Suddenly we stop. Dead ahead stands a squad of United States Marines.

I'd been wondering when they would put in an appearance.

There are seven of them, not a full squad, commanded by a second lieutenant who looks as if he could pass for a high school sophomore. The marines wear their winter uniforms: white jumpsuits filled with down, wool caps, Gore-Tex gloves. They stand tall and steely on their long, thin skis. All but the lieutenant carry a semiautomatic rifle at the ready. A shiny new revolver in a leather holster hangs from the lieutenant's hip.

Several seconds pass before anyone says a word. That word comes, finally, from Conrad Whitman MacKenzie. "Don't you marines have the sense to salute your commander in chief?"

The lieutenant hesitates, then snaps to attention. His enlisted men do the same. Willy flicks his right hand across his temple. "Did you boys want something?"

Again the lieutenant hesitates. He doesn't go anywhere near his revolver.

Finally he says, "I was told to protect you here on the island, sir."

"Step aside, son," says Willy, sounding almost presidential. "I'm sick of being held prisoner on my own island. We're leaving, heading for the mainland. Come along or stay behind. Your choice."

The small army of Tamaqua Valley residents immediately begins to move forward. The marines have to scurry out of the way. As I slide by the lieutenant I give him a verbal jab: "Nice work, kid. You'll go a long way in the corps."

He catches my sarcasm. "I can't detain my commander in chief."

I ignore his excuses. "Are there others in town?"

"Yes, sir," he says, "an entire battalion."

I nod and hurry to catch up. The marines follow some distance back.

We ski across the cove and out onto Lake Katydeeray. The moment we reach the lake the wind slams into me and almost knocks me off my feet. But before it does we turn east and put that gale at our backs. It shoots us across the frozen, snow-covered lake. I barely have to do more than maintain my balance. But still my feet throb. I can feel the blisters swelling on my heels and toes. I'll bet that damn Henry Bender gave me these tiny boots on purpose.

In the distance I can see Cedar Bluffs. I doubt I'll need to ski much farther than that. The military will put an end to Willy's folly. He never should have left MacKenzie. He was safe as long as he stayed on the island.

"Come on, Fred, let's make our way forward. See if we can get a word with Willy."

We push a little harder, slowly work our way toward the front of the pack. Even in this intense cold I start to warm up. A pretty good sweat breaks out across my forehead and under my arms.

These Blue Mountain folk don't have much on: boots, wool pants, wool sweaters, some with hats, some without. They slide across the snow without the slightest sign of strain. They all look as though they could compete for the Norwegian cross-country ski team.

Me, I'm feeling the pain.

It takes some time, and too much toil, but finally Fred and I get close enough to Willy that he should be able to hear my questions if I yell them loud enough into the wind. I just hope I can ask a few before I poop out. All this extra work has left me overheated and out of breath.

"Willy, can you hear me?"

"Sure, Steel, I can hear you."

"Where are we headed?"

"Where do you think?"

"I don't know. You tell me."

"We're heading for Washington, Steel. For the United States Capitol. I have a date there to be inaugurated. Remember?"

"Sure, Willy, I remember. But you'll never make it. Too much opposition. Too many obstacles." I can feel myself losing energy, running out of steam.

Fortunately, Willy takes up the slack. "You'd really like me to resign, wouldn't you, Jack? Step aside for the good of the country. And maybe you're right, maybe I should. The job, I'll admit, is probably too big for me. Probably too big for any man. Or woman. I thought about quitting, I really did. Just about an hour ago I made the decision to pack it in, to spare myself and my family the burden of taking and holding office. But then my mother reminded me of my responsibilities and my birthright, of my connection to Hiawatha and the terrible condition of the planet. So we're going, Jack, come hell or high water, we're going to Washington."

All this while he skis with power and precision. I'm impressed. In fact, I think Willy started skiing faster as he made his little speech. Either that or I'm skiing slower. I'm definitely falling behind. These Blue Mountaineers pass me like I'm standing still. I see them smirk as they slide by so easily. Luckily we have only a few hundred yards farther to Cedar Bluffs. Already I can see the military gathered on the waterfront: trucks, jeeps, tanks, and an impressive display of armed personnel.

I wonder what Willy has in mind.

Fred and I use all our strength to reach the mainland along with

Willy's army. I keep my head down and concentrate on pumping my arms and legs back and forth. I can feel myself rapidly running out of gas.

Less than a hundred yards from shore I look over and see Fred glide to a stop. "What's the problem?"

He stares straight ahead. "Take a look."

I stop, struggle to catch my breath. The air, raw and cold, catches in my lungs. I shudder, then peer into the whiteness. At first I see nothing but snow. Then I begin to focus. I see the United States military, members of the army and the marines, lining the lakeshore, calm and steady as they prepare for Willy's reception. But behind these armed and uniformed soldiers stands an even larger and more ominous army. They wear wool hunting jackets and leather coats and down parkas. They carry shotguns and .22-caliber rifles and bows and arrows. They fill the streets of Cedar Bluffs.

Willy does not even break stride. At full speed he skis off the lake and into town. He skis straight into the heart of that military presence. A long, tense moment settles over the valley. A perfect silence fills the crisp, cold mountain air.

And then Willy, without uttering a single word, begins to move again, to ski, to push forward, one small step closer to Washington, D.C. I fully expect to hear a gunshot, or at least some gruff Marine Corps colonel bark an order to halt. But nothing, not a sound.

Those military boys stand inert, powerless. They realize they have no choice but to open ranks and allow Willy, his family, friends, and neighbors to pass through unimpeded. No way do they dare challenge this crowd.

And then, beyond the vast citizen's army, I spot another reason why the military has decided to maintain a low profile. Yet another army, small but extremely potent, carrying tape recorders and notepads and television cameras, occupies the high ground above the town. It seems my friends and fellow journalists have returned to the Tamaqua River Valley.

President-elect MacKenzie takes note of their presence, then he continues to make his way through the streets of Cedar Bluffs. He is cheered and congratulated and slapped on the back every step of the way.

But Willy's not just rambling, looking for adulation; no, he has a goal, a destination.

He slides out Water Street, and in a matter of minutes he has reached the train station, the station built nearly one hundred years ago by his great-grandfather, Ulysses Simpson Grant MacKenzie. And sure enough, there's a train waiting. A giant locomotive spews smoke into the ice-cold air. A single Pullman car is attached to the locomotive, perhaps the same Pullman once owned by Willy's forebear.

Willy helps his mother onto the train car. Then his little girl, Emily. And his brother's wife, Alice. Then Conrad and Sanders step aboard. And Henry Bender. And one or two others I do not recognize. Then Willy waves, climbs aboard, and disappears. His supporters let loose with a wild display of cheers, hoots, hollers, applause, and foot stomping.

Willy suddenly reappears on the back platform of the Pullman. It take some time but the crowd finally grows quiet.

"Do not forget," he says, his voice loud and clear but barely above a whisper, "we still hold the power in our hands." Willy learned long ago that he does not need to shout.

The crowd's enthusiasm explodes once again. Willy waits patiently for them to grow silent.

"A violent and sinister wind," he continues, "blows across this vast and divided land. We need to put an end to this wind. We need to plant and nurture the Three Sisters. We need to worship and respect the three great elements: the earth, the air, and the water.

"Tomorrow, at dawn—and I don't give a damn about the weather or the press or the United States military or the United States Congress or the countless lunatics who want to see Willy MacKenzie dead and buried—tomorrow at dawn, on the steps of the United States Capitol, I fully expect to take the oath of office and be inaugurated as your forty-fourth president."

More hooting and hollering.

"Until then," he says, "I thank you. Godspeed to us all. May the Great Spirit mercifully intervene and save us from ourselves!"

Willy waves, then once more disappears into the Pullman car. And a moment later, amid the thunderous roar of the crowd, that locomotive blows its mighty whistle and slowly begins to roll south out of the valley. . . .

Will Willy survive the journey to Washington? Will he be inaugurated? Will he assume his duties as president of the United States?

I don't know. Difficult to say. In our relatively short history as a nation, we have weathered revolutions and rebellions, civil wars and civil unrest, assassinations and resignations. I suppose we will weather this storm as well.

And so, as his train rolls out of sight, I think we should take this opportunity to put aside our differences, wave farewell, and wish Willy all the best.

The sky has started to clear over the Tamaqua River Valley. The sun, dull and gray, hangs low over these beautiful Blue Mountains.

For now, so long. This has been Jack Steel reporting live from MacKenzie Island.